Foreign *Affairs*

SPANISH SEDUCTIONS

CATHY
WILLIAMS

ABBY
GREEN

CHANTELLE
SHAW

MILLS & BOON

FOREIGN AFFAIRS: SPANISH SEDUCTIONS © 2023 by Harlequin Books S.A.

CONTRACTED FOR THE SPANIARD'S HEIR
© 2019 by Cathy Williams
Australian Copyright 2019
New Zealand Copyright 2019

First Published 2019
Second Australian Paperback Edition 2023
ISBN 978 1 867 28743 8

REDEEMED BY HIS STOLEN BRIDE
© 2019 by Abby Green
Australian Copyright 2019
New Zealand Copyright 2019

First Published 2019
Second Australian Paperback Edition 2023
ISBN 978 1 867 28743 8

THE SECRET HE MUST CLAIM
© 2017 by Chantelle Shaw
Australian Copyright 2017
New Zealand Copyright 2017

First Published 2017
Second Australian Paperback Edition 2023
ISBN 978 1 867 28743 8

Published by
Mills & Boon
An imprint of Harlequin Enterprises (Australia) Pty Limited (ABN 47 001 180 918), a subsidiary of HarperCollins Publishers Australia Pty Limited (ABN 36 009 913 517)
Level 19, 201 Elizabeth Street
SYDNEY NSW 2000
AUSTRALIA

MIX
Paper | Supporting responsible forestry
FSC
www.fsc.org   FSC® C001695

® and ™ (apart from those relating to FSC®) are trademarks of Harlequin Enterprises (Australia) Pty Limited or its corporate affiliates. Trademarks indicated with ® are registered in Australia, New Zealand and in other countries. Contact admin_legal@Harlequin.ca for details.

Printed and bound in Australia by McPherson's Printing Group

CONTENTS

Contracted For The Spaniard's Heir

Cathy Williams

Books by Cathy Williams

Harlequin Modern

The Secret Sanchez Heir
Bought to Wear the Billionaire's Ring
Cipriani's Innocent Captive
Legacy of His Revenge
A Deal for Her Innocence
A Diamond Deal with Her Boss
The Tycoon's Ultimate Conquest

One Night With Consequences

Bound by the Billionaire's Baby
The Italian's One-Night Consequence

The Italian Titans

Wearing the De Angelis Ring
The Surprise De Angelis Baby

Seven Sexy Sins

To Sin with the Tycoon

Visit the Author Profile page
at millsandboon.com.au for more titles.

Cathy Williams can remember reading Harlequin books as a teenager, and now that she is writing them, she remains an avid fan. For her, there is nothing like creating romantic stories and engaging plots, and each and every book is a new adventure. Cathy lives in London, and her three daughters—Charlotte, Olivia and Emma—have always been, and continue to be, the greatest inspirations in her life.

CHAPTER ONE

'SHALL I BRING the girl in now, sir?'

Sprawled back in his swivel chair, Luca Ross looked at his housekeeper, Miss Muller, who was standing to attention by the door.

In short order, he had sacked the nanny, sat his godson down for a talk to find out what the hell was going on and now, item number three on the agenda, was the girl waiting in the kitchen. It was fair to say that his day had been shot to pieces.

He nodded curtly at his housekeeper, who was as forceful as a sergeant major and one of the few people not intimidated by her aggressive and powerful boss.

'And make sure those hounds don't come with her,' he said flatly. 'Lock them outside if you need to. If it's raining, then they'll get wet. They're dogs. They're built for that. Just make sure they don't destroy any more of my house.'

In the cold confines of his home office—which was better equipped than most commercial offices, with all the accoutrements necessary for him to keep in touch with his myriad companies that spanned numerous time zones—Luca Ross sat back and contemplated this latest, unwelcome development.

He had failed. It was as simple as that. Six months ago, out of the blue, he had inherited a six-year-old cousin once removed, a boy he had briefly met when he had accepted—with cavalier nonchalance, he now realised—the role of godfather.

Luca had few relatives, and certainly none with whom he kept in active contact, and the request, coming from his cousin, had seemed perfectly acceptable. A compliment, even.

His cousin had then set off for foreign shores to seek his fortune, breathtakingly naïve in his assumption that the streets of California were really and truly paved with gold, and Luca had promptly lost touch.

Life was hectic. Emails had been few and far between and his conscience when it came to the role of godfather had been easily soothed by the occasional injection of cash into the bank account he had set up for his godson shortly after his cousin and his young wife had set off to sail the seas and make their fortune.

Job done.

He had not banked on actually being called upon to take charge of anyone, least of all a six-year-old child, but fate, unfortunately, had had other plans.

Jake's parents had been tragically killed in an accident and Luca had been left with a godson who had no place whatsoever in his highly controlled and extremely frenetic life.

Naturally, Luca had done his best and had flung money at the unexpected problem. But now, sitting back in his office while he waited for the tiny, dark-haired thing who had returned his godson two hours earlier, he had to concede that he had failed.

That failure was an insult to his dignity, to his pride and, more than that, signalled a dereliction of the duty he had blithely taken upon his shoulders when he had accepted the position of godfather.

Once this chaotic mess was brought to a conclusion, he would have to rethink the whole situation or else risk something far worse happening in the not-too-distant future.

What, precisely, the solution to that problem might be, Luca had no idea, but he was confident he would be able to come up with something. He always did.

Standing outside the door, where she had been delivered like an unwanted parcel by the fearsome middle-aged woman with the steel-grey hair and the unsmiling face of a hit man, Ellie wasn't sure whether to knock, push open the door which was ajar or—her favoured option—run away.

She instantly and regrettably ruled out the running away option because right now, in the pouring rain, the dogs she was looking after were mournfully doing heaven only knew what in the back garden of this stupidly fabulous Chelsea mansion. She couldn't abandon them. If she did, she quailed to think what their fate might be. Neither the hard-faced housekeeper nor her cold-as-ice employer struck her as the types who had much time for dogs. They would have no problem tossing all three dogs into the local dogs' home faster than you could say 'local dogs' home'.

She licked her lips. Hovered. Twisted her hands together. Tried hard not to think about the towering, intimidating guy to whom she had spoken briefly an hour and a half previously when she had rung the doorbell to deliver one runaway six-year-old back to his home. She'd had no idea to whom the blond child belonged, but she certainly hadn't envisaged the sort of drop-dead gorgeous man who had greeted them with an expression that could have frozen water. He had looked at her and the dogs and then taken charge of the situation in a manner that had brooked no debate, dispatching her to the kitchen where she had been commanded to *sit and wait; he would be with her shortly.*

She tentatively knocked on the door, took a deep breath and then walked into the room with a lot more bravado than she was currently feeling.

Like the rest of the house she had glimpsed, this room positively screamed *luxury.*

In her peripheral vision, she took in the cool greys, the marble, the built-in bookcase with its rows of forbidding business tomes. On one wall, there was an exquisite little painting that she vaguely recognised. On the opposite wall, there was an ornate series of hand-mounted clocks, all telling different times, and of course the vast granite-and-wood desk on which were three computers, behind which...

'My apologies if you have been kept waiting.' Luca nodded at the leather chair facing his desk, his cool, dark eyes never leaving Ellie's face. When she had shown up at his front door, with Jake in one hand and a series of leads attached to dogs in the other, Luca had thought that he had never seen such a scrappy little thing in his life. Small, slender, with short hair and clothes he associated with the sort of people with whom he had minimal contact. Walkers, ramblers, lovers of great open spaces...

He'd barely been able to see what sort of figure she had because it had been hidden under a capacious jumper that was streaked with muddy paw-prints. Her jeans had been tucked into similarly muddy wellies and she had forgone the nicety of an umbrella as protection against the driving summer downpour in favour of a denim hat from beneath which she had glared at him with unhidden, judgemental criticism.

All in all, not his type.

'Sit. Please.'

'I don't know what I'm doing here, Mr Ross. Why have I been made to hang around, waiting to see you? My whole day has been thrown out of kilter!'

'Tell me about it. And I'm betting that your out-of-kilter day is somewhat less catastrophic than mine, Miss... Edwards, is it? When I left for work this morning, the last thing I anticipated was being called back here because my godson had done a runner.'

'And it was a good job I was there to bring him back!' Ellie stuck her chin out defiantly, recalling in the nick of time that she was really furious with this man, who clearly ran such a rubbish ship on the home front that his godson had absconded, crossing several main roads and endangering his life to get to the park where anything could have happened, because this was London.

Anger felt very good, because the alternative was that unsettling *awareness* in the pit of her stomach because the guy staring at her, as grim-faced as an executioner, was also one of the most ridiculously good-looking men she had ever set eyes on.

An exotic gene pool was evident in the rich bronze of his skin and the midnight darkness of his stunning eyes while his features were perfectly and lovingly chiselled to exquisite perfection. One look at him had been enough to knock the breath out of her body and, sitting here, the effect of those remote, thick-fringed dark eyes on her was threatening to do so again.

'You have no idea how dangerous London can be,' she emphasised, tearing her gaze away from his with visible difficulty. 'A young boy wandering through a park...? That's a disaster waiting to happen.'

'Yes. There is no doubt about that.' Luca sat back and stared at her coldly and thoughtfully. 'Incredibly fortuitous that you were on the scene, ready to return him.'

'Yes. Yes, it was.'

'Should I tell you at this point how fortunate you are that you're not currently being quizzed by the police?'

Ellie stared at him blankly while her brain tried to crank into gear and make sense of what he was saying.

'Police?'

'My initial reaction when my housekeeper phoned to tell me that Jake couldn't be found was to suspect kidnap.'

'Sorry?'

'Look around you, Miss Edwards.' Luca waved his hand carelessly to encompass the luxurious surroundings of his office, where an original Picasso rubbed shoulders with an impressive sculpture of an elongated woman that rested on a glass stand.

Ellie duly looked.

'I have never,' Luca continued, 'considered the necessity for bodyguards—or kidnap insurance, for that matter—but then I have never been in charge of a young and unpredictable child. Had you not shown up when you had, my next phone call would have been to the police, and you would now be sitting here being interrogated by them. However, here you are, and, in answer to your original question, the reason I kept you waiting was because I thought it necessary to establish what role, if any, you played in my nephew's disappearance.'

'I'm sorry, but I'm not following you.'

'In which case, I'll give you a few moments to digest what I've just said. I think, once you've done that, you'll know precisely where I'm going with this.'

'You think that I…that I…'

'I'm not a man who takes chances. I've always found that it pays to take what people tell me with a generous pinch of salt.' Luca shrugged. 'For all I know, you could have lured the boy out with the bait of those three hounds frolicking in my back garden.'

'*Lured him out?* Why on earth would I do that?'

'Now, Miss Edwards, you must surely realise that anyone living in a place like this would be able to pay whatever money you might ask for in return for the safe return of his charge? I won't go so far as to say that you kidnapped the boy. Perhaps it was an opportunity that presented itself, one you decided to take advantage of. Maybe you saw Jake out with the nanny at some point? Noticed where he lived? Temptation and opportunity often have a way of finding one another.'

'That is the *most outrageous* thing I have *ever heard* in my entire life!' Cheeks flaming, Ellie sprang to her feet and then stopped dead when he commanded her to sit back down.

'When you're sitting on a fortune, you find that people will do anything to try and get their hands on some of it. Had the police been called, trust me when I tell you that the line of questioning would have been far more intrusive.'

'Perhaps in your world, Mr Ross, people will do anything to

try and steal your money—maybe you're surrounded by people who have no scruples—but I can assure you that I'm not interested in getting my hands on any fortune of yours! I had no idea that Jake lived in a place like this. Thank goodness,' she added sarcastically, 'that he was wearing a convenient dog tag so that I knew his address.'

Luca had the grace to flush. 'He's six years old and he's only been in the country for a few months. It was important that he carried some form of identification on him, just in case he ended up lost for some reason. His nanny was instructed never to let him out of her sight, but as you can see for yourself my instructions were lamentably ignored. Jake is a bright boy, but he can't be expected to remember an address he is not familiar with.'

'Do you believe me when I tell you that I just happened to find him in the park, Mr Ross?' Ellie said tightly. 'Because I don't have to stay here and be accused of…being a criminal!'

'Yes.' Luca sighed and twirled the pen on his desk between his fingers before fixing his riveting dark eyes on her. 'I had a word with my godson and it would seem that he got bored. Alicia, the nanny, was on her phone—doubtless on a personal call, which is clearly against the rules—and he thought he'd go and do a little exploring.'

Luca preferred not to dwell on that conversation which, as with most of the conversations with his godson, had been monosyllabic and unsatisfactory.

He had sat on the bed, while Jake had conspicuously refused eye contact, and had done his best to elicit information from him.

'What did you think you were doing, leaving the house without the nanny?' Luca had asked, tempering an inclination to be impatient and critical.

Jake had shrugged.

'Not a good enough answer,' Luca had gritted, which had met with another shrug.

In the end, he had managed to drag a 'I hate it here and I was bored so I went outside to play' from Jake and that had been the sum total of words exchanged.

'It's what six-year-old boys do, unfortunately. They explore, especially when outside looks like more fun than inside.' Her voice was cold. She was still bristling at his insulting insinuation that she might have had something to do with his godson's absconding from the less-than-happy home sweet home. Whatever world Luca Ross inhabited, did he honestly think that everyone around him had some sort of underhand motive and had nothing better to do than to try and access his bank account?

That there wasn't a person out there who wouldn't do what it took to get their hands on what he had?

Except...

She, of all people, was uneasily aware that she should have known what power money and wealth could exert.

She had grown up with the disastrous consequences of a beautiful mother who had been one of those people Luca had talked about; one of those people who would have done anything for money.

Her mother had yearned for that very thing Luca Ross accepted so casually, and that yearning had created a war zone within the Edwards household. Andrea had, as she had made patently clear over the years, married beneath her. She had married a lowly clerk who had failed to rise to the heights she had initially hoped when they had both been young and hopeful. Riven with bitterness and disappointment, she had focused all her energies on ensuring that her youngest daughter, Lily, a beauty like her, could make good on the dreams and aspirations *she* had had to watch wither away.

And the casualty had been Ellie, studious, hardworking and a sparrow to her little sister's shimmering peacock.

Oh, Ellie knew just how damaging the quest for money could be. She had grown up loathing the way people were prepared to behave to get it. Her father had been the one with the strong moral compass and she had adhered to him from a very young age.

The arrogant billionaire sitting in front of her was just the sort of guy she loathed.

The fact that he could sit there and casually accuse her of deliberately trying to con him out of money by snatching his nephew and then returning him in the guise of a Good Samaritan said it all.

'If that's all, Mr Ross…? I have to return the dogs to their owners. I've texted to tell them that there's been a bit of a situation but I can't afford to antagonise any of them.'

'Let me have the addresses of these people. I will ensure that their pets are returned to them.'

'I've already been here for nearly an hour and a half. I have things to do. You said you wanted to talk to me and I'm thinking that you wanted to establish whether you had to bring the police in to arrest me. Now that you've seen I'm not a criminal, I shall leave and take the dogs back to their owners myself. They're tired and they need to be fed.'

'There are a couple of things I still want to straighten out. I can assure you that the dogs will be delivered safely back.'

'By your housekeeper?' Ellie smiled at him without warmth. 'I think she blew the bonding bit when she chucked them out into the pouring rain and locked the door behind them.'

'My orders. I had no intention of letting those dogs drag any more mud into my house than they already had. They're dogs. Enjoying the great outdoors is what they do. My driver has two dogs. He will deliver them, unless you want to hang onto them for another hour or so. Your choice.'

'What else is there to say, Mr Ross? I've told you everything that happened. I saw Jake playing with the dogs and, when I went over, he let slip that there was no adult with him. At first I didn't believe him, because kids are clever when it comes to twisting the truth to get what they want, and I thought that perhaps he wanted to have a bit more time with the dogs, but

I very quickly realised that he was telling the truth. He was in that park on his own. Naturally, I was horrified.'

'Naturally.'

'And I got him back here as fast as I could. And, no, I don't want any money for returning your nephew. I'm just relieved that—'

'Yes, got the drift. As for the money element to your statement, why don't we return to that later?'

'There's nothing to return to, Mr Ross.'

'You rescued my godson. I feel we can step away from formalities. Why don't you call me Luca? And you... Ellie, I believe you said?'

Ellie flushed. Luca. Strong, aggressive name for a strong, aggressive male, was the thought that ran through her head. She squashed it flatter than a pancake and gave him a little half-shrug.

'You seem to imply that you're familiar with children.' The dark eyes watching her were careful and speculative as he continued to command the conversation, thinking on his feet as he talked, observing—something he was extremely good at. 'Have you any of your own?'

'I'm twenty-five. I would have to have started very early.'

'And you're not married...'

'How on earth do you know that?'

'No ring on your finger. Jake took to you as well as the dogs. If he hadn't, he would never have allowed you to walk him back to the house. He would have scarpered. It's obvious he trusted you. He was also holding your hand when he returned.' He tilted his head to one side and inspected her in silence for a few long seconds. 'None of this may seem like much of a big deal to you, Ellie, but I can assure you that it is. Since he came over here, he has found it difficult to...settle.'

'Can I ask what happened?'

Luca's initial response to that was to shut down, because answering questions posed by other people was seldom within his remit, unless those questions were work-orientated. Personal questions were off-limits. This was a personal question, but for once he wasn't going to drop the shutters, because he was in a jam and he was beginning to think that part of the solution could be sitting right there in front of him.

'His parents were killed in a car accident,' he intoned flatly. 'Freak situation. They left Jake an orphan. By virtue of the fact that I was Johnny's closest blood relative—his cousin, to be precise, not to mention Jake's godfather—and the fact that Ruby, his wife, had no close family members, I inherited Jake.'

'So you're Jake's second cousin as well as his godfather...'

Luca frowned. 'As I have just said.'

'And yet, despite that connection, things must be a bit strained between you for him to have run away.'

Was he being called to account? For a few seconds, Luca's mind went blank because *being called to account* was not something with which he was familiar.

'A bit strained?' he questioned in a voice that would have had grown men quaking, a voice he had perfected over the years, one which was very handy when it came to controlling anyone who had the temerity to breach his barriers.

The slender, dark-haired gamine sitting opposite him wasn't quaking.

'It happens,' she said, her voice rich with sympathy. 'Just because you're family doesn't always mean that the relationship is close.' She thought of her own relationship with her sister, which was anything but close even though, once upon a time, they had been far closer than they were now.

'Jake and his parents,' Luca said heavily, 'went to America to live. Keeping in touch was difficult.'

'I'll bet.'

'I'm an extremely busy man.' Luca heard the irritation in his voice and was exasperated with himself for launching into explanations that were, frankly, unnecessary.

'It wasn't meant as a criticism,' Ellie murmured, lowering

her eyes and thinking that that was exactly how it had been meant—because what she was deducing was that Luca would have been way too busy making money to remember some cousin on the other side of the world.

'The fact is that we have both found ourselves in a situation where adjustments have had to be made and Jake has found those adjustments somewhat difficult.'

'Poor, poor kid. No wonder he's had trouble settling down. I've come across that sort of thing a couple of times, usually involving kids who have come to London from another country, and in one instance to stay with a distant relative they really didn't know very well. Adjusting was an issue.'

She sat up straighter, on more solid ground now that she was in possession of a few facts. 'I don't suppose...' she had nothing to lose by speaking her mind '...it's helped that he's been farmed out to a nanny and a housekeeper, and heaven only knows who else, when all he probably needs is one-on-one time with you as the adult responsible for his welfare.'

'Is that a criticism?' Luca asked coldly. 'Because I've been sensing a few of those under the demure replies and the polite questions.'

Ellie dug her heels in and shrugged. 'I can tell you don't appreciate it,' she said eventually, when the silence threatened to become too tense, 'but I'm just speaking my mind. I'm a teacher, and I have quite a bit of experience when it comes to young kids.'

'So you're a teacher? That's very interesting.' Luca dropped his eyes and doodled something on the pad in front of him.

'Is it? Why?'

'I feel I would have worked that out eventually,' he murmured, and she reddened.

'Why is that, Mr Ross?'

'Luca.'

Ellie stared at him, lips tightly pressed together, and just like that Luca smiled.

Her expression—thorough disapproval even though she was let down by having such a delicate, feminine face, all huge green eyes, short, straight nose and a mouth that was a perfect Cupid's bow. The more defiantly she tilted her chin, narrowed her eyes and aimed for severe, the more amused he was.

'I'm not seeing the joke.' Ellie's heart was slamming against her rib cage, and not just because she knew that he was laughing *at* her. That smile was so *sexy* and, just like that, she glimpsed someone other than the ice-cold billionaire who had rubbed her up the wrong way the second she had met him and who represented everything she had no time for.

And this *someone other* was dangerous. She felt it. This *someone other* wasn't just drop-dead gorgeous. He was sinfully sexy, the sort of *sexy* that should come with a health warning.

'You should see your face,' Luca drawled. 'Tight lips, pursed mouth, disapproving eyes. Could you be anything *but* a school teacher?'

He made that sound like a source of amusement instead of consternation, which somehow made his criticism all the more offensive.

'Maybe most of them are too scared,' she snapped with reckless abandon.

'I don't care for that tone of voice.' Cool eyes fastened on her flushed face. He realised that she had signally made no effort to try and impress him from the second she had walked into his house, just as he realised that most people did, which was something he took for granted.

'And I don't care for the fact that you think it's okay to sit there and laugh at me. I'm a teacher, an excellent teacher, and if you think that it's hilarious that I speak my mind then too bad.'

'Not hilarious,' Luca said slowly, speculatively. 'Refreshing.'

His mobile buzzed and he took the call, which lasted a matter of seconds. Not for a second did his eyes leave her face.

Ellie had the strangest sensation of intense discomfort under that scrutiny. It was as if her body was on hyper-alert, sensitive in ways she couldn't quite understand. She felt restless in her own skin and yet frozen to the spot, barely able to breathe.

'The dogs have gone. I'm sure their owners will be overjoyed to have them home.' He sat back and inclined his head to one side. 'Can I ask you something, Ellie?'

Ellie felt that he would anyway, whatever answer she gave, so she tilted her head to one side and didn't say anything.

'Why are you walking dogs when you have a job?'

That wasn't what she had been expecting and she went bright red.

'I don't see what that has to do with anything,' she muttered.

'The nanny has gone.' He changed tack so abruptly that she was left floundering and wrong-footed.

'The nanny…?'

'Second in six months.'

'That can't be a good thing. The poor boy probably needs continuity,' Ellie said when he made no attempt to elaborate on this. 'Children really need defined boundaries and, especially in Jake's situation, stability would be very important.' *Tight lips… pursed mouth…disapproving eyes…* Ellie was impatient with herself for letting him get under her skin, because who cared what the man thought one way or another?

'I fully agree with you. It's been disappointing but what can one do? The first nanny was a middle-aged lady who was clearly out of her depth dealing with Jake. He's extremely clever and very strong-willed underneath that quiet exterior. It would seem that he simply refused to go along with any plan he didn't agree to.' Luca paused. 'He also created such a fuss about going to school that, as it came out in the wash, the woman was browbeaten into keeping him at home on a couple of occasions which, naturally, didn't work.'

'Has he not settled into school life either?'

'It's been a difficult period,' Luca murmured with exquisite understatement.

Confused, because she had no idea where this roundabout

conversation was leading, but very much aware that there was a definite destination in sight even though it eluded her at the moment, Ellie stared at Luca with fascination.

Everything about him was compelling, from the graceful, economical movements of his hands when he spoke to the proud angle of his head and the harsh beauty of his features.

For the first time, she was awkwardly conscious of the gaping chasm between them—and not just in the money stakes.

He was so breathtakingly beautiful that he made her aware of her shortcomings, and that was a place she hadn't visited for a long time.

Growing up, she had learned to accept that when it came to looks she was second-best.

Lily was the one with the looks. Like her mother, she was tall, willowy and blonde, her vanilla hair dropping like a waterfall down her narrow back. From the day she'd been born, she had been attracting attention, and that had only become more pronounced as she had grown and eventually matured into a stunningly beautiful adolescent.

With a sister blessed with such spectacular looks, Ellie had quickly learned to fade into the background, developing skills that did not rely on physical appearance. She had studied hard, got A grades in everything, helped out during summers at the local kennels and played as much sport as she could, because being outside the house often beat being inside it.

So it was irritating now to find herself thinking about her looks and wondering what Luca saw when he stared at her with such a veiled expression.

'I had hoped,' Luca said truthfully, 'that Alicia might have worked out. I'd come to the conclusion that it might have been a mistake relying on experience to deal with Jake, without taking into account that experience might come with the downside of being a little too stuffy to handle a kid of six.'

'Mr Ross... Luca... I'm sorry that your nephew hasn't settled over here as well as he might have. I would advise you to try and bond with him a bit more, but I'm sure you'll ignore me. Perhaps, after this little incident, his nanny will be a little more vigilant. Maybe she just needs to get him out and about a bit more. It's the summer holidays and there's an awful lot going on in London at the moment for kids. Or she could even take him out of London. To the seaside, perhaps.'

'That would be difficult,' Luca said gently, when she had finally tapered off into silence, 'considering the nanny has been sacked.'

'Sacked? But why?'

'Why do you think?'

'Yes, well... I'm sure she will have learned from this episode...' Ellie vaguely wondered whether the sacked nanny could take him to some kind of industrial tribunal for unfair dismissal but somehow she couldn't envisage anyone, least of all a young nanny, having the courage to do anything of the sort.

And sadly, whilst the poor girl probably did deserve a second chance, it was fair to say that letting her charge escape did come under the heading of *dereliction of duty*.

'I would hope so but it doesn't matter because it's not my problem.' Luca pushed himself away from the desk and linked his fingers on his washboard stomach. 'My problem isn't what the sacked nanny does now. My problem is what *I* do now...'

CHAPTER TWO

LUCA HAD REACHED a decision. He'd done what he did best. Faced with a problem, he had brought his natural creativity to the situation, thought on his feet and come up with a solution.

He'd sacked the nanny. He needed cover. And it wasn't going to fall on his shoulders because he didn't have enough hours in the day.

Miss Muller, efficient though she was, could hardly be expected to turn her hand to child minding a six-year-old. She'd never had children and, from the little he had glimpsed of her interaction with Jake, an eagerness to make up for that lack was not there.

And the agency wasn't going to be much help in the immediate future. They were painstaking when it came to the business of sourcing nannies. Leave it with them and he could be collecting his pension before they came up with a replacement, especially given the short, chequered history of the previous two, both sacked.

Cover was staring him in the face. The girl was perfect. He was good when it came to reading people and he could read that this one would be up to the job.

He would lay his cards on the table soon enough but first he would find out as much as he could about her personal circumstances because her personal circumstances could be used to his advantage.

He would at least have to determine her availability.

It didn't occur to him to ask her directly whether she would be able to step into the breach because getting what you wanted always panned out better once you'd got a feel for the lie of the land. A lifetime of dealing with people had given Luca a healthy scepticism when it came to making sure he got the best possible deal from them.

This girl was no gold-digger, but that didn't mean she wouldn't be tempted to try her luck if she thought she could pull a fast one.

'You never told me why you were walking dogs.' He lazily returned to the question he had earlier directed at her. He tilted his big body at an angle that allowed him to watch her closely from under lowered lashes. 'You have a job. I don't know what teachers get paid, but I'm assuming it's not so little that they have to take a begging bowl onto the streets.'

'Walking dogs isn't the same as *taking a begging bowl onto the streets.*'

'Figure of speech. Shouldn't you be enjoying your respite from tetchy kids and classrooms?'

'I...' Ellie reddened. 'I like dogs,' she said lamely. 'And I like walking.'

'And that's very commendable, but you surely must do it because of the money?'

'I... As it happens, I find the additional income very useful.' Ellie heard herself stutter out the truth and immediately told herself that it was nothing to be ashamed about and that she shouldn't let herself be cowed into editing her personality which was, by its nature, open and honest.

'Why?'

'*Why?* Mr Ross, *Luca,* I'm not one of your employees. I don't actually have to tell you anything.'

'Instead of getting worked up because I'm asking you a few

questions, you need to sit back and listen to me without interruption for a few minutes.'

Ellie's mouth dropped open.

'You probably want to get back to your house as much as I need to return to work, but there *was* something I wanted to propose to you, and I think you would be open to my suggestion—especially if you tell me that you need money.'

'I never said that I *needed* money.'

'You don't have to but I'm good at joining dots. I heard the anxiety in your voice when you talked to me about reuniting those dogs with their owners. You were apprehensive about upsetting them. You don't want to upset them because, however much you love dogs and love walking, it's not a labour of love for you. Ergo, you need the money.

'Now, don't get me wrong. I don't give a damn what you want the money for—addiction to fine wine, an obsession with designer clothes...or maybe you're saving for a round-the-world cruise. I don't care. It's all the same to me. You have no criminal record, because checks would have been done on you before you became a teacher. Here's the deal.'

He leant forward, palms flattened on the desk. 'I no longer have a nanny and I can't afford to spare the time out for babysitting duties. Miss Muller isn't going to be able to step up to the plate here and I would not ask her to. However, as I said to you, my nephew took to you and that in itself speaks volumes. Combined with the fact that you clearly need the money, we could work together towards a satisfactory solution to my problem.'

Ellie stared at him in a daze. She was accustomed to controlling situations. It was part and parcel of her job, but right now she felt as though she had handed the reins over to someone who was cheerfully steering her in the direction he wanted her to go.

'I'll admit my immediate reaction to you showing up at my front door with my godson was one of instant suspicion.'

Ellie was fascinated by Luca's lack of apology for behaviour that frankly had been pretty outrageous. When she had walked

Jake back, she had anticipated gratitude. She had mentally prepared an informative speech about the importance of family and of understanding the psyche of children. It was going to be a severe speech, as befitted the situation. She had even mulled over the possibility that she might step into a quagmire that would necessitate outside intervention. She worked in a school where that sort of thing had occurred on a couple of occasions, although something about Jake had made her think that his family life wasn't going to be a disaster zone. His clothes had been dishevelled and muddy from the dogs but expensive all the same.

She hadn't anticipated a series of events that had seen her told coolly that she could have been hauled down to a police station, accused of staging the whole thing for money and then eventually been given the all-clear without a hint of remorse.

'I got that,' Ellie said tightly as her mind continued to whirr. She couldn't take her eyes off him. He was larger than life in every sense of the word and in his presence every nerve-ending in her body was on red alert, every sense and pulse stretched to breaking point. From the proud angle of his head to the luxuriant dark hair and exotically sculpted features, the man oozed more than just sexuality and it knocked her for six.

And now he was offering her a job?

'Naturally I would do my own background check on you anyway,' he murmured, half to himself.

'You're offering me a job?' Just in case she'd got hold of the wrong end of the stick.

'The circumstances are a little unusual,' Luca admitted. 'It's not in my nature to jump into anything without first testing the water, but I need someone to look after Jake, and sooner rather than later...'

'But you could always just take a couple of weeks off work. Maybe go on holiday with him whilst the agency finds a replacement. If he's had trouble settling down then a holiday might be just the thing he needs.'

'I don't have time for holidays,' Luca said flatly.

'Never?' Ellie asked incredulously, wondering what the point of being rich was if you never took time out to enjoy your hard-earned cash. If *she* had money, then she would travel the world. It was a luxury she had never had.

'There's no time off when you're running a business the size of mine.' Luca shrugged. 'It may sound harsh but I'm simply being realistic.' He leaned back and sighed heavily, with a hint of impatience. 'This escapade has made me realise that Jake needs someone who is not only capable of taking him from A to B and making sure he is fed and watered, but someone with whom he has some kind of bond. He clearly didn't bond with either of the previous nannies, but in the space of a very short time he managed to do that with you, and I'm guessing your experience as a teacher has something to do with that.' He looked at her shrewdly. 'So here we are.'

'I already have a job,' Ellie said. As job offers went, this one certainly hadn't been wrapped up in any pretty packaging. He was in a jam and she was a possible solution. No beating about the bush with any niceties.

'Teaching, and walking dogs for the additional income.'

She decided not to go down the 'needing money' road again. Luca made her nervous and uncomfortable and she couldn't think of anything worse than working for him. 'There's no way,' she said politely, 'that I would ever consider jacking in my full-time job to become a nanny to your godson. I love my job. I enjoy working with lots of different kids.'

He would make a terrible employer. It was obvious that he was as warm and cuddly as a rattlesnake. He thought nothing of getting rid of people who didn't live up to his high expectations and, while he was quick to blame, he didn't seem prepared to accept that he might be the root cause of Jake's behaviour.

Work for him?

She would rather walk on a bed of burning coals. Part of the reason she enjoyed what she did, aside from the satisfaction of working with the kids, was that she really loved the people she worked alongside.

They were on her wavelength. They were all part of the greater caring community who didn't rush to put themselves first.

Luca Ross was part of the cut-throat community who thought nothing of taking what they wanted whatever the cost. He was arrogant, ruthless and manipulative. She'd been in his company for a handful of hours and already she felt wrung out.

'I'm not talking about a long-term position,' he clarified, still fully confident that he was going to get what he wanted because, frankly, he always did. 'Of course, a suitable nanny will be found in due course, but that's going to take time, and this time around I will have more input to the procedure than previously.'

Ellie was making a mental list in her head of all the things she disliked about him and she tacked this new one on. *He probably left choosing the nannies to his secretary because he was too busy and couldn't be bothered...*

'I'm sorry,' she said, standing up so that he could take the hint that their conversation was at an end. Her body broke out in light perspiration as he slowly rose to his feet. He strolled towards her, in no hurry.

His long, lean body oozed latent strength and suffocating masculinity. She could almost see the flex of sinew and muscle under the charcoal-grey trousers and the white shirt, which he had cuffed to the elbow. His forearms were liberally sprinkled with dark hair. She wondered whether his chest would likewise be sprinkled with dark hair and she furiously stopped herself in crazy mid-thought.

He cast an ominous shadow as he finally paused to stand in front of her, and Ellie had to will herself not to cower.

The mental checklist of things she disliked about the man was growing by the second. Not only did he think he could get whatever he wanted but he was not averse to using sheer brawn and intimidation tactics to get there.

'Sorry?'

'I'm not interested in working for you.' She cleared her throat and their eyes collided, causing the air to rush out of her body in a whoosh. 'I appreciate the offer, but you're better off going back to the agency, and maybe taking more of a hands-on approach this time, because you seemed to imply that you hadn't on the previous occasions.'

'How can you appreciate my offer when you haven't heard the details?'

'I don't need to.'

'Care to tell me why?'

'I know you think that you can get whatever you want because you're rich, but you can't.' She tore her eyes away with difficulty. He was standing so close to her that she could breathe in whatever woody, intensely masculine aftershave he was wearing.

Breathing was proving to be a problem. It was unnerving. She forced herself to remain calm and composed because he was just standing there; he wasn't trying to prevent her from leaving the room. She remembered how to breathe and then looked at him.

'Jake ran away for a reason.' Her voice, thankfully, did not betray the utter turmoil his proximity was bringing on. 'Okay, so maybe he didn't like the nanny very much, or perhaps he got bored and decided to venture out, but the bottom line is that there's obviously something missing on the home front and that something can only be provided by you.'

'We're going round in circles.'

'Because we're on completely different wavelengths.' She cleared her throat and wished that he would back off by even a couple of inches so that she could get her act together. 'And that's just one reason why I could never work for you. We're from different worlds.'

'Since when do people have to think alike in order to have a satisfactory working arrangement?'

'It matters to me,' Ellie persisted. Since she had nothing to lose, she said, bluntly, 'I don't like what you stand for. I'm not into money and I don't approve of people who focus all their energy on making it. I'm happy doing what I'm doing, and I wish you all the best in your search for a replacement for the nanny you sacked.'

Luca stared at her in silence then he nodded slowly.

He backed away, leaving a cool void behind him. Desperate to leave only seconds earlier, Ellie now hovered uneasily. He had moved back to the desk but was now perched on the edge and was watching her with a thoughtful expression.

'So...' She licked her lips nervously.

'You were on your way out?'

'Yes, I was!' She pulled open the door and an odd thought suddenly sprang into her addled brain—*this will be the last time you set eyes on this man.* She blinked, surprised and bemused at the discomfiture that thought provoked out of nowhere.

Ellie thought he might have tried to stop her, one last stab at persuading her to hear him out, and she was disconcerted to find that she was almost disappointed when he remained in the office while she let herself out of the house, pausing and looking up the stairs on her way out.

Should she try and find Jake? Say goodbye? She wanted to. In a short space of time, he had touched her with his shy overtures of friendship.

No. She'd already become way too involved in his backstory. She'd done her good deed for the week and delivered him back to his home and it was doubtful she would lay eyes on him again.

Whatever nanny Luca got, Ellie's money was on the poor girl being monitored more closely than a convict on parole. She would be manacled to the poor child while Luca carried on making money and kidding himself that he was being a good guardian by flinging cash at the problem that had landed on his doorstep.

Hateful and obnoxious, she thought, barely aware of the walk back to the park and then on to the nearest bus because she was so busy thinking of him.

Ellie shared a house with three other girls. Every time she approached the front door, she recalled the far nicer little place she had rented previously where she had been able to relax in peace; where she hadn't had to jostle for space in the fridge; any time she wanted to herself now had to be spent in a bedroom that was only just about big enough for a bed, a chest of drawers and a wardrobe that was a whisker away from being held together by masking tape. But needs must.

She wondered, but only briefly, whether she should have listened to whatever offer Luca had been prepared to put on the table...

Twenty-four hours later, Ellie was on her way back home when she noticed a long, sleek, black car pull away from the kerb, picking up speed and then slowing down until it was right alongside her.

The persistent rain of the past couple of weeks had stopped and, at a little after six-thirty in the evening, a watery sun was trying to remind everyone that it was still summer.

The road was quiet, practically deserted, and with a flare of panic she quickened her steps, only almost to collide into the passenger door of the car which had been flung open, barring her path.

'Hop in, Ellie.'

She recognised the voice instantly and, when she peered inside, her heart did a quick flip and her breathing hitched. Luca was the last person she had been expecting to see again.

The tinted windows had prevented her from seeing the driver and now she wondered how on earth he had managed to do that?

Show up just when she was on her way back to her house. Did he have some sort of telepathic X-ray vision?

She blinked, her mouth opening and shutting while Luca looked at her in total silence.

'How did you find me?'

'Hop in.'

'No!'

'Don't slam the door. Just get in the car and listen to what I have to say.'

'How did you find me?' she repeated, reluctant to get in the car yet not wanting to draw attention to herself. She slid into the passenger seat and slammed the door behind her.

In the enclosed space, she was uneasily conscious of the raw sexuality that had accosted her the last time she had been in his company. He was so staggeringly *male*, so devoid of any soft side, so unapologetically masculine.

She looked at him and didn't know whether it was because he had been on her mind, or whether it was just the shock of seeing him when she hadn't expected to, but her body was suddenly filled with a disturbing electric charge.

Her nipples pinched, scraping against her tee shirt because she seldom wore a bra except to work. What was the point when there was precious little to hold in place? And there was a stickiness between her legs that horrified her, made her want to slam her thighs together tightly.

'Don't forget, I know where your dog-walking clients live,' Luca intoned smoothly. 'I asked them whether you were out with their dogs. Actually, I struck jackpot with owner number one. You're a creature of habit, Ellie. Same routine. It was a pretty simple process of deduction that you would be heading back to your house around now. Mrs Wilson was kind enough to let me have your address. She also gave me your mobile number but I thought it best if I surprised you.'

'She had *no right* to hand over my private details!'

'Maybe she could tell at a glance that I wasn't a homicidal maniac.'

'That's not the point.'

'Which is your house?'

'I don't want you in my house!'

'Then we can sit here and have this conversation,' he said calmly. He killed the engine and reclined in the chair, angling his big body so that he was facing her.

'We've covered everything there is to say. I'm not going to work for you.'

'You've moved.'

'I beg your pardon?'

'You never used to live in this part of London. You used to rent a tidy little flat in West London, but you gave that up two months ago so that you could move to this area which is, at the very best, dodgy.'

'How did you find all of that out?'

'I can find out anything I want to,' Luca told her without batting an eyelid. 'And I wanted to find out about you because I want you. You're saving money, and a brief background check leads me to believe that it's because you're helping your father out of a hole.'

Ellie stiffened, shocked and dismayed. How far was his reach?

'Tell me about it,' he said, but his voice was curiously gentle. 'And don't let your feelings for me and your pride get in the way of your common sense, Ellie. Like I told you, we can help one another. As business arrangements go, this could be an extremely rewarding one for both of us. I need someone there for Jake. Did you know that he's asked after you?'

Suspicion poured out of every pore in Ellie's body but that question, tacked on at the end, made her hesitate, even though she suspected that he was a man who would work the cards in his hand any way he chose if it could get him what he wanted.

You didn't get to the top by being kind and caring and making allowances for the weak and feeble. You got to the top by being ruthless, and he was at the very top.

'It's the first conversation I think I've had with Jake since he came over here. Or, at least, the first conversation that wasn't like squeezing blood from a stone.'

Ellie opened her mouth to inform him that she wasn't interested, and besides she resented the fact that he had been investigating her behind her back, but instead she heard herself say, 'What do you mean?'

'We've barely spoken. I've had reports from the nannies but the times we've sat down together over a meal, he's only managed to mutter a few monosyllabic answers to the questions I've asked. This morning, he asked after you, and after those mutts you introduced him to. He wanted to know whether he would be able to return to the park so that he could walk with you.'

His expression was shuttered but Ellie was good at reading body language and what she was seeing was genuine emotion from a man who probably found it difficult to express himself in terms of feelings and who was at a loss with a situation he couldn't control.

'This would not be a permanent position,' he told her softly, shifting, because a car was not the most comfortable of places in which to have a protracted conversation. 'It would be a matter of a few weeks, no more than the duration of the summer holidays, during which time you could perhaps help source a replacement nanny for Jake. I think your input would be helpful on that front. It's clear you have an instinctive empathy with children, which is something I clearly lack.'

Ellie opened her mouth and he raised his hand.

'No, allow me to finish before you start digging your heels in.' He shot her a crooked smile and Ellie blinked because, shorn temporarily of that authoritarian streak in him that she had previously glimpsed, he was curiously *human*. It was unnerving.

'I could have found out the details of whatever commitment you may have towards your father, but I stopped short of that because it doesn't matter, and I also felt that if you wanted to fill me in then you would. I will pay you enough to more than cover the entire debt your father has incurred.'

'That's a crazy assurance,' Ellie said shakily. Her eyes dropped to where he was resting his hand lightly on the gear shaft and she inconsequentially thought what shapely hands he had.

'My pockets are shockingly deep,' Luca returned without a trace of false modesty. He paused and inclined his head to one side. 'What happened? Do you want to talk about it?'

The vision of being released from the stranglehold of a debt that would take her years to clear dangled in front of Ellie's eyes like an oasis in the desert.

'If you'd rather not go into the details, then that's fine. All I want to know is this: are you prepared to consider my offer? In return for a handful of weeks working for me, your father will never have to worry about his debts again. You don't have to like me to agree to this. That doesn't enter the equation. All you have to do is ask yourself whether you're willing to prolong your father's unhappy situation because of misplaced pride.'

As trump cards went, Ellie knew that he had pulled out the ace of spades. Her father was stressed beyond belief and frankly so was she.

Did she want him to know the situation? Ellie already knew that she would agree to what he wanted. He'd somehow managed to find the precise spot where his appeal would hit pay dirt.

'It would be a relief to clear my father's debts,' Ellie said stiffly.

'Before you continue, do you want to carry on this conversation in your house? I'm too big to sit in this car indefinitely. I need to stretch my legs.'

'I share the place with other girls.' She involuntarily grimaced. 'But I guess we could go to a pub. There's one not far from here. I could direct you.'

Having secured the deal, Luca had no intention of letting the grass grow under his feet. They were in the pub with a bottle of chilled wine in front of them within fifteen minutes.

'So...?' he pressed urgently.

'My dad has found himself in a bit of a pickle.' She opened up, because she did want him to know more than just the bones of why she was taking this job. He'd found out so much about her that he could easily have found out the entire story and the fact that he hadn't softened her impression of him. Just a little. If she chose not to explain anything, she knew that he wouldn't try to find out off his own bat but, for some reason, she didn't want him to be left with the suspicion that her father had blown away his savings on rubbish.

'He got taken in by a scam on the Internet. He didn't admit to what had happened for a while. In fact, I only found out because I happened to come across a letter from the bank he had left on the console table in the sitting room. When I asked him what was happening, he admitted to everything. The bills have been piling up and he hasn't been able to meet his mortgage payments for the past few months. He's been having panic attacks.'

She looked down quickly. 'Apologies,' she said huskily. 'My dad and I are very close and I can't bear to think what he must have been going through. Anyway, of course I earn enough to keep body and soul together, but I've had to move into somewhere smaller temporarily. It's been very stressful and you should know that if it weren't for...this situation there is no way I would be sitting here having this conversation.' She looked at Luca, her green eyes challenging.

The clarity of her gaze was so disconcerting that for a few seconds words failed him.

He was staring at someone from another planet. He had offered her an easy, hassle-free job and instead of biting his hand off and naming her price she had turned him down. She was only accepting the offer now because she would have been insane to refuse it.

Luca was accustomed to women who accepted his generosity without batting an eyelid. He was made of money and he had never yet come up against any woman who didn't enjoy spending some of it when it was on offer.

He hadn't cared why she'd needed money when he had first suggested the job. He'd been confident that she would snap at the chance to get her hands on some to fund whatever lifestyle had left her in debt. He'd assumed a credit card crisis and had banked on her trying to manoeuvre to get the maximum out of him.

He was quietly pleased that he hadn't been able to buy her.

'Tell me how much your father owes,' he said, not beating around the bush, and Ellie reddened and hesitated.

'Do you think I'm going to laugh because he's been the victim of a scam?'

She didn't answer that, instead naming a figure that seemed so huge to her that she looked away in embarrassment.

'Naturally I don't expect you to cover that stupid amount...'

Luca told her what he was willing to pay her, and for once in his life he wasn't interested in driving a hard bargain.

The woman had such fundamental integrity that he was surprised to discover a side to him that wasn't utterly cynical. Born into wealth, Luca had seen from the sidelines how ugly the pursuit of money could be after his mother had died. As an eligible middle-aged widower, his father had become a magnet for women from the ages of twenty to seventy. Many of the women, having admitted defeat with his father, had turned their attentions to him, even though Luca had been a mere boy of seventeen at the time.

His own experiences as an adult had hardly served to change his opinion that there wasn't a woman alive who wouldn't do whatever it took when the stakes were high.

Luca didn't mind. He was happy to be lavish with the women he dated but he had no intention of settling down with any of them. He had no intention of settling down, full-stop.

He was fascinated by Ellie's clear-eyed gaze as their eyes met.

Predictably, she was staggered by the sum he was willing to pay. Even more predictably, she hotly refused to allow him to part with such a vast amount of cash.

'You're overreacting,' he dismissed, reaching to top her glass up. 'I'm not offering you the crown jewels...'

'As good as. It goes against my nature to accept a sum as large as that.'

'And it goes against my nature to be stingy when it comes to a situation like this. You'll be doing me a service, and I'm a man who rewards good service.'

A quiver of excitement rippled through her as their eyes met and tangled. This was a business arrangement, but right now it felt like an adventure...

CHAPTER THREE

THE FOLLOWING DAY, Ellie finally made contact with her sister.

Lily had called their father the night before and it hadn't taken him long before he phoned Ellie to tell her all about their conversation. But by then Ellie was on her way out to meet Luca for dinner. He would have her contract of employment and had told her that it was essential she knew what was expected of her. Ellie thought that top of the agenda would be not making personal calls while her charge slipped out of the house.

'Did she leave a number, by any chance?' Ellie asked when there was a break in the conversation.

She was going to be late for dinner but if she didn't talk to Lily now then there was no guarantee that she would talk to her at all. Over the years as Lily had pursued fame and fortune, using her incredible looks to open doors, she and Ellie had grown increasingly distant. It took a lot of will power to resist the temptation to let things slide until their contact was reduced to birthday cards and polite conversation over the turkey with their father on Christmas day.

Ellie had no time to beat about the bush.

'Did Dad mention anything…er…about his situation over here?' she asked bluntly, because the long-distance call was costing her money, and if she didn't stop her sister in mid flow then she would have to spend the entire phone call listening to Lily wax lyrical about all the exciting things happening in her life and the agents who were hunting her down with scripts for movies.

'What situation?' her sister questioned cautiously, so Ellie explained.

She decided that throwing out hints wasn't going to work. 'I thought that since you've found your feet over there you might think about helping me out, Lily. I earn a teacher's salary and I don't have to tell you that it's not much…'

'*You* chose to be a teacher,' Lily snapped defensively. 'So please don't tell me to start feeling sorry for you because you haven't got any money!'

'This isn't about me, Lily. It's about Dad. I've had to take… er…another job to help raise money to clear his debts, but if you could contribute then it would give me some flexibility…when it comes to accepting the offer. Luca will clear the debt but obviously it goes against my pride to accept that level of generosity.'

'What job?' Lily asked curiously. 'Luca? Who's Luca?'

In a mad rush to leave, Ellie briefly explained the situation, that Luca was a Spanish businessman who had hired her to look after his godson for the summer. Lily knew where she stood when it came to money. She would know that accepting such a vast sum of cash would have been tough.

'Oh, for God's sake,' Lily said, although her voice was more thoughtful now. 'Stop with the pride thing and just accept what's on the table. Jeez, the guy is obviously loaded and he needs you to look after the kid. Instead of beating yourself up about it, you should be trying to suss whether you can't get more out of him! Anyway, I can't commit to anything, Ellie, and even if I could I'd be nuts to hand over hard-earned cash when there's some rich guy willing to clear all Dad's debts for a few weeks of playing happy families with his kid.'

So that was that.

Despite the fact that her sister was in the enviable position of having producers banging on her door, she was being true to who she was and refusing to help.

In a rush, Ellie barely glanced at herself in the mirror before flying out of the house.

She was meeting Luca at an Italian bistro in Covent Garden. He had only ever seen her in clothes used to walk dogs, but this was going to be a more formal meeting, and she had dressed accordingly, in the same outfit she pulled out of the wardrobe for parents' meetings. A neat grey skirt, a white blouse and a pair of ballet pumps.

It was an outfit that reminded her of the businesslike nature of their relationship, and for that Ellie was grateful, because when she thought of him her mind started playing games, and what she saw in her head wasn't someone in a suit discussing terms and conditions and holding a fountain pen, it was a man with smouldering sexiness and a smile that could give her goose bumps.

She was half an hour late by the time she stepped into the bistro and looked round her, spotting Luca instantly.

She smoothed down her skirt and took a few seconds to gather herself. The restaurant was busy, with every table filled, and despite the casual sense of waiters hurrying with trays, the open-plan kitchen and the unfussy furnishings, Ellie could tell that the food would cost a fortune.

The clientele was all well-heeled. The food passing her on plates was delicate, artistic creations.

She weaved her way towards Luca and, the closer she got, the more nervous and self-conscious she felt. Her outfit, which had seemed sensible and appropriate when she had put it on an hour earlier, felt cheap and drab and she slid into her chair with a palpable feeling of relief.

'You're late,' Luca opened.

Ellie's initial reaction was to snipe back at him. Her glass-green eyes were narrowed as he glanced at his watch and then relaxed back in the chair to look at her.

Unlike the other people in the restaurant, who were all clearly kitted out in designer gear, Luca looked as though he had dressed in a hurry and without any thought for the end result. His dark hair was combed back and there was a scraping of stubble on his chin. Yet it suited him—he looked even more dangerous with a five o'clock shadow and her nervous system went into free fall.

He was in black. Black tee shirt. Black jeans. Loafers without socks.

Her mouth was suddenly parched and she gulped down some of the water that had been poured into a glass in front of her. A glimpse of her prissy grey skirt was a timely reminder of why she was sitting in this upmarket bistro.

And she also realised that his observation was pertinent. If she was going to be working for him, then punctuality was going to be important.

'I'm sorry,' she said, composing herself. 'I was delayed by a phone call. My sister phoned and I haven't spoken to her in quite a while. I couldn't brush her off.'

'Your sister? For some reason I thought that you were an only child.'

'Lily lives in America.'

Luca picked up something in her voice and he inclined his head and waited. This woman was going to be a key part of his life for the next few weeks. Two or three at the very least but almost certainly longer. The contract sitting in the envelope in his pocket offered a clever inducement should she need to stay longer than she might have anticipated. A sliding scale of pay, rising with each week over a two-week tide mark. Irresistible to someone who needed the cash.

Under normal circumstances, he wouldn't be sitting here right now. When it came to employees, it was pretty simple. He paid them well and they either did their job well, and were further rewarded, or else they didn't and they were booted out.

But the last nanny had been a learning curve for Luca. Normal rules didn't apply when it came to something as personal as his godson.

He had hired Alicia, paid her handsomely but he had taken his eye off the ball. In other words, he had treated her the same as he would have treated any of the people who worked for him.

And where had it got him? A runaway child who had had the good luck to be found and delivered back safely by a woman who was obviously charity and goodwill on two legs.

This time round, he was going to have to liaise with the woman looking after Jake and not simply rely on reports, emails and a debrief once a fortnight.

If he was going to have a more hands-on approach, then it would pay actually to find out about her. He needed her to feel comfortable with him because, if she did, she would be a lot more relaxed and forthcoming.

As things stood, she felt about as comfortable with him as a minnow felt in the company of a shark. He knew that. She didn't like him, she disapproved of him, and she'd only taken the job because he had done what he knew how to do so well. He'd put her in a position of being unable to refuse what was on the table.

Luca knew the power of money and he knew how to use it to his advantage.

But you couldn't buy trust and you couldn't buy openness and he would need both if he was to make headway with Jake—and that was what he needed to do.

'Whereabouts?'

'Los Angeles, as a matter of fact. Or at least,' Ellie couldn't help tacking on in the name of perfect honesty, 'I'm assuming that's where she is.'

'Do I hear the sound of the pot calling the kettle black?' Luca asked coolly. 'If I recall, you were pretty vocal on the subject of my losing touch with my cousin when he moved with his family to the very same place your sister now lives. Coincidentally they both ended up in America...'

'Not really. Lots of people go there because they see it as a land of opportunity.'

'But you weren't tempted?'

'I… I don't chase dreams. I'm too grounded.' Ellie flushed. 'Lily and I are very different. Anyway, to get back to what you said, my sister was the one who lost touch with me,' she said uncomfortably. 'Not the other way around.' For some reason, she didn't want to carry on talking about Lily. She remembered the curiosity in her sister's voice when she had mentioned Luca and the huge amount of money he was paying her, enough to clear their father's debt. 'This is a brilliant place.' She looked around her but she could feel his dark, penetrating gaze boring into her. 'You can imagine that, on a teacher's salary, this kind of restaurant is way out of my league.'

A waiter came and Luca gave his order without bothering with the menu, which he hadn't opened, while Ellie made a deal of scrutinising hers and picking what she wanted carefully.

'I have a stake in this place,' he said, casting his eye around him briefly. 'A decade ago, I decided to dabble in the restaurant business, so I bought a few failing ones to add to my portfolio. This was one of them.'

'Right,' Ellie mumbled. 'Of course. It's really important to have a varied portfolio, I've found.'

Luca burst out laughing, then he sipped his wine and was still smiling as he looked at her. 'Is that why you chose to teach? Because your sister was the one who had the monopoly on dream-chasing?'

Startled because he was closer to the truth than he probably imagined, Ellie stared at him for a few seconds. 'Like I said, I'm grounded. I don't have that risk gene in me that's willing to take a chance that everything's going to work out the way I want it to.' Ellie wondered why that made her sound so dull. She was no different from the majority of the human race.

She looked at him with a trace of defiance but his expression was bland and, when he next spoke, it was to change the subject. He had the contract, he told her, fishing it out of his pocket and sliding the envelope towards her.

'We said two to four weeks. I think it's possible that it might be longer. The longer it is, the more you'll be paid.'

Ellie opened the envelope and read the contract. It couldn't have been more straightforward but the sums of money involved made her feel even more uncomfortable now because it was all officially written down, waiting for her signature.

'The job isn't worth what you're willing to pay me,' she said simply and Luca clicked his tongue impatiently.

'We've been over this.'

'I know, but seeing the amount now, in black and white...'

'You need to dump the social conscience, Ellie, or else we'll be having this conversation on a loop, and it's not going to get either of us anywhere. Take the money and run. That's what any sensible person would advise.'

'You'd probably have a lot in common with my sister. You both think along the same lines because that was exactly what she said.' Plus, she thought absently, looking at the lean, beautiful lines of his face, he would probably do what every other guy did when they were confronted with Lily—he would want her.

Ellie thought that she had grown out of feelings she had had when she'd been an impressionable adolescent but now, suddenly, as though Pandora's box had been opened, they all flew out at her and she blinked in dismay.

Lily had always stolen the limelight, but that had been fine. It had only been less fine when she had stolen the one and only guy Ellie had been serious about.

Serious, hard-working, head-firmly-screwed-on Paul had been such a sensible choice and Ellie had liked him a lot. He had been the PE instructor in one of the local schools and she had met him on a night out with some friends. They'd got along and then, of course—oh, why hadn't she seen it coming?—he had been introduced to Lily and Lily had done what she had always done. She had charmed him. She had paraded in front of him in next to nothing, long, slim legs everywhere, blonde hair tousled, blue eyes wide and innocent.

'He actually asked me out,' Lily had said later. 'So really, I did you a favour, because if you'd ended up with him then it wouldn't have lasted. Besides, he was boring.'

The fact that Ellie had not suffered serious heartache following the break-up didn't detract from her annoyance that her sister had had no qualms about proving the point that she was prettier, sexier and more appealing to the opposite sex. After that, Ellie had quietly determined that she would keep any involvement with guys under wraps until she was sure that they were interested in *her* for who she was.

That hadn't been difficult because none had appeared on the horizon since. She had backed away from involvement with the opposite sex because it was easier than risking disappointment.

She was annoyed at the direction of her thoughts and even more annoyed when Luca asked casually, 'If your sister is on the other side of the world making her fortune, why have you been walking dogs to help pay off your father's debts?'

'Because...'

'Got it. So, moving on, you'll have to sign the contract. That will include an agreement to extend cover as necessary.'

'I haven't signed up to an indefinite situation...' *What had he meant by 'got it'?*

'I'm not asking for anything beyond the official school summer holidays—and have a look at the fine print. Stay on and you'll retire with enough money to do more than pay off your father's debts.'

He handed her a pen and nodded. 'You're doing me a favour, Ellie,' he said quietly. 'I'm not just paying you to look after Jake because I've sacked the last nanny and I'm in a tight corner. I'm paying you to be much more than a competent babysitter. I'm paying you because I think you'll be able to bond with Jake and I know that he's going to benefit from that.'

Ellie saw the raw sincerity in Luca's face and any hesitation was wiped out of her mind faster than dew melting on a summer morning. She signed the paper and shoved it back to him.

'Did you mean all that?' she asked, 'Or were you just making sure that you got what you wanted?'

'You think I'm ruthless enough to lie in order to get what I want?'

'Probably,' she said truthfully, and he delivered another of those rare, utterly charming half-smiles that made her thoughts go into a tailspin.

'Lying's not my style,' Luca told her. 'I don't need to use underhand tactics to get what I want in life. I've always found that the art of persuasion is far more successful.'

'And an ability to throw money at a problem.'

Luca shrugged. 'Money talks and usually has the loudest voice. Now, when will you be able to start?'

Since she had nothing planned for the long summer holidays—having assumed that they would be filled with the joys of dog walking to earn some money and perhaps, if push came to shove, some bar work, which she thought she would have rather enjoyed—the answer was *immediately*, but she took her time giving it a lot of undue thought.

'I should go and visit my father before I start,' she answered. 'I'm going to have to explain how it is that I'm suddenly in a position to pay off all his debts, and that's a conversation best had face to face.'

'Understood. Want me to accompany you to do the explaining?'

'No!' Horror laced her voice and she looked at him in alarm.

'Why not?' Luca asked bluntly, irritated by her reaction, because since when had women rejected the offer of his company?

'My father would be astounded if you showed up and he was told that you and I had worked out a deal whereby you were going to be paying me a fortune for looking after your godson for a few weeks.'

'Why?'

'Because…you're not the sort he would ever associate me coming into contact with, far less doing business with.'

'Ah. I'm not the sort you would get along with…unlike the elusive sister. We're back to the sliding scale of your disapproval, are we?'

'It's just easier if I handle this on my own. But thanks for the offer.'

'How long do you intend to stay there?'

'A couple of days at most and then I can start.'

'I should tell you that my preference would be for you to live in, Ellie. I can't always account for my working schedule and it's going to be a nuisance having to find someone who can fill in when necessary. Naturally, you will be compensated.'

'I'm not sure about that,' Ellie muttered, flushing. She thought of the discomfort of her shared house and, when their eyes met, she had a sneaking suspicion that he could read her mind.

He said, 'You'll have your own suite on the top floor. I assure you it will be very comfortable. Very quiet.'

Ellie had missed quiet. She'd never realised how important that was until she'd been thrown into the situation of sharing her space.

'Okay,' she agreed. 'On one condition.'

Luca raised his eyebrows in a question and she told him firmly, 'No extra money. Please. You're already paying me enough to do something that I will enjoy doing anyway.'

The spendthrift and the saver, Luca thought with curiosity. *One seeking fame and fortune in America, the other teaching and working her butt off to clear debts her father had incurred.* In his head, a picture was being put together, and for the first time he was genuinely interested in knowing the dynamics behind the relationship between the woman sitting opposite him and her family.

He felt the stirrings of something inside him. Something novel. His love life had become all too predictable and, yes, whilst he enjoyed the predictability, and certainly wouldn't have traded it for anything out of his control, with predictability came a certain amount of boredom.

He'd been celibate for the past two months and the last woman he had dated had only been on the scene for a few weeks. He couldn't really remember what she looked like although he knew that she had run to type—beautiful, blonde, leggy and very amenable. He hadn't been interested in her back-story, although she had insisted on filling him in anyway.

And since then? His libido had gone on holiday.

Luca sat back and looked at Ellie, his lush lashes veiling his expression.

God only knew where she had bought her outfit. Had she specifically looked for something designed to do absolutely nothing for the female form?

And yet the delicacy of her features was strangely arresting, and the fact that he wanted to find out more about her wasn't just about him knowing that he needed to get her onside if the situation with Jake were to work out. She sparked his interest. Her unwillingness to confide spurred on his curiosity. Her lack of interest in his money tickled him pink. She wasn't impressed and she didn't bother to pretend, and that seemed to fire up his jaded soul.

'Now that you're working for me,' he drawled, 'you'll find certain things will be at your disposal. I'll arrange a driver to take you to see your father.'

'My father doesn't live in London.'

'I don't care if he lives in Glasgow. You will also have the services of my driver on tap for when you need to go out with Jake. In addition, I will deposit a sizeable amount of money into your account which you can use when it comes to paying for anything Jake might want or need.'

'Anything?'

'Anything.' Luca shrugged nonchalantly. 'Money is no object.'

Ellie drew in a deep breath and tried hard not to be intimidated by the powerhouse sitting across from her. Everything inside her reacted to him in ways that were embarrassing and unwanted. He wasn't the type of man she could ever be remotely interested in, yet her body went up in flames when she was around him, and that unnerved her. How could she be so uncontrolled in her responses? She'd never been that way and, especially after the debacle with her last boyfriend, she had firmly put the lid on her emotions—not that Paul had roused anything like the idiotic sensations Luca seemed to. That had been a measured relationship, which she had liked. If she had been cautious then, well, she was even more cautious now, so why did sitting within touching distance of Luca make her feel all hot and bothered?

The bottom line was that she was going to have to get her act together because this was a business arrangement and there was no room within any business arrangement for a disobedient body. Luca was a staggeringly good-looking man and the fact that she was so keenly aware of him on a physical level just said something about her hormones. They were in full working order. She should be thankful for that, considering they had done a disappearing act after Paul had left the scene. It was good to know that she was *normal*, and maybe when she was back at work she would think about jumping back into the dating scene. This time round she would make sure that whoever she dated wasn't into leggy blondes.

'Now that you've told me all the terms and conditions about my employment,' she said carefully, 'there are just a few things *I* would like to say.'

Luca's eyebrows flew up and she took a deep breath because she knew that, given half a chance, he would tread all over her and the whole point of this exercise would be lost. It didn't matter how much *she* bonded with Jake, it was far more important that *he* did, and throwing money around like confetti wasn't the way to do it.

'Have you sat down with Jake and actually talked to him about what happened?'

'The runaway episode?'

'The loss of his parents. That episode.'

Luca flushed darkly. 'I thought it best not to bring that up because it's sure to revive bad memories. It's better to move on from that place.'

Ellie held his stare. Food had come somewhere along the line but she had been so preoccupied with the conversation that she had hardly been aware of eating what was on her plate. Now, plates cleared, Luca dismissed a hovering waiter who wanted to find out about dessert.

'I disagree,' Ellie told him firmly, ignoring the way his mouth tightened in automatic rejection of the criticism. 'Just because you don't talk about it doesn't mean that it's all going to disappear. It was something momentous. He's only young, but you can mention his parents naturally so that the subject doesn't become taboo. Have you any pictures of them?'

'I...' Did he have any pictures? All their worldly goods had been shipped back to him and he had had the lot put into the attic. He hadn't checked to see what was there and had thought that at some point in the future, when he had time, he would go through it all. That thought had come and gone and he had done nothing about it.

Ellie was looking at him curiously.

'You don't know?'

'It's not that shocking.' For once on the back foot, Luca shifted irritably, his fabulous eyes pinned to her face. 'I haven't had time to go through the crates that were shipped over,' he muttered.

'You're busy.'

'Is that a criticism?'

'It's an observation.' Ellie paused. 'And if we're going to have a successful working relationship then I have to feel that I can be honest and truthful with you when it comes to Jake.'

Luca lifted both hands in a typically Spanish gesture that could have indicated impatience, annoyance, resignation or a combination of all three. Accompanied as this gesture was by a scowl, Ellie thought that it probably wasn't resignation, but that was tough.

'Feel free,' he delivered smoothly. 'I'm all ears.'

'The first thing you should have done should have been to go through those possessions one by one. There are probably all sorts of things there that would have been cherished by Jake, that would have made him feel more secure in an alien environment. He's still very young. He would have had toys that have been with him probably since he was born.'

Luca looked at her in stony silence but she ignored it. So what if he thought she was a prissy schoolmarm who disapproved of pretty much everything about him?

'Also, what about photos?'

'Do photos exist any more?'

'Then his parents' computers or mobile phones, or any place where digital photos might have been stored.'

'I...' Luca was about to repeat what he had said, that time was a valued commodity and he just hadn't got round to finding any to sift through his cousin's bits and pieces. Not much had been shipped over. Johnny and Ruby had not exactly accumulated a treasure trove of memories but then, from what he had gathered, they had rented and had moved on a fairly regular basis. Souvenirs and baby photos on the mantelpiece probably hadn't been their thing.

But he should have done more than just dump the lot in the attic with the vague thought that he would go through it all on a rainy day. In his world, rainy days when you did stuff like that never happened.

'I will ensure that the oversight is rectified,' he conceded and she gave him a nod of approval.

She ordered a coffee, because he was beginning to wear the hunted expression of someone who was keen to leave, but since she had a few more things to say she would have to ensure that he stayed put, at least for a short while longer.

'When?'

'Soon.'

Ellie didn't say anything and eventually, on a note of frustration, and raking his long fingers through his hair, Luca gritted, 'Tomorrow.'

She beamed. 'Brilliant.' She looked at him and her tummy did a flip. When she was talking business, she could almost forget the impact he had on her, but as their eyes tangled she thought how gorgeous he was, how astoundingly, sinfully sexy. On the looks front, no one could deny that Luca was without comparison.

She would have to get past that if she was going to be working for him and she knew that if she could accept the magnetic pull he had over her and shrug it off then there would be no problem dealing with him.

Establishing the nature of their relationship from the outset would be a good start.

'And there's something else. I think you'll need to get more involved with Jake. Money is no substitute for time. I realise you're busy with work, but you're going to have to find the time to leave it now and again so that you can begin to build a relationship with him. He didn't run away,' she said bluntly, 'because he was so happy to be living here in London with you.'

'Anything else?' Luca asked silkily. 'Should I go on a parenting skills course to make sure I'm covering all bases?'

'Not funny.' She tilted her chin at a combative angle and outstared him. 'When I leave, it would be nice to think that you and Jake had built something a bit stronger than what's there now. He needs to really know that he's loved and wanted in order to settle properly.'

His discomfort was palpable. Luca Ross didn't do these sorts of conversations. Ellie waited, half-expecting him to shut down the dialogue and move back into his comfort zone. Instead, he said at last, 'You win. I will take some time off work.' He shook his head and shifted his piercing gaze away from her. 'I've never failed at anything in my life before and I don't intend to fail at this. I'll do what it takes.'

CHAPTER FOUR

WITHOUT ANY FANFARE, Ellie vacated the house in which she had been renting a room. Most of the business of balancing the books was amicable and largely done over text. Rooms to rent in London which were cheap and in a relatively good location were as rare as hen's teeth and there was a list of alternative tenants—mainly friends of friends—waiting in the wings. The girls were all a pleasant bunch and they took her defection without grumbling.

Ellie didn't know whether she was relieved at the lack of fuss or saddened because she'd made so little impact, then she robustly reminded herself of the lucrative nature of her new temporary job and told herself that she would be able to afford something far better by the end of summer. A definite date hadn't been set but it would be determined by the speed with which a suitable replacement nanny was found which in turn, Ellie thought, depended on how fussy Luca intended to be. He might have given the go ahead on the last two with a casual wave of his hand but that was pre-runaway godson. Now, he had been shocked into taking stock.

She'd been bought lock, stock and barrel for the foreseeable future, and as she looked around her vacated room and reminded herself of the small fortune she would be earning over the next few weeks she couldn't prevent an uneasy shiver from running through her.

When she thought back to that conversation three days ago, she realised just how much he had controlled the outcome. He had sought her out, having done his homework, and he had baited his hook in just the right way to catch the fish he needed.

He'd known her weak spot and he had subtly but effectively played on that without appearing to be manipulative in any way—but here she was, room emptied of her possessions and stepping into waters she couldn't predict. Luca would be a fair employer but he would have impossibly high standards and she couldn't afford to let his overpowering personality suffocate her professionalism.

She knew that she would have to do more than just engage with Jake. She would have to try and build a bridge between little Jake and his older cousin. He would be cool and practical and he would expect her to be the same. She would have to squash the temptation to get hot and bothered in his presence, because if she did then all attempts to be cool and practical like him would take an instant nose dive.

Her visit to her father had been brief because, she had said, she had to return to London to start her job.

'It's quite specialist.' She had spun the truth in a way that had somehow justified the exorbitant salary she was being paid. 'This isn't just a normal situation… Jake is a very confused and mixed-up young lad…'

She was guiltily aware that in one sentence she had somehow managed to go from a primary school teacher walking dogs to a top psychologist capable of dealing with a troubled young child but, if she'd stuck rigidly to the truth, her father would have been worried sick. He wasn't an idiot. Why would someone pay over the odds for the simple job of looking after a misbehaving child? Why wouldn't he get a professional in? It would have been impossible to explain either Luca's personality, that was geared to see and take what he wanted whatever the cost, or that he had wanted her because of the peculiar nature of the situation.

Lily, she was told, was making noises about returning to England for a spell, if she could spare the time. Ellie had grimaced and concealed the bald truth that her sister had refused to contribute a penny towards paying off her father's debt.

She had had just one conversation with Luca since their dinner. She had phoned to thank him for the initial sizeable deposit of cash into her bank account and, getting to the point as he always did, he had said bluntly, 'I hope you're not getting cold feet.'

'What makes you ask that?'

'I'm good at detecting anxiety in people's voices,' he had informed her drily. 'If you're worried that you'll be working with someone you don't like, then don't be. It's immaterial whether you like me or not. You just need to respect me. The world is full of people whose values don't happen to dovetail with yours. Being an adult means training yourself not to be affected by that.'

Which had told her!

For the duration of the summer holiday, she would have to be prepared to commit fully to the job, to be there twenty-four-seven for his godson. No last-minute appointments that couldn't be broken, no dog-walking duties that had to be fulfilled and no men claiming priorities over her time.

He had asked her, at the tail end of that conversation, and almost as an afterthought, whether there was a man in her life.

'You don't have a husband,' he had delivered in a voice that was cool and a little bored and she could picture him doing something else while he was talking to her on the phone—perhaps checking emails on his computer or reading some high-level report. 'And you don't have a live-in partner, but is there someone lurking in the background that you may have failed to mention?'

He had wanted her positioned in just the right place to suit his needs, and having anyone making demands on her time was not going to work, especially as she would be living under his roof. Considering she had only just been gaping at the sum of money in her account, she had realised in that instant just how detailed the trade between them was going to be. In short, he would call all the shots.

'As a matter of fact, I haven't at the moment.' She had stumbled over her words and her cheeks had reddened in embarrassment. Luca didn't have any interest in her personal life, except insofar as it might affect their arrangement, but she had winced with self-consciousness at the picture that admission had painted—the teacher who walked dogs, dressed in shabby clothes, with no one in her life.

Where most girls her age, with eight weeks of summer to fill, would have been booking holidays with boyfriends, she was trying to find a way to save money so that she could bail her father out of the desperate hole he had contrived to dig for himself, and there was nothing going on in her life to prevent her from doing that. She hadn't had to cancel any hot dates or rearrange any holidays with a significant other so that she could fulfil her obligations to Luca.

It had been a moment to think seriously about the direction her life had taken. She hadn't really thought about it before, but now she could see that she had thrown in the towel after her last crash-and-burn relationship. She had buried herself in her job—had breathed a sigh of relief that she hadn't actually *loved* Paul but had more been in love with the idea of being in love—and had taken the safe option of not getting involved with anyone again. She would wait for the right guy to come along.

But having to admit to Luca—sex-on-legs Luca, who had probably never spent more than a handful of nights in an empty bed—that she was resolutely single had been mortifying.

Was this where she wanted to be in a year's time? Two years' time? Okay, maybe walking dogs to earn some extra cash, but still on her own with no particular reason to look forward to the long summer holidays? Maybe getting together with a clutch of similarly single female friends so that they could go somewhere together? Was that how she had been affected by living in the shadow of her fabulously beautiful younger sister? Had she had her self-confidence sapped over the years? Even though she would always have asserted proudly that you didn't have to rely on something as superficial as looks in order to lead a brilliant and fulfilling life, had she known, somewhere deep down, that she had in all truth given up on making any effort?

When she had been dating Paul, she had made an effort. Back then, she had fussed over her appearance and done all those girly things her sister had spent a lifetime doing. She had experimented with make-up, done her nails and grown her hair, and it had all been for nothing, because he had dumped her for her sister. That had been a wake-up call for her, and after that she had promptly lost all interest in stuff that she wrote off as being superficial.

When she met someone, appearance would not make a jot of difference to how he felt about her. He wouldn't be the sort of shallow type whose head could be turned by a sexy blonde with big boobs and legs up to her armpits.

Except, she was never going to meet anyone if she didn't get out there, was she?

She was going to be living in a gilded cage for the next few weeks, and once she was back in her own world things were going to change.

Right now, the gilded cage was a joy to behold, and Ellie did a full circle of the room.

On her bed, Jake was lying in starfish mode, staring up at the ceiling, trying to think of as many things as he could that began with the letter A.

Ellie flung herself down next to him and tickled him until he started squealing for her to stop.

'Shall I tell you a secret?' she whispered, laughing, and Jake giggled.

'What?'

'This is the nicest room I've ever slept in in my entire life.'

'My room's nicer,' Jake whispered back, hugging her. 'I have a Spiderman duvet.'

'You're right,' Ellie said, in a serious hush-hush voice. 'That's the only thing that's missing and I'm going to make sure to put that right as soon as I can. No Spiderman for me, though. Maybe something princessy...'

Jake made a face and she laughed and ruffled his hair. 'Are you saying I'm not like a princess?' she teased, slipping off the bed. 'Because you'd be right! I'm more like...*the big, bad wolf* and I'm going to *gobble you up* if you don't fly down to the kitchen this very minute and start eating your dinner! Miss Muller called you ages ago, you little horror!'

She might not have seen Luca since the deal had been done, but she had seen a lot of Jake, and she could already feel the bond between them growing.

Luca was prepared to pay the earth for her services and she realised that this was what he wanted—this bond between herself and his godson—because that very bond would be the foundation for his own way in to Jake. To put it loosely, he would use her, and for that he was willing to pay over the odds. This was the nature of their relationship and it helped to put everything in perspective.

Her settling-in period had been made even smoother because Luca had had to go to New York on business for the first few days after her arrival. He had kept in touch by email and text, and spoken with her every evening without fail to ask penetrating questions about Jake, but she had been relieved that he wasn't around while she found her feet.

She'd had time to relax with Jake and, bit by bit, was finding out about his background.

The picture he was slowly painting, much to her dismay, was of a broken household with his young and irresponsible parents largely absent. As he gradually opened up, she realised that he talked more about the elderly couple in the flat next door to where he had lived, who had obviously borne the brunt of baby-sitting duties when his parents had been busy chasing the dream.

As promised, his possessions had been sorted through while she had been visiting her father, and she had flicked through a scant amount of photos of his parents on the laptop which had been charged up. A young, beautiful couple, largely posing against dramatic backgrounds that made the photos resemble photo shoots, with only a handful of pictures of Jake as a baby and so forth.

Little wonder that he had shrunk into himself, bewildered and confused, when he had been torn from the familiarity of his surroundings and thrust into the care of an aggressively powerful workaholic who had no patience with having his life disrupted. From the sounds of it, his life had contained precious few rules. He had attended school *sometimes* and had been allowed to do what he wanted whenever he wanted. Luca, with his authoritarian approach to life and his rigid sense of control, would have been a terrifying contrast to Jake's largely absent, easy-going, very young parents.

She would talk to Luca the following evening when he returned to London. It was going to be a two-way street and, if he thought that he could call all the shots, then he was going to be in for a surprise.

She was busy mulling over a scenario in which she could pin her demanding and arrogant employer to the spot, and force him to listen to things he would probably not want to hear, when there was a knock on her bedroom door.

Ellie answered it without thinking. Probably Jake bouncing back up for something or other.

It was Luca. For a few seconds Ellie stood and stared because she hadn't been expecting him.

She'd spent days dismissing her nonsensical response to him and now all of that flew out of the window faster than a speeding bullet as their eyes collided.

She marvelled that she had somehow forgotten how breathtakingly *vital* Luca was, even when he needed a shave and he looked dishevelled and weary. Nothing could detract from the man's enormous sex appeal. His impact was as powerful as if she'd run headlong into a brick wall and been left dazed and disorientated.

He was in a suit but the tie had gone, as had the jacket, and he had cuffed the sleeves of his white shirt to the elbows.

She lowered her eyes, heart beating harder than a sledgehammer in her chest, and her mouth went dry, because all she could see somehow was his muscular forearms and the sprinkling of dark hair that seemed weirdly, aggressively, over-the-top *masculine*.

'What are you doing here? I thought… I wasn't expecting you until tomorrow evening.'

'Things got wrapped up earlier than expected. It's not yet seven-thirty. I expected to find you downstairs.'

'I was on my way down.' She tried hard not to focus on her stunningly casual outfit—old jogging bottoms, tee shirt and bedroom slippers. These were not clothes with which she could project her professional face.

'I thought that this would be a good a time to have a face-to-face conversation before I start work. I have a hundred emails to get through but I can spare an hour or so.'

'What, now? I realise I'm being paid a lot, but that doesn't mean that you can barge into my bedroom and summon me downstairs for a chat.'

'I'm afraid it does,' Luca returned coolly.

This was what you signed up for, a little voice whispered in her head.

'I can't predict my hours,' he continued in the growing silence. 'With the best will in the world, I can try and have a more reliable work schedule, but there's no guarantee that that will work out.'

'I do understand that, but I don't get why you can't arrange your schedule to accommodate Jake. You keep reminding me that you're the boss of your own company, so why can't you decide when you can leave and when you can't?'

Luca looked at her narrowly. 'I don't care for the tone of your voice.'

Back down now and cower, Ellie thought, and she would set a precedent for their relationship that would last the duration of the time she was under this roof, and it would make for a very uncomfortable situation. There would be things she would need to say to him that he would not particularly want to hear and he would need to be less of a control freak to deal with it.

'I apologise for that,' she said in a composed tone. 'And of course, I do appreciate that you can't tailor your working hours as much as you may like, but I think Jake would benefit from a predictable schedule from you, at least to start with. And that aside...' she drew in a deep breath '... I won't be disturbed any and every time you think you might want to catch up. It's not on.'

Thick, humming silence greeted this and, eventually, Luca raked his fingers through his hair and stared at her, as though debating what he should say next.

Ellie stepped into the breach and continued in a more placatory voice, 'If you give me fifteen minutes, I'll come downstairs. I just need to change.'

She used the fifteen minutes of allotted time to dress quickly into a pair of trousers and a pale blue polo shirt.

On her way down, she passed Jake, who was heading up.

'Read me a story tonight?' He looked at her and then sighed with disappointment when she told him that she couldn't.

'So you get two tomorrow night,' she promised, kneeling down and giving him an affectionate squeeze. 'Plus, Luca is back tonight. Isn't that great?' Her keen eyes noted the way his whole body tensed and he shook his head vehemently.

'Why does he have to come back?'

'Because he wants to spend some time with you.'

'I don't want to spend any time with him.'

Ellie didn't say anything. As far as mountains to climb went, this was going to be a steep one.

Ten minutes later, she was sitting at the long metal and wood table when Luca walked in; she could see he'd had a quick shower because his dark hair was still damp. He positively glistened with robust good health, an alpha male in the prime of his fitness radiating energy from every pore, and no longer looking tired.

'So.' He strolled towards the fridge and peered inside. 'Talk to me.'

Ellie gritted her teeth and wondered whether the word *polite* had ever been used to describe Luca's take on conversation.

Was he *that* short with everyone to whom he spoke? Or maybe just with the people who worked for him? Surely not? There were moments when she glimpsed such overpowering charm and charisma that she could only imagine the guy just didn't believe in wasting any of that charm or common courtesy on her because she worked for him.

And he doubly wouldn't be bothered because not only did she work for him but she was also a *woman* and therefore would not even register on his radar.

He asked her about Jake, and she repeated a lot of what she had communicated to him via email. He was a very good listener. She could tell that he was taking in every word she was saying, and was probably working out how her activities with Jake compared to the previous two nannies.

He'd abandoned the fridge in favour of a glass of wine, and offered her a glass as a token gesture of politeness, not pressing her when she shook her head.

'I know this is going to work out,' he said when there was a pause, 'because Jake asked for you when you went to see your father.'

'He probably needed a comforting shoulder after everything

he's been through. We looked at some of the photos together.' She hesitated. 'Did you go through them with him?'

'I began.' He shrugged. 'But it wasn't a success.' He didn't add that Jake had stared stonily at the ground in absolute silence, his small body stiff with tension, until Luca had flung his hands up in surrender and packed in the exercise.

'It takes time.'

'That's a commodity that's in short supply with me.' He hesitated, then added with hard-won honesty, 'I'm afraid I don't know a huge amount about children. I have no idea how to communicate with them. I don't suppose that helps.'

'You just have to be interested and genuine,' Ellie told him. 'Talk to Jake the way you would talk to…well…anyone, really. Bearing in mind he's six, so discussing world politics isn't going to get you anywhere.' She smiled and he returned it with a crooked smile of his own.

'I prefer giving orders,' Luca said. 'Or else it's down to world politics, I'm afraid.'

'You'll pick it up.' She hesitated, then explained what she had found out about Jake's background and the way he seemed to have been left to his own devices while his youthful parents had got on with their lives.

'I wouldn't say that Johnny and I were the best of friends,' Luca expanded thoughtfully. 'He was much younger and very different from me. I only met Ruby, his wife, once. At the christening. She seemed very much like him.'

'How so?'

'In love with a dream that was never going to materialise,' Luca said flatly. 'And with a baby in tow, to make matters worse. Naturally, I advised against the whole thing.'

'Naturally.'

Luca frowned. 'I'm picking something up here. What is that remark supposed to mean?'

'Being in love with a dream is just another way of saying being hopeful.'

'Which, if you don't mind me saying, is another pointless waste of time.'

Ellie wondered, in astonishment, where that depth of cynicism had stemmed from but the conversation was already over and he was standing up, restlessly prowling back to the fridge and frowning into it until she asked him, reluctantly, whether he had eaten.

'Not since yesterday,' Luca confirmed, without looking at her.

'If I had known, I would have told Miss Muller… She stayed on later this evening because she left early yesterday. Her neighbour was poorly. She had to do some shopping for her. She prepared something for Jake and I would have—'

'Forget it. I didn't know myself that I would be returning a day early.'

'I could do something for you. Make something…'

Luca swung round to face her. 'Cooking for me isn't one of your duties,' he said flatly.

'It's no trouble,' Ellie said, standing up and making her way over to one of the cupboards, but he halted her in mid-stride, one hand on her wrist.

At that fleeting contact, a charge of electricity raced through her, sending hot sparks through her body and igniting all her nerve endings. Her nipples pinched into urgent, responsive buds and she could feel a horrifying melting between her thighs that made her want to rub her legs together. Her mouth ran dry and she stared up at him, pupils dilated, only galvanising her treacherous body into action when he removed his hand and stood back to stare at her narrowly.

Dismayed that she might have revealed far more than she wanted to, Ellie stepped back, but her heart was thundering and her skin was hot and prickly.

It didn't matter how much she told herself that she needed to be businesslike and efficient, she couldn't seem to help the way her body reacted when it was around him.

She had never suffered that sort of weakness before and she was baffled as to how she could suffer it now with a man who, however drop-dead gorgeous he was, did not appeal to her on any other level at all.

'No.' Luca pinned his fabulous dark eyes on her flushed face as he helped himself to bread and unearthed some cheese from the fridge. He didn't bother with butter or anything else. 'Like I told you, cooking for me isn't part of the deal, and I won't have it.'

'Right.'

'You're offended,' he said shortly, sitting down and then re-laxing back to look at her with brooding intensity while she hovered in the middle of the sprawling kitchen like a fish out of water, wanting desperately to leave, but knowing that she would have to be formally dismissed before she could do so.

'Why should I be? Of course I'm not. I was merely being po-lite. Of course I know that cooking for you isn't part of the deal.'

'I don't do *women cooking for me,*' Luca told her, releasing her from the suffocating stranglehold of his stare and eating the bread and cheese without enthusiasm. 'I don't like it, and I never encourage it, so there's no need to feel piqued because I turned down your offer.'

'I told you, I don't,' Ellie said stiffly. It was now fair to as-sume that she wasn't going to be dismissed just yet so she si-dled across to the chair facing him and sank into it with relief. 'And, while we're on the subject of deals, you've spent the past couple of days abroad and after this you're off to work. Maybe you should look in on Jake? Say goodnight? I'm sure he'd re-ally appreciate that.' She crossed her fingers at the little white lie. Horror would be a more predictable reaction from Jake if Luca were to show up on a godfather-godson bonding mission.

'I...' Luca looked at her and, for a moment, she saw some-one who might be top of the food chain when it came to mak-ing money, but who when it came to the relationship with his godson was touchingly vulnerable.

'He's probably asleep,' she said quickly. 'You wouldn't want to wake him.'

Luca nodded briskly. The whole thing was a bloody nightmare and he was only now really appreciating the extent of it because he was being called upon to interact instead of throwing money at the problem and leaving it to the professionals. He'd sworn to himself that this was a challenge he would overcome, but how equipped was he to handle the demands of a screwed-up kid?

Highly equipped, a little voice inside him whispered.

Introspection had never played a part in his life. Luca was someone who powered through, eyes firmly set on the present and the future, because nothing about the past could be changed so why dwell on it? He particularly didn't dwell on his emotional past, which had always been better secured under lock and key, but he unlocked that place now.

His background was, on the surface, so different from Jake's. He had known happiness right up to the point when his mother had died. After that, his father had retreated behind impenetrable walls and, when he had, he had taken Luca's childhood with him, leaving behind a young boy forced to grow up fast and to find his independence at an age when he should still have been playing with toy cars and Action Man heroes. All the money in the world had not been able to compensate for the absence of his father.

Had that been a childhood? Yes, he had certainly learnt to thank his years spent at that boarding school for providing him with the sort of backbone that could win any fight. But could you have called it a *childhood*?

You didn't have to be a genius to work out that Jake would tread a predictable path if Luca didn't get his hands dirty and engage with the situation.

'I'm glad you're here,' he said gruffly. He stood up and she followed suit.

She smiled and he moved towards her, his expression unusually hesitant.

When she looked up, he was so close to her that her heart seemed to skip a beat.

He reached out. She wasn't even sure whether he was aware he was doing anything but what he did was devastating. He brushed her cheek with his finger. A soft, brief gesture that was there and gone in a heartbeat.

'And if I don't tell you that,' he finished awkwardly, 'it's not because I don't think it.'

The moment was gone but her heart was still thumping long after he'd disappeared off to work.

CHAPTER FIVE

'THINKING OF COMING HOME? When?' Ellie was having this rushed conversation on the phone to her father whilst keeping one eye on the front door.

The past week had been a busy one. At the start of this job, she had been determined to keep some distance and to remember that she was doing this purely for the money. She wasn't in it to build a lasting relationship with Jake, far less his complicated godfather.

Unfortunately, she had felt herself being sucked into the family dynamic as the week progressed. Luca had made big efforts to keep to his side of the bargain, to put in more of an appearance than he had previously.

Jake had tolerated his presence. One step forward, two steps back. She had watched and noted Luca's frustration, for once playing a game the rules of which he hadn't made and didn't get.

She had tried to limit her interventions, but they had both turned to her variously to mediate their awkward interaction, where neither side seemed to know quite what to do.

Luca, on the back foot, was not the arrogant guy she had so disliked on first sight.

Jake, tiptoeing around like a shy deer hoping to sneak past a predator to get to a stream, was increasingly working his way into her heart.

'Not giving a date yet,' she heard her father say with pleasure in his voice. 'She'll be busy over there. Said she can snatch a week or so to return. Can't spare longer than that. Something about agents hounding her.'

'Well, that's nice anyway.' Ellie wondered whether the little chat she had had with her sister a couple of weeks ago had galvanised her into doing something to check up on their father. She hoped so. It was no longer important whether Lily contributed to the financial situation because that was, miraculously, in hand but she knew that her father would be thrilled to have his youngest daughter come and visit.

'Told her you weren't going to be around much to come up here and visit,' her father continued. 'Told her you were hard at it in London, sorting out that little lad.'

'Yes, indeed,' Ellie mumbled guiltily.

'She'll want to see you, Els. She specifically mentioned how keen she was to meet up. Think she might be impressed by what you're doing.'

Ellie couldn't see that herself because Lily had never been particularly impressed by anything that hadn't involved being in the public eye and preferably surrounded by adoring admirers. So why was she suddenly interested in a job that involved looking after a child? But Ellie swallowed back a tart reply while manoeuvring to conclude the conversation.

This evening she would be going out with Luca, leaving Jake with a babysitter who lived three doors down.

This was about business. It was a perfect opportunity to broaden Jake's horizons when it came to interaction with other adults on the home front. They would be discussing progress. There was a script to be obeyed and Ellie was going to make sure she stuck to it.

But she hadn't stopped thinking about the way he had oh-so-casually touched her. She'd been set alight and, deep inside, there remained something smouldering, waiting to re-ignite.

For a few seconds, their eyes had met, and she had felt *something* stir between them, something hot and dangerous, but it had been over in the blink of an eye. It preyed on her mind, though, that brief connection.

It was a relief, in a way, that he had made sure to keep everything between them businesslike since then. They had semi-formal discussions in his office, employer and employee discussing work-related matters. She sat opposite him, perched forward, hands on her lap, and reported on the day's events, and stopped short of actually submitting a written report only by a whisker.

Tonight, though, it would be an experiment in getting Jake accustomed to a change of face. It had been Ellie's idea, because there was no point in allowing Jake to settle into such a comfort zone that any new person on the scene would be viewed, once again, with suspicion and mistrust.

She had suggested the young girl a few houses away because the girl owned a dog and they had chatted briefly on a couple of occasions. She had visited the girl's parents and satisfied herself that she was an excellent babysitting option.

Ellie had imagined the girl popping over to babysit during the day, even if Ellie remained upstairs in her suite catching up on work prep for the forthcoming term. She hadn't foreseen an evening out with Luca, but here she was.

She was alarmed at the level of excitement racing through her, touching all her nerve endings like little electric charges pulsing through every pore of her body. The minute the lines between employer and employee were even a tiny bit blurred, Ellie found that she was frighteningly far from immune to his raw, animal sex appeal which he exuded in punishing waves without even having to try. She had caught herself looking at him—sidelong, surreptitious glances that felt like the stolen glances of a lover. When she was within a metre of him, she could feel the heat of his body as though she was standing too close to an open flame—and the only saving grace was the fact that talking about Jake was a constant reminder that she was in paid employ.

Tonight, though…a meal out.

She had debated whether to wear her parents' meeting outfit of neat skirt, responsible, worker-bee blouse tucked into the waistband and her no-nonsense pumps, but on the spur of the moment she'd opted for something less formal because it was a lovely summer evening.

She had treated herself to a couple of summer dresses and she looked at her reflection in the mirror now. She didn't have the curves of a lingerie model but she looked okay.

The colour suited her dark colouring. It was a pale bronze and made her look ever so faintly exotic. The dress was short and skimmed her slender body lovingly and the shoes, with a little heel, did great things for her bare, brown legs. She'd also made the most of her eyes which she had always considered her best feature.

This wasn't a date and *she knew that*, but why shouldn't she wear what any other twenty-something would wear if she happened to be going out for a meal?

She would have worn this very outfit, she thought, running lightly down the stairs towards the kitchen where Luca had told her he'd be waiting, if she'd been going out with a bunch of girlfriends. No big deal.

She entered the kitchen unhurriedly and took a few deep breaths as Luca, who had been absently gazing through the kitchen window, slowly turned to face her.

He was tugging at his tie, loosening it, and for a few seconds he stilled.

'You're on time. Good.' Luca had perfected the art of glancing at Ellie without really taking her in fully. His reaction to her—one that continually caught him off-guard, the tug she induced in his groin—was unwelcome, inappropriate and incomprehensible because she wasn't his type at all. Too slight, too fierce, too outspoken and too flat-chested.

He had gone out of his way to underline their working relationship. No casual chatting in the kitchen, which would smell of something more intimate than he wanted. In the formal sitting room, they interacted in the way an employer interacted with someone he happened to be interviewing for a job.

He didn't get why she affected his libido the way she did, but he was working overtime to control his wayward response. That one and only moment, when he had given in to the urge to touch her, had galvanised his body into a reaction that had shocked him in its intensity. Her skin had been as smooth as satin under his fingers. He had had to fight down the urge to slip a finger into her mouth, feel her suck it then tug her close to lose himself in her sweetness.

Now, though…

There was no need for this so-called meeting to be conducted at night, nor was it necessary for the venue to be an expensive country pub. Lunch at the noisy local wine bar would have sufficed, but his rational brain had decided to take a break when that choice had been made.

He lowered his eyes, lashes concealing his expression, but he didn't have to stare at her because the image was imprinted in his head. She was in a dress that hugged her slender body and accentuated her ballerina grace. Her breasts were pert and rounded. Her legs were tanned, slim and shapely, and the shortness of her dark hair emphasised the contours of her delicate face and the swan-like grace of her neck.

'I usually am,' she responded quickly, heart picking up speed as she tried and failed not to look at him. 'Last time, there was a reason I was a little late.'

'I believe you. You're not one of these women who shows up late to prove a point or stage a grand entrance.'

Ellie sensed that this was one of those vaguely offensive remarks loosely gift-wrapped as a compliment of sorts.

Old feelings of insecurity rose to the surface like scum. She'd thought she'd put those feelings to rest. Living in her sister's shadow, knowing that she was the plain Jane with the brains, had been tough, especially because their mother had made no attempt to disguise her preference for Lily. But it was only now, in the company of Luca, that she realised just how deeply old wounds could cut.

Luca was so imperfect when it came to every single thing Ellie used as a benchmark for men. Yes, she had had glimpses of someone so much more complex than he appeared on first sight, but the truth was that he was still a billionaire with all the traits of a billionaire. Arrogant, ruthless, intolerant of imperfections, uncompromising. Faced with the arrival of his little charge, he had made no concessions until Jake had absconded, at which point he had got his act together. To some extent. If Jake had never run away, God only knew how much interaction he would have had with his forbidding and powerful godfather, the man from whom he was destined to inherit a multi-billion-euro business. None, Ellie suspected.

All those downsides and yet… Luca was so physically perfect a specimen. So sinfully sexy. Once she started looking at him, she couldn't seem to tear her eyes away, and her brain went into hibernation, leaving her at the mercy of all sorts of confusing, unwelcome reactions.

Ellie knew that she could keep at the forefront of her mind the fact that Luca was the sort of guy who would always be attracted to leggy blondes like Lily. It was galling that she was attracted to him. She could blame her hormones, and tell herself that he *was* ridiculously attractive, so it was no wonder she found him so, but none of that counted for anything. He wasn't her type, so why did she find him so compelling?

The way he was looking at her, his dark, intelligent eyes shielding all expression, made her wonder what was going through his head. Was he amused because she had dressed up? Did he think that she might be getting ideas into her head and maybe thinking that this was some kind of date instead of just an alternative venue for their usual daily debrief about his godson? Maybe he thought she hadn't taken the hint when he'd begun conducting their brief meetings in the more formal sitting room.

'I don't do grand entrances and I'm almost always on time,' Ellie said, grinding her teeth together, because that was just the sort of prissy statement that a truly boring person would come out with. 'It…it goes with the job.'

'Goes with the job?'

'When you teach, there isn't an option to swan in and out of class at whatever time happens to take your fancy. You have to get in at a certain time and it's a habit that's become ingrained. It's not the sexiest trait in the world, but there you go.'

Ellie went bright red and averted her eyes as he smiled slowly and walked towards her.

'I like it,' Luca told her honestly. 'It's a fallacy that men enjoy being kept waiting because a woman needs five hours to apply some war paint. Speaking of which…' He paused, and in that pause Ellie could feel herself tingling all over and waiting for him to *do something*. He had that look in his eyes. The dark depths were lazy and slumberous. He was so close to her, so close that she could feel the warmth of his body heat radiating and enveloping her. 'We should be heading off…'

Ellie blinked. He was still looking down at her. Her throat was parched but she managed to croak, 'Where are we going?'

'I thought we'd get out of London.' For once, he left the driver behind and she followed him to the garage where his Maserati was housed. He opened the passenger door for her and she slid inside a car that smelled of leather and walnut and breathed shameless luxury.

He turned to her just as he switched on the engine which roared into life. 'Forty minutes and we can sample the joys of a country pub. I don't do rural, but I also don't get many opportunities to take this car out, so why not?'

He drove with the skill and confidence of someone comfortable behind the wheel of a fast, powerful car. In between talking about Jake and the advances she was seeing in him, Ellie let herself linger on the flex of his muscled forearm as he changed gears, and the lean beauty of his profile as he stared ahead, concentrating on the road and listening to every word she was saying.

'It's taking longer than I thought,' he mused.

'What is?'

'Relationship building.' Luca shot her a sideways glance.

'It's not an overnight process.' Ellie stared ahead as they left the busy hustle of London and began cruising out towards Oxford. 'Think of your own childhood,' she urged, 'and how complex the relationship you had with your parents was. It's all about having the trust there so that you're free to make mistakes, on either side, knowing it's not going to affect the balance of the relationship. In this case it's made all the more complicated because of the situation.'

'I can't really fall back on personal experience, as I may have mentioned,' Luca said drily. 'Please don't paint rosy images of me as a kid. I was sent to boarding school when I was quite young after my mother died. My relationship with my father was, in actual fact, a very simple one. He paid the school fees.'

'You're so...*matter of fact* about it,' she observed, drawn to the tight line of his lips, the expression of someone who had few touching memories when it came to his past.

'Where's the point in getting worked up over a past that can't be changed? You work in a tough school. You must have encountered kids with more pressing problems than an eight-year-old from a rich background who ends up in a boarding school.'

'I guess that's one way of looking at it,' she said slowly. But the way he had bluntly stated those facts...*mother dying, boarding school, absentee father...and eight years old!* Somehow the situation in Luca's case felt quite different from Jake's insofar as there were alternative parental choices that could have been made. Luca's father had still been around but instead of reaching out he had chosen to walk away.

'You *would* find it difficult to bond if you…er—'

'Let's drop the Good Samaritan take on this. Bottom line is that we need to speed the process up,' he interrupted her. 'Jake is with the neighbour this evening, but sooner or later the hunt for a nanny has to commence, and by the time it concludes he should feel more confident in my relationship with him to make for a happier home environment.'

'Speed it up? How do you intend to do that?' That glimpse of humanity underneath the icy exterior was as fleeting as those other glimpses of him that showed her a man who was not the intimidating powerhouse he projected to the outside world, but it touched her in ways she couldn't explain. She pictured a bewildered child, holding back his grief as he was dispatched into the care of efficient strangers. No wonder he found it impossible to bond with his nephew. He had no experience of family life to fall back on. For all the ups and downs within her own family, who had been far from perfect, she at least had known the ebb and flow of how families operated.

'You're the touchy-feely one with the people skills,' Luca told her flatly. 'You should have one or two ideas. Here's the thing—with the best will in the world, time isn't on my side. You need to busy yourself thinking about how we solve this problem. Anyway, we're here.'

Ellie realised that they had either been driving longer than she'd thought or faster than she'd imagined because they were now in a very civilised part of the world. The houses were all set back from the road and dotted in between fields. Only the distant sound of the motorway served as a reminder that they weren't in the deepest countryside.

The pub was a chocolate box concoction of old beams, cream walls and a sprawling courtyard in which were lined up high-end cars interspersed with a couple of motorbikes.

It was still warm, even though the sun was no longer high

in the sky, and the garden at the back was packed, with only a couple of free tables, one of which Luca took, settling her before returning with a bar menu and a bottle of wine.

'My driver can get here and return to London in the Maserati.' He poured them both a glass of wine. 'And we can take a taxi back to London. Now, let's talk ways forward with Jake.'

'I don't know how you think I can work miracles and suddenly speed up his recovery process and cement the relationship you two have.' She frowned and stared off into the distance, seeing but not really noticing the crowd of expensive-looking people filling out the place. She rested her eyes on his cool, beautiful face. 'You may think that you don't need to have any input into trying to find a solution to this, that so long as you unbend enough to get back from work a little earlier than you're accustomed to doing, it's enough, but you're wrong. You won't thank me for saying this, but throwing money at the situation isn't going to work the way it may have done for you when you were a child.'

Ellie didn't mean a word of that. Personally, Luca's cold, unemotional take on the world was probably directly related to the way his father had dealt with the situation and no one could say that the end result had been a blazing success, even if the guy was as rich as Croesus.

She looked at the uncompromising, unwelcoming lines of his lean, striking face and had an insane desire to reach out and stroke his cheek, the same way he had casually reached out and stroked hers. His boundaries were steel-clad and she wondered whether anyone had ever come close to breaching them. Any of those women he had dated? She thought not. He would never allow any of them near enough.

'Don't get me wrong...'

'No need to butter me up before you drop the axe.' Luca grinned because, against all odds, he was amused by the uncomfortable tinge of colour in her cheeks. 'You have amazing eyes,' he murmured, in a voice that implied that he was as surprised by what he had just said as she was.

'I beg your pardon?'

'It's an unusual shade of green, as clear as glass washed up on a beach.'

Ellie could feel herself burning up under his lazy, dark eyes. 'I... I don't think that's...appropriate, do you?'

'Possibly not,' Luca murmured. His eyes drifted to her mouth, full lips the colour of crushed raspberries and made for kissing.

'Stop looking at me,' Ellie whispered, breaking the silence with difficulty.

'You don't like it?'

'No, I most certainly do not!'

Luca raised his eyebrows and smiled and she wondered whether he thought that she might actually *like* him staring at her. She'd never played with fire and this felt as though she had a box of matches in one hand and a tank of petrol in the other. It wasn't a game she cared to begin.

'You need to spend a bit more undiluted time with Jake.' Back to the reason they were sitting here! 'I think that might be the way to go if you want to speed things up. Half an hour in the evening is better than what you were putting in before but it's not nearly enough.'

He surfaced to something she was saying and realised that he'd dropped the ball for a minute there because he'd been too busy looking at her. *Spend more time.* Time was money for him, but he was being pinned into a corner, and somehow his brain wasn't functioning at optimum level.

He heard the voice and recognised it almost before he registered that he was being addressed.

Heidi Troon had been his last girlfriend and she had not accepted the parting of ways with philosophical equanimity. She had screeched and squawked and accused him of leading her on, then she had wept and wailed and finally, in the absence of a suitable response, she had flounced out of his apartment, having called him every unladylike name under the sun and swearing darkly that he would get what was coming to him. That had been some months previously and since then her vitriolic departure, along with a certain boredom with the prospect of wooing a replacement, had propelled Luca into increasing his workload. Jake, in retrospect, had not been a happy beneficiary of the situation.

He turned around with visible reluctance as she arrived at his side, her big blue eyes staring at Ellie with open curiosity before zeroing in on him.

This was a woman designed to make men swoon and bump into lamp posts. With legs up to her armpits and hair that fell in a golden sheet to her waist, she knew how to play up every single asset she possessed to perfection, and her assets were many.

She was wearing a small red skirt and a small, cropped black-and-white sleeveless top that clung to every curve, and the striking length of her legs was accentuated by six-inch strappy sandals.

'I've been trying to get in touch with you,' she crooned and Luca gritted his teeth. 'We left on bad terms and afterwards, well, I thought I could make it up to you. I've phoned and texted...'

'I know.'

'Why haven't you replied?'

'I've been busy. Heidi...this is Ellie.'

Ellie had never seen anyone as stupendous as the blonde towering over their table. She wasn't sure whether to stand, sit, smile, stretch out her hand or explain why she was sitting in a country pub with Luca. Or maybe just curtsy. She opted for the path of least resistance and looked away in silence, leaving Luca to deal with the situation.

'I wanted to talk to you, Luca. Without your...*who are you anyway?*...earwigging.'

Luca sighed and stood up, his lean, handsome face tight with disapproval. 'I'll be back shortly,' he grated, while Ellie grinned like a wind-up toy until her jaw ached.

Hot embarrassment was coursing through her. Had she been lulled into thinking that this was *a date*? Well, she'd been brought right back down to earth with a bump, and let that be a lesson to her.

By the time Luca returned, the blonde was no longer with him, and Ellie was halfway through her food.

'Apologies,' she said stiffly.

'For what?'

'For getting in the way if you would rather have dined with your friend.'

'If I'd wanted the woman around, I would have asked her to stay. I didn't ask her to stay because the last thing I wanted was her company.'

'She must have been curious about me. What did you tell her?'

'Nothing.' His expression was cool and unrevealing. 'Why would I tell her anything? It's none of her business.' He shrugged and said, by way of brief explanation, 'We went out some time ago. It didn't last long but she took the break-up badly, even though I'd been nothing but honest with her from day one. She has been trying to contact me and I've been ignoring her texts. I had said what had to be said and that, as far as I was concerned, was the end of the story. My apologies if you felt uncomfortable with the situation.'

'Not at all,' Ellie lied. 'But don't you care if she gets the wrong impression?'

'Wrong impression?' Amusement lightened his features. 'Ah, I get where you're going with this. I repeat: what she thinks is her concern. I can't legislate over her thoughts and I have never seen the need to explain myself to anyone.' That *had* occurred to him, and he'd thought, so what if she thought that Ellie was her replacement? Wouldn't it stop her thinking that there was still a chance for them and bring an end to the nuisance calls?

Why would he shut down that line of thought when it was beneficial to him that she run with the misconception?

'Has it occurred to you that *I* might care what someone else thinks of me?'

'No,' Luca answered truthfully. 'You don't know the woman so why would you care what she thinks of you? You'll never see her again and, if she chooses to gossip a bit with her crowd, then it won't make a scrap of difference to you because you'll never know.'

Everything he said made sense, but Ellie was still dismayed at the thought of having her reputation used as gossip fodder for people like the stalking blonde. Being seen with Luca, being thought of as the latest in his line of mistresses, did not sit well with her. She had noticed the way the other woman had looked at her with those icy blue eyes—with pitying speculation.

'Don't think about it,' he said dismissively. 'If you worried about what everyone thinks, you'd go mad.'

'Thanks for the tip,' Ellie muttered, lowering her eyes and half-wanting to slap him, because maybe that was how it worked in his world, but it wasn't how it worked in hers. Plus, somehow the atmosphere had been ruined, and while she knew that there should have been no atmosphere to ruin in the first place she still felt flat all of a sudden.

'You're welcome,' Luca drawled. 'You'll thank me for it one day, even though right now you look as though you'd ram your foot on the accelerator and run me over if you happened to be behind the wheel of a truck.'

'Not everyone sees the world the way you do.' Ellie looked at him defensively but he had obviously put that moment of unpleasantness behind him and was already half-smiling at her.

'What a shame.' The smile turned into a grin. Her breathing hitched, and some of that determination to remind herself that this was *business and not pleasure* was chipped away. 'Now, moving on, there was something I wanted to discuss with you before that untimely interruption. You say that I need more time with my godson and I happen to agree with you. The only way I can think of doing that is to remove myself from the office altogether.'

'What does that mean?'

'Take time off. Two weeks. I won't be able to fully escape the workload, but there will be considerably fewer demands on my attention. I own a villa in Majorca. I can't remember the last time I went there and I'm thinking that this would be a good opportunity to pay it a visit. Naturally you would have to come along.'

'Two weeks? Out of the country?' Ellie was thinking *sun, sea, sand...and Luca. What kind of a mix was that?*

'You'll find that it will be a luxurious two-week holiday. Yes, it'll be a busman's holiday insofar as your interaction with Jake is concerned, but I can guarantee relaxation. The villa is a short walk down to a private cove. When we return to London, the hunt for your replacement can begin in earnest, and I'm hoping that some undiluted time with Jake will build more of a bridge between us than currently exists.'

'When would we leave? I had hoped to go up north next weekend. My sister is planning on coming over and seems keen to meet up...'

'I should be able to tie up all loose ends and get my calendar cleared within three days. Aim for that. The sister can be put on hold. Three days should give you time to buy whatever you want to take with you in terms of summer clothes, as well as whatever Jake needs. It'll be hot out there. Questions?'

None, Ellie thought, as her life hurtled into fifth gear and the predictability which had been the mainstay of her existence threatened to vanish altogether. She'd taken his deal and signed her soul away in the process. So how could she have any questions?

And then, at five the following evening, questions became redundant anyway because fate decided to speed things along.

In the kitchen with Jake, Ellie was startled by the sound of the front door slamming and then, seconds later, Luca strode into the kitchen, face as black as thunder.

He tossed two tabloids on the table and said, before Ellie could recover from her astonishment at seeing him, 'Turn to the gossip column. Jake.' He spun to look at his godson. 'Exciting news. We're going on a trip. Find Miss Muller and start packing whatever you want to take with you. Ellie will be up in a minute.'

'We bought some Lego. Can I take it?' Jake hovered, nervous eyes locking on Ellie.

'Whatever you want.' Then Luca seemed to think about it because he knelt to Jake's level and said, tone slightly softened, 'But there will be a lot to do out there. A pool, the sea... There's even a boat.'

'A boat?' Jake's eyes lit up and, for the first time, Ellie could see real interest there in what Luca was saying just as she could see the effort Luca was making to remember that he was dealing with a six-year-old child and so had to exercise patience.

'Nothing fancy, but you don't need fancy to do a bit of sailing.'

'Will you teach me how to sail?'

'I could do that.'

Luca smiled and Ellie felt a lump form in her throat. Something inside her bubbled up, something quite different from the fierce sexual awareness that gripped her whenever she was in his presence.

The way he was now with Jake—a certain softness in his manner, as though he was deliberately slowing himself down—touched her.

Then, Jake gone, things were back to normal and Luca was focusing on Ellie, striding forward to help himself to some water while he tugged off his tie with one hand and flung it on the table. 'It seems that my ex has had a little mischief at our expense. You're the newest acquisition in my long and chequered line of women.'

The colour drained from Ellie's face. She snatched up the paper and there, in bold print, were riveting revelations about a non-existent relationship which, Heidi had made sure to reveal, could really be serious because, for once, the most eligible man on the planet was not dating to type.

'I'm even more furious than you are,' Luca said with audible loathing in his voice.

'You have to tell these reporters that none of this is true!' Ellie was horrified at what her dad would think. He would be bitterly disappointed. She had never been the type of girl to sleep around and get herself emblazoned in tabloid papers. He might never find out, but Lily was going to be around, and she read tabloids as thoroughly as a student cramming for an end-of-year exam.

'I don't discuss my private life with reporters,' Luca informed her, his movements restless and lacking their usual grace. 'And for the record, never get into a dialogue with the paparazzi unless you want every word misconstrued.'

'So what do you suggest? You might not care about any of this but *I do*!'

'It'll be a five-minute wonder. You can tell your father the truth but that isn't going to make the article disappear. There will be reporters trying to take pictures of you out and about and embellishing a non-story as much as they can until some other nonsense comes along to distract them.'

'Pictures of me?' Ellie squeaked, paling at the thought of that intrusion into her privacy.

'Not if we leave the country. I have my private jet on standby. You just need to pack your bags and I'll ensure we leave this house without being followed. My villa is more secure than the Bank of England and, by the time we return, all of this will have blown over.' He glanced at his watch, dumped his empty glass in the sink and looked at her. 'I will see you in the hallway in an hour, Ellie.' Then unexpectedly his voice was gentle when he added, 'I realise I have a different take on this to you, Ellie, but everything will be fine in the end. You just have to trust me on this...'

CHAPTER SIX

WITHIN AN HOUR and a half, they were being driven in his Jag out to the airstrip where his private jet would be ready and waiting for them. There were no reporters in sight, but there were two black Range Rovers driving behind them at a discreet distance, and they had been ushered out of the house via a side door straight into a waiting chauffeur-driven car.

She hadn't managed to cobble anything together by way of summer clothes, so her case was full of the stuff she wore every day. Jeans and tee shirts. A couple of pairs of shorts and some flip-flops. Jake, fortunately, had an ample supply of designer summer gear, which had been provided along with all the expensive trinkets and gadgets that Luca had ordered in for him as a replacement for *quality time*.

The sun was fading by the time they made it to the airstrip which was forty minutes outside London. In the car, Luca worked and Jake stared excitedly out of the window before asking repeatedly when they were going to be there, and Ellie…

Ellie marvelled that her well-ordered, neat little life had detonated without her even realising that there had been a hand grenade waiting to go off.

This was an adventure, and it felt like one. Except she didn't do adventures. Her sister did. Which, for most of the silent drive, brought her right back to the business of her father and hoping he didn't read all the rubbish that had been circulating in the tabloids...

The private jet—which clearly Luca took for granted, as he barely glanced at it—was amazing.

Sleek, black and powerful, bearing the logo of his company in dull, matt silver along the side, it oozed crazy wealth and Jake was so impressed that he sidled closer to Luca, who had paused to look down at his godson.

The promise of a sailing lesson had opened a crack in the door between them, even if neither of them was quite aware of that, and Ellie took a back seat, allowing them both awkwardly to try their hand at communicating without her intervention.

Jake asked questions about the jet and Luca broke down his answers into bite-sized replies, easily digested by a curious six-year-old.

'Perhaps you could teach me how to fly?' Jake asked as they boarded, and Luca burst out laughing.

'That might have to wait,' he said, looking down as Jake strapped himself in. 'A pilot's licence is the one thing I haven't yet had time to get. But don't worry. You want to fly my jet? You'll get the chance in time.'

'Wow,' Ellie murmured with heartfelt sincerity when Luca was sitting next to her, while behind them Jake occupied himself with something on his tablet. 'I think you're working out how this whole father-son thing works...' Then she blushed and clumsily amended, 'I meant godfather-godson.'

'Stick to the former.' Luca pulled out his laptop, eyes not on her. 'It's more appropriate considering he will inherit the throne.'

'Inherit the throne?'

'What I have will one day be his.' He looked at her thoughtfully. 'I would like to have a meaningful relationship with the child who will, one day, take over my empire.'

'More than the relationship you have with your own father,'

Ellie heard herself say, but instead of slamming down the shutters hard Luca nodded abruptly.

'Something like that.' He stared at her for a few seconds, then adjusted his position and murmured softly, 'And, Ellie, don't think about what other people are going to say or how they're going to react to a couple of trashy articles printed in some tabloids. I can see it's on your mind. Don't focus on it.'

She nodded but didn't answer as the jet began taxiing for take-off. It thundered into the heavens with the power of a rocket and she couldn't contain a gasp of excitement, which took her mind off the whole sorry business for a couple of minutes.

'Did you get through to your father?' Luca asked as soon as they were airborne.

'No,' Ellie told him glumly.

'It's more than likely he won't read those articles. Is he the sort who has a penchant for trashy tabloids?'

'One of them isn't a trashy tabloid.' Her green eyes were filled with anxiety. He lived in such a different world from her, she thought again. He occupied a world where he was such a top dog that other people's opinions didn't matter and he had complete freedom to do exactly what he wanted. Looking at him was like looking at an alien from another planet.

'You're getting lost in the details.' Luca smiled. Her worry was palpable. He should have been irritated because he disliked hand-holding, especially when it came to situations where the hand-holding concerned something he personally considered trivial, but he wasn't irritated. In fact, he wanted to smooth away her anxiety. He felt a tightening in his groin as his gaze dropped to her full mouth and he breathed slowly and deeply, regaining control. It would help if she wasn't staring at him with eyes that could have melted ice.

'It's a storm in a tea cup. Trust me on this one. The paparazzi are fickle. I might be marginally newsworthy but I'm a businessman, not a celebrity. The only reason they've picked up on this at all is because I'm rich and because Heidi is a model who enjoys getting her name and face out there. Reporters love her and she knows just how to throw mud around.'

'Your storm in a tea cup is my personal nightmare,' Ellie said, worrying her lower lip and then leaning back against the leather seat to close her eyes briefly. 'And even if my father doesn't read tabloids, which he doesn't, my sister devours them, and she'll be reporting the incident in great detail.'

'Ah, your sister, the one who has so much in common with me. I recall you saying something of the sort.'

Ellie shrugged one narrow shoulder and kept her profile averted. She didn't want to talk about Lily. She didn't want him to be curious about her sister. Why was that? she wondered. It wasn't as though they were ever going to cross paths. She hated the thought of that happening but refused to analyse why.

'I'll try and take it all in my stride,' she said, eyes still closed, which made this awkward conversation a lot easier. 'But I don't live in your world where this kind of thing happens. You're used to dealing with it, and besides, you don't really care what people think anyway. We're chalk and cheese.'

'I won't argue with that.'

'That's why this whole situation is so stupid,' she thought aloud.

'Why?'

'Because...' Ellie turned to him then drew back a little because it felt as if he was way closer to her than she'd thought. She could smell the clean, woody scent of whatever aftershave he used and could see the tawny glitter in the dark depths of his eyes. 'Because anyone would take one look at us and know that there was no way we could be anything other than employer and employee.'

'You don't do justice to yourself,' Luca said softly. 'What makes you think I don't find you sexy?'

Ellie's eyes widened and then she said, angrily, 'Please don't think you have to compliment me to make me feel good about myself. I feel very good about myself. I'm just realistic.'

'Look in the mirror, Ellie.' Luca's voice was mild and un-revealing.

Ellie's head was swimming. She couldn't maintain eye contact. What was he saying? That he found her *attractive*? She refused to believe it. She had seen his last girlfriend and she was nothing like her.

If she had looked like Lily, well, that would have been a different matter.

Ellie hated all the old insecurities that had somehow been revived ever since she had met Luca. She didn't understand why that was so and it was frustrating that those insecurities were pursuing her so doggedly when she thought she'd left all that behind a long time ago. Was it because he was the sort of beautiful person she had trained herself to ignore over the years? She'd hunkered down after the boyfriend that never was. She knew the limits of her sexual appeal and was very content to work with what she had. But Luca's compliments? Why should he be allowed to feel sorry for her?

'I look in the mirror every day,' she said crisply, 'and I'm not exactly a six-foot blonde whose best friends are reporters and who enjoys having her face splashed across gossip columns in tabloid newspapers, am I?'

'No, you're definitely not that.'

'And thank goodness for that!' Ellie was stung by his easy acceptance of what she had said.

'But as my ex made clear in that article, what about the theory that opposites attract?'

Ellie laughed shortly. 'I don't think so.' She was beginning to squirm because the conversation seemed to be meandering down all sorts of unpredictable roads and, the more it meandered, the more out of control she was beginning to feel. 'Men always go for the same types.'

'Is that your personal observation?'

'As a matter of fact, it is,' Ellie said coolly. Their eyes tangled and she powered on, determined not to be the first to look away. 'Not,' she added gamely, 'that my private life is any of your business.'

'No, of course it isn't,' Luca murmured, his interest piqued in ways that took him by surprise. 'And I won't muddy the waters by pretending that it is. Although...'

'Although what?' The lengthening silence threatened to wreak havoc with her fragile composure.

Ellie hadn't had much choice when it had come to this arrangement. In fact, she'd had *zero* choice. For the amount of money he was paying her, she would have been obliged to follow him to Timbuktu for the job, had she been asked. In the absence of any choice, she had tried not to give house room to the tricky technicality of what it would feel like being cooped up with him all day for hours on end with very little reprieve.

Trepidation soared inside her as he continued to look at her with lazy, brooding intensity, his dark eyes so unsettling and so compelling.

'We're going to be in one another's company for longer periods of time than we have been so far.'

'Yes, I realise that, but I'm here for Jake, and I suppose it's no different than if you were to go somewhere on business with your secretary.'

'Very, very different,' Luca corrected without batting an eyelid. 'I've never shared a villa with my secretary before. Not to mention the fact that the business of Jake takes this to a very personal level.'

'Perhaps *personal* is the wrong word.'

Luca shrugged. 'My point is that there's a limit to how formal things are going to be once we get to the villa. I feel it's only fair to warn you of that in case you're beginning to feel nervous about the situation.'

'Thank you for that,' Ellie said politely, eyes sliding away from this dark, beautiful face.

The jet began dipping and she jumped up to check on Jake.

'Come sit up by us,' she urged, and by the time they were both buckled up the jet was descending to land.

The villa was breath-taking Ellie thought when, two short hours later, the four-wheel drive Luca had hired finally came to a stop. They had driven through lush mountains, where both she and Jake had exclaimed at the glimpses they'd caught of turquoise strips of ocean in the distance.

Far behind them lay the buzz of the nearest town, replaced by hillsides dotted with whitewashed houses, and ribbons of tarmac winding away from the main road climbing the sides of the hills to disappear into the greenery.

All of it was barely visible because night had descended, although the villa itself was brightly lit.

It was peaceful, it was tranquil and it was telescopic-lens-proof.

'CCTV,' Luca pointed out as they headed to the front door. 'And the perimeter walls are crawling with cameras.'

'Extreme for somewhere you don't visit very often,' Ellie returned as she was offered a glimpse of how the really rich conducted their lives.

'I like my privacy.'

Which made Ellie think how furious he must be that it had been so efficiently invaded by his ex.

To Ellie, it had seemed like overkill. It was only after the first couple of days that she thought just how *safe* the place felt.

No prying eyes, and that lack of any intrusion from the outside world was like a pick-me-up tonic.

She had got through to her dad on the first evening they'd arrived and had stammered through an explanation for whatever tacky article he had read which, thanks to Lily, who was now back in the UK, had been all of them.

Then she had spoken to Lily who had been barely able to contain her curiosity and had asked so many questions about Luca that Ellie's head had been aching by the time she'd hung up.

But she hadn't been able to hold on to her worries for long because the villa was magical. Pale colours, shutters everywhere and a veranda that circled the entire house like a bracelet and was strewn with sitting areas. The breezes wafted through the open windows like a lullaby. The infinity pool was stupidly stunning, like something lifted straight out of a classy house magazine.

All the tension drained out of her body and, whatever charm the place wielded, Jake wasn't immune to it either.

His thin, pale face relaxed and the tentative advances he had shown towards Luca continued, slowly but surely. He began to play without reserve and to show some of the spirit a normal six-year-old boy should have.

On day one, they took it easy. Luca showed them around the villa. They strolled down to the private cove where Ellie sat in the shade reading while Luca spent an hour with Jake in the shallow water before calling it a day and retiring to take a series of business calls.

From where she was sitting, Ellie was able to hear their conversation, with Jake asking what fish lived in the sea, squealing apprehensively when the water got too frisky around his ankles and then finally drifting back towards her so that he could sit and focus on building a sand castle.

It was relaxed in the villa because Juanita, the housekeeper, was there, popping up with furniture polish and dust cloths in a very reassuring fashion.

She came in once a week, Luca told Ellie, regardless of whether the property was in use or not, to air it and make sure the roof hadn't fallen in. While they were there, she would come daily and also be responsible for all the cooking.

'So if you don't use this villa,' she asked, bemused by this display of wealth, 'then who does?'

'Friends.' He'd shrugged. 'Employees. Clients occasionally.'

'It's so beautiful. What a waste for you.'

'It's an investment. What's wrong with that?'

Ellie thought it was sad that he really couldn't see where the flaw in that argument was but she wasn't going to go down any more personal roads with him.

She was relieved when, on the first night, Juanita was bustling in the kitchen while they ate the dinner she had prepared after Jake had been settled. Luca had spoke to Juanita in fluent Spanish and then, meal over, Ellie excused herself and retired to bed.

Bit by bit, Ellie noted that the periods of time Luca spent with Jake increased. It was very small steps but all heading in the right direction.

She took a back seat, explaining to Luca that it was a good idea for him to have one-to-one time with Jake without her being there twenty-four-seven because when she was there Jake's attention was conflicted.

'Right now,' she confided when, on their third day, Luca and Jake had spent close to an hour together without Luca climbing the walls with boredom and looking at his watch, 'you're really making strides. Keep this up and by the time we get back to London, you can really begin the search for another nanny. Jake will be comfortable enough around you to see you as the primary adult in his life with the nanny as a secondary figure. He'll feel he belongs and that'll be more than half the battle won.'

They were on the sprawling veranda, Ellie sitting in a wicker chair with her book on her lap while Luca leaned against the wooden railing, looking down at her from his towering height.

Inside, Juanita, who had taken an instant liking to Jake, was continuing with her project to teach him Spanish. After all, as his godfather's heir, he would need to speak the language like a native.

Ellie stared up at Luca, shielding her eyes with her hand. Being alone had been rare so far. Juanita was around all the time, arriving at eight in the morning and leaving at seven, and when she wasn't around Jake filled the gap. Being alone with

Luca was unexpected, and she had been lulled into complacency, so out here alone with him she was jumpy.

Just a handful of days in the sun had turned his skin to burnished gold, and there was a lot of that burnished gold on display, because he hung around in loose khaki shorts and tee shirts that did a brilliant job of showing off his lean, muscular physique.

Right now, his hands were jammed into the pockets of his cream shorts, dragging them down, which emphasised his lean hips and hard, washboard stomach.

She looked away quickly but her skin was prickling all over and she was suddenly self-conscious in her tidy pair of denim shorts and loose cotton tee shirt. And her bare feet. Somehow a pair of sandals went a long way to making her feel suitably attired.

'I hope,' she said into the lengthening silence, 'you don't feel that by giving the two of you time together I'm somehow shirking my duties...'

'If I felt that, trust me, I would tell you.' Luca raked his fingers through his hair. 'I can see that there has been an improvement in my relationship with Jake,' he admitted. 'So the last thing I would feel is that you're shirking your duties. You're doing exactly what I'm paying you to do. That said, you can relax in your spare time, Ellie. Have you been to the pool once since we got here?'

'I... Not yet...but I plan to...' She'd cringed at the thought of getting into her very proper, sporty black one-piece in front of him, choosing instead to watch from the sidelines while he and Jake took to the water.

'You can swim, can't you?'

'Yes! Of course I can swim! I was very sporty when I was a teenager!'

'Then enjoy the pool, Ellie. You can take the working hat off now and again.' He pushed himself away from the wooden railing and strolled towards her, then he leaned down, hands on either side of the chair, caging her in and bringing her out in a fine film of nervous perspiration.

'Luca...'

'You're beginning to make me feel like a taskmaster.' Luca watched the delicate sweep of colour in her cheeks and his keen eyes noted the way she had pressed herself so far back into the chair that she was in danger of breaking it. 'I'm not keeping tabs on you, Ellie.' His voice had sunk to a low murmur.

She smelled of flowers, fresh, clean and *young*. He found that he couldn't move because he was entranced by the delicacy of her face. She glowed over here. Her short hair had lightened in the sun and a sprinkling of freckles had appeared from nowhere on the bridge of her nose. She looked like a fairy. A ridiculously sexy fairy. He had to will himself to stand back, and when he did he made sure to put some distance between them, but his breathing remained thick and uneven.

'I know you're not,' she said evasively.

'Good. I'm going to work now and I'll be busy until early evening. Something has come up with a deal in Hong Kong and I have a series of conference calls to chair. Jake's busy with Juanita. You can sit out here reading your book or retire to your room, but you can also explore the grounds and enjoy yourself. If you like, I can arrange for you to be driven into the village. No one knows where we are so there's not much chance of any flash bulbs going off in your face. Besides, the village is small, and even if I don't get here very often I contribute quite substantially to various projects and organisations. They are reassuringly protective of my privacy.'

'I... I'm fine here, Luca. Thank you.' Her heart was thumping as though she'd run a marathon. 'I like reading, and I'm very relaxed, so please don't worry about me.'

For a few seconds he stared down at her, his expression veiled, then he straightened, eyes drifting downwards to the small, delicate points of her breasts. A surge of hot blood made his groin ache. He felt giddy, out of control, and he abruptly stepped back, scowling.

'Good.' His voice was cool and sharp. 'Just so long as you know that you can actually have fun—that you're not my servant, or on call twenty-four-seven.' At which, he swung away and headed at a pace towards his office.

Hurt by the abruptness of his voice, Ellie realised that whatever occasional shiver of camaraderie she sometimes felt with him, whatever weird feeling that he sometimes *saw her as a woman*, was an illusion because it was obvious the guy thought she was a bore. The sort who faded into the background and had to be forced to enjoy the massive grounds, the gardens and all the things that were on offer. She had brought her computer over and had mentioned that there was a backlog of school stuff to do, which had so far been put on the back burner. Hardly riveting stuff for a twenty-something singleton to be doing in a place the likes of which she would never, ever see again.

On the spur of the moment, Ellie headed straight up to her bedroom, slipped into her swimsuit, armed herself with sun lotion, a towel, a sarong and her oversized sunglasses and headed straight down to the cove.

Jake was with Juanita and, really, she'd had no time to herself since they had arrived.

It would be good to relax and enjoy the scenery without feeling self-conscious that Luca was around, or in teacher mode because Jake was there. What with all the business with her dad and his debts, relaxation had been a distant dream for so long now. She would be an idiot to pass up the opportunity to grab some while she was here in this little slice of paradise.

It was a little after five but the sun was still warm and the sound of the water whispering against the sand was soporific.

On the very verge of falling asleep, Ellie decided to take to the water. She'd represented her school in swimming and it felt great to be scything through the sea. It had been a long time. Public swimming pools were fine, but usually far too crowded to do anything but weave in and out of other swimmers, and there was nothing like the freedom of the open water.

Oblivious to everything but the feel of the water as she sliced through it, she was barely aware of the distance she was swimming.

After twenty minutes she stopped, lay on her back, floated and let her thoughts drift in and out of her head. She closed her eyes.

Luca's sexy image swam into her head and she didn't bother trying to chase it out.

She shivered when she recalled how her skin had burned when he had touched her. She thought about the dark beauty of his face and the way his eyes lingered, watching her and thinking thoughts she couldn't begin to imagine but about which she could speculate for England.

She wondered…

Floating like driftwood, she wondered what it would feel like to have him touch her intimately. To have those long, clever fingers explore her body, rouse her passion. She could feel the warmth of her wetness mingle with the sea and she shifted, restless and suddenly aching between her legs.

She wanted to touch herself to ease the tingle there.

She wasn't expecting her lazy reverie and the pleasant ebb and flow of her fantasies to be brought to a sharp halt by the feel of someone grabbing her, gripping her waist and sending her into a panicked meltdown.

She thrashed like a wild thing as the sea water poured into her eyes and her mouth until she was spluttering and quite unaware, for a few terrified seconds, about what was happening.

Then she snapped out of it when Luca growled into her ear, 'What the hell do you think you're playing at!'

Her stinging eyes flew open and there he was, like a dark, avenging angel, glaring at her, out of his depth in the deep water but still holding her as though she was as light as a feather.

Ellie pushed, hands flattened against his rock-solid chest, and he circled her wrists with his fingers.

'What are *you* playing at? Let me go!'

'So you can bloody carry on drifting out to sea while you're in La-La Land? No way! You're coming right back to shore!'

'I'm fine!' Ellie yelled, dropping all pretence of professionalism, because she'd been taken by surprise, and because the feel of him so close to her, wearing next to nothing, was making her feel giddy and faint, especially when she'd been having such pleasurable and such, such taboo fantasies about him.

'You can't see the shore line, Ellie!' He was treading water but now he began to swim, making sure that she kept pace with him.

He was a strong swimmer, but so was she, and pride made her swim as strongly as she could so that he didn't think she was a wilting female in need of being saved from her own idiocy by a knight in shining armour.

By the time they finally made it to land, she was exhausted as she staggered upright.

He didn't wait for permission. Water pouring off him, he picked her up and ignored her half-hearted struggles against him.

'Put me down!'

'Shut up.'

'How *dare* you tell me to shut up?'

'Have you any idea how long you've been out here?'

'I must have forgotten my waterproof diving watch back in my room!'

'The sun's practically disappeared!' Luca roared, striding up the beach towards a rug that he had brought with him and dumped alongside her towel. 'You've been missing in action for over an hour and a half, Ellie!'

'No, I haven't!' The sun *had* begun to fade and… *An hour and a half?* Where on earth had the time gone?

In her raunchy thoughts! That was where!

She stopped struggling, choosing to hold herself as rigid as a plank of wood against him, which he ignored, and then she found herself on the rug, staring up at him and hastily shuffling herself into a half-sitting position, resting on her elbows.

She could barely catch her breath because the swim back had been so tiring.

Legs apart, Luca stared down at her, thin lipped, eyes narrowed, oozing anger through every pore.

'You suggested I take some time out,' Ellie said weakly. Okay, her eyes had been closed, and she might have dozed off out there, because darkness was rolling in at speed. Her heart was beating hard and fast.

'I didn't suggest you head out on a suicide mission into the open ocean! Do you know *anything* about the currents that can sweep along these shores without warning? Have you any idea how many people get into difficulties because they think that the sea is a safe place just because it's calm? No lifeguard here, Ellie!'

'Well, then.' She sprang to her feet, because lying on the rug just made her feel helpless with Luca towering over her like a skyscraper. 'Good job *you* came along to rescue me, isn't it?'

She was breathing brimstone and fire. This was a side to her that Luca had never seen. Her eyes were flashing, her hands were placed squarely on her hips and she was leaning into him with open aggression.

'Damn well is,' he growled. 'And there's no way you're going to attack me for being worried about your bloody welfare!'

'Well, I'm very grateful! Even though I *wasn't in any difficulty whatsoever*! How would you like me to thank you, Luca?'

'How? Well you can start with this…'

CHAPTER SEVEN

HE KISSED HER. Even when he reached to cup his hand behind the nape of her neck and lowered his head Ellie still wasn't expecting him to *actually kiss her.*

The touch of his mouth against hers was as potent as an electric shock ripping through her body, heating her blood and firing her nervous system into frantic overdrive.

A soft kiss…but only for a second, just long enough to break down all her defences, and she stepped towards him, hands positioned to push him away but instead curving over his warm, naked skin and seeking out his flat, brown nipples.

She was straining up, on tiptoe, and she sighed into his mouth. She'd just been fantasising about this and it felt unreal for the fantasy suddenly to become bone-melting reality.

The teasing delicacy of Luca's kiss changed tempo and he pulled her towards him, tasting her with urgent hunger, tongues meshing, and their damp bodies sticking together, salty and hot.

Ellie's head fell back as he carried on kissing her and she wound her hands around his neck.

He was so impossibly strong and muscled and she dropped her hands to trace the contours of his corded shoulders.

She was on fire, flames licking through her slender body, tightening her nipples and causing her legs to tremble unsteadily. As if sensing that, he swept her off her feet, without his mouth ever leaving hers, and this time when he rested her on the rug he lay down next to her.

Ellie moaned softly.

The sun was disappearing rapidly and they were bathed in soft twilight.

She squirmed against him, half of her aghast at what she was doing while the other half was sinking into the physical contact like a man deprived of water suddenly led to a flowing stream.

She'd never wanted anyone as badly as she wanted this man. She never wanted to come up for air, and she was so overwhelmed that 'right and wrong' and 'crazy and sensible' were just a jumble of words that made no sense.

Luca flattened her, hand on her hip, and he began stroking her thigh.

Her legs dropped open and he placed his hand over her crotch and gently massaged.

For a few seconds, she couldn't breathe. His touch was firm but he was caressing her in such a leisurely manner she could barely think straight.

She sifted her fingers through his dark, spiky hair and then felt the rough stubble on his chin and arched up to push her small breasts against his chest.

The damp swimsuit was an intolerable barrier, and when his hand drifted away from her crotch to cover her breast she hooked her finger under the strap, wordlessly leading him to do what she was desperate to do.

It was funny but *lust* was a word that had never exerted any curiosity for Ellie. She'd read a million articles about women who flung themselves into bed with some guy because he was irresistible.

Privately, that was a concept she had always held in contempt.

Really! Irresistible? No wonder the world was full of miserable divorced couples! If they were guided by lust, then where was the longevity in that? She'd always reckoned that her mum had married her dad because she'd been carried away by lust, only for reality to insert itself and begin its destructive work once the lust had tapered off.

She could never have imagined being swept off her feet and doing anything that went contrary to good, old-fashioned common sense.

She had watched and seen the way boys hung around Lily with their tongues out and their hormones all over the place. 'Recipe for disaster' was what she could have told them, and sure enoug, they always ended up retreating, wounded.

Even when she had had her one big affair with Paul, yes, Ellie had found him attractive enough, but she hadn't found herself wanting to fling herself at him.

In fact, the whole sexual side of things had been controlled and pleasant and that had suited Ellie fine.

She'd been devastated when he had succumbed to Lily's charms but not particularly surprised when, like all the others, he had fallen by the wayside as soon as her sister had decided it was time to move on.

Lust, Ellie had worked out a long time ago, was for the birds.

Except, caught in the grip of it now, she was finally discovering what all the fuss was about.

Luca's hands on her had the same effect as fire melting wax and her body was molten hot with need. She clung to him shamelessly and, when he eased the straps of her swimsuit down, she shuddered with heated anticipation.

It was dark now on the beach. The calm, glassy water was inky-black and the trees and rocks dark silhouettes against a starless horizon. The breeze was as ineffective when it came to refreshing their bodies as the whirring of a sluggish overhead fan.

But Ellie cooled as the swimsuit exposed the pert, rounded orbs of her breasts, pale in contrast to the rest of her, which had turned pale gold over the past few days in the sun. Against her pale breasts, her nipples were dark-pink circles, enticingly large compared to the size of her breasts.

Luca bent down, took one nipple into his mouth and began to suckle on it. He lathed the tight bud with his tongue and Ellie groaned and wriggled, feverish in her want.

Hand cradling the back of his dark head, eyes squeezed tight and mouth open as she breathed thickly, Ellie pressed him harder against her aching, sensitive breast, desperate for some attention to be paid to the other one.

She shuddered when he did just that, turning his attention to her swollen, pulsing nipple and, at the same time, easing his hand underneath the stretchy swimming costume to feel the slick wetness between her thighs.

'This is what heaven feels like,' Luca broke free to mutter. He meant it. She was so hot, so responsive and so damned sexy. It was as if he had discovered a different person behind the armour of prissy clothes—or had that person always been there? Had he seen the passion lying dormant behind the calm exterior? Surely he had, because she had piqued his sexual interest long before now.

His erection was rock-hard and he had to control his breathing so that he didn't do the unthinkable. One touch from her and he knew that he would come as fast as a randy teenager, and he didn't want to do that. He wanted to take his time even though, at the back of his mind, he knew that they would have to stop. Right now, time was definitely not on their side.

But when?

Luca had no desire to lose the moment.

But the moment was lost when they both heard the distant reedy voice of Jake calling out for Ellie.

There was no way that either Jake or Juanita would take the steps that led down to the cove. They were lit but at this time of the evening it would be a hazardous trip down for a six-year-old and Juanita, despite living close to the sea, was terrified of water.

No matter.

That voice penetrated their cocoon and Ellie pushed Luca away with shaking hands and stumbled to her feet.

'What are you doing?' she cried, and it was such a stupid question that Luca didn't bother responding.

Ellie spun round and began running along the cove, grabbing her stuff en route, heading for the stone steps up to the villa.

Horror was spreading through her with toxic ferocity. How on earth had they ended up doing what they had? What had possessed her? How could she have lost all control like that?

Lust...was the word that sprang into her head, mocking and jeering at her prim, horrified reaction.

She recalled the feel of him in the water when he had surprised her, the hardness of his body lying next to her and the sensation of his mouth on hers, on her lips...her breasts...her nipples.

She wanted to groan with frustration and despair because this sort of thing just *wasn't her.*

She headed up the steps at speed, half-stumbling as she neared the top to see Jake and Juanita on the lawn outside the front door.

Behind her, Luca was taking his time and not saying anything, and Ellie was more than happy to ignore him.

What sort of conversation could they have? The thought brought her out in a cold sweat.

She threw herself into scooping Jake up and hurrying inside. She knew she was chatting far too much, with high-pitched, feverish intensity, and she knew that it was to distract herself from the horror of remembering what had happened down there on the beach.

To her relief, Luca vanished, probably to bury himself in whatever he had been doing before he'd been rudely interrupted and taken it upon himself to play knight in shining armour.

It gave Ellie time to shower quickly, change and then return to the kitchen where she took up where she had left off with Jake.

'I was scared,' he confided in a small voice.

'And I was silly,' Ellie admitted, giving him a huge cuddle. 'I swam a little too far out, and that was incredibly naughty.'

'But Luca saved you,' Jake piped up in a voice that was full of admiration. 'When I told him I was scared, he told me there was no need to be because he'd make sure you were okay, and you were. He saved you.'

'I'm sure he'd like to think that.' Ellie couldn't help injecting a touch of sarcasm into her response. 'Although I used to swim a lot when I was your age, right up until I was a big girl.' Which led to a long discussion about sports, hobbies and swimming and allowed her mind way too much freedom to roam and agonise over what she had done.

Ellie knew there was no way she could lay the blame on Luca's shoulders.

He had been dragged away from his work and had been furious at having to rescue her. Yes, he might have instigated that kiss, but she had flung herself wholeheartedly into it and had practically accosted the poor guy.

As if there was any chance that he could actually fancy her! Ellie cringed when she thought about that. He was a man and he had responded the way any man would have when a woman flung herself at him with abandon.

He had probably gone into hiding just in case she wanted a repeat performance.

Juanita had gone, Jake had been settled and Ellie was finishing the salad she had prepared for herself when she looked round to see that Luca had quietly entered the kitchen behind her.

She froze. She desperately wanted to blank him out but instead hungrily took in the lean, muscular lines of his body and remembered the way it had felt pressed up against her, wet, slick and hard.

'What are you doing here?' she questioned tightly.

He'd changed, as she had. Where she had got into some faded

jeans and a tee shirt, he was in all black—a black V-necked tee shirt that clung in just the right way and black jeans. And he wasn't wearing any shoes. That seemed disproportionately intimate.

'It's my villa.'

'I... I've just eaten,' she gabbled, backing away as he strolled towards her then swerved to fetch a bottle of water from the fridge. 'I was just on my way up. I... I... I hope you remembered to say goodnight to Jake! It's a brilliant routine. Have I told you that? He really enjoys that.'

'We need to talk, Ellie.'

'Talk? Talk about what?'

'What do you think?' He raised his eyebrows and shot her a dry look.

He raised the bottle to his lips and began drinking and Ellie frantically asked herself how it was that someone drinking water from a bottle could look so sexy.

It was an effort to tear her eyes away and she had to work hard at channelling her thoughts into some kind of order.

So beautiful, she thought weakly. It wasn't fair! How was she supposed to stand a chance against someone so beautiful? She'd thought she was as tough as nails when it came to making judgement calls on men. She'd always found it easy to scoff at people who were swept away by something as superficial as *looks* because, after all, there was so much more to a person than appearances.

Yet here she was! Scratch the surface and what you found was a guy who had nothing at all in common with her, whose principles contravened everything she believed in, whose arrogance got up her nose...

It angered her so much that none of that seemed to count for anything because she took one look at him and something inside her melted. And then there had been those moments, like when she had seen him stooping down to Jake, slowing down, trying so hard to connect, willing to step out of his comfort zone. Those had been moments when something inside her had opened up, letting him in.

'I don't want to talk about that,' Ellie whispered.

'You want to pretend that none of it ever happened?'

'And none of it would have if you hadn't overreacted! I'm an extremely strong swimmer! I represented the county at one point when I was a teenager!'

'Academic.'

'What does *that* mean?'

'It means that whether you swam in the Olympics makes no difference to the fact that if we hadn't been interrupted we would have ended up making love on that beach.'

The colour drained from Ellie's face and then, just as quickly, rushed back to turn her cheeks beetroot-red.

'We wouldn't.' She turned away to busy herself by the sink. When she felt his hands on her shoulders, her whole body stiffened. For a few panicked seconds she forgot how to breathe. She didn't dare turn around to look at him.

'Why can't you just drop it?' she half-cried under her breath.

'And why do you find it so impossible to talk about it?'

'We would have come to our senses. *I* would have come to my senses. There's no way...'

'I wanted it, Ellie.'

'No! That's crazy!'

'And so did you.'

'Stop putting words into my mouth, Luca! Yes, I admit you're an attractive man, but that doesn't mean that I'm a complete fool!'

'Why don't you look at me when you say that? Or are you afraid to?'

'Afraid?' Ellie burst out laughing but even to her own ears her laughter sounded hollow. He'd thrown down a gauntlet and she turned slowly to look at him.

Luca dropped his hands and stood back.

'I apologise,' she said stiffly.

'For what?'

'For throwing myself at you.'

'I'm a big boy, Ellie. If I hadn't enjoyed it, I wouldn't have ended up lying on that rug with you, with the straps of that swimsuit down, feasting on your breasts.'

Ellie closed her eyes. Her breathing was laboured. She didn't understand why he had to be so provocative, so graphic.

'It was a moment of madness,' she whispered, helpless against the onslaught of wild emotion Luca's words had roused in her. Her body was responding in just the way she didn't want it to; she folded her arms protectively across her breasts and looked at him with deep reluctance.

'I want you,' Luca said flatly. 'I'm not saying it makes sense.' He raked his fingers through his hair, suddenly ill at ease but utterly unable to back away from what he wanted to say. 'I'm not saying that it's something I need. That either of us needs. But since when does everything have to make sense?' In his world, everything *always* made sense, and he was annoyed and frustrated that in this instance he couldn't bring his formidable intellect into play to control a situation that was, as she had said, no more than a moment of madness.

'I work for you, Luca.'

'And I have always kept very distinct lines between business and pleasure.'

He reached out to touch her cheek and felt her shiver under his touch. 'Until now.' He heard the unsteadiness in his voice with some surprise.

She was gazing at him, lips parted, pupils dilated, and she didn't pull away when he lowered his head and oh, so gently covered her mouth with his.

He tasted her.

This wasn't frantic and urgent, as it had been on the beach. This was slow and tender, and she lost herself in the moment, curving her body into his, her softness moulding against his hardness.

Their tongues were entwined and her eyes were closed as he took his time exploring her.

He wasn't rushing. He wasn't touching her anywhere at all and, the less he touched, the more she wanted him to. When he finally pulled back, they stared at one another in silence and he was the first to break it.

'I want to make love to you.'

'I don't understand why.'

'You do something to me. Have done for a while. There's something about you. I want to take you to my bedroom and I want to taste every inch of your body.'

'Luca...'

'Yes or no, Ellie? It's a simple question that needs a one-syllable reply.'

'I've never been the kind of girl who does this sort of thing. We're chalk and cheese...' She thought of the towering blonde mischief-maker who had been his last conquest. Men ran to type. Men who were attracted to towering blondes didn't suddenly find themselves unable to resist small brunettes.

But then again, small brunettes who went for serious, relationship-focused guys with a social conscience didn't suddenly find themselves unable to resist arrogant billionaires who expected the world to obey their commands.

So what was this about, for either of them? Was it because being here, in a place that was so peaceful and so magical, had turned their heads? Had it taken those first stirrings of attraction she had felt for him and magnified them into something irresistible? And was it all about novelty for him? A change being as good as a rest?

He was waiting for her answer. He said it was a simple yes or no but she knew it was far from that.

'Maybe opposites attract,' Luca murmured, because he couldn't think of any other explanation for why he found her so incredibly enticing. 'Yes, Ellie, or no? Say no and this is something that will never rear its head again.'

'Yes.' Apprehension and excitement flared inside her like a blowtorch. She looked at him and cleared her throat. 'Opposites attract. I guess that must be it.'

Luca wasn't sure whether to be flattered that she had agreed with him or disgruntled because it was hardly the level of adoring enthusiasm he was accustomed to from the opposite sex.

He wasn't going to waste time debating the issue.

'My bedroom?'

'This is so crazy...' But her head was so full of him that crazy made sense in a weird kind of way.

Wordlessly they headed for his bedroom. The effect of the silent villa felt like tacit encouragement, egging her on to do something that felt wildly, madly daring. She'd played it safe all her life and especially when it came to men. Living with a beauty queen for a sister, and a mother who wasn't backward when it came to drawing comparisons, Ellie had made a virtue out of never punching above her weight. Sensible choices meant she'd never be let down. Although that hadn't exactly worked with the boyfriend who had leapt for her sister faster than a Jack-in-the-Box, had it?

But still...

Heart racing, she paused as Luca pushed open the door to his bedroom and stepped inside.

Two banks of windows overlooked the sprawling back gardens and the windows were both open so that a cool breeze blew through, rustling the nude-coloured voile drapes. The bed was enormous. Ellie stood still and gazed at it. Was this really what she wanted—a meaningless one-night stand with a guy because she happened to find him irresistible?

Because she knew that, if it wasn't, then this was the time to back away.

'Cold feet?' He switched on the overhead light but then immediately dimmed it so that the room was infused with a mellow, warm glow. He turned to look at her, his beautiful face all shadows and angles.

'No,' she whispered, although she hadn't actually stepped into the room, but was hovering just outside, as though an invisible but impenetrable force field were keeping her out. 'You?'

'I don't get cold feet when it comes to sex.' Luca reached out and linked his fingers through hers, gently guided her into his bedroom and then shut the door behind them.

'Will you promise me one thing?'

'What's that?'

'We don't talk about this in the morning. I mean, we pretend it never happened.'

'We pretend it never happened...?' Luca murmured with low incredulity. Had any woman ever said that to him before? Nope.

'A one-off...' She placed her hands on his chest and stared at her pale fingers then raised her eyes to his. 'I've never done a one-off.'

'Nor have I.'

'Don't tell lies, Luca.' But she smiled and some of the tension left her. Of their own accord her hands were stroking his chest and loving the hardness of his torso under the tee shirt.

She was fascinated by the perfection of his physique. She itched to feel the flatness of his nipples again and to explore lower, to feel the throbbing pulse of him.

'I don't do one-night stands,' he murmured, cupping her rear and inching them both towards the bed. 'I may not do permanence but I don't do one-night stands.'

'So this is a first for both of us...'

'Both virgins when it comes to this, yes.'

Everything she said made sense and was what he should have wanted to hear. It was a complication that could end up a massive headache. She wasn't built like him. She still had ideals and illusions. She still believed in the power of love and all those fairy-tale stories that got people walking up an aisle before everything turned sour and the starry-eyed sweet nothings became high-pitched arguments in a divorce court.

She could get hurt.

'Just don't go falling for me.' He kissed the side of her face, trailed his mouth along her jawline, tasted the sweetness of her lips.

'That would never happen.' Ellie sighed and curved against him.

'That's good. We both know the score. This is an itch that needs to be scratched.' He nuzzled her neck and then broke apart to hook his fingers under his tee shirt, stripping it off in one easy movement.

He guided her hand to his erection, which was a prominent bulge under his jeans, and she gasped.

'My turn now,' he murmured into her ear, and he undid the button of her jeans and pulled down the zip, then worked his way into her panties until he found her sweet spot, the throbbing nub of her clitoris. 'Now touch me.' He groaned unsteadily as he slid his finger along and into her.

Ellie unzipped his trousers. She felt clumsy and gauche, and then nearly passed out when she actually touched him. He was huge, his shaft rigid and thick.

Touching one another without taking it any further was making her head swim. She was so wet between her thighs that she just couldn't keep still.

He broke from her but his eyes never left hers as he stripped off the rest of his clothes and then stood in unashamed glory in front of her. So lean, so beautiful, his physique perfect in every way. He let his hand rest loosely on his erection and smiled crookedly when she found she couldn't tear her eyes away from the sight.

'Your turn,' he commanded, watching.

Lack of experience showed in her first nervous fumblings, but when she looked at him the flare of desire was so apparent in his dark, intense gaze that her inhibitions were discarded along with her clothes.

She'd never thought of herself as desirable before and that look in his eyes made her heady with feminine satisfaction.

It seemed hard to believe that this drop-dead gorgeous guy wanted her but he did. It was there in the flare of his nostrils and the burning darkness of his eyes.

In the grip of lust, Ellie was realising that there was so much more than love when it came to relationships.

There was...*this*. Wonderful, incredible, short-lived, like a firecracker burning bright until it was extinguished in a poof.

Somehow they made it to the bed. Her breathing was staccato-ragged.

He straddled her, and Ellie wriggled up to lick his thick, pulsing manhood, then he shifted and lowered himself to kiss her.

With a groan, she pulled him closer. He couldn't get close enough. She wanted to feel his body against hers, his heartbeat in tune with hers, his breathing warm against her skin.

Their lips met and she arched up to him, one hand behind his head, the other in a closed fist under the small of her back so that she was pressed against him.

Tongues meshed. Her groans merged with his. When he finally reared up, she wanted to do nothing more than yank him back again so that they could carry on kissing.

She had never dreamt that the physical demands of her body could be as powerful as this.

He pushed her gently on her shoulders and she tilted back, her small, pointy breasts a succulent feast waiting to be enjoyed.

She gasped as his mouth circled a breast, sucking deeply as his tongue teased the rigid peak. She couldn't contain her mounting excitement and she shifted her hips from side to side, and up and down, desperate and greedy for him in a way she would never have dreamt possible.

She was barely aware of panting his name or begging him to *hurry up because she couldn't take it any longer.*

She was breathing fast, and even faster when that devastating mouth finally left her breasts to trail a path down her flat stomach, pausing only to circle her belly button.

Luca parted her legs and with expert fingers stroked through her wet folds to tease her clitoris until her pants became hitched cries of pleasure.

Then he dipped down to taste her with the tip of his tongue, a gentle, delicate exploration that made her whole body stiffen in urgent response.

She curled her fingers into his dark hair, pressing him lower even as she opened her legs wider. She felt the waves of her climax begin to build, stiffening her body, and then, with explosive force, she spasmed against his questing mouth, bucking just as he'd said he wanted her to do.

She'd become a slave to her body. She'd reached heights that made her cry out in a voice she didn't recognise. She had no time to apologise for her premature climax, because surely it would have left him frustrated? She came down from her high and slowly he began to build her back up with expert finesse.

He knew just where to touch and how so that her sensitised body was once again roused.

When he sank into her, thrusting hard and deep, she was taken to whole new heights of pleasure, soaring and cresting, higher and higher as he plunged harder inside her, filling every ounce of her body.

Her climax this time was so powerful that it swept her away, and she cried out, jerking and arching as he angled his hips and his shaft in just the right way to take her soaring.

She felt him come, felt him stiffen on one final thrust, and then she was sated and so satisfied that what she wanted to do most was fall into a deep sleep.

Luca rolled off her, disposing of the condom she'd hardly noticed him donning, but then he immediately turned and pulled her close against him so that their naked bodies were pressed against one another.

'I should go,' Ellie said drowsily, although she didn't want to.

'I've decided to renege on my promise,' Luca responded without a hint of shame.

'What do you mean?'

'I still want you and I have no intention of waking up in the morning and pretending that nothing happened between us. A lot has happened between us, and one night isn't going to be enough for me. So, if you want to play the pretend game, then you're on your own.'

'But you promised!' Ellie said with consternation.

Luca shrugged. He circled his finger over a rosy nipple that was peeking out above the cover.

'Promises get broken. This one has.' He fastened his dark eyes on her. 'Are you going to tell me that one night will be enough for you? Because, if you do, then I'll say now that I won't believe a word of it. We're here and I don't intend to watch you from a distance and kid myself that I don't want to touch you.'

'We're not children, Luca! We're grown up enough to know that you don't always get what you want!'

'That's right. We're not children, we're adults, and we still want one another and we can have one another. Ten more days and then we return to London and this thing between us…this virus…gone. It's as easy as that…'

Luca was in no doubt that he would be more than ready to conclude things by then anyway. He bored easily and, though she might be stimulating now, in a fortnight that allure would have worn off, and it would certainly disappear under the weight of reality that would be waiting there for him. Besides, whatever ground rules had been agreed, he was still uneasy at the thought that she might start looking for more than was on the table.

'It's not as easy as that, Luca.' Her brain was refusing to function. It really wasn't as easy as that. Was it?

'Oh,' he murmured silkily, 'but it is. Trust me…'

CHAPTER EIGHT

LUCA LOOKED ACROSS the width of the infinity pool to where Ellie was teaching Jake some swimming tricks of the trade. She swam like a fish. She could have rescued *him* if he'd been in trouble in deep water as efficiently as he had thought he'd been rescuing *her* a week ago when he'd spotted her on the distant horizon.

Now that he was looking at her, he decided that it beat reading the *Financial Times* on his tablet. She was so graceful, so slight, so supple when she moved, and she had a laugh that could light up a room. From behind his dark designer sunglasses, reclining on the lounger in the shade, Luca indulged in thinking about all the things he found strangely attractive about her, from the way she looked to the way she smelled and definitely the way she responded to him when he touched her. She was a firecracker between the sheets.

He was guessing that this was what a lot of people might call paradise. Overhead, the sky was a milky blue with just a few wispy clouds here and there to interrupt the perfect turquoise expanse.

The sun was beating down. At a little after five, it no longer bore the fiery intensity of the midday sun, but it was still warm enough for them all to be out here fooling around in the swimming pool.

Luca hadn't been to this particular property for some time and the last time he *had* been, with a handful of high-achieving employees being rewarded for their hard work on a particularly fruitful deal, he had spent the majority of the long weekend working, signing off on yet another deal, barely venturing outside except to a couple of highly rated local restaurants. He hadn't been tempted by the swimming pool and, indeed, he had barely spared any time actually to appreciate his surroundings.

He was appreciating them now. Maybe it was because, for the past week, he had seen them through Ellie's eyes, and viewing his possessions through other people's eyes was not something he spent a lot of time doing.

He had always been indifferent to the fact that women found his wealth impressive. It came with the territory.

With Ellie it was…different. She was impressed, but fundamentally she didn't attach a huge amount of importance to money, and she certainly didn't have pound signs in her eyes at his displays of wealth. She teased him about how much he owned and told him that he was too rich for his own good. She was insistent that she do her bit around the villa, always tidying up behind Jake, even though the hired help descended every morning, paid to do that. He didn't get it but he had to give her credit. She took absolutely nothing for granted and was at pains to explain to him that, when you grew up with not very much, you learned to appreciate everything you had.

When pressed, she admitted that, yes, some people reacted by realising the importance of all those things that money couldn't buy while others reacted by doing their utmost to get rich, whatever the cost.

Luca, in this roundabout manner, had found out about her sister and had formed a picture in his head of a woman who was very different from Ellie.

And of course, on rote, she reminded him how grateful she was for the way he had rescued her father.

'Which makes me think,' he had drawled as they had lain entwined in the sheets after a particularly energetic bout of love-making, 'that filthy lucre does, actually, have its uses.'

'Yes,' Ellie had said, 'it has purchase power. I can't deny that, but there's a lot more out there that can't be bought and, when you sell your soul for it, you lose sight of all those other things.'

'Very philosophical.' But Luca wasn't buying any of that because he'd seen too much avarice in his lifetime, and way too many women who would have sold their souls to the devils a thousand times over for money, but he was tickled pink at her sincerity.

'I have no idea how we got where we have.' She'd shaken her head in wonderment. 'Our perspectives on life are polar opposite.'

Luca didn't know, himself, how things had got to where they were between them.

The one-night-stand plan had been kicked to the kerb on night one, and their original intention to keep their liaison within the four walls of the bedroom had quite quickly got lost when he had absently held her hand in front of Jake.

Was that when, subtly, the relationship with his godson had changed? Had that been the turning point when Jake had begun to trust him? Yes, he had been making headway before, but things had definitely taken an upturn at that point.

Luca guessed that this was as good as it got when it came to playing happy families.

It wasn't about love and it wasn't about selling your soul to someone else safe in the knowledge that sooner or later you were going to get hurt. Those were options he had shut the door on, and that was a door he would never thinking of opening, but yes...there was something to be said about this arrangement.

He gazed idly at his phone then re-read the text he had received from his PA, who knew how to handle the press with the dexterity of a magician, and whose contacts within those dubious circles had always been invaluable.

The salacious rumours started by his ex were about to go up a notch. It was becoming a headache. Being linked with a woman in a six-inch column in a tabloid was one thing. Taking the rumour that step further was something else.

Across the pool, Ellie was laughing at something Jake had said. She had a wonderful, engaging laugh, and for a few seconds, eyes concealed behind sunglasses, Luca watched her thoughtfully.

He thought that sometimes life had a funny way of dealing hands that looked unfortunate until you sat back and worked out how to play with them.

Under normal circumstances, he shouldn't have been here, but here he was.

If life had carried on as it had been, he would have been working and Jake would, in due course, probably have ended up in therapy because of him. Who knew? He might have suffered an even worse fate. Drugs...drink... There was a world of temptation out there for kids who had been screwed over by life.

But this turnaround... Well, he couldn't have asked for better.

Luca stood up, glanced at his watch and strolled down to where the pair of them were recovering on the semi-circular marble steps in the warm, shallow end of the pool, exhausted after frolicking in the water.

Ellie shielded her eyes and watched as he approached.

Her heart flipped in her chest and her mouth went dry, her nipples pinched into tight buds, and every pore in her body responded in ways that were all too familiar now.

She didn't think she would ever tire of watching him, of listening to him, of the way he touched her, the way he made her body come alive.

For as long as was humanly possible, Ellie had kidded herself that the way he made her feel was down to lust. He was irresistible. She was too inexperienced to ward off the potent effect he had on her. She had capitulated and fallen into bed with him because her body had refused to listen to common sense, but the nature of lust was that it didn't last. She wouldn't be the first and she wouldn't be the last. Blah, blah, blah.

She didn't know when she wised up to the truth that what she felt for him—and it was a feeling that seemed to grow ever stronger by the second—left lust standing in the shade.

Unguarded, protected by all those common-sense check lists she had always had when it came to the opposite sex, or so she'd thought, she hadn't been prepared for her heart to be ambushed by the very sort of guy she should have been equipped to walk away from. She'd been side-swiped by his arrogance, his self-assurance, that way he had of always assuming that he was the leader and the duty of everyone else was to follow and obey.

She had barely really noticed when the little things had started piling up. The way he laughed. The occasional look of searing vulnerability she had seen when he looked at Jake, when he thought no one was observing him. His quick wit and the way he balanced his outrageous arrogance with magnificent generosity. He was a contradiction and he had sucked her in until it was hard to think of a time before him.

Where she had always imagined that love would be something that grew, after months of watering and nurturing, she had discovered, to her dismay, that it was something that just appeared from nowhere like a weed, with the power to smash her foundations to smithereens, and there was nothing she could do about it.

Except enjoy him while she could.

The end of their allotted time out was a heartbeat away and she intended to lose herself in loving him and then face the consequences when it was all over and she returned to normality.

She took great care in making sure he didn't suspect a thing, because she had her pride, and she couldn't bear the thought of him laughing at her, or looking at her with pity from the depths of those dark, fabulous eyes.

'Are you coming in?' she asked lightly now. She was already moist between her legs at the unconscious hunger in his gaze as he stared down at her.

She had brought her one and only black one-piece swimsuit, something she wore to the public swimming baths near her in London, because her other two were at the family house. It was so modest that she could have gone and done her weekly supermarket shop in it and no one would have batted an eye but, when Luca looked at her in it, it was as though she was the most stunning lingerie model on the planet.

Nothing could have made her feel more wonderful and more at home with herself and her body than that fierce gaze of un-hidden approval and appreciation.

She'd discovered that it was like a drug and she knew that she was guilty of feeding off it, hungrily taking it in, because pretty soon it would no longer be available.

'Tempting,' Luca drawled. His dark eyes followed Jake who was splashing around with a toy Juanita had bought for him the day before. He turned his gaze to Ellie. 'Will you make it worth my while later if I do?'

Ellie blushed. 'Is sex all you ever think about?' she asked in a low voice as he settled on the stair next to her, leaning back and closing his eyes.

'No, work takes priority, but there's not a lot in it.'

'We should go in.' She stood up and called to Jake, then went to towel herself dry. Sex, sex, sex. It really was all Luca thought about. On every other level he was so complex and three-dimensional but, when it came to relationships, he was as shallow as a puddle.

'Just a minute, Ellie.' Luca held her arm, staying her, and when their eyes met his were so serious that she felt a shiver of panic ripple through her. 'Juanita's there. She can play with

Jake for a couple of minutes, and I've arranged for her to baby-sit this evening.'

'Oh, okay.' His words were unthreatening but her panic levels were up all the same. 'I guess you want to discuss progress with Jake. I'm sorry. It's been far too easy to lose track of the fact that this isn't a joyride for me.'

'Stop.'

'Stop what?'

'Apologising for things you should never feel obliged to apologise for. We don't need to have formal discussions about Jake any more. We're lovers. Interviewing you across a desk is no longer relevant. I think we've gone past that point, don't you? But…there *are* other matters I need to talk to you about.'

'What other matters?'

'This isn't the right place. We need to talk and what I have to say will require a certain amount of privacy, hence the reason why I've arranged for Juanita to stay on. I'm going to book us into one of the local restaurants I recall as having excellent food, as well as a certain amount of privacy.'

Ellie felt the surge of tears prick the backs of her eyes because she knew what this talk was going to be about. She was about to get the 'Dear John' speech and icy fear settled in her heart. She looked away quickly but, when she next spoke, her voice was light, in keeping with the no-strings-attached, sex-only non-relationship they were supposed to be having.

'I know…' She shrugged and stared off into the distance. '"The time draweth near". We're going to have to wrap this up and actually start putting our heads together about finding a replacement for me. I've got a good idea of the sort of girl Jake would take to, and I don't think there's going to be any problems with adjustment.'

'Save the bracing words of encouragement, Ellie. Like I said, we need to talk, and a rushed conversation here isn't appropriate.' When he glanced down, he was treated to the sight of her cleavage, and the small bumps where her breasts were outlined by the fine fabric of her swimsuit.

He veered his eyes away from the delectable sight and breathed in deeply.

'I've got work to do. I wish I hadn't, but you're right. The time is drawing near and the rabble in London are getting tetchy.' He stood up. 'I'll swing by when Jake's in bed to tell him good-night and then I'll meet you in the hallway.'

'Sure.' She followed suit, moving to fetch her towel from the lounger, along with all the other stuff that followed her out whenever she came to the pool. Sun cream, sunglasses, her sarong, her e-reader, her phone and an assortment of puzzle books she never got round to doing but always felt she might.

Luca veered off ahead of her to his office and she called out to Jake, but this time not even his six-year-old chatter could distract her.

It was the first restaurant they'd been to together since they had arrived at the villa and it felt odd to dress up when most of her time had been spent in shorts and tee shirts with flip-flops. She wondered whether his taste for shorts and tee shirts with flip-flops had reached the end of its natural cycle.

For the first time Ellie was nervous, and she wished that he could just text her the bad news, give her some advance warning so that she could get her facial muscles to behave and not let her down. Her stupid facial muscles were always letting her down when she was around him and she didn't want to give him any sign that there was anything amiss about calling it a day.

She'd brought a couple of summer dresses and, like Cinderella stripped of the fancy ball gown, she looked at her reflection critically. Yes, she'd got a good colour out here in the sun, and, sure, her short hair was now streaked with auburn and gold, but aside from that… Now that she knew what this dinner was all about, now that her walking papers were about to be handed over, the ridiculous self-confidence he had inspired in her was seeping away like water down a plug hole. She was back to being who she really was. Just an ordinary woman whose moment in the spotlight was over.

Luca was waiting for her and she plastered a bright smile on her lips.

'I'm not late, am I?' She chatted as she slipped on the shoes she had carried from her room, dangling them on one finger. She didn't look at him but she was ultra-aware of him standing within touching distance of her.

He was coolly, elegantly sophisticated in a white linen shirt and a pair of dark jeans and loafers. The ultimate dream man, the stuff that women's fantasies were made of. She would have to work hard at making sure not to use him as a benchmark when it came to future relationships because, if she did, then she was going to be in for a rough ride.

'How was Jake when you went in to see him?' She settled on something impersonal as they headed out to the rugged four-wheel drive he had rented for the duration of their stay.

'Jake was…' Luca turned to her once they were in the car, before switching on the engine. 'Unrecognisable as the sullen little boy who first walked through the front door of my house seven months ago, but then you know how far I've come with him.' He smiled and slid his gaze across to her. 'Two days ago you gave me a gold star for progress.'

Ellie blushed when she remembered how he had demanded she reward him for that particular gold star. She also remembered telling him that he should aim for several a day because she quite liked the reward schedule he had in mind.

Bad time for that kind of memory. She decided to bring it down to business. It was what Luca understood best. Business and sex, and there was no way she was going to talk about sex. Or even remind him of what they had shared. She'd seen the way he had dealt with the ex who had ended up with her walking papers. She'd seen the annoyed impatience on his face because, once he'd dispatched a woman, the last thing he wanted was to have to go through the bother of working to disentangle her from clinging to his neck.

'Let's put the business chat on the back burner for the moment,' Luca drawled after she'd made a few fruitless attempts to discuss the qualities a replacement nanny might need. 'Talk to me about something else.'

'Like what?'

'Surprise me. I want some soothing conversation. I don't want to exercise my brain just yet with an in-depth discussion about what a successful nanny needs to be.'

'Well...what's the restaurant like? I... I hope I'm dressed okay. I haven't been abroad very much. Well, I can't tell you the last time, to be honest, but I always think that in hot countries the dress code is casual, even if the restaurant is fancy.' At this rate, Ellie thought desperately, she was going to exhaust her repertoire of nervous, pointless small talk before they made it to the restaurant.

For a few awkward minutes, Luca didn't respond, and when he did it was to say, pensively, 'I had an interesting message from my PA.'

'Yes...?' Ellie shot him a confused look from under her lashes.

'My expectations that gossip about our so-called relationship would die a convenient death over the two weeks we were here seem to have been misplaced.'

'I don't understand what you're saying.' Ellie frowned because, in truth, she'd barely given a second thought to the silly rumours that had hastened their departure from London. She'd spoken to her dad when she'd first arrived. Her sister had been frantic with curiosity and Ellie had taken to dodging the calls and ignoring the text messages.

She was living in a bubble and there was no way she was going to let Lily burst it.

'My feeling is that Heidi had hoped for a more dramatic response from me when she spoke to the press. Anger, retaliation, a dialogue. Anything but silence. So she decided that leaving well alone wasn't going to do.' He looked at her and grimaced. 'There's nothing more dangerous than a woman scorned.' His voice had cooled. 'Especially one who clearly had a great deal more ambition when it came to our relationship than I ever had. Or, for that matter, ever hinted at. But we can talk about that over dinner.'

They'd arrived at the charming restaurant, white-fronted and cluttered with clambering, colourful flowers. The courtyard at the front was half-filled with high-end cars and she could see diners inside, outlined in mellow lighting. Inside, there were sofas, rustic wooden tables, little honeycomb-shaped private areas and so many plants that the oxygen levels must have been through the roof.

However, Ellie was too tense by this point to take it all in.

'What's going on?' she asked urgently, as soon as drinks orders were taken, menus inspected and decisions made about food.

'Hear me out without interruption.' Luca leaned towards her, elbows on the table, his lean, beautiful face unsmiling. 'The rumour about us has gathered pace and, on hearsay alone, the paparazzi will be printing a piece about our secret engagement. My PA has only managed to unearth this gem because she has some contacts with the tabloid press—a consequence, I'm afraid, of working for me. Naturally, she has neither denied nor confirmed the rumour. She thought it best to get in touch with me immediately.'

'Engagement? Secret?' Ellie blanched.

'The last thing I intended to do was to give credence to my ex's ridiculous rumours, because there would be nothing that would please her more than to think that she'd managed to throw my life out of joint.'

'You should have denied all that rubbish from the start!'

'I don't do conversations with hacks.'

'This isn't just about you, Luca!'

'There's no point crying over spilt milk.'

'Well, you're going to have to say something now. You're going to have to tell them that they've got it all wrong.' She thought about her friends who had been texting, and Lily who hadn't *stopped* texting.

'And naturally I will.' Luca sat back, sipped some wine and gazed thoughtfully at her over the rim of his glass. 'Although...'

'There's no *although* about it, Luca!' Ellie exclaimed in dismay. Running through her head were the horrible and embarrassing ramifications of an article printed about an engagement that didn't exist. Luca might be able to ignore the gossip, because he didn't care what anyone thought about him, but *she* wouldn't. She would have to be the one to face inquisitive reporters and tell them that it was all a load of nonsense. She'd managed to laugh off the original article as malicious nonsense, and no one had questioned it because they all knew her, knew the sort of person she was. But *an engagement*?

'This is awful.'

'It's true that it's an unexpected development and yet...it's made me think.'

'Think about *what*?'

'Strangely enough, marriage. Not something I've wasted much time on.' He swirled his glass of wine, swallowed some and looked at her thoughtfully. 'My father never loved anyone but my mother and, when she died, so did he—or so did the better part of him, but you know that. However, he was a rich widower, and there was no shortage of gold-diggers trying their luck. They would have sold their mothers for a slice of his fortune. From every angle, love and marriage have never come out tops when put under the microscope. But...'

'But?'

'But although I don't do love...' he absently reached for her hand and played with her slender fingers '...and hence never considered marriage because the two seem to go together, I'm beginning to think that there can be another aspect to a very successful union. The situation in which we now find ourselves has opened up that possibility to me.'

'I have no idea what you're talking about. I *know* you don't do love so *what* situation and *what* possibility?'

'The second you entered Jake's life, things began to change. It was almost as though fate had decided that the wheels had to start going in a different direction. He met you and he immediately responded to you and you've brought out a side to him that I don't think anyone else would have been able to.'

'Thank you very much.' *She* did love, and it was just her bad luck and rubbish judgement call that had landed her where she was. Loving a guy who *didn't do love.*

'And things have only got better since we've been over here. I've talked more to him than I have done in the six months before and, if you don't think that we have extensive conversations now, then you're getting the picture when it comes to how little communication there was between us before.'

She opened her mouth to say something and he raised one hand to stop her.

'Hear me out, Ellie. Someone coming in to replace you isn't going to work in the way I originally thought it might. What Jake has with us, what this little holiday has made me see, is that we're family for him. The two of us. Not exactly the traditional family but one that seems to be working for him.' He raised his eyebrows. 'When it comes to traditional families, who's to say that they're any better than the non-traditional ones? So now it seems that, in the absence of denial, we're engaged. And why not?'

'I beg your pardon?'

'If the world thinks we're engaged, then who are we to tell them they're mistaken?'

'But we're not engaged.'

'Every word I say will probably jar with you, but I'm proposing that we continue our relationship, because it works, and not just for us, but for Jake.'

'*Continue our relationship?*'

'I'm asking you to marry me. For me, it's something that makes sense, and what I bring to the table would be considerable.'

Ellie's mouth dropped open. She wondered whether she had misheard him or maybe misinterpreted what he had just said. Or maybe that snazzy little fish starter she'd just eaten had contained some hallucinogens.

'You would never want for anything in your life again. You would have security and stability, and let's not forget the sex.'

'You're asking me to *marry you*? Because Jake's happy and because you and I rub along okay and have a good time between the sheets?'

'Doubtless, it's not exactly the romantic dream you've been harbouring…'

'No, it's definitely not that.'

She had a load more to say on the subject but she was sideswiped by the thought of her parents' marriage. That had started out as the romantic dream. It had descended into bitterness and resentment when the romantic dream had turned sour and her mother had realised that the middle manager she had married was never going to become anything more than a middle manager. A good man who would have done anything for her but who wasn't enough. She thought of her own upbringing. The way she had been casually side-lined by her vain and shallow mother, the way the relationship with her sister had suffered for that. She had had the traditional upbringing but it certainly hadn't been an entirely positive one.

'It's a crazy idea!' She robustly pushed that interrupting thought aside.

'Why? Because I'm not your ideal man?'

'And I'm not *your* ideal woman! You're in a different place to me, Luca. You see marriage as a business proposition with plus and minus columns that should all tally up to determine whether it's successful or not.'

She thought of Jake. Okay, so maybe he'd been lulled into a false sense of security, and okay, yes, maybe she and Luca had been remiss in being openly demonstrative in front of him, but she wasn't going to be steamrollered by Luca into thinking that the natural outcome of that was a walk up the aisle because Jake was in need of a family unit.

She could feel a tension headache coming on.

'There's no such thing as an ideal soul-mate, Ellie. We could make this work.'

'You don't love me.' *But could he learn to?* That possibility crept into her head like a thief in the night, and she shivered. 'And what happens when someone comes along to capture your interest? One of those women you've always been attracted to? Where would that leave this so-called business arrangement?'

'We could let this rumour stand and see how it plays out.' He sat back and watched her with a keen gaze. 'But when it comes to someone else coming along? You turn me on and I like you. Why would I want to look anywhere else?'

Ellie could think of a hundred reasons, starting and finishing with six-foot blondes with long, tanned limbs and big hair. He could talk the talk here, where there was no temptation, but what about when temptation *did* appear? What then?

'Don't dig deep to find faults with my idea,' he counselled levelly. 'Let's finish dinner, talk about anything but relationships and you can sleep on it.' He lowered his midnight-dark eyes then raised them slowly to look at her with frank appraisal. 'You can tell me what you really think when you're warm and drowsy after we've made love.'

CHAPTER NINE

WITH THE DEXTERITY of a magician, Luca had spared no effort in pulling out all the stops to persuade her to his way of thinking.

He knew that she had her theories about soul-mates and the flowery promises of romance. He knew that his sensible suggestion for a union based on practicality was not high up there on her wish list... But there was this amazing chemistry between them and, however much she might waffle on about the importance of love, he knew that she had been sucker-punched by the power of their mutual physical attraction. She hadn't seen it coming.

She had never thought to work *that* into her long-term happy-ever-after plans.

And then there was Jake. He had watched them together and had seen the affection in her eyes when she looked at the boy. Would she be able to walk away from her little charge with the suspicion that she might take with her all the good work she had achieved?

From the heights of his cynicism, Luca knew that what he wanted was selfish. She was the glue between him and Jake. How successful would the happy family scenario be if a critical component of it went missing in action? He'd come far, but had he come far enough?

That aside, she was also a woman who appealed to him on many levels. The sex was stupendous but he could also appreciate her easy wit and the way she never deferred to him. Without the hindrance of wanting more than was possible, it would be a match that stood a better chance of working than any rush down the aisle between two starry-eyed people.

With the sharply honed instincts of a born predator, a man who always got what he wanted, Luca knew that making love was the way to get to her. He saw no down sides to using that ploy because to him it made perfect sense and bolstered his argument.

What he was proposing transcended the coldness of logic because it was infused with the passion of lust.

His fingers were linked through hers and he urged her up the stairs, stopping on every other stair to touch her. Action always spoke louder than words and he planned to put a lot of his persuasive powers into action.

Once in the bedroom, he kicked the door shut with the heel of his foot and propelled her towards his bed, stripping her off as they made progress across the floor until she was practically naked, with the dress pulled down and dropping to the floor as she shuffled backwards.

'Luca...' Did he think she couldn't see through his ploy?

'Shh...' He placed a finger over her mouth and then replaced the finger with his lips, kissing her without letting her surface for air.

He was doing what he did best. Pesky conversations could always be put to rest between the sheets, but this was bigger than a pesky conversation.

Ellie knew that there was still a lot more to say, but when he was touching her like this, kissing her senseless, rubbing his hands over her breasts, skimming them across her stomach, touching her between her legs...she lost the ability to think and turned into a mindless rag doll.

She fell back onto the mattress, arms spread wide, and watched with the usual level of shameless fascination as he stripped off in a hurry.

She could spend a lifetime doing this, she thought abstractedly, if she married him. They could give Jake the sort of stable home he would thrive in. *If* she married him. She'd be able to touch him whenever she wanted. *If* she married him.

But…but…but…

The agonising battery of questions tried to press onto her consciousness, but she didn't want to think of any of that, so she pushed them away and concentrated on the luxury of watching him stand for a few taut moments in front of her at the side of the bed, naked and unashamedly aroused.

She propped herself up, then knelt and took him into her mouth. He had been a masterful tutor and she an enthusiastic pupil, and she put all his lessons to use now as she licked and sucked him, feeling the rough ridges of his shaft, knowing just how to tease him until he was on the verge of losing control.

He juddered and urgently tugged her away from him, but then held her still for a few seconds while he regrouped his self-control.

The sex was fast and furious, a tangling of bodies as they met their needs, pleasuring one another in ways that were so finely tuned that neither could put a finger on why, really, they seemed physically to meet with such ease and freedom.

Afterwards, spent, they lay back and eventually Luca turned to her, propping himself up on his side. He pulled down the sheet which she had hoiked up to cover herself because, to his amusement, she was always strangely prudish in the wake of their love-making; he traced a line over her collarbone with his finger.

'I won't lie to you, *querida*, my proposal is something that works for me. I don't do love and empty promises, but you add something to my life, and you add something to Jake's. Like I said, I never gave house room to thoughts of marriage, but this is an arrangement that has an excellent chance of success. It would certainly put paid to the nuisance of having to return to London and start pouring water on all the engagement rumour fires stoked up by my vindictive ex.'

Ellie knew that this level of honesty was commendable. He wasn't wrapping things up with pretty paper and ribbons and trying to pretend that what was in the box was more than it actually was. He was being truthful when he said that rumours of a phoney engagement had made him consider the advantages of a union that was actually for real. Jake would have a family. Luca would not have the bother of explaining himself to nosy reporters. As a bonus, he would have the satisfaction of knowing that whatever his ex had hoped to gain by stirring false rumours would be scuppered. And if he changed his mind? Well, it wasn't as though there was a wedding ring on her finger, was it?

'It all sounds very selfish, Luca.'

'Jake wouldn't agree.'

'So Jake wins and you win...and what about me?'

'You really think that love is a guarantee of happiness?'

'That's not the point, is it?'

'Well, Ellie, I think it is. We go into this with our eyes wide open. We respect one another. We get along. You'll have financial security for the rest of your life but, if you want to continue working, then that would be fine by me. I'm not a dinosaur who expects his woman to stay at home. Added bonus...the sex is great.'

'And what about when the sex isn't great any longer? Your track record doesn't exactly promise longevity on that front, does it?'

'You've broken the track record already. I'm not even beginning to be bored by you.'

'Because we've known one another for five minutes!'

Luca looked at her seriously. 'I've spent more undiluted time with you than I've ever spent with any woman in my entire life.'

Ellie hated the way hope had taken root and was making

inroads. Hope that that meant something. Hope that he could come to love her. Hope that she could become indispensable. Things like that happened, didn't they?

'No girl dreams of a marriage proposal in the form of a business deal.'

'I don't get into bed with anyone I've ever done business with.'

'You know what I mean.'

'I can't force your hand, Ellie.'

'So if I say no, you wouldn't care one way or another?'

'I've found that life goes on, whatever disappointments crop up along the way. There's not much I've ever found I can't handle.'

'Because you've had to handle quite a lot from a young age...'

'Playing the therapist on me?' He wasn't nettled because he was enjoying looking at her. She was here, in his bed, flushed from love-making. This wasn't a woman who was going to turn him down flat.

'You're asking me to get engaged to you, and yet we don't even know one another.'

Luca burst out laughing, then manoeuvred himself so that she was resting in the crook of his arm. He played with her breast and brushed her hair with his lips.

'I think you'd be surprised at how much we know one another.'

'I'm not talking about sex.'

'Good,' Luca purred, stirring back into heavy arousal at the sight of her pink, pouting nipple. 'Because right now, there's too much talking going on. I'm happy to talk, Ellie, but only if the conversation is of the dirty variety. And don't tell me you don't want it. You know it turns you on when I tell you just what I want to do to your body...'

She opened her mouth and he shifted so that he was straddling her. He lightly ruffled the soft down between her legs and, while her body was busying itself trying not to succumb to what he was doing, he lowered himself, edging down to lick gently between her legs.

He teased the swollen bud of her clitoris until she was shifting with urgent little mewls of pleasure. He pressed his finger into her until she squirmed. He parted her thighs and hoisted her so that her legs were wrapped around him, allowing him to explore her wetness without hindrance.

He touched her everywhere until there were no more words and no more questions.

If she had doubts about his proposal, then this was as effective a way of showing her what, exactly, would be on the table.

Ellie wondered whether the proposal and her ambivalent response would affect their relationship but the following morning nothing was mentioned and there was no coolness from him.

Had he forgotten about it or just shrugged off her negative response as *'one of those things, you win some you lose some'*?

She didn't bring it up and nor did he. Luca wasn't accustomed to obstacles and either he had decided to jettison the idea because he'd hit a bump in the road, or else he was playing a waiting game.

Either way, Ellie wasn't going to be put on the back foot by bringing it up.

Nerves all over the place, she could barely focus on the day trip to a secluded bay that Luca took them on on a small motor boat he kept. It was a billionaire's plaything that was small, compact and kitted out to an eye wateringly high standard. The fabulous picnic which had been prepared for them tasted like cardboard to Ellie. She swam and did a little nature tour with Jake, and she knew that she said all the right things and held his interest for the full forty-five minutes as they walked and looked at stones, plants and rock pools, but she was so keenly aware of Luca, right there alongside her. So sexy, so tempting... so *suddenly attainable...*

It was a relief when seven o'clock rolled round and Jake was settled in bed. For the first time, when Ellie asked whether he wanted Luca to read him a story, he shrugged and said, 'Okay, I guess so.'

Major headway. Prompted by the security of the family unit he thought he now had...?

Luca was waiting in the kitchen when she entered at a little after seven-thirty, his back to her as he stared out of the window. But, before she could say a word, she felt the buzz of her mobile phone in her jeans pocket and she absentmindedly pulled it out as she headed into the kitchen, moving towards Luca.

'Lily!' For a few seconds, Ellie was so disorientated that she couldn't quite match the sound of the voice on the end of her phone to the sister whose nosy text messages she had been studiously ignoring. 'Is Dad okay?' A feeling of nausea crept into the pit of her stomach. She'd been living in a bubble. The sound of Lily's voice was the pin that had been stuck into that bubble, bursting it immediately. It was the harsh sound of reality and it made Ellie feel suddenly sick.

'You haven't been answering any of my texts!'

'Sorry, Lily. I'm back in a few days and I thought I'd...er... wait and, you know, talk to you face to face.'

'I've looked this guy up online and he's loaded, Ellie! Plus he looks like a rock star. So what the hell is he doing getting engaged to you?'

'Thanks very much!' Ellie bit down the temptation to press the disconnect button on her phone. She knew her sister so well. Lily wasn't about to congratulate her on landing a great catch. Lily was thinking ahead, working out how much more suitable a guy like Luca would be for *her*...

'You know what I mean. Remember boring Paul Jenna?'

'I try not to, Lily,' Ellie said through gritted teeth.

'Dad says you told him that it's just a load of nonsense. Is it?'

'Let's not talk about me.' She glanced at Luca who was shamelessly earwigging into the conversation and staring at her with undisguised interest. 'Let's talk about you.' Usually this was guaranteed to get Lily off the thorny subject of Luca. 'Tell me what you've been up to in America. Lots of important...er...exciting jobs and offers?'

'Have you slept with him?'

'Lily!'

'Okay. Out of order. Sorry.'

'How are you enjoying being back in the UK?'

'Finally! She's asked the question! I'm not in the UK! I'm calling from your part of the world! Dad told me where you were and I thought I'd fly over and pay you a visit! He's worried.' Lily's voice was suddenly pious. 'So I offered to check and make sure you're okay.'

'You're...*here*?' Ellie looked around her wildly as though anticipating a dramatic entrance from her sister via a cupboard.

'Just making sure you're not in a pickle! You have to admit it's not every day you get engaged! I know what Dad said, that it's all a load of rubbish, but still...what are sisters for if not to look out for one another? Anyway, Els, I'm running out of juice on my cell phone, so text me the address, would you? I'll take a taxi.'

Put in a position from which there seemed to be no easy way out, Ellie gave Lily the address. Her head was swimming, though. How long would it take her sister to hit the villa? How long did she intend to stay? As expected, there was no shame on Lily's part when it came to showing up uninvited at a stranger's house.

Because there would be an agenda.

If, once upon a time, her sister had nabbed the guy Ellie had been seeing just for the hell of it, then what might her intentions be when it came to a man like Luca, the most eligible man on the planet?

Only now did Ellie realise that she had actually begun to give house room to Luca's crazy proposal. She might have laughed at his preposterous marriage proposal but it had set up a series of tantalising scenarios. Lily showing up on the doorstep? It didn't bear thinking about.

Five minutes later, Ellie was staring at the phone and feeling as though she'd been run over by an HGV.

'Family?' Luca encouraged.

'My sister.' She heard a note of dismay creep into her voice and she summoned up a smile from somewhere. 'Guess what? She's here, right here, a taxi ride away, and she's coming to visit. I can't wait to see her. It's been months and months…'

'Ah, the famous sister you think is right up my alley.'

Ellie stiffened and remained silent. He extended a glass of wine to her and she swallowed it in one gulp.

'Dutch courage?' he murmured with keen interest, and Ellie blushed.

'Thirsty.'

'For wine. Interesting. Normally a glass of water does the trick when it comes to quenching thirst. You should sit down. You're looking a little green round the gills.'

'I should tell you that she knows about the…er…fact that… well… I happened to tell Dad ages ago that if he read some silly nonsense about us being together then it was a complete lie and he wasn't to believe a word.'

'And now that there's an engagement story doing the rounds and your sister thinks that there's no substance to it…'

'Something like that.'

'And would she be right?'

Something wicked and daring nudged past the sudden onset of anxiety Lily's call had generated.

Wow. How dared her sister be so openly shocked that Ellie could actually be engaged to someone gorgeous, rich, exciting and *eligible*? How dared Lily take it as read that the engagement thing was obviously a sham?

And why should Ellie automatically begin surrendering at the thought of her sister coming along? Why should she just lie down and wave a white flag simply because she knew that Lily would get the guy, as she always did?

Ellie was suddenly sick of all the insecurities she always seemed to have to put to bed whenever Lily was around.

Luca had given her confidence she hadn't known she possessed—why should she dump it all because Lily was coming out here on a fact-finding operation? A so-called fact-finding mission because sisters had to look out for one another. Since when had Lily ever played by those rules?

For the first time in her life, Ellie had done the unthinkable and stopped playing it safe. And it felt good.

'We could take a chance.' She threw caution to the wind along with her long list of pros and cons.

Engagements didn't always lead to weddings... They *could* take a chance. So Luca didn't love her, but she could have some stolen time to try and make herself indispensable to him and, if that was through Jake, then so be it.

She couldn't bear the thought of never seeing him again and why kid herself that that was something she would be able to handle?

Luca smiled a slow, lazy, satisfied smile and drew her towards him. Then he kissed her and all the doubts she had had about this wild decision flew out of her head with a whoosh. She reached up to link her hands around his neck and kissed him back with hunger and abandon.

Was she doing the right thing? This felt like a little rebellion but it also felt good. She couldn't suffocate that little sliver of hope that what she and Luca had cultivated over the weeks would be strong enough to counter the Lily effect.

She was trembling as her slight body pressed against his rock-hard erection.

For some reason, that phone call had galvanised her into accepting his proposal and Luca wasn't going to question it.

'You're making the right decision,' he murmured, drawing

back to look at her, while gently sifting his fingers through her short hair.

'You *would* say that.' Ellie's voice was breathless and teasing. 'If someone agrees with you, then you're always going to think that they're making the right decision.'

Luca grinned. 'But I'm always right,' he said piously, making her smile, relax and momentarily forget the fact that her sister was heading towards her at speed, a force to contend with.

'Stop looking so anxious,' he counselled, kissing her again and pulling her against him.

'My sister has always had that effect on me,' Ellie confessed, resting her head in the crook of his neck.

'Makes you anxious? Charming.'

'Charming,' Ellie muttered inaudibly, 'is exactly how you'll probably end up describing her.'

'Come again?'

'Nothing.' She smiled up at him and squashed the thread of apprehension running through her. 'Anyway.' She stepped back and tidied herself and decided that some more wine was necessary. 'She'll be here shortly…'

But it was another twenty-five minutes before the doorbell went. Ellie dashed out while Luca waited in the kitchen, intensely curious to see what the sea had decided to wash up.

He had a rough idea of what to expect and he wasn't disappointed.

'Luca, this is my sister, Lily.'

Ellie watched the interplay with eagle eyes and, to Luca's credit, if he was impressed then he wasn't showing it.

She felt an uncharitable spurt of satisfaction because Lily, just his type, was even more stunning after months spent in the Californian sunshine.

She had been toasted golden-brown and her long white-blonde hair fell in a glossy curtain down her back. She was dressed in next to nothing—a little crop top that rose to reveal her firm belly and the tattoo of a swallow just below her belly button, low-slung ripped jeans that seemed designed to show off legs that went on for ever, and flip-flops.

Plus she was in full flirtatious mode, talking quickly with lots of engaging hand gestures, and using her body language to suggest that what he could see was only the tip of the iceberg.

Ellie had seen her sister in action a thousand times but her heart was still thudding painfully because this was the first time she was really sickened at what might happen if she weaved her magic charm and sucked Luca in with those big, blue eyes.

'You'd take to life over there like a duck to water,' she was trilling as she tossed her blonde mane over one shoulder and made herself at home at the kitchen table. 'It's full of movers and shakers in the media world and you'd really fit in. Have you ever thought about making a movie? I have a lot of connections... not that you'd need any!' She dimpled a smile, batted her lashes and pouted. 'I know you've gone out with a number of celebs.'

'Not my thing,' Luca responded politely.

'You could even be an actor.' Lily tilted her head to one side and looked at Luca narrowly while, standing to the side, Ellie gritted her teeth. 'You have just the sort of dashing, dark looks. Such a catch, Els!' She winked, making sure that Luca saw that wink, making sure he knew that she knew that it was all an act.

'I'm going to catch up on some work.' Luca was making for the door. 'Give you two time to catch up.'

Ellie hovered, but in the end didn't say anything, because she was too busy agonising over her thoughts. She'd just agreed to his proposal but was already beginning to see the holes in it. Here in Spain, in this bubble, it was easy to forget the outside world. Lily had wafted through the door, bringing that outside world in with her, and Ellie questioned whether, once they were back in London, Luca would be able to resist the charm offensive of all those beautiful Lily lookalikes who flocked around him. Playing happy families because of his godson might begin to look a little less alluring.

'He is *gorgeous.*'

Startled out of her introspection, Ellie moved to top up her sister's glass and asked politely, 'Have you eaten, Lily? I could fix you something.'

'Ever the home maker. No thanks. Dieting.' She patted her stomach. 'You wouldn't believe the competition out there.'

'But it's going well? You've barely mentioned what you've been up to.' *Too busy flirting with Luca.*

Lily brushed aside the show of interest and strolled through the kitchen, taking everything in. 'Course it's going well. Why wouldn't it be? Anyway, I would have helped out with Dad, you know that, but it was a bad time financially for me just then. You have to invest to create and just then I'd sunk quite a bit into portfolios and the like. You know how it is.'

Ellie had no idea.

'But, doesn't matter now anyway! Tell me all about the hunk. I know you're just here for the kid but you two must, you know, socialise now and again... Fill me in.'

Ellie began opening cupboards, fetching stuff from the fridge, ignoring her sister and the avid curiosity etched on her lovely face.

Lily hadn't come to make sure everything was okay. She had come because curiosity had got the better of her. How had the sister who had always faded into the background suddenly found herself in a position where she was being written about in a gossip column? Was there any truth behind that engagement story? Surely not?

'When was the last time you ate?' She knew that she was clinging to her composure by a thread, fighting against habits of a lifetime which compelled her to fade into the background.

Because she *had* accepted Luca's proposal, hadn't she? She really *was* going to have a ring on her finger, wasn't she?

Admittedly, it wasn't actually there yet, and would probably not materialise now that Luca had been given a tantalising glimpse of the sort of thing he'd been missing out on ever since he had become a hermit living in a villa in the middle of nowhere, but still…

In a flash, Ellie knew that Lily would make a pass at Luca without a second's thought.

Just as she had done with Paul.

Lily would make a pass at Luca because he was the sort of man she had spent her entire adult life trying to get. He was rich, he was powerful, he was good-looking. He was the kind of man that other people hung around, looked up to and tried to be friends with.

He was, in short, the ultimate catch.

'I told you, Ellie, I'm not hungry. Stop fussing and sit and tell me about Luca. Is he single? I mean, really? Or is there some celeb stashed away somewhere waiting in the wings until this whole stupid engagement nonsense blows over?'

'Why do you ask?' Ellie's voice was tight as she sat in front of an unappetising omelette and dug into it, making sure not to look at Lily.

'Okay, tell me if you're all right with this—and I'm sure you will be—but if he isn't taken then I might, you know…'

'No, explain.'

'Well, he's pretty fabulous, and I'm not going out with anyone at the moment. So many gays out there, you wouldn't believe, and most of the guys I meet are a lot more into themselves than they are into me. None of them can walk past a mirror without crashing into it.'

'I'm sorry to hear that,' Ellie said with genuine sympathy because, like a plant needed nutrients, Lily needed the adoration of men to thrive.

This was the first chink in that coat of armour her self-confident sister always presented to the world.

Which didn't mean that Ellie was going to let herself fall right back into the status quo, fading into the background and accepting that her sister would always get what she wanted because of how she looked.

'Well.' She sighed and pushed her plate away from her. She linked her fingers on the table, then looked gravely yet kindly at her sister. 'I hate to be the bearer of bad tidings, Lily, but as matter of fact Luca is most definitely taken.'

'Is he?' Lily narrowed her eyes and Ellie could see her mentally working out how she could trump the opposition.

'He is. By me.'

'You're having a laugh, Els.'

'I'm not. The fact is…we're engaged. For real.' Empowered, she sat back and cocked her head to the side, as though deciding how much to tell and how much to withhold. Her heart was hammering inside her chest. Her skin was clammy at the enormous leap into the unknown she was taking. 'Okay, I admit when that story first broke about us seeing one another it was all a load of bunkum. Luca had taken me to a country pub to discuss Jake, and his ex had shown up and seen us together and then decided to wreak a little havoc.'

'I can't believe this.' Lily was flabbergasted. Ellie could have told her that the sky was falling in and she wouldn't have received a more stunned reaction.

'And then there was that business in the tabloids about an engagement. By then—and this is just between the two of us—Luca and I were…well…*you know…*'

'Sleeping together?'

'Falling in love. Truly, madly and deeply. I don't know how it happened, but I tell you what, it's the most wonderful thing I've ever felt in my life.' She could feel herself welling up. Lily might think she was welling up with tears of joy. Ellie knew that she was welling up because the picture she was painting was half-true and she wished that it was all true.

'He's terrific, Lily. He comes across as arrogant at first, but as soon as you get to know him you see that there's so much more to him than meets the eye. He's smart, funny, thoughtful, and incredibly frustrating sometimes, but I don't think I could love anyone as much as I love Luca.'

'And he feels the same way about you?'

'Why else would he have asked me to marry him?' Ellie neatly evaded a direct answer to that question.

'I don't see a ring on your finger.'

'That's because he wants to take me to his jeweller's in London when we get back. Don't forget, this wasn't planned. I mean, it's taken both of us by surprise. But, when love strikes, what can a person do?'

She laughed gaily, stood up to take her dishes to the sink, simultaneously avoiding her sister's sharp, probing eyes, and heard a deep, dark, velvety and very familiar drawl behind her.

'What indeed?'

Ellie swung round, almost dropping the plate and glass because her hands were suddenly as slippery as if they were coated in oil.

Her mouth fell open and colour rushed to her cheeks in a tidal wave of bright red.

'Luca!'

'My darling.' Luca looked at Lily whilst strolling across to wrap his arms around Ellie, before dipping to kiss her on the side of her mouth. 'I'm very glad you listened to me and told your sister about us.'

He turned and pulled Ellie towards him so that he was standing with his back to the kitchen counter with Ellie in front, her back against his stomach, his hands draped loosely over her shoulders.

'She wanted to break it to her dad at the same time, put paid to all those pesky rumours doing the rounds. Yes, it may have been a piece of malice on the part of my ex coming up with that story, but how was she to know that the engagement she'd fabricated would turn out to be the real deal?'

Lily made a strangled sound and rose to her feet, suddenly looking very young and vulnerable in her confusion.

'So, just for the record,' Luca said without batting an eye, 'I'm not up for grabs.'

'I... Well, of course...'

'And I know you wouldn't be so tactless as to make a pass at the man your sister intends to marry, but if you do you should know that I wouldn't take to it kindly.'

'I wouldn't dream of... No... Well, congratulations to both of you. I'll... I'm off to sleep and I'll leave first thing in the morning!'

'I'll make sure there's a taxi waiting for you. You can have full use of my private jet. Say eight-thirty tomorrow morning?'

The silence that settled as Lily shut the door behind her could have been cut with a knife.

Luca slowly turned Ellie round to face him.

'Well, well, well...'

CHAPTER TEN

ELLIE CATAPULTED HERSELF out of his arms and spun round to face him, arms folded defiantly, eyes blazing.

'How long have you been standing outside that kitchen door *eavesdropping*? Do you think that listening to other people's conversations is *acceptable*? Because *I don't*!'

'Totally unacceptable,' Luca conceded smoothly. 'But I couldn't resist once your sister started asking whether I was open territory. I was curious to see where the conversation was going to go.'

'Lily's always thought that she could do what she wanted when it came to guys,' Ellie gritted stiffly. 'I was just being *human* when I decided to show her that there were limits!'

Luca poured himself a long glass of water then pulled up a kitchen chair and sat down. 'Let's talk.'

'Let's not.'

'Forget about those declarations of love for a minute. I want to ask you about your sister.'

'Why?'

'Ellie, stop inching towards the door. We either talk here or we talk in the bedroom but we're going to talk.'

'Isn't that a bit dangerous, Luca?' Ellie threw back at him. She was frantically trying to work out what, exactly, she had said. Lots of incriminating stuff. She'd poured her heart out to Lily, blissfully unaware that the wretched man was lurking outside the door with a glass pressed against it, hearing every word.

'What do you mean?'

'*Talking.* Isn't *talking* dangerous for someone who likes keeping it superficial? For someone who gets into a panic if there's a woman in the kitchen with a frying pan in her hand and a recipe book on the counter? Isn't that why this *arrangement* of ours is so convenient for you, because it bypasses all that nasty domestic stuff you feel trapped by?'

'If we get married, then I'm assuming you'll have a frying pan in your hand and a recipe book on the counter from time to time. Did you think that your sister was my type because of the way she looked? And for God's sake, stop hovering! Sit down.'

'Stop yelling at me,' Ellie muttered, shifting to sit, mostly because her legs were beginning to feel wobbly.

He was tying her in knots. He didn't do love and he didn't do domestic. What he did was *business arrangement; no emotional ties, thanks very much.* So why wasn't he peeved at the thought of her doing something such as cooking for him? Wasn't he suspicious that that might be the start of something unfortunate?

She looked at him in defiant silence.

'Answer my question.'

'Of course I thought that! She's blonde and beautiful and she's not backward at coming forward!'

'I'm surprised you didn't give her the green light to strut her stuff for me,' Luca said drily, and Ellie reddened. 'It crossed your mind, didn't it?' He looked at her narrowly, his dark eyes cooling by several degrees, and she shook her head.

She felt drained. So what was she going to do now? How was she going to handle this situation? Lie? Pretend? She was fed up pretending.

If he was so keen for them to talk, then talk she would, and she was going to tell him the truth—how she felt, when she'd started feeling what she felt, what she really wanted out of any relationship with him.

If he didn't like it, then he would be free to walk away.

She'd been stupid to buy into the notion that marrying him was going to be the better option because she would be able to indulge her love for him and then maybe, just maybe, he might start returning some of that love.

This arrangement had been formulated with Jake in mind. If Luca had any feelings for her at all, then they largely revolved around feeling *turned on* because he fancied her, and that didn't count.

Okay, so maybe he liked her well enough, but that wasn't love, was it?

Was she really going to be satisfied with him *liking her well enough*?

Wouldn't it be better for her, in the long term, to walk away and hope that one day she might meet a guy who could love and cherish her the way she deserved to be loved and cherished?

Yes!

'No,' Ellie told him truthfully. 'It really didn't occur to me. Or if it did, I barely registered that. Thing is… I had a boyfriend once. His name was Paul and I thought that it was the real deal. That was a couple of years ago. He was a good, solid guy. Really nice. Very caring.'

'Sounds deadly.'

Ellie frowned and realised that Paul, whilst ticking quite a few boxes, hadn't been a riveting match, especially when she compared him to Luca.

'He wasn't at all Lily's type,' Ellie mused, gazing off into the distance. 'Lily always went for good-looking, solvent and hunky. But she turned her attention to Paul. I don't know if she did that to be mean, or if she did it unconsciously because flirting with guys just came as second nature to her. Anyway, whatever. He fell for her hook, line and sinker. One minute, he was talking about holidays and a life together with me. The next minute, he was drooling after my sister. So was I tempted to tell her to have a go with you, if that was what she wanted? No.'

'In fact, you decided to do just the opposite,' Luca murmured, expression veiled, and Ellie shrugged and looked away.

She now expected him gently but firmly to set her straight on what he had overheard. Probably tell her ruefully that there was no way he could fulfil the arrangement because he wasn't looking for what she wanted.

'I'm only human.'

'Has it always been like that?'

'Like what?'

'Living in your sister's shadow.'

'Pretty much. She had the looks and my mother cultivated that. She wanted Lily to succeed where she thought she had failed. My mother was a disappointed woman. She was very beautiful, and I think she thought that she deserved more in life than to be married to my dad, who was just an ordinary guy.'

'An unhappy marriage,' Luca murmured. 'And yet you still have all those romantic notions about love and marriage.'

'What's wrong with that? Because my parents didn't have a good marriage, doesn't mean that good marriages don't exist.'

'Did you get a kick out of telling your sister that the engagement was for real?'

Ellie blushed and said grudgingly, 'Huge.'

'Bigger question coming here. Did you mean any of it?'

Ellie looked at him. This was it. Crossroads time. She had a choice. The truth would free her, whatever the outcome, whether he fled the scene in terror or not. But a little white lie was so much more compelling...

She would be able to clear off with her pride intact and her head held high. She could laugh gaily and tell him that *of course, she hadn't meant a word of it!* He'd laid down the rules of the game and he would be relieved that she had stuck to them.

'All of it.' Her eyes were clear and steady, and she took a deep breath and forced herself not to look away. 'Every last word. I'm sorry. You warned me enough times about keeping emotions out of this, and I wish I could have done that, but I couldn't.'

Ellie wished he would say something. Anything, really. But he just sat there, very, very still, his dark eyes revealing nothing. Which meant that she had to play a guessing game, and she hated that.

However, now that she had started, she felt compelled to carry on and lay herself bare.

'I'm in love with you. I know you never signed up for that, and I know I probably shouldn't be telling you this because you're the guy who's locked his heart away somewhere and thrown away the key, but there you go. I'm in love with you. I don't know why or how or when I fell in love with you. I wish I could be noble and say that I agreed to the whole engagement thing because I thought Jake would benefit from having both of us on the scene, and I suppose there was a bit of me that was persuaded by that argument, but truthfully? I wanted to do something out of the box just for once in my life and I also thought that, if we did end up together, I might stand a chance of somehow getting under your skin.'

'I have never let any woman get under my skin.'

Ellie cringed, even though he wasn't exactly saying anything she didn't already know.

'I know, but you've never been engaged to anyone before, have you?' she threw at him. 'Or have you?'

'Never been stupid enough.'

'Why are you so cold?' She looked away. Her skin was prickling, her heart was beating so hard she felt in danger of passing out, her mouth was dry and her head was throbbing.

'Practical.'

'No, it's not *practical*, Luca! Packing sunblock when you go on holiday to a hot country is *practical*! Being ice-cold and having no emotions…' She gazed at him helplessly.

'I saw what my mother's death did to my father,' Luca grated. 'I think I've told you this already.'

'Doesn't mean I agree with you!'

'He never recovered. You'd have to be a fool to let yourself feel so strongly for another human being that you end up losing your way if something happens to them! And after she died? Let's not forget that I witnessed first-hand how callous and greedy women could be when it came to money. Hell, I was just a teenager at the time, but there were some who didn't think twice about trying it on with me when their advances hit a dead end with my father!'

'You'd rather spend the rest of your life being lonely than take a chance?' Ellie was pleading. She could hear it in her voice and it shamed her.

'I've never been lonely in my life.'

'I'm not talking about having a woman in your bed! I'm talking about having a woman in your heart!'

'I'll take my chances on being just fine without that complication.'

'Right.' She leapt to her feet. Tears were stinging the back of her eyes but there was no way that she was going to let him see her break down in front of him. 'I think it's a good time for me to head upstairs.'

'Ellie...'

'Don't say anything else, Luca.' She spun round on her heels and headed straight for the kitchen door. No way was she going to get up early tomorrow to bid a fond farewell to her sister. She'd be seeing her soon enough, and how Lily was going to have a bit of fun at her expense.

Strangely, Ellie didn't care.

She couldn't hurt worse than she was hurting right now.

She had become accustomed to sleeping with Luca. She almost went to his bedroom through force of habit. Instead, she swerved and quietly let herself into her own bedroom.

Her suitcase was stuffed in the wardrobe and she pulled it out and opened it. When she had packed to come over, she had been filled with excitement and trepidation. It had felt like the greatest adventure of her life.

Now, she looked at that suitcase and knew that this time, when she was packing it, she would be filled with misery.

She had no idea how long she'd been stuffing clothes into the case, but the knock on the door carried the impact of a hand grenade because she knew who it was going to be. Lily might have scuttled out of the kitchen when faced with Luca, but her curiosity would be boundless, and Ellie knew that she probably would have heard her coming up the stairs.

She hurriedly flung the suitcase into the wardrobe and composed herself into the image of a woman in love who, mysteriously, was not sharing a bedroom with the guy she was supposedly all set to marry.

She was smiling as she pulled open the door. It was a rictus smile but it was the best she could muster given the circumstances.

She expected Lily with a list of questions.

She got Luca.

She didn't budge.

'Let me in, Ellie.'

'Go away.'

'What are you doing?' He peered around her and Ellie followed his gaze to the half-open wardrobe.

'Packing.'

'Let me in.' Luca shifted uneasily, raked his fingers through his hair. 'Please. I... I've been a fool, Ellie.'

'Really?' Her voice was the temperature of ice. 'I thought that was my terrain.'

'I was a fool,' Luca muttered with low urgency, 'to think that I could live without you.'

Their eyes tangled and Ellie glared at him.

'Right. And I'm supposed to believe that?'

'I don't want to have this conversation with you out here.' He shuffled when she didn't say anything. 'I've never begged for anything in my life. I'm not sure I'd know how but, if you don't let me in, then I'm going to have to give it a go.'

Ellie stood aside with visible reluctance and, as soon as he was in the bedroom and the door was shut, she removed herself to the broad window sill and perched against it with her arms folded, staring at him.

Undeterred, Luca positioned himself right next to her. 'You told me you loved me.'

'I don't want to be reminded of that,' Ellie muttered viciously.

'You told me that you loved me and I did what came naturally to me. I turned away. It's the way I've been programmed. My life was as placid as a lake until you swept in like a whirlwind, breathing brimstone and fire. You didn't care what I thought. You said whatever you wanted to say and I had no idea how addictive that would become.'

'If you're saying all that to butter me up into reconsidering the engagement thing for Jake's sake, then forget it.'

'If I were terrified of being with a woman who loved me, then there's no way I would be considering any engagement, Jake or no Jake.'

'Just say what you have to say, Luca.' Hope was beginning to send out alarming tendrils and, before they became too profuse, Ellie wanted him to spit it out.

'I thought that there was strength in building an ivory tower around myself,' he said quietly. 'I was protected and no one had ever been able to breach my ramparts. And then along you came and you managed to find a way through within seconds. I asked you to come out here because I needed you to be here for Jake—but where I would have been cautious about having any woman around, sharing my space for that length of time and in that capacity, with you I felt…comfortable.'

'Comfortable.' Why did that word sound so…*dull and boring*?

Luca laughed. 'It's a compliment, Ellie. It's also something that should have alerted me to the fact that you weren't just different from the women I've known. It should have alerted me to the fact that I was falling for you.'

'Falling for me...? Is that why you listened to me pour my heart out and then sent me on my way?'

'Like I said, I responded on cue. A lifetime of telling myself that love was the one thing I didn't do swung into action. I'd say I was shocked by what you said, but in fact I wasn't. I'd say I felt trapped, but no, that would be a lie as well. As soon as you walked out of the kitchen, I felt sick.'

'But you never let on...'

'I didn't have it in me and, anyway, I didn't recognise the signposts because I'd never walked down that road before and I'd never wanted to. Honestly, I didn't get the appeal,' he confessed with wrenching honesty. 'You were nothing like what I was used to and, to start with, I just figured that you were different, that you were a tonic for my jaded palate, but then we slept together and you blew me away.'

'You blew me away, too.' Ellie rested her hand on his chest and felt the fast beating of his heart. 'I guess I was as rigid in what I wanted as you were. I guess some of that was down to my own insecurities. If I didn't punch above my weight then I would never be let down. Lily is the one who gets the good-looking guys, and I told myself that that was fine because I wasn't attracted to that sort anyway. When I met you, you were the last person I thought I could ever have a connection with.'

'I'll bet.' Luca smiled crookedly. He covered her hand with his, lifted it to his lips and dropped a kiss on her palm. 'We didn't exactly meet in circumstances that cast a glowing halo around me, did we? I can only imagine what you were thinking. Arrogant bastard, too much money, runaway kid...'

'But I still couldn't take my eyes off you, Luca. You mesmerised me and I hated it. It's like I wasn't really alive until you came along and then, boom, life was Technicolor-bright.' She sighed. 'You made me face all the old insecurities and come to terms with them, and finally you made me overcome them.'

'And you, my darling, made me realise that life isn't worth living unless you're prepared to take chances.' He swept her off her feet, carried her to the bed and gently deposited her as though she was as fragile as porcelain. Then he stood back and looked at her for long minutes before sliding into bed next to her and immediately curving her towards him so that their bodies were pressed against one another.

'So...can I ask you that question once again?'

'What question?' As if she didn't know. Ellie squirmed against him, fingers itching to rip his clothes off.

'Will you marry me? For real? Because I can't contemplate a life without you. I want you to be there for me, for Jake and for all the kids we're going to have together. I love you, *querida*, now and for ever...'

'How,' Ellie laughed, 'is a girl supposed to say no to a proposal like that?'

It was a fairy-tale story for avid reporters and, for the first time in his life, Luca actually gave them what they wanted because he was just so proud to show off the woman who was going to be his wife.

They were married without fanfare in the local church in the village where Ellie had grown up although several days later, and before they departed on their honeymoon to the Maldives, they threw a bash worthy of any A-lister to celebrate their union.

And not only were her father and all her friends in attendance, but so was her sister.

She and Lily had had a long talk when they had finally met up back in the UK and Ellie had been startled to learn that for every insecurity she had had, her sister likewise had her own.

'You were so bright,' Lily had admitted. 'I could never get higher than a C but you were a straight-A student and sometimes it felt as though Dad only had eyes for you. I could slog my guts out and I knew I'd still never be able to make it to university. It was easier in the end to just let Mum have her way and, you know... I got accustomed to making the most of my looks. But your brains will last for ever. My looks won't and I know that.'

Then it had all come out in an outpouring of emotion that had left Ellie feeling closer to her sister than she had in a very long time.

Lily had gone to seek fame and fortune but instead she had just joined the quagmire of hopefuls all out there looking for the same thing. She'd become just one of many pretty faces trying to clamber up the same tree.

'I ran out of money,' she'd admitted. 'That's why I couldn't send any over for Dad. I had none. I was waitressing by night and then going round and round, looking for agents, trying to get hold of connections. Everyone was doing the same thing. You wouldn't believe what it's like...'

The steps Jake had made in forming a bond with Luca had been quite remarkable. The memories of his parents would never leave him; Ellie knew that. But he was no longer the lost child who had felt the need to run as fast and as far as he could from a place he didn't like.

And the Maldives...

Ellie looked at the wedding band on her finger and smiled. Sitting out here, with an orange sunset dropping over sea that was as calm as a lake, she almost had to pinch herself that she wasn't playing the lead role in a dream, one from which she would cruelly awaken at any minute.

Back in England, Jake was with her father and her sister, who had given up dreams of stardom and was slowly realising that there was a lot to be said for ordinary.

Here... She swivelled around and absorbed the stunning scenery. Rich foliage was bathed in a mellow light cast by strings of lanterns that zip-lined through the trees and shivered and twinkled in the lazy evening breeze. The sound of invisible insects was a background orchestra of soothing sounds. Ahead, the dark sea was as flat as glass. It was hard to believe that, as soon as dawn broke, that black body of smooth water would become turquoise and alive with colourful fish.

The place was paradise but what made it really special was the fact that she was here with her husband.

She heard Luca behind her and turned around, smiling and already tingling because he never failed to impress her. He was just so spectacular, prowling with the grace and strength of a panther. And hers! She felt a hot flare of possessiveness.

Their two-bedroom cabin was the height of luxury and so secluded that they could practically walk around naked without fear of being seen. But right now, fresh from a shower, he had a towel slung low on his lean hips.

His hair was still damp and he raked his fingers through it then stood behind her before inclining to slip his hands underneath the silk strappy dress, finding her bare breasts and gently massaging them.

Ellie squirmed and twisted round then knelt on the chair so that she could hold his face in her hands and kiss him.

'Sometimes I can't believe it's possible to be so happy,' she murmured and Luca smiled.

'Nor can I,' he admitted. He sauntered round to sit next to her on the padded two-seater on the wooden deck of their cabin.

'You were the man who felt claustrophobic at the thought of a woman cooking for you,' she teased, holding his hand and linking her fingers through his. 'Remember?'

'How could I forget when you got me an apron saying "domesticated and proud of it" to show me the error of my ways?'

'You never wear that apron.' She sighed, smiling.

'I wouldn't want to invade your territory. I know you like cooking for me so why spoil your fun?'

Ellie burst out laughing. He didn't wear the apron but he could cook a mean steak.

'I look back at the man I used to be, afraid of letting go in case I got hurt, and I marvel that I could ever have been so short-sighted. Although, maybe I was just waiting for the right

woman to come along and show me the error of my ways...'
He pulled her towards him and kissed the tip of her nose, then
covered her mouth with his, stroking her rib cage and firing
her up so that she just wanted to haul him back into the cabin
so that she could have her wicked way with him.

'And now that we're married,' he continued with a smile
in his voice, 'maybe it's time we took this to the next level...'

'Next level?'

'I think it's time for Jake to have a sibling, don't you?' He
chuckled and then swung round the chair so that he could hoist
her into his arms, caveman style, carry her back into the cabin
and into the bedroom with its four-poster bed. 'And why put off
for tomorrow what can be done today?' His grin was wicked
as she began stripping off the slip of a dress under which she
was completely naked.

'Just today?' she teased.

'Today,' Luca said with tenderness, 'tomorrow and every
day for the rest our lives.'

* * * * *

Redeemed By His Stolen Bride

Abby Green

Books by Abby Green

Harlequin Modern

The Virgin's Debt to Pay
Awakened by the Scarred Italian

Conveniently Wed!

Claiming His Wedding Night Consequence

One Night With Consequences

An Innocent, A Seduction, A Secret

Wedlocked!

Claimed for the De Carillo Twins

Brides for Billionaires

Married for the Tycoon's Empire

Rival Spanish Brothers

Confessions of a Pregnant Cinderella

Rulers of the Desert

A Diamond for the Sheikh's Mistress
A Christmas Bride for the King

Visit the Author Profile page
at millsandboon.com for more titles.

This is for Heidi Rice, who came up with the idea of giving the jilted fiancée from *Confessions of a Pregnant Cinderella* her own story. X

CHAPTER ONE

LEONORA FLORES DE LA VEGA couldn't seem to take her eyes off the man standing at the back of the crowd in the glittering ballroom. He towered over everyone around him, putting him at well over six feet.

He was also scowling, which only made his hawkish good looks even more forbidding and intimidating. And even from here Leonora was aware of his sheer masculine magnetism. As if there was an invisible thread tugging her attention to him whether she liked it or not.

She knew who Gabriel Ortega Cruz y Torres was. Everyone did. He came from one of Spain's most noble and oldest families. They owned huge swathes of the country and generated an income from banking, vineyards and real estate—just to name a few enterprises.

He was an intensely private man, but even so he had a reputation for being as ruthless in the bedroom as he was in business. Single, he was considered one of the most eligible bachelors in Europe, if not the world. But he appeared to be in no hurry to settle down. And when he did it would be with an undeniably well-connected woman who breathed the same rarefied air as he did.

And why should that even concern her? Leonora chastised

herself. She might come from a family almost as well-connected as Gabriel's, but there the similarity ended. Her family had lost their fortune, and had been subsisting on scraps and the funds from opening up their *castillo* just outside Madrid. It was an ignominious state of affairs. And one that was becoming increasingly unsustainable.

She had never spoken to Gabriel Torres and was never likely to. A man like him wouldn't lower himself to consort with someone from a family of very faded glory. But she'd always been aware of him. From the moment she'd first laid eyes on him when he'd been about twenty-one and she'd been twelve. She'd watched him play polo—that had been before her family had lost everything due to her father's gambling habit, a long-standing source of shame that had kept her parents from venturing out in public for years.

She hadn't been able to take her eyes off Gabriel that day. He'd been so vital. So alive. He and the horse had moved as one, with awesome athleticism and grace. But it had been the expression on his face that had caught her—so intense and focused.

She'd overheard one of the opposing team say, 'Hey, Torres, lighten up. It's just a friendly game.'

He'd said nothing, just glowered at the man. Leonora could remember feeling an ache near her heart, as if she'd wanted to soothe him somehow…make him smile.

Which was ridiculous.

She became aware of the hubbub in the ballroom. Of the hundreds of eyes looking at her. And suddenly she came out of her reverie and back into the present moment. A moment that was going to change her life for ever.

A spurt of panic clutched at her gut and she breathed through it.

She was doing this for her family. For Matías. She had no choice. She was their only hope of redemption.

A light sweat broke out on her palms as she forced her gaze away from the man at the back of the room and found the man she *should* be looking at. Her fiancé. Lazaro Sanchez. He was devilishly handsome, with overlong dark blond hair and mesmerisingly unusual green eyes. Tall. He was almost as tall as—

She shook her head briefly. *No.* She had to stop thinking about him. She was about to become engaged to *this* man. This man she hardly knew, if she was honest. They'd had some dates. She didn't feel anything when she looked at him. Not like...*him.*

But Lazaro was kind and respectful. And, more importantly, he was prepared to bail her family out of their quagmire of debts and in so doing restore their respectability and secure Matías's future. In return... Well, Leonora was cynical enough to recognise ruthless ambition when she saw it. Lazaro Sanchez wanted to marry her in order to achieve a level of acceptance into the world she inhabited. Her only currency now was as a trophy to someone like him and she had no choice but to accept it.

She noticed then that Lazaro had a glowering expression on his face, not unlike the one on Gabriel Torres's. Something about that caught in Leonora's mind, but before she could unpick what it meant she realised that one of Lazaro's staff was making a motion, as if to say, *It's time.*

She tried to get his attention, 'Lazaro?'

He looked at her. Still glowering.

'Are you all right?' she asked. 'You look very fierce.'

His expression cleared. He held out a hand and she slipped hers into his. *Nothing.* No effect. She berated herself again. People in this world didn't marry for love or chemistry. They married strategically. Exactly as she was doing.

'Yes, fine...just a little preoccupied,' he said.

Unable to help herself, Leonora glanced back across the room, and this time Gabriel Torres's dark, compelling gaze met hers. A flash of heat went straight through her abdomen. Her fingers tightened reflexively around Lazaro's.

'Are *you* okay?' he asked her.

A surge of guilt blasted her. How could she be so compelled

by another man when she was about to commit publicly to this one? She looked at Lazaro and forced a smile. 'Yes, I'm fine.'

His hand tightened around hers. 'I'm glad you have agreed to marry me, Leonora. I think we can have a good marriage, I think we can be…happy.'

Did he?

A semi-hysterical bubble rose up inside her. She had a sense of the massive room closing in around her, suffocating her. Lazaro let go of her hand and slipped his arm around her waist. The feeling of claustrophobia got worse.

His hand tightened on her waist, almost painfully, and Leonora hissed at him. *'Lazaro—'*

He looked at her with a strange expression on his face, his eyes burning.

'You're hurting me.'

Immediately he released his grip. 'I'm sorry.'

Leonora forced a smile. The sooner they got this announcement over with, the sooner she could get out of this room and get some air. She resolutely forced herself to keep her eyes averted from where Gabriel Torres stood, towering over everyone else around him. Powerful. Magnetic. Disturbing.

A waiter approached with champagne and she took two glasses, handing one to Lazaro. She saw movement nearby and said, 'Your advisors are making motions that it's time to make the announcement. Ready?'

Lazaro looked at her, and she clung to the resolve she could see in his eyes.

He clinked his glass to hers. 'Yes, let's do it.'

He put his arm around her waist again and Leonora forced a smile through the lingering claustrophobia. He started speaking, but she didn't really take in his words, letting them roll over her.

Against every effort, her eye was drawn back across the crowd to where Gabriel Torres stood. He was still watching her, with a disconcertingly intense gaze. Leonora started to tremble lightly under the force of it.

Suddenly a voice rang out. *'Wait! Stop!'*

It shook Leonora out of her trance. It was a woman, who'd pushed through the crowd near the dais. She was being held back by security guards. She was dressed like the wait staff, in a white shirt and black skirt. Vibrant red hair, up in a bun. She was very pretty. Bright blue eyes.

She was looking at Lazaro, and then she said, 'You need to know something. I'm pregnant. With your child.'

For long seconds time was suspended, and then everything seemed to go into slow motion as Leonora felt Lazaro's arm leave her waist. She watched as the woman said something else, not hearing what it was through the buzzing in her head.

Lazaro stepped down off the dais to talk to the woman, holding her arm. She looked very petite next to him. Vaguely, ridiculously, Leonora appreciated that they looked good together.

She couldn't hear what they were saying, and then the woman was being led away.

Lazaro turned back to look at her, his expression veering between shock, anger and contrition.

He came back up on to the dais and said something to the crowd—she wasn't sure what. Too many feelings were rolling over her—chief of which, she was ashamed to admit, was a sense of relief. But that was quickly eclipsed when she looked around and saw the crowd whispering. Some people were looking at her with pity and others with something far less benign. A malicious glee at the fall of one of their own.

She'd tried to buy her way out of debt and shame and now she felt as exposed as if she were naked. And *he* was still there. At the back. Looking at her with a grim expression.

She turned away and saw Lazaro. She backed away and then she stopped. Maybe this was just some hideous case of mistaken identity.

'Is it true?'

But Lazaro said nothing, and his silence said everything.

He looked guilty.

He held out a hand. 'Leonora, please…let me explain.'

It was real.

She became aware of the burn of humiliation. She shook her head. 'I can't agree to marry you. Not now.'

She sent up a silent *thank you* that her parents weren't there to witness this moment. Or Matías. He would see that she was upset and that would upset him.

She cast a look around, instinctively seeking an escape route. All she saw were judgemental eyes. Mocking eyes.

She looked at Lazaro for one last time, dismay and humiliation scoring her insides like a knife. 'How could you do this to me? In front of all these people?'

Without waiting for a response, she put her glass down on the nearest surface and turned and fled, making for the nearest exit with no clue where to go.

The first thing she saw was a Ladies' sign, and she followed it to the bathroom, which was mercifully empty. She locked herself into a stall and sat down on the closed toilet.

She was trembling, her heart pounding. She forced herself to take deep breaths, and just as she was starting to feel marginally calmer the door opened. It sounded as if at least three women were coming in, all chattering. About her and Lazaro.

'Who'd marry her now? She's so desperate she was willing to marry some nouveau riche billionaire…'

'Where did Sanchez even come from?'

'Some say he grew up on the streets.'

'The de la Vegas can't survive this. All they have is her and that brother of hers, who everyone knows is a—'

At the mention of Leonora's beloved brother she opened the door and stepped out of the stall, coming face-to-face with the three gossipers. The chatter stopped instantly.

One blanched, one went red, but the other one was totally unrepentant. Leonora was too upset to speak. She just watched as they collected their things and walked out in silence, taking no sense of satisfaction in having routed them because she knew they'd only start gossiping again as soon as they were out of earshot.

She went over to the sink and put her hands on the counter, looking at herself in the mirror but only vaguely registering that her outward appearance—relatively calm—belied the storm inside. She could only give thanks that the women hadn't witnessed her falling apart.

She took a deep breath and ran some cold water over her hands and wrists. She hoped that by the time she emerged there would be no one else waiting to witness her walk of shame.

At that instant a face popped into her head. *Gabriel Torres.* His hawk-like features were as vivid as if he were standing in front of her. She went hot and then cold at the thought of *him* having witnessed her public humiliation.

But she wouldn't see him again. Because she wouldn't be emerging in public for a long time.

She took a breath and steeled herself before heading back out and into the lobby, hoping for a discreet getaway.

Where was she?

Gabriel Torres looked left and right outside the function room, but there was no sign of the dark-haired woman in the long strapless red dress. The dress that clung to her elegant curves in a way that had made his blood pound for the first time in a long time. The compulsion to follow her prickled over his skin now; he wasn't someone normally given to such impetuosity.

He had only come here this evening to see for himself what Lazaro Sanchez was up to, because he didn't trust the man as far as he could throw him. Especially when everything he did seemed to be designed personally to get under Gabriel's skin. And because they were both involved in a very competitive and lucrative bid for a public project.

Recently Sanchez had even gone so far as to concoct a story that he and Gabriel were half-brothers. He'd accosted Gabriel at an event they'd both attended and when Gabriel had tried to walk away, disgusted at the insinuation that they could be related, Sanchez had stopped him, telling him of a day, many years before, when he had confronted Gabriel's father, claiming to be his son.

To Gabriel's surprise and shock he'd remembered the incident—and the skinny kid who had been waiting for them outside a restaurant in central Madrid. It had been his birthday—one of the very rare occasions when his dysfunctional family had put on a united front.

Gabriel had never been naïve about either of his parents. It was quite possible that his serially philandering father might have sired a bastard along the way. For a family like the Cruz y Torres, whose vast dynasty stretched back to the Middle Ages, such occurrences by opportunists were frequent and, frankly, to be expected.

So, for all he knew, Sanchez could be his brother but he suspected it was more likely to be a ruse to get under Gabriel's skin.

Ironically enough, Gabriel's father was at this event too, this evening, but Gabriel had ignored him. They barely tolerated each other at the best of times, and he'd had no doubt that the only reason his father had been there was probably the free-flowing booze or a woman.

Since Sanchez's claim to be related to Gabriel, he'd been kept at a certain distance. But tonight had been one of his most audacious moves yet: announcing his engagement to one of Spain's most well-connected women, whose own family rivalled Gabriel's in lineage and legacy.

Marriage to someone like Leonora Flores de la Vega would elevate Sanchez to a place that would make it that much harder to ignore him. Gabriel had to hand it to him for sheer chutzpah.

Clearly he hadn't been intending on marrying Leonora Flores for her money—her family were famously broke after her father's well-documented gambling problems. Her worth came in her name and lineage.

Gabriel had heard the whispers in the crowd. Whispers that Sanchez had offered her a deal—he'd pay off her family debts and in return buy his way into the world he was so desperate to be a part of that he claimed to be Gabriel's blood relation.

Gabriel didn't know Leonora personally, but he knew *of* her, and their paths had crossed over the years at social events. But coming here this evening, seeing her standing up on that dais beside Sanchez, had reminded him that there was something about her that had always snagged his attention. He'd noticed it again this evening. Enough to distract him from Lazaro Sanchez.

Her beautiful face had been composed. Revealing nothing. Her long dark hair pulled back and sleek, showing off the exquisite bone structure of her face. Wide almond-shaped eyes. Dark lashes. A full mouth that hinted at a level of sensuality Gabriel sensed she wasn't entirely comfortable with.

He'd racked his brains to think of the last time he'd seen her. It hadn't been recent. She'd grown up in the meantime. Now she was a woman—and a stunningly beautiful woman at that.

Gabriel had found himself staring at her, willing her to look at him, *needing* her to look at him. And then she had. He'd felt the impact of that contact from across the room. An instantaneous jolt of sexual awareness surging through his blood.

She'd kept on looking at Gabriel and he'd seen the flicker of panic in her eyes. Along with something else far more potent. *She wanted him.*

That awareness, together with seeing Sanchez's arm around her waist, had caught at something unexpected inside Gabriel. Something hot and visceral. A sense of...possessiveness.

When Sanchez had announced their engagement, Gabriel had felt an inexplicable and almost overwhelming urge to disrupt proceedings, but just at that moment another voice had rung out. A voice coming from the petite red-haired woman near the dais, claiming to be pregnant with Sanchez's child.

Leonora had fled, and Gabriel had watched her go, knowing

immediately that he would go after her. He'd never felt such a primal pull towards anyone.

He'd looked at Sanchez and the animosity he'd felt towards the man had compelled him to mock him for his abortive attempt to buy respectability and for bringing his domestic dramas into the public domain.

But all thoughts of Sanchez were gone now, as he looked left and right for Leonora Flores.

She was gone.

An alien sensation stopped Gabriel in his tracks and he realised it was the sensation of something having slipped through his fingers.

For a man who generally obtained his every want and desire, it was unwelcome. And an unpleasant reminder that he was acting out of character. Pursuing a woman when he didn't need to. If he wanted a woman that badly he could walk back into the room behind him and take his pick. But a new restlessness prickled under his skin. He didn't want one of *them*. So eager, so desperate. He wanted *her*.

And then, as if answering his silent call, he saw her, standing behind the elaborate foliage screening the lobby and entrance from the rest of the hotel. He saw what she saw: a bank of waiting paparazzi outside the main door of the hotel, and no other means of escape.

There was no way he was going to let her out of his sight again. And if the opportunity presented itself to remind Sanchez of where he belonged, Gabriel would be a fool not to exploit it.

Leonora cursed silently. Between the fronds of the exotic plant she could see where the photographers were lined up, no doubt ready to capture the smiling couple emerging from the hotel. There was no other way out without going through the lobby. One way or another they would see her, either scuttling away as if she was the one in the wrong, or walking out without her new fiancé.

Just as she was steeling herself to run the gauntlet, she felt the back of her neck prickle with awareness and her skin tingled all over.

She turned around and Gabriel Ortega Cruz y Torres was standing a couple of feet away, looking at her. She gulped. He was even taller up close. Broader. Thick dark hair swept back off his forehead. Deep-set dark eyes. Strong brows. A patrician nose and a firm, unyielding mouth.

His bottom lip was surprisingly lush, though, softening the hard edges of his face and making her wonder what it would feel like to touch...kiss... She could imagine him lounging on jewel-coloured cushions, summoning his minions.

Summoning his lovers.

A wave of heat flashed through her body. She was losing it. She *never* imagined kissing men. She was a twenty-four-year-old virgin, because her life had revolved around her parents, the castle and her disabled brother. She'd been more of a mother than a sister to her brother, since their world had imploded after her father's gambling excesses. She'd literally had no time for anything else. Anything normal. Like relationships.

Before she could even think of something to say Gabriel came forward and his scent reached her nostrils, sharp and infinitely masculine. Exotic.

'Would you like me to get you out of here?'

His voice was deep and compelling.

Leonora's response was swift and instinctive. She nodded.

'We'll go out through the main entrance. Don't look left or right, just let me guide you.'

He plucked something out of his pocket and Leonora saw that it was a phone. He issued a curt instruction and put the phone back, his eyes never leaving hers.

'My car is outside. Let's go.'

Before Leonora knew what was happening Gabriel Torres had taken her elbow in his hand and they were already halfway across the lobby. Flashes erupted from outside, and as soon as they got through the doors there was a barrage of noise and calls.

'Leonora! Where's Lazaro Sanchez?'

Leonora ignored it all and followed Gabriel's instructions, looking straight ahead.

A sleek low-slung silver bullet of a car was parked by the kerb and the doorman sprang aside as Gabriel helped her into the front passenger seat. The door was shut, cocooning her in expensive leather and metal and blissful silence, which was only broken briefly when Gabriel came around to the driver's side and opened the door, settling himself into the car.

Within seconds they were moving through the throng of press, who had to part to let them through. Leonora flinched at the bright flashes from their cameras as the paparazzi pressed cameras up to the window to get their shots.

'I should have tried to leave through a back entrance. I'll be on every front page tomorrow.'

She felt Gabriel glance at her. 'Why should you? You've nothing to be ashamed of.'

Leonora's heart was pounding. She saw Gabriel's hand work the gearstick. Square-shaped long fingers. Short, blunt nails. Masculine.

Her lower body clenched.

'You didn't have to do this,' she said.

Her voice was husky. She looked at Gabriel, whose jaw was tight.

'It's nothing. You shouldn't have been thrown to the wolves like that.'

She got the impression that he was angry. On her behalf. She barely knew him. Her relief at being out of that situation was taking the edges off her own anger at Lazaro.

'Well...thank you.'

She noticed then that they were driving through one of Madrid's exclusive city enclaves. Leafy streets and chic cosmopolitan bars and restaurants. Expensive antique shops and designer boutiques. Elegant buildings mixed with new architecture.

Feeling embarrassed now, and thinking that Gabriel might be regretting his good deed, Leonora said, 'You really don't have to take me home. I'm the other way, anyway. I can jump out here and get a taxi.'

He shook his head and glanced in the rear-view mirror. 'Not if you don't want them to follow you home, you can't.'

Leonora looked behind them and saw a couple of motorbikes weaving in and out of traffic, following them. Her heart sank at the thought of them outside the family estate. If Matías saw them he'd get confused and upset...

At that moment Gabriel said, 'Hang on,' and then surged ahead as a traffic light turned to red. He negotiated a couple of rapid turns down dark side streets that had Leonora's heart jumping into her throat, but at no point did she feel unsafe. It was exhilarating.

With the next turn into a quiet residential street Leonora sucked in a breath. It looked as if they were going to drive straight into a wall, but it quickly revealed itself to be a door that opened and allowed them entry down into a private garage under the building.

Gabriel pulled to a stop beside a row of equally sleek cars. 'I think we lost them at the last traffic lights.'

Silence descended around them. 'Where are we?' she asked.

'At my city apartment. You can wait here for a bit—let them lose you. I'll organise for you to get home later. If you want.'

If you want.

Leonora looked at Gabriel, still reeling at everything that had happened and at the fact that he was her rescuer. His eyes were on her, dark and unreadable, and yet she felt as if some silent communication was taking place. Something she didn't understand fully. Or didn't want to investigate fully.

'Okay...if you're sure. I don't want to bother you.'

He shook his head. 'You're not bothering me. Don't worry.'

He undid his seat-belt and uncoiled his tall frame from the car. He came around and opened her door and held out a hand.

Leonora almost didn't want to touch him, afraid of how she'd react. She could still feel the imprint of his hand on her elbow. But she couldn't dither, so she put her hand in his and let him pull her out. And she'd been right to be afraid, because a jolt of electricity ran up her arm and right down into her core.

By the time she straightened up she was breathless. And she was so close to Gabriel that one more step would bring her flush with his body. She could sense the whipcord strength beneath his bespoke suit. Her eye line rested just below his bowtie.

His hand wrapped around hers. 'Okay?'

She looked up and forced a smile, trying not to be intimidated by the sheer masculine beauty of the man. His proximity. 'Fine... Just a bit shaky after the paparazzi. Normally I don't register on their radar.'

Not the way this man did. He was slavishly followed and speculated upon by press eager to get a story on the reclusive billionaire. She thought of the papers tomorrow. Her head hurt at the prospect of her parents' reaction. They were depending on her to redeem the family name and finances, not to embroil them in another scandal.

Gabriel let her hand go and Leonora suddenly realised something with dismay. 'My bag and coat!'

Lazaro had arranged for someone to take them to the cloakroom at the hotel.

Gabriel said, 'Come upstairs and I'll arrange for them to be delivered here.'

He opened a door that led out into a dimly lit foyer. A security guard stepped into the light. 'Good evening, Señor Torres.'

'Good evening, Pancho. One of my team will be delivering something shortly. Let them in and send it up, please.'

'Of course, sir.'

Gabriel put his hand on Leonora's back, guiding her with a barely perceptible touch over to an elevator. Even so, she could feel his hand through her dress, and had the ridiculous urge to sink back against him, let him take her weight.

It unnerved her how much he made her *feel*, so she stood apart from him in the small space as the doors slid shut and he pressed a button. It rose silently and stopped a few seconds later with a small jerking motion.

The doors slid open and Gabriel put out a hand, indicating for Leonora to precede him. She stepped out and into a stunning penthouse apartment. It had all the original features of the building's era—around the nineteenth century, Leonora guessed—but none of the fussiness.

It was a very contemporary apartment in the shell of one of Madrid's classic buildings. Modern art hung on the walls, with spotlights directing the eye to bold slashing strokes and colours. Surprisingly sensual. Something about the design—the lack of clutter, the open spaces—soothed her. The furniture was deceptively plain and unobtrusive, letting the interior speak for itself. She'd never seen anything quite like it.

She watched as Gabriel strode over to French doors, opening them to let some air in. Leonora only realised then how close it was. The late-summer city heat was still oppressive. He took his phone out of his pocket and made a call, speaking in low tones. She assumed he was arranging to have her things collected.

He turned around to face her then, tugging at his bowtie, undoing it. Opening the top button of his shirt. She almost looked away, feeling as if she was intruding on some intimacy.

He gestured with a hand to a couch. 'Please—sit, make yourself comfortable...'

Leonora stepped further into the room, feeling naked without her wrap or bag. 'I'm fine, thank you. You have a beautiful apartment.'

No doubt it was just one of the hundreds of properties owned by him and his family all over Spain and the world.

It was well known that he was seen very much as the patriarch of his family, even though his father was still alive. And

Leonora was vaguely aware of a rumour about his younger sister going off the rails and how she'd been sent abroad to clean up her act.

She shivered slightly at the thought of what it must be like to face a disapproving or angry Gabriel Torres. She didn't even know his sister, or if the rumour was true, but she already felt sorry for her.

'Would you like a drink?' He walked over to an elaborate drinks cabinet. 'I have whiskey, brandy, champagne, wine, gin—'

'I'll have a little whiskey please,' she blurted out, needing something to settle her clanging nerves.

He poured dark golden liquid into a small tumbler and brought it over to her. 'It's Irish. I believe it's meant to be very good.'

Leonora took it, distracted by the bowtie dangling at his neck and the open top button of his shirt. She could see dark bronzed skin. A hint of hair.

'You haven't tasted it?'

He shook his head. 'I don't drink.'

She watched as he moved back, giving her space. It fitted that he didn't drink. He seemed far too controlled. Exacting. Alert. She wondered why he didn't, but wasn't going to ask.

As if he could read her mind, though, he supplied, 'I was put off after watching how alcohol affected people's judgement and their decision-making. Not least my father's. He almost ruined the family business.'

So that was why Gabriel now ran their extensive operation.

'I'm sorry to hear that...' Impulsively she added, 'I have some idea of what you're talking about.'

She wondered why she'd said that, but there was something about being in this space with this man that didn't feel entirely real.

To her relief he didn't say anything, or ask her to elaborate on the fact that her father's vices had driven them to the brink and over. Anyway, he probably knew the sordid details. Most people did. But for the first time she didn't feel that burning rise of shame. Maybe it was his admission that his family wasn't perfect either.

He said, 'I'm sorry for what happened to you this evening. You didn't deserve that. You're too good for a man like Lazaro Sanchez.'

Leonora clutched the tumbler to her chest. She'd yet to take a sip of the drink. 'You don't have to be sorry. It wasn't your fault. And how can you say I'm too good for him? You don't even know me.'

'Don't I?' he asked softly, raising a dark brow. 'We come from the same world, Leonora. We might not have had a conversation before now, but we know more about each other than you realise—and I'm not talking about idle gossip. I'm talking about the lives we've led. The expectations on our shoulders. The life built on legacy and duty. Responsibility.'

CHAPTER TWO

GABRIEL MARVELLED AT how expressive Leonora was. She clearly hadn't expected him to say that. He'd caught her unawares. Her eyes were wide on his, as if he'd shocked her.

He realised now that they weren't dark brown, as he'd assumed. They were grey. Like a stormy ocean. But even as he had that fanciful notion she seemed to come back to herself and her face resumed its serene mask. The same one she'd been wearing earlier, standing beside Lazaro Sanchez. Before all hell had broken loose.

She took a sip of her drink and he noticed her hand wasn't entirely steady. He had to clench his fist to stop from reaching out and taking her hand in his. He saw her throat work as she swallowed and he imagined the burn of the alcohol as it slipped down into her stomach, radiating heat. Mirroring the heat he felt in his blood.

Dios, but she was stunning. Possibly the most beautiful woman he'd ever seen. And she was getting to him in a way that made him distinctly uncomfortable. Usually when he desired a woman it was a manageable thing. Right now it was taking all his restraint not to seduce Leonora to within an inch of her life and demand the satisfaction his body was crying out for.

A kind of satisfaction that he knew instinctively would eclipse anything he'd ever experienced before.

He stepped back and gestured to a nearby couch. 'Please, sit down. Your things should be here soon.'

For a long moment Leonora couldn't move. She was still in shock at how succinctly Gabriel had summed up her existence.

'The lives we've led... The expectations on our shoulders... The life built on legacy and duty. Responsibility.'

She'd never felt that anyone could possibly understand what her life was like. She had very little to complain about and yet sometimes she felt as trapped as if she was in jail.

He was looking at her. He'd just asked if she wanted to sit down.

She shook her head jerkily. 'No, I'm fine. Thank you.'

She felt restless, and she walked over to where floor-to-ceiling windows looked out over a terrace and further, to the skyline of Madrid under a clear starlit sky. She had a very fleeting moment of wondering what Lazaro was doing right now. Dealing with the mother of his child?

A tiny sense of hysteria at what had happened rose up and she took another hasty sip of whiskey to try and force it back down.

Gabriel came to stand near her. She could see him in the reflection of the window. He'd taken off his jacket and his chest and shoulders looked impossibly broad under the snowy shirt.

She saw her own reflection. The strapless red dress. She'd hoped its elegant simplicity would prove to be timeless, because it was many seasons out of date. She saw the glittering drop earrings hanging from her earlobes that looked like diamonds. But they weren't diamonds at all. They were cubic zirconia. It was a long time since she'd worn any real family jewels. They'd all been sold by her father to get money for gambling.

She felt like a fraud, and the humiliation from earlier rose up again. She quickly downed the last of her drink, guiltily relishing the last dregs of comfort from the alcohol.

She turned to face Gabriel, avoiding his eye. 'I should leave—go home. My mother and father will be worried.'

And Matías.

Just thinking of him made her heart hurt. What would happen to them now? If they lost the castle then that was it. They would have hit rock bottom with no way back. An entire dynasty and legacy wiped out through the actions of her father...

'Don't go yet.'

She looked at Gabriel. Her heart thumped hard. His face was all lean angles and harsh lines. And then softened by that ridiculously sensual mouth.

'We're still waiting for your things.'

Leonora was torn. She wanted to appear totally at ease and sophisticated, draping herself artfully on one of the sofas while wittily regaling Gabriel with inconsequential chatter. But that wasn't her. Had never been her.

'I can get them tomorrow. They're not that important.'

She felt that the longer she stood there the quicker he'd see that he was having an effect on her.

He came closer and moved to take the empty glass from her hand. He put his fingers over hers. A deliberate move? The breath stuck in her throat. He was so...*vital.* Lazaro had never had this effect on her and she'd believed that it would make for a better marriage. No extreme feelings or wants.

Gabriel said, 'The paparazzi will know for sure by now that your engagement wasn't announced. They'll be actively hunting you down. Waiting for you. You should call your parents—warn them to stay inside.'

Leonora swallowed. Gabriel's fingers were still on hers. 'But I can't just...stay here.'

'Of course you can.' He took the glass out of her nerveless fingers and in the same motion, with his other hand, he handed her his phone. 'Use this.'

It seemed to be a foregone conclusion. And she knew he was right. She couldn't go back home now and face a barrage of lights and questions. Out of concern for Matías as much as anything else.

Leonora moved away from Gabriel and dialled her home number. Her mother answered, immediately concerned, and Leonora rushed to assure her that everything was okay. She filled her in on the broad strokes of what had happened and told her not to worry. She told her that she'd spend the night elsewhere, to draw the press away from the de la Vega home. Her mother sounded disappointed—and then just weary. They'd been here before, with the press camped outside.

When she'd ended the conversation, after checking that Matías was okay, Leonora handed the phone back.

Gabriel said, 'Your brother is not well?'

Leonora gave a small tight smile. 'He has...learning difficulties. Since birth. He's home at the moment—from the school he attends just outside Madrid.'

The school that was paid for out of the receipts from tours around the Flores de la Vega castle. And with the money from the designer clothes and jewellery Leonora sold over the years online. The school that he loved and thrived in. The school that was offering him a real chance at a life in the outside world as he moved into adulthood.

The school that they would no longer be able to afford if they had to sell the castle—the only thing keeping them afloat in a sea of debts.

'He picks up on moods and tension very acutely, so he'd be upset if he knew the press were outside, or if there was anything wrong with me.'

'You're close?'

Leonora looked at Gabriel, expecting to see the same look most people had when they heard about Matías, varying between mild disdain and salacious curiosity. Or pity. But Gabriel's face and eyes held none of those things. Just a genuine question.

She nodded, feeling emotional. 'The closest. He's eighteen

now, and when he was born I was six. He was like my baby more than my little brother.'

'That would have been before your fortunes...changed.'

Leonora appreciated his attempt at tact. He was obviously referring to the fact that her parents had once been such fixtures on the Spanish social scene that they probably hadn't been around much to parent. Making their fall from grace even more explosive. They'd gone down in a ball of flames and infamy when her father had been thrown out of the casino in Monte Carlo with his wife clinging to his coat, weeping uncontrollably.

That was one of the reasons for their reclusiveness these days. Her parents' shame. Hence their desire and need for redemption. Through Leonora.

She diverted her mind from that and said, 'Something like that. Yes.' She looked away, embarrassed.

'That was them—not you. You're not like them.'

Leonora looked at him. Had he moved closer? The way he made her feel—the way he seemed to be looking deeper into her than anyone else ever had—made her prickly.

'You don't know that I don't have a gambling habit.'

He seemed to consider this for a moment, and then he said, 'True, I don't. But I don't believe you do.'

He was definitely closer now. Close enough for Leonora to see the stubble lining his jaw. And that his eyes had golden flecks—they weren't just brown.

She shook her head. 'Why are you doing this? Why do you care what happens to me? We've never met before this evening. I mean...not properly.'

Even with Leonora's family connections they'd moved in a lesser sphere than the Torres family.

'No. But our paths have crossed—even if just peripherally. I realised something this evening—I have always noticed you... on the edges. As if you'd prefer to disappear.'

Leonora blushed to think she'd been so transparent.

'And I realised something else.'

She looked at him.

'You have become a very beautiful woman.'

A tingling rush of heat coursed through her blood. The way he was looking at her was so...*intense*. She could almost feel it...as if he was touching her.

He took another step closer. Almost close enough now that she could imagine him bending down and pressing his mouth to hers.

Leonora was barely breathing. She was hot—so hot. All over. Deep down where no man had ever had any effect on her before.

'I want you, Leonora.'

For a long, suspended moment neither one of them moved. Gabriel was watching her as she struggled to absorb this information. So, all these sensations making her melt from the inside out...it wasn't just her.

For a second it was too heady to consider. The fact that he thought she was beautiful. And that he wanted her. *Her.* A woman who lived a more sheltered existence than most nuns.

At that moment there was a chiming sound. Gabriel emitted a curse under his breath and said, 'Don't move. That's the concierge with your things.'

He turned and she watched him walk across the vast room with athletic grace. He disappeared and she heard a door open, low voices. She saw the French doors and suddenly needed—craved—oxygen. She walked outside, drawing in deep lungsful of the night air. The sounds of traffic floating up from nearby streets helped to ground her in reality a little.

What was she doing? Practically falling into Gabriel Torres's arms after mere words? He was probably just being polite, helping to soothe what he assumed was her damaged ego. But in all honesty relief was her overriding feeling when she thought about Lazaro and the wreckage of their engagement.

It had been an audacious plan in any case—agreeing to marry a man purely for strategic reasons. Because it would benefit them both. It shamed her now. Yet she knew it was silly to feel shame, because her parents' marriage had been a strategic one. In their world *every* marriage was a strategic one. Too much was at stake when legacies and dynasties had to be passed down to the next generation for emotion to be involved in making a marriage.

The fact that her parents got on and had some affection for each other was just a bonus. It had helped them weather the storm of infamy and their son's vulnerabilities.

But Leonora—much to her eternal embarrassment—had always secretly harboured a desire for more. For a *real* relationship. For love. Happiness. She saw visiting tourist couples walking through the castle and its grounds, sharing kisses, holding hands. Whispering things to each other.

She'd met an old English couple, married for fifty years. They'd exuded such an aura of contentment and happiness. She knew what they had was rare, but not unobtainable. For normal people. Not for her.

When Lazaro Sanchez had shown an interest and taken her on a few dates, and when he'd put forward his proposal and the fact that he was offering to pull them out of their quagmire of debts, Leonora had known that she had no choice. She had responsibilities, just as Gabriel had said. The Flores de la Vega legacy was bigger than her secret hopes and dreams for a different life. A more fulfilled life.

'I want you, Leonora.'

She shivered, even though it wasn't cold. She shivered with awareness. With desire.

'I have always noticed you...on the edges. As if you'd prefer to disappear.'

How could a man who was little more than a stranger—no matter how much their worlds might have collided over the years—*get* her? More than anyone had ever got her before?

She'd never felt seen in her life. She'd hovered on the edges, exactly as he'd described. Out of the innate shyness that she had to work hard to overcome. Out of her concern for Matías, who found social situations very challenging.

And also because she'd never really enjoyed the social scene of their world. It had always reminded her of a medieval royal court, with its intrigue and politics. Petty cruelties. The way so-called friends had treated her and her parents and her brother like pariahs ever since they'd become *persona non grata* had been a formative lesson in human nature.

Had Gabriel Torres really told her that he wanted her? So bold? So direct?

Yes. He was that kind of man. He would just say what he wanted and expect results.

Leonora looked out over the city stretching before her. Millions of people living their lives. Millions of possibilities.

It was as if she'd stepped out of her life and into an alternative realm. Where anything could happen. She was in a moment out of time. In a place she'd never expected to be. With a man she would never in a million years have expected to know her name. Let alone...*desire* her.

Unless it wasn't desire.

It must be pity.

A wave of humiliation rose up through her. Oh, God, was she so desperate that she really believed—?

She heard a noise and tensed to face Gabriel again. She needed to leave. *Now.*

Gabriel saw the moment Leonora heard him return. Her slim shoulders were suddenly a tense line. He stood behind her, drinking in her graceful figure. The smooth pale olive skin of her back. The sleek dark ponytail that he wanted to wrap around his fist so he could tilt her head back, giving him access to her lush mouth.

He might have started this evening fixated on Lazaro Sanchez, and wondering what the man was up to, but now all he could see was this woman.

'I have your things.'

She turned around but he noticed that she avoided his eye.

She held out a hand. 'Thank you. I really should go now. There's a back entrance into the estate. I can use that. I'm sure they won't see me.'

Gabriel handed her the wrap and bag, noting how she avoided touching his hand. A novelty when he was used to women throwing themselves at him. Especially if he told them that he wanted them.

'Are you really willing to take that risk?'

She put her wrap around her shoulders, covering up her skin, crossing it over her chest like a shawl.

Eventually she looked at him. 'Look, thank you for helping me, but you really don't need to go out of your way to do any more.'

Gabriel moved closer to her, watching how her eyes flared and colour tinged her cheeks. She wanted him. He knew it.

'Did you not hear what I said?'

She swallowed. Her fingers clutched her wrap.

For a second the possibility trickled into Gabriel's mind that she was different from other women he knew in terms of experience, but he batted it away. She was twenty-four. To be inexperienced at her age, with her stunning beauty, in this modern cynical world, was practically an impossibility. Far more likely she was playing him. She knew he wanted her and she was getting off on watching him work to seduce her.

There was little novelty in Gabriel's world and he suspected it was the same for her. She was hardly a wide-eyed innocent when she'd been about to announce a business arrangement masquerading as a marriage.

'I want you, Leonora. You felt it too this evening. I saw it.'

She flushed and her eyes were huge. 'But...we don't even know each other. How can—?'

'How can it be possible?' Gabriel decided he'd indulge her

faux innocence. 'Because chemistry transcends such mundanities.'

Every line in her body was tense.

'You don't have to do this, you know.'

There was a fierce pride in the aristocratic lines of her beautiful face. Her eyes had turned stormy.

'I don't need your pity, Gabriel.'

Leonora was resisting the pull she felt to this man with every atom of her being. He was toying with her. He had no clue how inexperienced she was and she wasn't about to let him expose her any more than she'd already been exposed tonight.

She went to move past him, intent on getting out of there before she could unravel completely, but he caught her hand, stopping her. Heat travelled up her arm. She clenched her jaw.

'You seriously think I *pity* you?'

The incredulity in his tone compelled her to face him, her hand still in his. He was frowning. Suddenly she was very aware of their proximity, and of the darkness of his chest under the white shirt.

She swallowed. 'Maybe you just feel sorry for me...for what happened. You feel some kind of responsibility to make me feel...better.'

Even as she said this out loud she wanted to cringe. It sounded ridiculous.

He shook his head. 'You give me far too much credit. I'm not that nice. I told you I want you because I meant it. And I believe you want me too. You wanted me even as you stood beside your fiancé.'

Leonora flushed with guilty heat. She tried to pull her hand back but Gabriel didn't let go. He tugged her closer. She couldn't breathe.

'You don't believe I want you? I can prove to you that I do. And that you want me.'

Leonora knew that if she tugged hard she'd be free. She

knew that if she did that, and if she turned and walked away, he wouldn't stop her. He was too proud for that. Too sophisticated to chase a woman or force her. And yet...she couldn't move. *Didn't want to.* That sense of being in a moment outside time, outside of her life, was acute.

As if sensing her vacillation, Gabriel said, 'Here you are beholden to no one. There's no duty or responsibility. We're just two people. A man and a woman who want each other. Who are free to indulge our mutual desire.'

Leonora searched the hard planes of his face, those dark eyes. Was it really that simple? Could it be that simple? *Was* she free?

She thought of where she would be now if that woman hadn't interrupted the announcement of her engagement.

She would be in a very similar situation with a man she'd liked, but hadn't wanted. Maybe he would be kissing her now and she would be feeling nothing, resigning herself to the fact that this was as good as it would get. Because so much more was at stake. The future of her family. Her brother's security.

She considered the vagaries of fate and timing and how she might not be here at all, how she wouldn't be feeling this terrifying but exhilarating wildness coursing through her blood right now.

But she was. And it sank in that Gabriel Torres was deadly serious. He wasn't being nice. Or pitying her. He wanted her. And she wanted him. For one night. One night out of time.

The wildness rushing through her body turned into something far more reckless. Tonight she really was free. Tomorrow she would return to reality and pick up the pieces of her life.

She wanted to seize this moment that fate had handed her. A chance to experience true desire with a man who wanted her for *her*. Not because of who she was or what her name represented.

Gabriel was watching her. Reading her.

Without saying a word, letting his actions speak for him, he let her hand go and reached for her wrap, tugging it out of her hands, pulling it off her shoulders slowly. The silk trailed across her skin and she shivered minutely at the sensation. She'd never thought of herself as sensual before, but she felt sensual now. Under his gaze.

His eyes not leaving hers, he draped the wrap over the back of a nearby chair and Leonora could see it out of the corner of her eyes, a vivid red splash of colour.

Danger. *Passion.*

He took her bag out of her hand and put it down. Anticipation built inside her, deep down. Coiling tight. She couldn't take her eyes off his face.

He said, 'I've told you I want you and I mean it. I haven't wanted a woman like this in a long time. But you owe me nothing. I brought you here to give you refuge, and my guest suite is at your disposal for as long as you need it. It's your choice what happens next.'

She let out the breath she'd been holding unconsciously. She hadn't expected that kind of consideration. And at that moment Leonora almost resented him for not just kissing her and taking the decision out of her hands.

She knew it would be so easy to gather up her wrap and bag and say, *No, sorry...not now.* But something inside her had bloomed into life and she suspected he knew that very well. Better than she did.

She felt totally out of her depth. Another woman, more experienced, would no doubt be sliding her arms around his neck, pressing herself against every hard muscle of his body. But she felt paralysed with sudden shyness.

Gabriel's gaze narrowed on her face. He frowned slightly. 'Leonora, if you don't want to—'

'I do,' she blurted out before she could lose her nerve. 'I do...want you.'

She stepped closer. They were almost touching. His sheer physicality was overwhelming but it didn't intimidate her. It excited her.

He put his hands on her arms and tugged her closer. She

rested her palms on his chest. It was like steel. A spasm of sheer lust gripped her insides in a vice of tension. She pressed her thighs together to stem the heat flooding her core. But it was impossible. Every nerve quivered with anticipation and her heart was thumping so loudly she was sure it had to be audible.

Slowly, Gabriel took his hand off one of her arms and brought it up behind her head. She felt him undo her hair, so that it was loosened out of the ponytail. He massaged her scalp, his long fingers strong but surprisingly gentle. It made something else quiver inside her. Not just desire. *Emotion*.

But before that could really register he was lowering his head to hers, and as if in some desperate bid to cling on to a semblance of reality she kept her eyes on his, on those gold-flecked pools of brown. Intense and direct. Anchoring her to the moment.

But any hope of clinging to reality dissolved in a flash flood of heat when his mouth touched hers. Firm and unyielding. Soft but hard. Masterful. She was helpless against the giddy rush of desire that ripped through her body as his mouth moved over hers, enticing her to further intimacy, coaxing her to open up to him, pressing her closer so she could feel every inch of his long, lean body.

She opened her mouth, and even though she wasn't a total novice—she had kissed boys a long time ago before her life had been reduced to staying in the shadows—she wasn't prepared for Gabriel's expertise.

His mouth and tongue demanded a response she wasn't sure how to give. She could only react instinctively. Tasting, exploring. Mimicking his movements. She felt rather than heard a growl deep in his throat as he pulled her even closer, delved deeper.

She couldn't breathe, couldn't think, but she knew she never wanted this moment to end. She'd never experienced anything so thrilling. Transporting.

When Gabriel took his mouth off hers she moved with him,

loath to let the contact end. Her heart was pounding. It was a struggle to open her eyes. When she did, it took her a second to focus. Both her hands were clinging to his shirt. She was pressed so close against him that she could feel his desire, long and thick, against her belly.

It should have shocked her. But she pressed closer in an instinctive move, emboldened by a feminine rush of confidence she'd never known before. By the evidence of this man wanting her.

He smiled, but it wasn't a gentle smile. It was hard. Knowing.

Not even that could dent Leonora's desire. She wanted this man to be her first lover, so that whatever happened next she'd always have this experience locked inside her. That was why she'd said *yes*. Because she'd realised how close she'd come to never experiencing this.

'Make love to me, Gabriel.'

He picked up one of her hands and interlocked his fingers with hers. A pulse throbbed between her legs.

His mouth quirked on one side. 'Your wish is my command.'

Even through the haze of arousal and desire making her feel drunk, Leonora doubted that this man was anyone's to command.

He kept their hands linked and led her from the living area, down a hall and to a door. He opened it and Leonora took in a vast bedroom. In contrast to what she'd seen of the apartment so far, this room was almost ascetic. Nothing but bare white walls and a few pieces of modern furniture.

Gabriel let her hand go to switch on a light. It sent out a warm golden glow, softening the hard edges in the room. She wondered about that. About its starkness. And yet it soothed her, coming from a castle stuffed to the gills with oversized furniture and dark décor more suited to the Middle Ages.

Her eyes fell on the bed—the most decadent thing in the room. Massive, and luxuriously dressed with sumptuous dark grey sheets and pillows. Unashamedly masculine. And modern.

'Come here, Leonora.'

She took her gaze off the bed and looked at Gabriel. She sucked in a breath. He filled the space. She pushed down her trepidation and walked the couple of feet over to where he stood. He was taking his cufflinks out of his shirt and placing them on top of a chest of drawers. She stood before him.

'Take off your jewellery.'

She didn't think. She obeyed. Giving herself up to this night and this man with total commitment. She took out her earrings and placed them down next to his cufflinks. Then she removed the matching bracelet. He'd probably already guessed they weren't real, but she didn't care any more.

'Take off my shirt.'

Leonora stepped closer, some of her bravado faltering as she reached for his buttons and started undoing them, revealing his impressive chest. She hoped he wouldn't notice the faint tremor in her hands. When it was open, she pushed it back and looked. Her mouth went dry. He was more like a warrior than a civilised businessman. Hard muscles. Hair curling over his pectorals and descending in a dark line at the centre of a six-pack to disappear under the waistband of his trousers.

He tugged his shirt off completely, letting it drop to the floor. 'Now you. I want to see you.'

No one had ever seen Leonora naked. Not since she was a child. When she was a teenager, fooling around with boys at after-school parties, it had always been an awkward fumbling in the dark, under clothes. Not this stark *'I want to see you'* while standing in the golden glow of a lamp in front of the most intimidating man in the world. A connoisseur of women, by all accounts.

Before Leonora could overthink it she turned around, presenting Gabriel with her back and the zip to her dress. She pulled her hair over one shoulder and steeled herself for the moment she would feel his hands at her zip. But instead of going there first, his hands landed on her shoulders, and then she felt his breath at the back of her neck, before he pressed his mouth there, the moist tip of his tongue flicking out to taste her skin.

Her legs nearly gave way completely.

She was dealing with a consummate seducer—not an over-eager boy.

His hands trailed over her skin as if he had all the time in the world to learn her shape. Goosebumps popped up even though she was warm. *Hot*. Melting...

Then his hands moved to the top of her dress and he started to pull her zip down, all the way, until it stopped just above the curve of her buttocks. His knuckles brushed her skin there and it felt as intimate as if he'd kissed her.

The dress was loosened around her chest but she brought her arms up, stopping it from falling down.

'Turn around.'

Her heart pounding, Leonora turned. After a moment she looked up and saw Gabriel's face. It was...stark. Hungry. She shivered.

He put his hands on her arms and slowly pulled them apart. The dress stayed up for a moment and then, under its own weight, fell down to her waist. She wore a matching strapless bra. Red lace.

Gabriel let her arms go and reached behind her to undo her bra. It fell away to the floor before she could worry about him noticing how frayed and worn it was.

He looked at her for a long moment. Saying nothing. And then, 'You are more beautiful than anything I've ever imagined.'

Gabriel reached out and reverently cupped her breasts. Leonora had always felt self-conscious about their size, but they fitted Gabriel's palms perfectly. He rubbed his thumbs across her nipples and she had to bite her lip to stop herself from moaning out loud as they stiffened under his touch, almost to the point of pain.

He stopped for a moment, bringing his hands up to cup her face before seeking her mouth again and drawing her deep into a drugging kiss. Her hand clasped his wrist, needing something, anything, to root herself in this dream.

The friction of her bare breasts against his chest was sensory overload. But that was nothing... He stopped kissing her and trailed his mouth across her jaw and down the side of her neck to her shoulder, and then down to her breast. He cupped the plump flesh again and lifted it to his mouth, teasing her stiffened flesh with his tongue and teeth.

She couldn't stop the moan this time. It came out like a guttural plea to stop...never to stop...to keep going. Her hands were on his head, her fingers in his thick hair as he lavished the same torture on her other breast until they were both tingling and wet from his mouth.

When he stopped and lifted his head Leonora could barely keep standing. Gabriel pushed her dress down the rest of the way, over her hips. It fell to the floor with a barely audible swish of silk.

Now she wore only panties and stockings. Her shoes. She kicked them off, dropping a few inches in height. It made Gabriel seem even taller, more impressive.

Then, before she could worry about how to stay standing on her wobbly legs, she was lifted into the air against his chest and carried over to the bed, where he lay her down as reverently as if she was made of spun glass...

CHAPTER THREE

GABRIEL WASN'T SURE how he'd managed not to ravish Leonora before now, but he knew something was holding him back. Her reticence—which he felt sure had to be an act—was having an effect on him.

For a man who had slept with some of the world's most beautiful women, and who'd been sexually active since he was a teenager, he was finding lately that sexual liaisons had become merely satisfactory. More often than not disappointing. But here, now, he hadn't done much more than kiss Leonora and already he was having the most erotic experience he'd had in a long time. If ever.

His instincts about her had been right. She was exquisite. Every line of her body sleek and perfect. Her skin was like silk. Her breasts were perfectly shaped. And her nipples— His mouth watered again, just at the thought of how they'd tasted and stiffened against his tongue.

She was looking at him with huge eyes. As if she'd never seen a man before. Part of him was irritated that she could get to him with such a rudimentary act—was he so jaded that faux innocence turned him on?

Enough playacting.

Gabriel divested himself of the rest of his clothes.

* * *

Leonora watched as Gabriel efficiently undressed, revealing a body honed and densely muscled. And hard. She couldn't stop her eyes widening on his arousal, thick and long.

He came down on the bed, resting over her on both hands. She suddenly felt trepidatious. What if he noticed straight away how inexperienced she was? What if it hurt? What if he was too—?

'You don't have to do this, you know...'

He bent down and surrounded one still sensitised nipple in the hot wet heat of his mouth. Leonora's back arched.

She panted, 'What...? Do what...?'

He lifted his head, a sexy smile playing around his wicked mouth. 'Put on the innocent act. You don't have to play games to entice me, Leonora. I'm enticed.'

Before she could respond to that he was ministering the same exquisite torture to her other breast. *Act? What act?* She couldn't think straight. Not when he was massaging one breast with his fingers and nipping at the other with his teeth before soothing it with his tongue.

His tongue trailed down under her breasts to her belly, dipping into her navel before moving further. Leonora tensed as he came close to the juncture of her legs. He tucked his fingers under her panties and tugged. She lifted her bottom off the bed in silent acquiescence. He pulled them down her legs and off completely. Then one stocking and the other followed them to the floor.

Now she was totally naked—like him. And yet she didn't feel self-conscious. Just...hungry. Aching. Empty inside. As if something was missing.

He was looking at her, his eyes roving over her body, and her self-consciousness returned. She was suddenly acutely aware that she didn't conform to current beauty trends by waxing every inch of her body. But Gabriel wasn't looking remotely repulsed.

He came down beside her, his hand resting on the cluster of dark curls between her legs. 'I like a woman to look like a woman.'

He kissed her then, stopping any words or more coherent thoughts. The feeling of pleasure that he liked her as she was quickly became something far more urgent as he pushed her legs apart and his hand explored further, through those tight curls to the secret place where she ached for his touch.

She gasped into his mouth when his seeking fingers found her, wet and ready. He massaged her, stroking her with expert fingers into a level of excitement that had her arching off the bed, pleading incoherently for something just out of reach, a shimmering promise of ecstasy she could almost taste.

He was relentless, teasing her to the point where she thought she would die if he didn't just—

But then, with one deep thrust and a twist of his fingers, Leonora was finally released from the tension, and she soared high on a wave of pleasure so exquisite she cried out, her hands instinctively reaching for Gabriel's wrist to stop his movements, her throbbing flesh over-sensitised.

Gabriel looked down at Leonora, transfixed by the pleasure suffusing her face. Her skin was dewed with perspiration, her cheeks pink. When she looked at him her eyes were unfocused.

'That was... That was...'

He shook his head, trying to fathom how she could manufacture a response so...earthy. Responsive.

He answered for her. 'That was amazing.'

It had been. And he was literally hanging on to the last shred of his control. Seeing her like this, her breasts moving up and down jerkily with her breaths, long dark hair tumbled across the pillow, it was all he could do to find and roll on protection.

He settled between her legs, where the core of her body was still hot and damp. She looked at him, her mouth swollen from his kisses. He'd never seen a more erotic sight, had never felt such a visceral need to join with a woman.

He couldn't wait any longer.

He put his hands on her hips, positioned himself where she was so wet and ready, and plunged deep into the hottest, tightest embrace he'd ever known.

The sensation was so exquisite that he almost climaxed in that moment.

It was also unexpected.

She was innocent.

Unbelievably.

Her eyes were wide and shocked. He saw her silent entreaty to move…to do something to alleviate this alien sensation. And Gabriel could no more deny her that silent plea than he could force his mind back to some rational place and absorb this revelation fully.

It took supreme skill and control to claw himself back from the brink and move slowly in and out…

Leonora's brain was white-hot with the sudden pain of Gabriel's body thrusting into hers and now, as the pain ebbed, with the building of a whole new level of tension. He'd looked at her just now as if he'd realised she was a virgin, but to her profound relief he hadn't said anything…

She didn't want him to say a word to take them out of this moment. She was joined with this man who had taken her over, body and soul. He lifted her buttocks up, so he could deepen his thrusts, and every single part of her body spasmed with a wave of pleasure, cancelling out any last vestige of pain.

He caught her hands, both of them, and twined his fingers with hers. He brought them over her head and held them there as he moved in and out in a relentless rhythm that made her writhe against him, seeking release from the growing tension.

She could do nothing but hold on as he wound her so high she thought she would break into a million pieces—and then, with no warning, she did break apart, on a thrust so deep that she gasped at the majesty of his body pulsing deep inside hers. She saw an expression of almost pain on his face as he stared down at her, as if he'd never seen a woman before.

Wave upon wave of ecstasy racked her body. She could feel her inner muscles clamping around Gabriel's hard length. She was his captive of pleasure and yet she'd never felt more free as she soared on a high that was breathtaking.

He jerked against her and she bit her lip to stop crying out as yet another mini-orgasm wrenched her apart all over again.

She had been so totally unprepared for this overload of sensation that she didn't even notice when Gabriel extricated himself from her embrace, slipping into the deep oblivion of deep and total satisfaction...

When Leonora woke the faint light of dawn was painting its pink trails across the sky. It took her a second to absorb the fact that she wasn't in her own bed and that she felt different.

Because she was different.

She was no longer a virgin. She had been thoroughly initiated into the art of lovemaking by a master.

She turned her head and saw Gabriel's dark one beside her. Even in sleep he looked powerful. Her gaze moved down his naked body hungrily, lingering over the densely packed muscles of his abdomen and lower, to where his masculinity looked no less impressive at rest.

Her lower body clenched. After they'd made love that first time she'd fallen into a pleasure coma. And then she'd woken a couple of hours later with her bottom tucked into Gabriel's body, his growing erection stirring against her. He'd demonstrated that that wasn't the only way to bring about intense pleasure and had brought her slowly and inexorably back to life with his hands and his mouth, showing her that what had happened hadn't been a dream.

No. It hadn't been a dream.

It had been very much an explosive and transformative reality. She held the sheet to her body, going cold inside as the full significance of the night sank in. Just hours ago she'd been about to be publicly betrothed to Lazaro Sanchez. And yet here she was, having been thoroughly bedded by a totally different man.

This behaviour was so out of character for her. She hadn't even kissed Lazaro beyond one chaste kiss on the lips. And yet she'd spent mere hours in Gabriel's company and tumbled into bed with him with barely a moment's hesitation.

She'd felt responsible for so long—since her parents had lost everything when she was a teenager—that she'd almost forgotten what it was like to want something just for herself. And now she felt supremely selfish. The paparazzi had probably been camped outside the *castillo* all night, while she'd been here indulging in sheer sensual decadence.

She felt as if millennia had passed since the previous day, when she'd set out from her home ready to commit to Lazaro Sanchez. And here she was in another man's bed.

She put a hand to her burning face.

She thought of how Gabriel had looked at her with that single-minded intensity. No one had ever looked at her like that before. As if they truly *saw* her. As a woman. Independent of her name and the scandal that had rocked her family.

And then she cursed herself.

Gabriel Torres was an experienced man of the world. A consummate lover. He probably looked at all his lovers like that. She was just one in a long line. She'd intrigued him last night, but even if he hadn't figured out she'd been a virgin she doubted very much he'd be expecting to see her again.

Terrified that he would wake and look at her, and see how profoundly he'd affected her, she stole out of the bed as quietly as she could. She held her breath when he moved, saying something incomprehensible in his sleep. When he didn't wake Leonora gathered up her things and tiptoed out of the bedroom, finding a guest suite down the hall where she dressed and repaired herself as best she could.

She avoided looking at herself in the mirror. She tried to ignore the tenderness between her legs. But then she caught a glimpse of the redness around her jaw and neck. The burn from Gabriel's stubble. The burn of shame.

She quickly pulled her hair back and tied it into a rough bun. She put her wrap around herself, hiding as much of the evidence of the passion of the night as possible. Then she crept out of the apartment and down to the lobby, where she got the concierge to call her a taxi.

Thankfully she didn't have to wait long. As it drove through the quiet early-morning streets she took a deep, shuddering breath, hating the awful bereft feeling stealing over her.

She thought of the man sprawled sexily in bed in his stunning apartment. He would wake up and get on with his life and not think about her again. Of that she was sure. Last night would barely register on his radar. How could it when she'd been such a novice?

She'd made a pact with the devil, agreeing to sleep with Gabriel Torres, telling herself that one night would be enough. Because now the empty feeling inside her mocked her. One night with Gabriel Torres had ruined her for ever.

Gabriel woke slowly, through layers of a deep sense of satisfaction. Not just any satisfaction. Sexual satisfaction. It was a long time since he'd felt like this.

His mouth curved into a smile as images came tumbling back into his head. Long dark hair, elegant curves, high, firm breasts with deliciously hard nipples... Brown curls covering the apex between her legs—the place where he'd lost himself and found ecstasy. The best sex he'd ever had.

With a virgin.

His eyes snapped open on that thought and he jack-knifed up in the bed, instantly awake.

She'd been a virgin.

He hadn't been able to process that information fully in the midst of the hottest experience of his life. She hadn't asked him to stop. She'd entreated him to go on with those huge grey eyes. And he'd tipped over the edge of his legendary control.

Uncomfortably, he had to concede now that he didn't think it had been her innocence that had elevated the experience beyond the realms of normality. It had been *her*. And their unique chemistry. He'd had no idea it would be so explosive.

Where was she?

There was a stillness in the bedroom that extended out into the apartment. He stood up from the bed and pulled on a pair of jeans, and only then noticed that it was bright outside. Already morning. He could hear the faint hum of city traffic.

He felt discombobulated. He always woke at dawn, if not before. He never slept in.

He padded through the apartment, an uneasy and unfamiliar feeling of exposure sliding into his gut.

There was no sign of her. Literally no sign. Had he dreamt it all? Then he saw the small tumbler that still held some alcohol. He didn't like the sense of relief.

He went back into his bedroom and something glinted in the morning light on his cabinet. Her jewellery. She'd left it behind. He went over and picked it up and recognised instantly that it wasn't real. Costume jewellery. To create a façade.

Leonora Flores de la Vega. The heiress with nothing to her name except her name. And her astonishing beauty. A virgin who'd left him behind in his bed.

No woman ever left him. *He* left women. And no woman left him with this hungry, clawing ache of need.

Even after only one night he could sense that the more he had of her, the more he would want. Unprecedented. One night with her was not enough. Not nearly enough.

As he stood under the powerful spray of his shower a few minutes later Gabriel knew that Leonora Flores was not like his usual women. There was a wildness under her serene exterior and it resonated with something inside him—a wild streak he never allowed to surface in his day-to-day life, when he had to be supremely controlled and on guard at all times. Too many people depended on him.

He'd been her first lover. And he couldn't deny that, along with the erotic charge he felt thinking of that, he also felt something else totally uncharacteristic. *Possessive.* It had been there the previous evening too, when he'd felt the electric current between them as she'd stood beside Sanchez with his arm around her waist.

Gabriel emerged from the shower and slung a towel around his waist. He caught a glimpse of himself in the mirror over the sink and stopped, looking long and hard at his reflection. He was thirty-three years old. He'd been ignoring his advisors' not so subtle whispers for some time now. Whispers that had been getting more insistent. Whispers about settling down. Putting forward a more respectable image. Being a family man.

Something lodged in Gabriel's gut at that thought. *Family man.* He'd always known that he would have to have a family some day. After all, he was the last in his line. But after his emotionally sterile upbringing, with two parents who had despised each other, he'd never relished the prospect.

And he'd never fully admitted to himself that while the thought of a family terrified him on one level, on another he'd always wondered if he could do it any differently? He'd grown up with one assertion—never to bring children into this world and leave them to their fate as his own parents had.

His younger sister had suffered more than he had, and he still felt guilty that he hadn't noticed her descent into chaos. But by then he'd been the only thing holding the Cruz y Torres empire together...

Both his parents had conducted extramarital affairs for as long as he could remember, and he'd routinely witnessed them lying to each other about their activities to the point when it had become farcical.

Gabriel was ashamed to recall that when he had been much younger, he'd had a fantasy of a relationship far removed from what he'd seen with his parents. Uncynical. Respectful. Kind. But life had shown him that he was a fool to have such dreams when he'd found his first lover in bed with his so-called best friend.

She'd told Gabriel she'd seduced his friend to make Gabriel jealous. He'd thrown his lover and his best friend out, and from that day forward had ruthlessly quashed his silly teenage fantasies.

But perhaps he had finally met someone with whom he could envisage embarking on the next phase of his life. He wasn't such a fool as to equate physical innocence with honesty, but there was something special and unique about Leonora Flores de la Vega.

She was stunningly beautiful, and she oozed elegance and class in spite of the fact that she was all but penniless. They had the most insane chemistry Gabriel had ever experienced with a woman.

And clearly, if she'd been prepared to marry Lazaro Sanchez, she was in the market for marriage.

The thought of her with that man made Gabriel's hands clench into fists. His expression in the mirror turned hard.

Sanchez had obviously been ready to make a lifelong commitment in a bid to garner respect. Perhaps it was a sign that Gabriel finally needed to deal with something he'd been pushing away for a long time. Saying a curt *Not yet* whenever another advisor tentatively mentioned the notion of settling down.

But maybe 'not yet' had become now.

Leonora Flores de la Vega was perfect on every level for what he envisaged in a marriage. He had never been so old-fashioned as to have expected a virginal wife, but he couldn't deny that her innocence appealed to a deeply masculine part of him. As did the knowledge that she hadn't slept with Sanchez.

She was from *their* world. She knew how these marriages worked. And after last night he didn't have to worry about compatibility.

Last night he hadn't seduced Leonora for any other reason than because he wanted her. Sanchez had been the last person on his mind. But now...

He relished the perfection of timing and serendipity. And the opportunity to show Lazaro Sanchez in a very comprehensive way that a woman like Leonora Flores de la Vega was out of his league.

For ever.

When Leonora arrived back at the *castillo* after driving Matías back to his school, she found her mother waiting for her, looking pale and agitated.

'What is it? Is it Papá?'

Leonora always had the fear that something would set her father off again. Something like this—his daughter getting jilted in public by her fiancé.

Her mother shook her head. 'No, nothing like that. Papá is having a nap. You got a phone call...from Gabriel Torres. He wants you to call him back.'

Her mother was handing her a note with a number on it before Leonora could fully register it. It had been two days since that cataclysmic night. Two days of feeling alternately shocked and shamed and giddy at what had happened. And two days of the knowledge sinking in that of *course* Gabriel wasn't going to be chasing her down.

Except now butterflies exploded in her belly. Along with a far more carnal tug of awareness. And the man wasn't even here.

She looked at the number. A cell phone number.

Her mother gripped her arm. 'Oh, Leo—*Gabriel Torres*. You must have made an impression.'

Leonora's face burned and she avoided her mother's eye. She'd been vague about Gabriel's involvement the other night, making it sound as if he'd just offered her a place to hide out. But she knew he'd offered her so much more. And delivered.

She scrabbled for something to say. 'Mamá, I'm sure he's getting in touch for something quite boring. Let me go and call him back.'

Her mother shooed her off, two bright pink spots in her cheeks, making her look girlish for her fifty-four years.

Leonora's insides cramped as she went into the castle's office, the administrative centre where they took bookings for tours. Tours that were falling increasingly in numbers because people inevitably wanted to experience something more exciting than just walking around a dusty medieval castle full of antiques and scary-looking portraits of long-dead ancestors and a tired and wilted walled garden.

Her family's dependence on her sat heavily on her shoulders today. She'd just had a painful conversation at Matías's school about overdue fees.

She sat down at the desk and put the piece of paper in front of her. She pulled her cell phone out of her pocket and keyed in his number. For an age she sat there, a little paralysed at the thought of hearing that deep rumble of a voice again.

Then, before she could lose her nerve, she pressed the key and after a second heard the long ring tone.

The call was picked up almost immediately with an impatient, brusque tone. *'Sí?'*

She almost cut off the connection, he sounded so forbidding, and then his tone changed and he said sharply, 'Leonora, is that you?'

She gulped. 'Yes, it's me.'

'Thank you for calling me back.'

She thought she detected a dry tone in his voice. She didn't imagine he had many women doing a disappearing act on him.

'I'm sorry for...for leaving the way I did the other morning... but I felt it was for the best.'

'For who? You? Or me...?'

Leonora squirmed in the chair. 'Both of us... It was—'

She stopped. She'd been about to say *just a moment out of time*, but that sounded far too whimsical.

'It was just one night.'

'An incredible night.'

His voice was low and it seemed to rumble down the phone and across Leonora's skin. Her mouth went dry and her palms got clammy just thinking about it.

Then he said, 'I'd like to take you out for dinner.'

Leonora pushed aside the X-rated memories. 'Dinner?'

'Yes...' He sounded amused.

'When?'

'Tonight. I'll pick you up at seven.'

'I...'

'Do you have plans, Leonora?'

Was it her imagination or was there a mocking tone in his voice now? Of course she didn't have plans—other than the endless worrying about what was to become of them.

She tried to sound as nonchalant as possible. 'No, I don't have plans this evening.'

He became brisk again. 'Good. I'll see you at seven.'

CHAPTER FOUR

BY ALMOST SEVEN that evening Leonora was a bag of nerves at the thought of seeing Gabriel again after sharing such intimacies, and also wondering what he wanted. A repeat of that night? Or was he just intrigued because she wasn't like his usual lovers?

The thought had slid into her mind over the past couple of days...wondering if he'd noticed her innocence. But he hadn't said anything. And certainly any pain had been fleeting.

She tensed when she heard the low purr of a powerful engine and crunching gravel, not remotely ready to see the man again.

Liar.

She went to the window and peeked out, feeling like a coward. She watched him step out of a low-slung sports car—a different one from the other night. This was black.

He was dressed semi-casually, in dark trousers and a lighter toned long-sleeved top. She could imagine the material was expensive, the way it moulded to the muscles of his chest as he came around the car.

He looked stern. Austere. But then she remembered how he'd smiled wickedly. Sexily. Her insides spasmed.

She was about to go into the hall to answer the door when he rang the bell, but just then she heard quick footsteps cross the marbled hall and cursed silently. Her mother. Seizing on the opportunity to meet the man who had been Leonora's knight in shining armour the other night.

Her mother's disapproval of Lazaro Sanchez's behaviour, as compared to the gallant actions of one of their own, had spoken volumes about what she'd really thought of Leonora's first fiancé. And yet, Leonora thought cynically, her mother would have been only too happy to have Lazaro's money paying off their debts and restoring their reputation.

The front door opened and Leonora heard voices—her mother's too high and girlish, and Gabriel's much lower. A light sweat broke out on her brow. She wished there was a mirror to check her reflection again.

Her black silk shirt dress with its wide belt had at one time been fashionable, with its thigh-high slit, but now she was afraid it was far too provocative and out of date. She touched the buttons again, to make sure they were done up as far as they could go—which didn't feel high enough. And should she have put her hair up?

Footsteps approached and she realised she was clasping her hands like a schoolteacher. She unclasped them just before the door opened.

Leonora only saw Gabriel, filling the doorway as if this massive house had been built around him.

Her mother said redundantly, 'Leo, Mr Torres is here.'

Leonora moved forward, shaky in high heels. For a ridiculous moment she wasn't sure if she should put out her hand to shake his, but then he reached for her, taking her shoulders in his hands and bending down to kiss her on each cheek.

His scent caught her unawares, hurtling her back in time to the other evening. She put her hands up to his arms—in a bid to stay standing as much as anything else.

'Señorita de la Vega. Thank you for agreeing to come and have dinner with me.'

There was a tone in his voice that made her look at him. Intimate. Complicit. It sent a flash of heat between her legs.

He straightened up and let her go. 'Shall we?'

Leonora gave her mother a quick kiss and walked out ahead of Gabriel while he exchanged a few parting words with her mother. He came out and opened the passenger door of the car, waiting until she got in. She tried to gather herself as he came around the car and got in.

He sat behind the wheel. But instead of starting the car he looked at her and said, *'Leo?'*

It took her a second to understand his meaning. 'Matías called me Leo when he was small. It kind of stuck...in spite of my father's distaste for shortening names.'

Leonora couldn't look away from those mesmerising gold-flecked eyes. His jaw was clean-shaven, but she could still remember the way her skin had felt so tender after kissing him. It had burned. Like she burned now...deep inside.

'Leo...' he said. Slowly. Testing it out. And then, 'I like it. It suits you. Makes me think of a lioness.'

His mouth curved into a small smile and then he turned the ignition on and drove down the drive and out of the property.

Leonora was breathless. So much for trying to regain her composure. She'd never thought driving a car could be considered sexy, but watching the way Gabriel drove, with nonchalant confidence, was undeniably compelling.

She was able to study him as he drove, taking in the thick hair swept back off his forehead. The long aquiline nose, more than hinting at his exclusive lineage. The hard jaw and that sensual mouth, made for sin. And that powerful body. Hard and honed. Not an ounce of spare muscle.

A warrior's body in the guise of a very modern man. All in all, an intoxicating package.

He glanced at her and she looked away, face burning. She realised her thigh was bared in the slit of the dress and hurriedly pulled it together, holding it with her hand.

'I've seen your thigh, Leonora.'

Her face burned hotter. She didn't know how to handle this... this flirting.

She blurted out, 'The other night... It wasn't... I don't usually behave like that.'

Something shifted in the atmosphere as Gabriel pulled up smoothly to a red traffic light. She risked a look at him and saw he was staring straight ahead, hands on the wheel.

'I thought as much,' he said after a moment, the car moving forward again.

Now she felt even more exposed. Clearly her inexperience had been woefully obvious. But hopefully not the full extent of it.

'Why didn't you tell me you were a virgin?'

Leonora felt the blood drain from her face. From hot to cold in seconds. 'How did you know?' she asked through bloodless lips.

Thankfully Gabriel needed to focus on the traffic, so he was looking ahead and not at her.

'Because I've never slept with a virgin before.'

Leonora wanted to slip down in the seat and disappear altogether, drowning in a pool of humiliation. But she forced herself to sit straight.

'Why did you ask me out this evening if you know I'm such a novice? I'm sure there are many women who can provide more experienced entertainment.'

She felt him glance at her but she stared straight ahead.

'You misunderstand me, Leonora. I did not say this was a negative thing.' He waited a moment and then he said, in a low voice that rubbed along every nerve-ending, 'In fact it was the most erotic experience of my life.'

That made Leonora even more rigid. 'If you've asked me out because I'm some kind of novelty to you—' Her flow of words halted when Gabriel swung abruptly into a layby and he came to a stop.

She looked at him and he turned to face her, the car idling. He looked stern and she swallowed.

'I did not ask you out because you're a novelty. I asked you out because I desire you very much.'

His gaze dropped to her mouth and he muttered something unintelligible to himself. Then, before she knew what was happening, he closed the distance between them, snaked a hand under her hair to the back of her neck and his mouth was on hers, possessing her so thoroughly that by the time he broke the kiss she was pressed against him, hands clutching at his jacket.

She was gasping, dizzy. After mere seconds. Her mouth throbbed. His kiss had been swift and explicitly sexual.

He raised a brow. 'That is no novelty. That is the kind of chemistry and desire that comes along very rarely. Trust me. And I want much more than one night with you, Leonora— much more.'

Leonora couldn't speak as Gabriel pulled back out into the traffic as if nothing had happened, his enigmatic comment reverberating in her head.

I want much more than one night...

What was he proposing? An affair? For her to become his mistress?

Everything in her balked at that because she knew she was not mistress material. She was a world away from the sophisticated women of the world he would know, in spite of her privileged upbringing. Until they'd lost all that privilege.

But then maybe he was only talking in terms of days...weeks. Gabriel Torres didn't flaunt his affairs. He was discretion personified—which was largely how he'd built up such a mythical reputation. And a man like him wouldn't be satisfied with one woman for long.

It was only when she saw that they were veering away from the city centre that she asked, 'Where are we going?'

He glanced at her and she felt it like a searing brand. *Dios.*

'We're going to my home. My family home.'

'Castillo Torres?'

Leonora was immediately intimidated. She'd visited the estate a few times in her lifetime, for social events with her parents. That long-ago polo match. Fundraisers. Galas. She hadn't been in a long time, but she remembered it as being a huge and intimidatingly grand place.

In comparison, it made her own family *castillo* look like a cosy country cottage.

'Yes. I trust that is okay?'

Leonora nodded. 'Of course.'

The truth was that even if he'd taken her to a busy restaurant full of people it wouldn't have lessened his intensity, or his power to intimidate. Maybe this was how he flew under the radar? He kept his liaisons confined to his elegant apartment or the *castillo*. Well out of the public eye.

Leonora didn't like to think that she was the latest in a long line of women who had been invited back to the *castillo*, but she told herself she was being ridiculous. There was a long line of women before her and there would undoubtedly be a long line after her. She didn't see a man like Gabriel Torres settling down to a life of domesticity any time soon.

She couldn't even imagine him in such a milieu.

He was turning off the main road now, onto a smaller road which led to a huge set of iron gates that opened automatically as soon as they drove up to them. Gabriel lowered his window and saluted the security guard in the box on the other side of the gate.

Leonora's family used to have security at their *castillo*—not any more. There was nothing of value left.

They drove in and Leonora tried not to let her jaw drop at the verdant splendour of the grounds. Tall trees lined the drive and beyond she could see lush landscaped lawns and blooming bougainvillea.

The winding drive opened into a massive courtyard with a fountain in the middle, behind which the *castillo* rose majestically. Not unlike Leonora's home, but on a far grander scale, it had a distinctly Moorish shape. And she noticed immediately that it was in pristine condition, which made her heart ache as she acknowledged how far her family had fallen.

Gabriel stopped the car at the bottom of the steps leading up to the main door. He got out and came around the bonnet, opening Leonora's door and helping her out.

A young man materialised seemingly out of nowhere and Gabriel tossed him the keys, asking him at the same time how his exams had gone.

The young man grinned and said, 'Passed them all, boss!'

Gabriel responded, 'Good for you,' and the young man jumped into the car and drove it around to the back of the *castillo*—presumably to a garage similar to the one under Gabriel's apartment, filled with expensive sports cars.

Keeping her hand in his, Gabriel led her up the steps. The door opened as they approached, as if by magic, and a uniformed butler bowed to them as she stepped over the threshold.

Gabriel said, 'Ernesto I'd like you to meet Leonora Flores de la Vega. Leonora, this is Ernesto, the only person holding this whole place together.'

'Not true, sir, but thank you. Señorita de la Vega, pleased to meet you.'

He bowed again and Leonora was charmed. She smiled shyly, 'Lovely to meet you too.'

She liked the way Gabriel acknowledged his staff. She was ashamed to remember how her parents had treated their own as very much beneath them. And now they had none. Karma?

Her hand was still in Gabriel's as he led her through a vast stone hall and out to an inner courtyard with a pool filled with colourful fish and lotus flowers. Stone pillars around the edges led up to a balcony running around the space.

Then they walked through to the other side and back into the main building, where another reception area led off to more rooms and a grand staircase up to the first level.

'This is...beautiful. I was here before, but only in the grounds.'

Gabriel stopped walking and grimaced as he looked around them. 'I've been working on bringing it into the modern era. For years it was dark and dank, full of useless antiques and mouldering paintings of long-dead relatives.'

Leonora couldn't help a small wry smile. 'That sounds like *my* family home.'

She caught Gabriel's eye and his gaze dropped to her mouth. Suddenly he looked...*hungry.* Leonora's heart thumped. Was he going to kiss her right here? Now? She wasn't ready—

But then the look on his face passed and he kept walking, saying, 'It's a painstaking and expensive process. I've been working on this for the last decade and we're not nearly finished.'

Leonora stayed silent, following where he led her, through a confusing labyrinth of corridors. She could see now why he might like his very sparse and elegant city apartment. It was a direct contrast to what he'd grown up with. That was why *she'd* liked it.

A sense of affinity struck her again...disconcerting.

They were approaching the end of the corridor now, and Gabriel pushed open a door which led into a massive drawing room, full of light and huge windows that looked out over the back of the *castillo*. All she could see was acres of lush green, trees, and what looked like an orchard in the distance.

'We grow lemons and olives here. Sell them to an organic company. Part of my restoration is an attempt to make the *castillo* and its grounds as self-sufficient and environmentally friendly as possible.'

He let her hand go and went over to a drinks cabinet.

Leonora said wistfully, 'That's what I'd love to do too. The day when these kinds of buildings can justify themselves by merely existing has surely ended.'

He cast her a look over his shoulder. 'Exactly.'

He came back then, with a glass of what looked like champagne in one hand and water in the other.

He handed her the tall elegant flute and said, 'Dinner will be ready in a short while, but first I have a proposal to put to you.'

Leonora took a sip of champagne and it fizzed down her throat. She swallowed, genuinely intrigued. 'A proposal?'

He looked at her carefully. 'Yes, Leonora. A proposal. Of marriage.'

CHAPTER FIVE

A PROPOSAL OF MARRIAGE. If Leonora had still had some of the champagne in her mouth or her throat she would have choked or spat it out. The shock of his words thumped her in the gut. She felt winded.

He was just looking at her. Assessing. As if he *hadn't* just said the most audacious thing she'd ever heard. A sliver of ice went down her back when she thought of the possibility that she might have hallucinated briefly.

'Did you just say—?'

He cut in smoothly. 'That I'm proposing marriage? Yes, I did.'

Leonora clutched the glass as if it was a lifeline. Her brain wouldn't seem to work. It felt sluggish.

'Do you...? *Why?*'

'For many reasons—chief of which is because I think we'd be a good match. I've known for some time now that I need to settle down, but it's always been an unpalatable prospect...until we met and connected.'

Connected.

Leonora's head was suddenly filled with X-rated images of them in bed, limbs entangled, his powerful body thrusting in and out of hers, transporting her to heights of ecstasy she'd dreamed about every night since.

Something else struck her and she felt slightly sick. 'Is this just because I was a…a virgin? Maybe you're old-fashioned and that kind of thing—'

He held a hand up, eyes sparking. 'Stop right there. This has nothing to do with your sexual innocence.' He lowered his hand. 'Although I have to admit that knowing I was your first lover is incredibly satisfying in a way that I never would have thought possible.'

Leonora's insides clenched. She had to admit that losing her innocence under the expert tutelage of Gabriel hadn't exactly been *un*satisfying. Far from it. But…*marriage*? And yet why should it be such an alien concept when she'd agreed to marry someone else only recently?

She struggled to understand Gabriel's motivation. 'But I'm not remotely suitable.'

He frowned. 'You couldn't be *more* suitable for my require-ments.'

Requirements.

A cold weight lodged in her chest. And it mocked her. Be-cause she realised that for a moment she'd fantasised that this might be a proposal stemming from emotion. Feelings. When she'd never even considered that with Lazaro Sanchez.

But you didn't sleep with him, reminded a small voice.

Leonora lifted her chin. 'Do I need to remind you that my family are considered pariahs in society? We haven't been in-vited to an event in years. I don't see you sullying the Cruz y Torres name by association with us.'

In answer he pulled out his phone from his trouser pocket and after a few seconds handed it to her, 'Have you seen this?'

'This' was a grainy paparazzi picture of her getting into his car that night outside the hotel. She looked like a rabbit caught in the headlights and he was staring directly down the lens of the camera, defiantly.

She handed it back, feeling sick. 'I tend to avoid looking at those websites or their headlines, considering my family were their sole fodder at one time.'

'I'm showing it to you to illustrate my point that I really don't care what anyone thinks of us getting together.'

Leonora looked at him. 'What would your parents think?'

Gabriel's expression hardened. 'My parents are not remotely involved in the running of my life and haven't been since before I came of age. If anything, I run *their* lives. My father spends most of his time in his city townhouse and at this point in time I'm not even sure where my mother is—she usually has the decency to conduct her illicit liaisons in discreet locations. They have no jurisdiction over me.'

Leonora shivered slightly, recalling how serious he'd been at twenty-one. No wonder, if he'd been running a massive business on his own.

'Don't you have a sister? Younger than you?'

His expression immediately softened. The cold weight in Leonora's chest warmed slightly.

'Yes. Estella. The bane of my existence.'

And yet clearly she wasn't, if that softened look was anything to go by.

Intrigued, Leonora asked, 'Where is she?'

'She's in New York, working as a model. She went through a rough patch a few years ago. Fell in with the wrong people. But she's doing really well now.'

The pride in his voice was evident. Then his focus came back to Leonora.

He said, 'Your family might have fallen from grace due to your father's actions, but whose grace? And who else hasn't? I despise that hypocrisy.'

At that moment there was a discreet knock on the door and Leonora looked around to see Ernesto enter. 'Dinner is ready, Señor Torres.'

'Thank you, we'll be right there.'

Leonora turned back to Gabriel, still feeling slightly winded, absorbing his words. She would never have expected him not to care about his family's reputation, but conceded cynically that he had that luxury because they were so powerful.

He said, 'I know you weren't expecting this when I brought you here, but I don't believe in playing games, Leonora. Life is too short. You're the first woman I've ever brought to the *castillo*. And you're the first woman I've ever proposed to.'

Gabriel was not used to being unable to read a woman easily. Usually they were so *unsubtle*. But Leonora was like the Sphinx. All cool and serene. He'd put a marriage proposal to her and she'd recovered quickly after her initial shock.

Their dinner plates had just been cleared away by his housekeeper and he asked, 'Did you go to university?'

A faint wash of colour came into her cheeks. She avoided looking at him and he had to curb the urge to tip her chin up so she had no choice. Once again, not usually an issue for him with women.

She shook her head. 'No. I wanted to do a business degree, but by the time I left school…things had changed. Matías was in school, but he came home every weekend and he needed me. And I had to work at the *castillo*—try to get it to make us some money.'

'I can imagine that experience probably taught you as much as a business degree.'

Leonora smiled ruefully. 'Perhaps, although it hasn't exactly been a resounding success. The *castillo* needs serious investment—like what you're doing here.'

Gabriel seized the opportunity she'd presented him with. 'I can help you with that kind of investment, Leonora.'

Now she looked at him, eyes wide, the flush in her face deepening. She stuttered, 'That isn't… I didn't mean to make it sound like—'

'I know you didn't. I'm merely stating a fact. If you become my wife, naturally your security and your family's, and the restoration of your *castillo*, become my responsibility.'

His cool, emotionless logic and the word *responsibility* made something snap inside Leonora. She blurted out, 'Why do you want to marry now?'

He sat back and looked at her. 'To be perfectly honest, because you're the first woman I've met who has inspired me to consider it.'

Leonora felt light-headed. 'Me? I inspired you?'

She really wasn't that special.

'I always knew I'd have to marry. I'm the last in my line. Not marrying and not having a family isn't an option for me. But it's something I've preferred not to think about. Until now.'

'But if it was an option you'd prefer not to?'

'I don't deal in *what ifs* or unknowns. I deal with reality, and this is my reality. And yours too, Leonora. Or are you going to tell me your engagement to Sanchez was born out of emotion or desire?'

Leonora flushed. 'No, of course not.'

She felt exposed, and tense. He knew full well she hadn't slept with Lazaro.

A sense of something that felt like hurt compelled her to push back. 'What makes you think I'm available? Just because I agreed to marry Lazaro? The other night you were reminding me that we're bound by duty and responsibility, but maybe I want more than that. Maybe I don't want to just become someone's *responsibility*.'

Or, maybe, she realised in the same split second, she didn't want to become Gabriel Torres's responsibility, because already she was feeling things for him that were dangerous and disturbing.

Gabriel sat forward. 'Are you telling me that you hadn't agreed to let Lazaro Sanchez take responsibility for your family's debts?'

At that moment the housekeeper came back into the room with a tray that held coffee for Gabriel and tea for Leonora.

Without taking his gaze from Leonora's, Gabriel said, 'We'll take it in the lounge, thank you, Tulia.'

He stood up and Leonora followed his lead from the dining room, glad of a momentary reprieve from the growing tension.

They followed the housekeeper into another surprisingly airy room, adjacent to the dining room. Sunset was bathing everything in a pink and golden hue. The furniture was classic, elegant. Timeless.

The woman set the tray down on a coffee table between two couches.

Gabriel said, 'Thank you, Tulia. That will be all.'

The woman left the room.

Gabriel said, 'Please, sit down.'

Leonora hesitated for a moment, torn between telling Gabriel that she wanted to leave, so she could get out of his disturbing orbit, and the stronger pull to stay. Hear him out.

Let him seduce you again?

Leonora sat down quickly before he might see the turmoil he'd unleashed inside her. Before he could see the want. Even now, despite his disturbing proposition. *Proposal.*

Thankfully he sat down on the opposite couch. She felt as if she could get her breath back and gather her wits as long as he kept his distance. She picked up her cup of tea and took a sip, hoping it would ground her.

He seemed to be waiting for her to speak. It unnerved her. She hadn't had so much focused attention on her from anyone, ever. And from a man like Gabriel Torres it was more than a little overwhelming.

She looked at him. He was sitting back, holding his tiny espresso cup in one big hand but looking no less masculine. One arm was stretched out along the couch, pulling his top tight across his tautly muscled chest.

She swallowed. *Focus.*

'Why do you want to marry me when you could marry any number of far more suitable women?'

He took his arm down and sat forward. A muscle ticked in his jaw. 'Why are you resisting my proposal when you agreed to marry a man you hadn't even slept with?'

Leonora tensed even more—so much that she felt as if she might splinter into a million tiny pieces. It was precisely because she'd slept with Gabriel that she was resisting this proposal. Because she was still reeling after what had happened and how explosive it had been.

She put her cup down and stood up, pride stiffening her spine. 'Maybe I should go. Just because I agreed to marry one man, it does not mean that I'm automatically going to agree to marry the next man who asks me.'

She turned, but stopped when she felt Gabriel's hand on her arm. Gentle, but with enough force to stop her. Reluctantly she faced him, and he let her arm go. She was surprised to see an expression of humility on his face.

'Wait—please.'

He ran a hand through his hair, mussing it up. It gave him a more approachable air. Less stern. Despite herself, Leonora felt something inside her weaken.

He said, 'I haven't articulated myself very well. Just hear me out...please?'

Leonora had the sense that this didn't happen very often with a man like Gabriel. She nodded her head slightly and sat down.

He sat down again too, but sat forward, with his hands clasped between his legs. He looked at her.

'It was not my intention to make you feel as though I thought of you as a wife for hire, based on your recent history. As I told you, there's been pressure on me for some time to marry and start a family, but no woman has ever made me feel remotely inclined to do so—until the other night and *you*. Every moment in your company only makes me feel more sure that this is the right decision for both of us.'

Leonora cursed him silently. His deep mesmeric voice was drawing her in, making it all sound so reasonable. Logical.

'You know this world, Leo, and you know how to navigate it. I think you share my disdain for it, and yet understand that we need it too. We are bound to it whether we like it or not.'

Leo. She should feel irritated by the way he'd shortened her name—only ever done by her family—but, dammit, she *liked* it. It felt intimate in a way that it didn't feel with her family. Private.

'You and your family need urgent financial help. Matías can't afford to stay at that school for ever. And what will you do if the bank takes your *castillo* as payment for the debts still outstanding?'

Leonora went cold inside. 'How do you know about Matías's school?'

'I know someone with a child in that school, so I know how expensive it is.'

Leonora refused to let herself feel vulnerable. 'I'm sure if we lost everything and Matías had to come out of the school we'd manage.'

'I don't doubt *you* would. But would they? Your parents? Who have only known a life of privilege and luxury, even in spite of what's happened? And would Matías survive without the care of special teachers and assistants? You'd have to work—you wouldn't be there all the time.'

Leonora knew he was right. Her parents would never survive in the real world, in a small apartment—if they were lucky enough even to get one. Neither would Matías. She had less sympathy for her parents, but Matías… She'd do anything for him. To keep him safe and secure.

Gabriel said, 'And there's something else you're not acknowledging.'

His voice was lower. Seductive. Leonora really wanted to avoid his dark, knowing gaze, but she couldn't.

She feigned nonchalance even as her skin tingled with anticipation. 'What's that?'

She knew, though.

She knew with every gathering rush of heat that pulsed through her body.

'We want each other.'

Just that. Stark. To the point.

'I don't like to play games, Leonora, life is too short.'

'And believe me,' he said, 'that's as solid a reason as any to embark on marriage. We have social compatibility and mutual chemistry. A powerful combination.'

Not really understanding why she felt such a need to resist his pull, Leonora said, 'But it won't last—it never does, does it? And what then?'

Gabriel raised a brow. 'This wasn't a concern of yours when you agreed to marry Sanchez? A man you hadn't even slept with?'

Leonora stood up abruptly, feeling cornered. She paced away to a window that took in the expanse of the *castillo*'s impressive back lawn. She was being a total hypocrite—she knew she was. And she was deluding herself. She *did* know why she was resisting his pull. But how could she explain that she had found it easier to agree to marry a man she hadn't been intimate with, who she hadn't even wanted, than *this* man, with whom she had been intimate and who she did want, with a hunger that made her feel so many things it was overwhelming?

She realised that Gabriel was infinitely more disturbing to her on so many levels because he affected not only her equilibrium, physically, but also her emotions. She'd grown up in a world where you kept your emotions hidden behind a polite front.

Her parents had never really approved of Leonora and Matías's affectionate relationship. But Matías didn't understand about keeping his emotions hidden and Leonora loved him for that. When her parents had sent Matías to the special school they'd told her that it was because he was becoming too attached to her. Too dependent. She'd always felt guilty that her need for his uncomplicated love and affection was the reason he'd been sent away, and while she knew now that he'd been sent away for lots of other reasons, to do with his own self-development in the right environment, she still felt guilty about that need in her for emotional sustenance. As if it was a weakness.

And that was why Gabriel scared her. Because he touched on those needs and wants inside her. That was why it had been easy to say yes to Lazaro. Because he hadn't disturbed her emotions on any level...

Gabriel looked at Leonora's graceful, willowy form. She oozed elegance in spite of the tense lines of her body. She was perfect. For him. For his life. And yet she resisted.

Irritation spiked in his gut when he thought of how she'd been willing to marry Sanchez with far less to go on.

He stood up and walked over to stand beside her. Her arms were crossed tightly over her chest. The irritation got stronger.

Before he could stop himself he said, 'Were you in love with Sanchez? Is that what this is about?'

She turned to look at him and he saw shock on her face. 'No! How can you even ask that? You really think I would have slept with you if I'd loved him?'

Gabriel didn't like the way her words soothed something jagged inside him. *Jealousy.*

She bit her lip. 'I just... I'm ashamed to admit it now, but I think I found it easier to make a commitment to him because it felt like a sterile business agreement. It's not as if I'm under any illusions. I know that people like us have to marry for reasons that are far removed from love...but I hadn't expected that I would...*want* my husband.'

Gabriel clenched his hand into a fist by his side to avoid reaching out to touch her. She reminded him of a nervy foal. Ready to bolt at the slightest sound.

'Is that such a bad thing?'

She looked at him and her eyes were dark pools of grey, searching his as if for answers. 'Maybe not...'

Gabriel took a step closer. 'Let me show you how it can be, Leo...'

Despite the turmoil in her head and her gut Leonora didn't move when Gabriel took a step closer. Close enough to touch. Her traitorous body craved his. Part of her wanted him to convince her, show her again how he could transport her. Transform her.

He was going to convince her to acquiesce—and, heaven help her, she was going to let him.

Desperately, at the last moment, she tried to assure herself that she wasn't saying *yes* yet. She was just allowing him to...to persuade her. But as his hands cupped her face and his mouth landed on hers she knew she was lying to herself.

She'd already made her decision and it was based on many logical reasons—everything he'd outlined. But it was also based on *illogical* reasons—reasons that had to do with motivations that came from a far more secret place. A place where she harboured dreams that she'd be a fool to believe a man like Gabriel would be able to fulfil.

Dreams of a happy marriage—of an old couple walking hand in hand together after a long life lived in love...

But he was kissing her now, and all those dreams dissolved under his hot touch.

When her legs no longer felt capable of holding her up Gabriel lifted her against his chest and carried her through the vast and echoing *castillo*, with the weight of history all around them, into his bedroom.

He undressed her. Undid her belt and pulled it off. Opened the buttons of her dress and pushed it apart, baring her to his gaze before tugging it over her shoulders and down her arms. Then undid her bra, releasing her breasts to his hands and mouth.

He laid her on his bed and pulled down her panties, pushed apart her legs and tortured her with his mouth until she was gripping the sheets and trembling with the effort it took not to shatter. But of course he wouldn't allow her that mercy, and he pushed her until she came in great shuddering waves, against his mouth.

And then, when she was still pulsating and dizzy from that shattering peak, he wound her up again, demonstrating the ease with which he could manipulate her. He thrust into her, stealing her breath and robbing her rational mind of any last coherent thought. He wound her higher and higher, until she was thrashing under him, begging, pleading for mercy.

And that was the moment when he stopped and said, 'Look at me, Leo...look at me.'

She forced her blurry vision to take him in, and it was a majestic sight as he reared over her, his body embedded in hers, every muscle straining with the effort it took not to let go. His face was flushed. Eyes burning.

Her whole body was poised on the precipice—one more thrust and she'd be set free. But he wasn't moving. She raised her hips but he pulled back. She scowled at him and he smiled wickedly. She was laid bare. Exposed. Nowhere to hide. And yet she felt a measure of power, the same power she'd experienced the first night they were together. A very feminine power.

Gabriel's body trembled against hers with the effort it was taking him to stop moving, over her, in her, and that gave her some solace.

And then he said, 'What do you want?'

His question got to her, breaking some last vestige of resistance. She suspected he was asking something deeper than just if she wanted release, but her brain was too melted to study it.

'You...' she said brokenly. 'I want you, Gabriel.'

For a moment he still didn't move. And then, just when she was about to beg him to release her from the tension, and from his too intense gaze, he finally moved, and with a broken cry she soared into bliss.

It was raw and visceral and she suspected that she'd just acquiesced to everything he'd asked of her without even saying *yes*.

The next morning when Leonora woke she felt deeply sated and at peace. It took a long moment for her to figure out where she was and why she was feeling like this. Then it all rushed back.

The proposal.

Making love.

She shivered under the thin sheet. 'Making love' sounded so...so benign, when it had felt more like breaking her apart and putting her back together in a new configuration.

She was alone in the room. She looked around it in the early morning light. It was surprisingly bare—not unlike the bedroom in Gabriel's apartment in the city. Like the man—no frills or flounces or flowery words. Just direct words like *I want you,* or *A proposal of marriage.*

Leonora got out of bed, afraid that Gabriel might appear at any moment and find her feeling so raw. She pulled on a robe that had been laid at the end of the bed—*considerate*—and went into the bathroom.

She looked at herself in the mirror, expecting to see a bedraggled mess. But her eyes were shining and her cheeks still had vestiges of pink in them. She cursed herself. Betrayed by her own body. She paced back and forth, knowing that Gabriel would be expecting an answer when she saw him again.

She sent up silent thanks that he hadn't extracted an answer from her in the throes of passion last night. She would have said anything not to have him stop his particular brand of passionate sorcery.

He made her feel as alive as she'd ever felt and he also made her feel scared. Scared for herself. For her heart. The heart she'd hidden for so long and the heart that longed for more than she'd witnessed growing up.

A little voice popped into her head: *Maybe a family can give you that if Gabriel can't?*

Before she could stop her wayward imagination she saw Gabriel in her mind's eye, returning home from work and scooping a dark-haired child up into his arms, before tugging Leonora close so that he could kiss her.

Leonora caught a glimpse of her reflection again and this time she looked slightly wild-eyed. This was precisely why she should say no to Gabriel. He stirred up too many illicit dreams and fantasies. Fantasies that could never materialise. No matter what she felt when they made love-like the only woman in the world.

And yet...did she have a choice? She had to marry. That was her duty and her responsibility. If it wasn't to Gabriel then it would have to be someone else. Because, no matter what she'd said to him the previous evening, the truth was that she *was* a bride for hire—whether she liked to admit it or not.

Was it so bad that she and Gabriel had this insane chemistry? Wouldn't it help a marriage? At the start at least... It couldn't last. He wouldn't want her like this for ever. But maybe by then they'd have children...

There was a knock on the door and Leonora jumped like a scalded cat. 'Yes?'

A woman's voice. 'Señorita de la Vega? Breakfast is being served downstairs in the dining room.'

Leonora's heart was thumping.

Not Gabriel.

'Thank you. I'll be right down.'

Footsteps went away.

Leonora got herself together and washed, and then went back and dressed in her clothes from yesterday, feeling the sting of shame that everyone would know.

But no one looked at her strangely when she went downstairs. If she passed anyone they just smiled politely, clearly busy with the upkeep of the *castillo*. That reminded her of what Gabriel had said about helping with their *castillo*'s renovations. How could she deny her family that?

She entered the hall and Ernesto appeared.

'Please, Señorita de la Vega, this way.'

Leonora forced a smile, even though inside she was cringing at what Ernesto must think of her. 'Please, call me Leonora.'

He smiled benignly at her as he opened the door into the dining room. She walked in and Gabriel stood up from where he was sitting at the head of the table, dressed in a pristine white shirt, tie and waistcoat, which only emphasised his lean body.

'Good morning.'

She avoided his eye, coming into the room, and wished she'd had more make-up to put on, or tied her hair back. She felt dishevelled. Undone.

'Good morning.'

She sat down and the housekeeper appeared with an array of food.

Leonora smiled at her. 'This looks delicious.'

The woman was pleased. 'Let me know if you want anything else.'

When she was gone Leonora still avoided looking directly at Gabriel.

Until he said, 'Look at me, Leo.'

See? Direct.

She put down the coffee pot and looked at him. All strong lines and that sensual mouth. Those mesmerising eyes. Her lower body spasmed reflexively with the memory of what it had felt like to have his powerful body thrusting in and out of hers.

Dios.

'You're a nice person, Leo.'

She blinked. That wasn't what she'd expected to hear. 'Well, I…thank you.'

'You notice people, acknowledge them.'

Now she was embarrassed. 'So do you,' she said, thinking of his interaction with the boy who had parked his car last night.

'See?' he said as he lowered his coffee cup. 'We're well matched.'

Leonora wanted to look away again, but she couldn't. She felt a sense of fatality wash over her. In all honesty, even though the thought of marrying Gabriel scared her to death, because he made her long for so many things, the thought of walking out of his *castillo* this morning and never seeing him again was nearly more terrifying. Never touching him again? *No.*

Before she could really think it through she blurted out, 'Yes.'

'Yes...to what?'

He arched a brow even as his eyes darkened with something that looked like desire but which she suspected was satisfaction. A part of her wished she could say no, just not give him that satisfaction. Did *anyone* say no to this man? She couldn't blame them.

She took a breath. 'You know what. Yes, I'll marry you.'

Gabriel was surprised at the level of tension he'd been feeling, which suddenly dissipated. He hadn't been sure what Leo would say even after last night.

He reached for her hand and lifted it, leaning forward to press a kiss into her palm. He saw how her eyes flared and an answering rush of desire made his blood hot. He wanted to tug her over onto his lap and crush that soft mouth under his, but he forced the desire down. They would have a lifetime for that. Right at that moment he couldn't imagine a day when he wouldn't want her with this fierce hunger, and surely that had to be a good indication that this union would and could work?

It was time to progress—with this woman by his side.

Not wanting to waste another moment of time, he said, 'Would you object to a private wedding service here in the *castillo*'s chapel at the end of the week?'

CHAPTER SIX

LEONORA'S HEAD WAS still reeling a couple of days after she'd agreed to a private wedding which would take place that very week. She'd protested, of course, but with his particular brand of cool logic Gabriel had asked her what advantage there could possibly be in prolonging the wait.

Gabriel had worn her down all too easily, and in the end she'd agreed—it had been the prospect of securing Matías's future sooner rather than later.

She'd come to Gabriel's office in Madrid this morning, to look over a prenuptial agreement. Cruz y Torres Enterprises was housed in a sleek and modern building made of glass and steel. Everyone looked very serious and efficient. She'd been whisked up with a private escort straight to his massive corner office that had a terrace overlooking the city.

'This is impressive,' she said, walking over to a window.

She could feel Gabriel looking at her and her skin prickled with awareness. They hadn't slept together since the other night.

'It's not bad.'

He came to stand beside her and she glanced at him. 'Not bad…? A slight understatement.'

He turned to face her. 'This will be your world too when we're married.'

Leonora balked a bit at that. Somehow she hadn't fully absorbed that aspect. She would be Señora Cruz y Torres.

Suddenly she felt conscious of her very worn suit. It was designer, but practically vintage at this stage, one she wheeled out when she had to look smart. And she'd wanted to look smart today. Professional. Because essentially this was just a business agreement, right?

It might be for Gabriel, but her thumping heart said something else.

A moment of panic made her turn to him. 'Gabriel, I know you think I'm suitable, but really—'

He put a finger to her mouth, stopping her words. He said, 'You're going to be absolutely fine. Trust me.'

He took his hand away.

Leonora swallowed. 'I just don't want to let you down.'

He shook his head. 'You won't.'

There was a taut moment when she thought he was going to pull her close and kiss her, but then there was a knock on the door and she looked around to see a series of officious-looking men and women enter. She was glad of the interruption. She didn't want Gabriel to see how needy she'd felt just then, for reassurance.

The prenup.

She calmed herself and took a seat at Gabriel's desk, where he'd pulled out a chair. She'd looked over the agreement herself at home, when Gabriel had emailed it to her, and she had no issues with it. It was exceedingly generous, actually, with provisions set out for her family and Matías in the event of their divorce. Essentially, he was promising to look after them for their lifetimes.

After she'd signed the agreement, and the legal staff had left, Leonora put down her pen and looked at Gabriel. She felt ridiculously emotional to think that this man, who really barely knew her, was making such a commitment to her family.

'Thank you—you've been very generous.'

He shrugged. 'Your family will become my family, Leo.'

She shook her head, 'But you haven't even met Matías.'

He paused for a beat and then said, 'So take me to meet him.'

Leonora's heart tripped. 'Now?'

'Why not?' He glanced at his watch. 'I can cancel my afternoon meetings—they're not a priority.'

Leonora put in a call to Matías's school. They had no problem with visitors that afternoon, so after some lunch in Gabriel's office they left the city in one of his sleek cars.

They were walking down the corridor, about to meet Matías in the common room area of his school, when suddenly Leonora stopped and said, 'Wait.'

Gabriel looked at her. 'What is it?'

Leonora was suddenly aware of the magnitude of introducing this man to Matías. 'You need to be gentle with him. He can be nervous with strangers and especially protective of me.'

Something crossed Gabriel's face. 'I have a younger sister. I know that's very different, and Estella doesn't have a learning difficulty, but I do know what it's like to worry...'

Leonora couldn't quite compute that Gabriel Torres was here, reassuring her about her own brother. 'Okay.'

She needn't have worried. Within mere minutes Matías was in thrall to Gabriel in a way she could only sympathise with. Staring at him as if he was a god.

It made Leonora's heart twist, because she'd witnessed so many people over the years shunning her brother because he was different. Gabriel seemed to have no such issue, and was talking to Matías as if he was any other young man of eighteen.

They were having an in-depth conversation about football and it turned out they both supported the same team—much to Matías's ecstatic excitement. When Gabriel offered to take Matías to a match some time, the young man—almost equalling Gabriel in height—launched himself at Gabriel, hugging him tightly.

Leonora immediately tensed, waiting for Gabriel to pull back at this display of affection from a stranger, to extricate himself, look awkward, but he didn't. He just hugged Matías back.

To her shock, instead of feeling reassured, she found that watching Gabriel so at ease with her brother was setting her on edge and bringing up emotions she wasn't sure she wanted to identify.

When they finally left, Leonora sat tensely beside Gabriel in his car.

'What is it?' he asked. 'I would have thought you'd be happy to see that Matías and I get along.'

'He really likes you,' she had to admit.

Gabriel shrugged nonchalantly. 'You say that like it's a bad thing.'

Suddenly she realised what was at the root of her unease. Gabriel was too used to getting his own way, having people fall in slavish devotion at his feet. He'd taken Matías's reaction for granted. She was aware that she was irrationally angry with him about that. But it was as if introducing him to Matías had brought home just how quickly and easily she'd let him upend her life. How quickly she'd let herself fall in with his plans.

She looked at him. 'Matías is vulnerable. If you say you'll take him to a football match he expects that to happen. If he likes you he trusts you implicitly, which makes him even more vulnerable. Once we marry, my responsibility to him doesn't disappear. He's only ever known me as his main carer outside of the school.'

Gabriel shot her a glance. 'Are you sure we're just talking about Matías, here?'

Leonora flushed.

'I have no intention of sidelining anyone once we're married, but the fact is that you will have other responsibilities. You'll be my wife, and I have a hectic schedule at the best of times. And once we have children, they'll obviously take precedence. We'll have as much support as we need, but I don't want to entrust my children entirely to the care of staff, as I and my sister were. And as I suspect you and your brother were, until there were no staff.'

That stunned Leonora slightly. 'You want to be involved in your children's lives?'

For a moment he said nothing. She saw his jaw clench, and then he said, 'My parents all but abandoned me and my sister. Left us to our own devices, sent us to schools as far away from them as possible. I was able to handle it. But Estella... she was more vulnerable. I had no idea how badly she was affected. Because of our age gap, when she was a teenager and home for the holidays I was already working in the business. I missed the signs...'

'The signs of what?'

'Signs that she was falling in with a wrong crowd. People happy to take advantage of her limitless wealth, her name and vulnerability.'

Leonora's chest tightened. 'What happened?'

Gabriel was grim, hands tightly on the wheel. 'I found her passed out at home a few years ago. She was unconscious. Nearly dead. I got her to hospital and into rehab and since then she's been doing really well. But the neglect of our parents was a direct cause of her pain and I'll never forgive myself for not seeing it.'

'You weren't her parent. It wasn't your job.'

He glanced at her, and the look on his face made her shiver. 'No. But I knew she wasn't like me. I won't lie—I don't know the first thing about relating to children—but I know that ours will not be neglected and left to fend for themselves.'

Ours. Their children.

They stopped at traffic lights and he looked at her. 'Unless you have other ideas?'

Leonora was still reeling from what he'd just said. She realised he was waiting for an answer. 'No. I want to be involved. Our upbringing wasn't so dissimilar. Until my father lost everything my parents were absent a lot. It was just me and Matías until he went away to school. I can't imagine having children and letting someone else raise them.'

Some of the harshness in Gabriel's expression softened. 'I know Matías is vulnerable and that he takes everything literally. I've made a commitment to you and he's part of that. All your family are.'

Emotion rose inside Leonora. For the first time in years she felt a weight being lifted off her shoulders. She looked away in case he saw it.

The lights turned green.

A car beeped behind them and Gabriel said, 'Leo, we're not moving till you look at me.'

She swallowed her emotion and turned her head. The car beeped again.

Gabriel was unfazed. 'Do you trust me?'

More cars beeped. But the awful thing was that Leonora didn't need the pressure of the traffic building behind them to tell her that *yes*, she did trust him.

She felt as if she was falling off a cliff edge, with nothing to hold on to. When had she allowed herself to trust him so implicitly? How had that even happened? Had it been just now, when he'd spoken of his sister? Or the moment she'd decided to sleep with him? Or the moment she'd seen him being so kind with Matías?

She nodded.

He said warningly, 'Leo... I need to hear it.'

More cars beeped.

A bubble of euphoria was pushing its way up from her chest and she blurted out, 'Yes! Yes, I do... Now drive! Please!'

They moved off smoothly back into the traffic. Cars were overtaking them, beeping their horns, but Gabriel showed no sign of being bothered. A small wicked smile played around his mouth and Leonora felt a lightness she'd never felt before, with anyone.

'You like causing havoc, don't you?'

He glanced at her and his smile grew more wicked.
'Always.'

Instead of being taken home, though, Leonora found herself being driven into the city centre—specifically to an exclusive shopping street in Salamanca. A place she'd avoided for some time, without the funds to purchase designer clothes.

'Why are we here?' she asked as Gabriel navigated expertly into a small parking space right outside one of the world's most expensive designer shops.

He turned off the engine and faced her. 'I've taken the liberty of organising for you to meet with a stylist. Unless you've already sourced a wedding dress and trousseau?'

Leonora flushed. Of course she hadn't. She'd been in denial, wondering how far her dressmaking skills would get her, cobbling together things from her wardrobe and her mother's.

'You'll be back on the social scene as my wife, and you'll need to maintain a certain...standard.'

Leonora swallowed. Again, that was something that had only hit home in that moment of panic at his offices earlier. Uncomfortably, she said, 'I don't like the idea of you buying me clothes.'

A slightly exasperated look came over Gabriel's face. 'You *would* say that, wouldn't you?'

'What's that supposed to mean? I'm sorry if I'm not making this easy for you by merely acquiescing to your every demand.'

Gabriel snaked out a hand and caught her behind the neck. He tugged her forward gently, so gently that she could easily have resisted, and yet treacherously she didn't want to. She *knew* this was part and parcel of marrying a man like Gabriel—so why was she winding him up? Because she wanted to provoke him?

'As long as you acquiesce to *this* demand we'll have no problems.'

His mouth landed on hers like a hot brand, immediately cauterising her thinking process.

* * *

'And Señor Torres said that we need to fit you for a wedding dress, yes?'

Leonora's attention came back to the efficient stylist, who had spent the last two to three hours helping her select more clothes than she thought she'd ever know what to do with. Or wear.

'Yes. I'm getting married this weekend.'

Leonora ignored the way the stylist paled slightly. She recovered herself and said, 'Very good. Please, come with me across the road to our bridal selection and we'll see what we have there. Luckily you'll fit most sample sizes.'

Leonora smiled weakly, following the woman across the road to another exclusive boutique. The stylist looked her up and down critically and Leonora said quickly, 'I don't want anything fussy. It's not that kind of wedding.'

What kind of wedding is it, then? a snarky inner voice prompted.

She ignored it.

The stylist disappeared behind a rack of voluminous dresses and Leonora called out, 'Honestly, the more simple the better. In fact maybe it could just be…'

The words died on her lips when the woman reappeared, holding a long dress under protective covering. 'Let's try this, shall we? And go from there.'

Afterwards, when Leonora was changing back into her clothes, she had to admire the skill of the stylist. They hadn't had to go anywhere after that first, perfect dress. Leonora scowled at that. She didn't want a perfect dress. She wasn't like other wide-eyed brides, believing in love and happy-ever-after. Her marriage was a business transaction, pure and simple. Gabriel was going to provide a dowry to save her family and she would bear him heirs to continue his line.

So why, when she had stood on the raised dais in the shop and looked in the mirror, had she felt ridiculously emotional?

Was it because she knew it was the perfect dress for a *real* wedding? Because in spite of everything she wished this was a real wedding?

Just because she trusted Gabriel Torres, she'd be a monumental fool to hope that trust would become something more substantial. If anything, what he'd told her about his parents only gave her more insight into why he was so self-contained. He'd had to learn from a young age to depend on himself. At no point had he mentioned love, wanting it or needing it.

She was still feeling a little raw when she walked back into the main area of the wedding boutique, and she wasn't at all prepared to see Gabriel sitting on one of the dusky pink chairs, reading a newspaper. He should have looked ridiculously out of place, but of course he didn't.

He looked up when she emerged, and immediately he frowned, standing up. 'What is it? Did something happen?'

She realised she must be still scowling and she forced a smile. 'Nothing is wrong. Everything is...fine.'

The stylist came out behind her, immediately fawning. 'Señor Torres, what an honour. Is there anything we can get for you?'

He glanced at the stylist, and then back at Leonora, a small smile playing around his mouth, as if he knew exactly the turmoil he caused in her heart and her gut and it amused him. She fought not to scowl again.

The stylist was saying, 'Purchases can be delivered to wherever you like.'

He said, 'Have everything but the wedding dress delivered to my *castillo*. After all, that's where you'll be living from next week—isn't that right, *querida?*'

Leonora felt dizzy at that reminder. But she refused to show it.

She went over and slipped her arm through his. 'Yes, of course it is, *mi amor.*' She wanted to see him as off-balance as she felt.

His jaw clenched, but instead of feeling a sense of satisfaction that she'd got to him, all she felt was an ache near her heart.

He thanked the stylist and then took Leonora's hand in his,

entwining his fingers with hers, and led her out of the boutique to the street. She slipped on her sunglasses, wanting some kind of armour against Gabriel.

He stopped outside the shop and looked at her. 'You weren't lying when you said you didn't like the idea of me buying you clothes.'

Leonora's heart thumped. 'It's not that. I'm very grateful—and I know I have to maintain a certain standard. I've just got used to doing without all the fuss and anxiety about what's fashionable and what's not...'

He made a non-committal sound and then he said, 'There's one more place I need to take you.'

He was walking down the street at a brisk pace before she could ask him where they were going. She saw women doing double-takes—men too, for that matter—as they cut through the shoppers. Leonora felt dowdy in her jeans and plain shirt and suddenly lamented that fact, in spite of her words to Gabriel. Right now she wished she was wearing something more flattering. And her hair was still in a rough bun, after the stylist had asked her to put it up to see how the veil would look.

'Where are we going?' She hoped it wasn't somewhere too public.

'My bank.'

Leonora rolled her eyes behind her glasses. Only someone like Gabriel could actually say *my bank* and literally mean *his* bank. The bank that he owned.

The ornate façade of Banco Torres, one of Spain's oldest financial institutions, used mainly now as an investment bank, rose up before them at the end of the street. And Leonora couldn't help but be intimidated as they went through the revolving door into the hushed exclusivity of the marble foyer. Classical statues were dotted around the space. Huge paintings hung on the walls. Presumably Gabriel's ancestors.

A woman approached them, beautiful and sleek in a dark suit. 'Señor Torres, the item you requested is ready in the vault.'

'Thank you.'

Still holding Leonora's hand, Gabriel led her over to where a uniformed security guard was holding an elevator for them. They got in and it went down to the basement level. They were met there by another sleek employee, male this time. He led them through open steel doors and into a long room filled with security boxes. There was a box on the table, and after unlocking it he left them alone.

Gabriel said, 'This is the family vault.'

Leonora looked around. 'Oh...' *Their* family vault had been cleaned out by her father.

Gabriel let her hand go and went over to the box, opening it up. He lifted out a tray and laid it down in front of Leonora. She sucked in a breath. It was a tray full of sparkling rings. Antique rings. Sapphires, rubies, diamonds.

'These rings have belonged to Cruz y Torres brides down through the generations. But if you don't like any of these we can buy a new one.'

Leonora shook her head faintly. As much at the thought of the unnecessary expense as because one ring in particular had immediately caught her eye. It wasn't as ornate as the others. It was much plainer. And yet it stood out.

It was an emerald cut diamond in a gold setting, with a detail of three smaller diamonds either side of the main stone. Classic and elegant.

Gabriel must have seen where her gaze was resting and he picked it out, holding it up. 'This one?'

She looked at him and nodded reluctantly, feeling like a fraud.

He took her hand and said, 'Let's see if it fits.'

Leonora held her breath as he slid the ring onto her finger. It fitted perfectly. She felt a shiver go down her spine as it sparkled up at her benignly.

'This ring belonged to my great-grandmother, actually. My father's grandmother. Apparently her marriage to my great-grandfather was a rare love-match. She died at the age of eighty, and he died less than a week later of a broken heart. Or so they say.'

Leonora looked at Gabriel suspiciously but he didn't look mischievous. He looked serious.

He said, 'This isn't a love-match, Leo—you do know that, don't you? We have insane chemistry…but that's just desire. I'm not denying that it's a boon for our marriage, but that's all it is. A boon. The important things are our compatibility and the fact that we come from the same world. We both want a different life for our children. But as for love… It's not something I've ever really hoped for or believed in. Sweet stories about my great-grandparents are just…fairy-tales.'

She pulled her hand back, the ring feeling heavy on her finger now. 'Why did you tell me about them?'

He looked at her far too assessingly. 'Because I think you want more from this marriage. More than I'll ever be prepared to give. And you need to know that now.'

Leonora's insides clenched tight. Was she so transparent? She felt the weight of the ring, the cold of the precious metal against her skin. He wasn't telling her anything she didn't already know, but her treacherous heart was shrinking in her chest at his words. In spite of everything, she had hoped for more.

She forced all emotion out of her voice. 'I know what's expected just as much as you do. I've never been under any illusions about what marriage means for me. Do I need to remind you that if the announcement of my engagement hadn't been so rudely interrupted I would be engaged to Lazaro Sanchez right now?'

His expression darkened. He moved closer. 'Do not mention that man's name again.'

Leonora tipped up her chin. 'I've known you intimately for less than a week—do you really think mere sex would turn my head so much that I'd forget a lifetime's lessons and start believing in fairy-tales?'

Gabriel looked at the woman in front of him. She was wearing a plain button-down shirt. He could see a hint of the lace of her bra. She wore faded jeans. Not a scrap of make-up. Her hair was up in a messy knot. She could pass for a student, and yet she had the innately regal grace that belied her lineage.

She was also the most exquisitely beautiful woman he'd ever seen. And every moment he thought he could read her, or figure her out, she slipped through his fingers like quicksilver.

The ring sparkled on her finger in his peripheral vision and something about that was immensely satisfying. Even though he still felt the spike of irritation at hearing her mention Lazaro Sanchez's name. Just the thought that she might possibly be with that man was enough to make Gabriel reach for her, tugging her into him so their bodies were flush.

'It's not *mere* sex—it happens to be amazing sex,' he said in a low, rough voice, already feeling the inevitable rush of blood to his groin.

Colour tinged her cheeks. 'We can't—not here.' She put her hands on his chest.

Gabriel clenched his jaw. She was right. As much as he'd love to turn her around, pull those provocative jeans down and bury himself inside her, he wasn't about to be the first of his line to desecrate the family vault in such a carnal manner. The fact that this behaviour was also totally out of character was something he didn't want to investigate.

'My apartment is less than five minutes from here.'

Leonora desperately wanted to pull back and say something cool, nonchalant. She still stung inside from his warning not to fall for him. But the sting was melting under the rush of blood to every nerve-ending. And she realised that she'd never felt so alive. Fizzing.

She was not a spontaneous person, and she wouldn't have figured Gabriel to be one either. But she was suddenly filled with an urge to unsettle him as he did her every time he looked at her. So she moved her hands down his chest to his waist and then cupped the growing bulge under his trousers.

Instantly his eyes flared with surprise and he sucked in a breath. 'Witch...you'll pay for this.'

Leonora smiled, even though she knew that every time she savoured a small victory like this she was fooling herself if she thought Gabriel's warning would serve as a deterrent. Nothing could save her from herself.

The thing that struck Gabriel most on the morning of his wedding was the equanimity he felt. He'd always imagined that on his wedding day he'd be suffocating with claustrophobia and chafing at the demise of his freedom.

But he wasn't feeling any of those things. He was feeling impatient.

Leonora was ten minutes late. And, while he knew that was traditional, this was hardly a traditional wedding, with only a handful of guests in the Cruz y Torres family church in the grounds of the *castillo*.

He'd managed to drag his mother back from the tropical luxury outpost where she was conducting her latest affair. His father was beside her, glowering. A parody of a united front.

All the more reason why Gabriel felt sure that Leonora was right for him. They wanted the same things for their children. A more holistic upbringing. They had respect and compatibility and that insane chemistry.

He shifted uncomfortably in his morning suit, recalling his totally out-of-character behaviour the other day—taking her back to his apartment mid-afternoon, where they'd lost themselves in a mutual frenzy of need. He couldn't remember feeling that desperate even when he'd been a hormone-fuelled teenager with his first lover.

Leonora's parents were here too. He'd talked to them the night before, when he'd hosted a dinner here at the *castillo* in order to meet them. He liked them. They'd been humbled by their experience and had paid a price that was disproportionate to what they'd done.

There was movement just beyond the church door and Gabriel tensed, surprised to find himself actually experiencing something that felt like...anxiety. A very unfamiliar sensation.

And then she appeared in the doorway. A graceful silhouette. Long white dress, veil obscuring her face. She was on the arm of Matías, whom she'd nominated to be her attendant. Gabriel's sister had desperately wanted to be here, but she was on a fashion shoot in South America and logistically wouldn't have made it in time.

Music began and they started walking down the aisle. Gabriel's breath stopped when Leonora was revealed more fully. The dress was a plain white column—no frills or flounces or ruffles. Just straight, elegant lines, skimming her perfect figure. Long sleeves and a round neck. And yet even from here he could see how the material clung to every dip and curve.

He forced his eyes off Leonora and acknowledged Matías as they arrived at the front of the church. He shook the young man's hand and then Matías went and stood beside his parents.

Leonora stood before Gabriel, face downbent. He willed her to look up at him. She finally did and he saw the shape of her face, the cheekbones, firm jaw. Lush mouth. Huge eyes.

'You look...stunning.'

The priest coughed and Gabriel turned to face him—but not before he found Leonora's hand and wrapped it in his, as if needing to touch her to make sure she was real.

Most of the wedding ceremony was a blur to Leonora. Gabriel taking her hand had been the only thing keeping her anchored to the spot as the enormity of what she was doing had sunk in when she'd reached the altar. She was committing herself to a man who would never love her. She was setting fire to all those secret hopes and dreams she'd nurtured deep inside her for years.

Somehow all this hadn't occurred to her with Lazaro Sanchez. Because she hadn't cared for him as she cared for Gabriel. That unwelcome realisation had made panic flutter in her chest. But then Gabriel had pulled up the veil obscuring her vision and she'd looked at him. And all she'd been able to see were those dark, fathomless eyes, and her panic had dissipated...

'You may now kiss your bride, Señor Torres.'

It was over.

But it was only beginning.

Gabriel cupped her face and lowered his mouth to hers, so slowly and deliberately that she was quivering all over by the time he made contact. Damn him. He knew exactly how to play her.

The kiss was short, but just as devastating as if he'd pulled her close and taken it all the way to deep and explicit. When she pulled back his eyes were glittering. Until now she'd barely even taken in his steel-grey morning suit or the white cravat. It made his skin look very dark.

He took her hand again and led her back down the aisle. Leonora smiled tremulously at her parents and Matías. He was the reason she'd been late. He'd been confused by all the activity and wondering why Leonora was dressed so strangely, and he'd wanted to know what it meant that she would now be living in this new place and not at home.

Very considerately, Gabriel had arranged for one of Matías's favourite teachers from his school to come to the wedding so she could keep an eye on him.

Leonora sucked in big breaths of fresh air once they were outside. A professional photographer took some pictures and then they were ushered into one of the *castillo*'s dining rooms for the wedding breakfast.

Leonora saw her parents awkwardly conversing with Gabriel's parents, who were looking unbearably aristocratic. As if all this was beneath them.

She had caught Gabriel's mother looking expressly at her midsection at one point, and had realised that she must suspect that Leonora was pregnant. Well, she wasn't. Not when she had the all too familiar cramps to prove it.

Leonora had always suffered from particularly painful periods, but it had never been diagnosed as anything but mild endometriosis. She hadn't even considered that she might be pregnant—Gabriel had used protection every time—but she'd been surprised at the tiny dart of disappointment when her period had arrived as usual just the other day.

Was she really ready for babies? Children? The thought was alternately terrifying and awe-inspiring.

She put a hand to her belly now, as she took a sip of champagne, unconsciously easing the lingering ache of the end of her period.

The wedding breakfast was nearly over, so she was surprised when Gabriel tapped his glass and stood up. He looked down at her and then he said, 'I would like to take this opportunity to welcome Leonora into the family, and also to welcome her parents and her brother Matías.' He looked at her and raised his glass. 'You're the future of this family, Leonora—you and our children.'

He took her hand and kissed it and the dull ache inside her was forgotten. She was curiously touched by his public endorsement of her, and the welcome he'd offered to her family. But she could see that his parents didn't totally approve, and they wasted little time in leaving once the party started to break up.

Gabriel had told Leonora that they would be leaving after the wedding for a short honeymoon—again, not something she would have expected of him, having assumed he'd waste no time in getting back to work.

She knew she should be grateful for this time to get to know him better, but as they set off for the airport later that day she couldn't control the butterflies in her belly at the thought of time alone with her new husband.

CHAPTER SEVEN

PARADISE. THAT WAS the only word Leonora could think of as she took in the sight before her. Gabriel had brought her to a paradise that had only ever existed in her imagination. It had a name of course. Costa Rica. They'd flown into the lush tropical country, bordered on two sides by sparkling oceans, late last night, and had then taken a smaller plane to the west coast, where Gabriel owned a villa.

They'd arrived so late and Leonora had been so exhausted that she'd barely noticed Gabriel taking off her outer clothes and laying her down on the softest surface imaginable. But now she was awake. Or was she still dreaming? She wasn't sure.

She'd woken in a massive four-poster bed, with muslin drapes gently moving in the warm breeze. When she'd pushed them back she'd seen the bedroom—wooden floors, rustic furniture. Then wide open doors leading out to a terrace and a glimpse of what could only be described as heaven.

A robe had been laid across the end of the bed, and Leonora had realised she was in her underwear. The strapless white bra she'd worn under her wedding dress and matching lace panties. Refusing to linger on thinking about Gabriel undressing her, she'd pulled the short robe on, and now she stood on a wooden deck, with an infinity pool in front of her, overlooking a forest and beyond that the sparkling Pacific Ocean.

'Not a bad view to wake up to, hmm?'

Leonora started and turned around with a hand to her chest. Gabriel was standing a few feet away, holding a cup in his hand. His hair was damp and he wore casual board shorts and nothing else. All she could see was that impressive expanse of hard-muscled chest.

She fought for composure. She was still disconcertingly in that space between waking and sleeping, and the view in general was not helping to bring her back to reality. *Either* view.

'It's absolutely stunning.' She turned back to the other view.

He came and stood beside her. 'Did you sleep well?'

Leonora smiled a little sheepishly. 'Like a baby.'

'Good. You deserve a break...'

Leonora didn't like the little warm glow near her heart when Gabriel said things like that. It was too...seductive.

She forced a breezy smile. 'I'm fine—why would I need a break?'

'Because you've been carrying the weight of your family's responsibilities for years.'

She rushed to defend them, but Gabriel put a finger to her mouth before she could.

'I'm your husband now, Leo. You're not on your own any more. It's not down to you. It's down to *us*.'

Leonora looked up at him. It would be so easy to lean on this man. So easy to let him just take her burdens and anxieties. And it was already happening. Her parents had told her that he'd already set up a meeting for them to talk with his assistant with regard to carrying out renovation work on the *castillo* and hiring staff again. And she knew their association with the Cruz y Torres family would soon have them accepted back into Spanish society.

Familiar anxiety knotted her belly, though. 'What if my father—?'

Gabriel shook his head. 'He won't. I spoke to him and he's agreed to get counselling to try and figure out why he became addicted to gambling. He's learnt a harsh lesson. I'm sure he won't go down that route again.'

Leonora was shocked that he'd discussed it with her father, who had always turned to obdurate stone when she'd tried to broach the subject of counselling or therapy. Perversely, she felt slightly jealous that he'd made more headway than she or her mother ever had.

As if reading her mind, he said, 'Sometimes it takes a person on the outside to communicate a little more effectively. Your father is ashamed of what he's done.'

Leonora swallowed her defensiveness. She realised that after living her life solely in service to her parents and her brother and their huge unwieldy home it would be a challenge to let someone else into that space.

'Thank you for talking to him. I think he does want to get better.'

'They're all thousands of miles away and being perfectly well looked-after. Forget about them now. Breakfast? Or would you like to work up an appetite first?'

Leonora's heart sped up. 'An appetite?'

He nodded. 'You owe me something.'

'I do?'

He nodded as he put down the cup and reached for the tie on her robe and undid it. 'You owe me a wedding night. But first…let's take a little dip.'

He pushed back the robe and it fell off her shoulders and down to the ground. Leonora blamed her semi-awake state for the fact that she felt so languorous as Gabriel looked her up and down while she stood there in nothing but two flimsy scraps of lace.

As she watched he opened the top button and his shorts

dropped to the ground. He was naked, and she took in the magnificence of his naked form as if she'd never seen it before. *Now* she was wide awake. Her body humming with electricity.

'Turn around,' he instructed.

She did, revelling in the warmth of the morning sun and the humid air. He undid the clasp of her bra and it fell away, floating gently on the breeze. He came up behind her and wrapped his arms around her, his mouth searching for and finding the sensitive spot between her neck and shoulder. She shivered in reaction. All that was separating them was that flimsy scrap of lace, and Gabriel's hands were there now, pulling it down over her hips.

Her panties fell to the ground at her feet and she turned around, heart beating so fast she felt light-headed. He stood back and held out a hand. She took it and followed where he led her to the pool.

As they descended the stone steps leading down into the clear cool water, with the backdrop of nothing but lush nature around them, she felt as if they were embarking on something very elemental.

The fact that this was so far removed from what Leonora might have imagined of a marriage was too huge to absorb at that moment. So when Gabriel reached for her she went willingly, wrapping her legs around his narrow waist, her arms around his neck, mouths fusing and passion drowning out all and any disjointed thoughts except for *this* bliss.

Breakfast turned into a very late lunch that day...

A few days later Leonora was dozing on a lounger under an umbrella by the pool. Since that first cataclysmic morning she'd discovered that Gabriel had a discreet, friendly staff, who melted in and out of the villa every day, leaving food and tidying away the evidence of the previous night's passion.

At first she'd been mortified, but now she was ashamed to

say she was already used to the sensation of invisible hands keeping her world pristine. It was a novelty after years of hiring only the most minimal help at the *castillo*, because she literally had not been able to do all the work alone.

Their days had fallen into a lazy, sensual pattern. Leonora would wake late, as she was generally only falling into an exhausted sated slumber as dawn was lightening the morning sky, and Gabriel would already be up, taking calls or doing some work in his airy study on the other side of the villa. He would join her for a late lunch, which would invariably end up with them back in bed.

Leonora blushed now under the umbrella. They were insatiable. She'd never known sex could be like this—so all-encompassing.

The previous night he'd been about to automatically don protection when she'd acted on impulse and put a hand on his, stopping him.

He'd looked at her for a long moment and then he'd put the protection aside and lain down beside her. 'Are you sure about this? Are you ready?'

Leonora had looked back at him, and even through the haze of desire she'd known they were crossing a line. She'd nodded and said, 'Yes. I want children with you. I know it's hard work, because I looked after Matías when he was younger, but these are different circumstances.'

Gabriel had put a hand on her belly. 'These are very different circumstances, *querida*. You're not alone any more. Our children will have two parents who want the best for them, who will support them no matter what. You'll be a great mother. You're amazing with your brother and you love your parents...'

Leonora's heart had felt suspiciously full. She'd reached for Gabriel, pulling him over her, opening her legs around him, guiding him into her body. Skin on skin. No barriers. Telling him without words that she wanted all those things too. *And more.*

That was why she'd stayed silent—for fear of what she might say.

She hated to admit it now, and she told herself it had only been because of the unique sensation of not using protection, but making love to him last night had felt almost...spiritual.

She put a hand on her flat belly, imagining a baby already taking root inside her. And then she told herself she was being ridiculous. It wasn't the right time. But it could happen within the next cycle. Soon.

She realised how badly she wanted it now. She wanted to show Gabriel that their family could be different. That there could be love. Her heart clenched. Her fantasy of a fuller, richer life wasn't just a fantasy any more. No matter what he'd said or how much he'd warned her not to build castles in the air. If Gabriel wanted a different life for his children then who was to say he couldn't fall in—?

'Afternoon, sleepyhead.'

Leonora's eyes snapped open behind her shades. Gabriel was standing beside her sun bed, tall and broad. Bare-chested. She was glad that the oversized glasses hid what had to be the soppy expression on her face.

She snatched her hand off her belly and sat up. 'Afternoon. Did you have much work to catch up on?'

Gabriel sat down on the lounger next to hers and reached for some of the fruit that his housekeeper had left out for Leonora in a bowl. He shook his head and his mouth tightened almost imperceptibly. 'A phone call about a project with someone from the other side. Intensely irritating but unavoidable.'

'That sounds...unpleasant.'

He dismissed it with a hand. 'It's not important.' He stood up, holding out that same hand. 'Come on, I want to take you somewhere.'

Leonora stood up, conscious of his eyes running down her body in the cutaway swimsuit. She let him take her hand, hating the way her treacherous heart tripped. He instructed her to put on a caftan and shoes, and then he took her around to the front of the villa, where there was a sturdy open-top four-wheel drive with a wicker basket in the back. She threw a sunhat in the back with the basket.

'Come on—jump in.'

Gabriel swung into the driver's seat, his naked torso gleaming. He looked like a buccaneer.

Leonora got in and Gabriel took off down the winding path. She put her head back and looked at the canopy rushing overhead, the sun breaking through every now and then in a bright flash. She felt...free. Unencumbered.

She didn't want to ruin the moment by saying anything so she let Gabriel drive, noticing his powerful hands on the wheel, the way he drove with speed, yet precision. There was a shadow of stubble on his jaw. His hair was messy in the breeze. He looked younger. Less...stern. When she'd seen him across that ballroom on that fateful first night she never would have imagined him in this kind of environment...carefree.

She had a sudden thought and hated herself for it. But she couldn't help asking, as massive trees rushed past the Jeep on either side, 'Have you ever brought anyone else here?'

She almost hoped he hadn't heard, that the breeze whipping past their faces might have snatched her words away, but she saw his hands clench on the wheel, momentarily.

'Have you ever brought anyone else here?'

The words landed straight in Gabriel's gut. No. He hadn't ever brought anyone else here. Because this was his secret private sanctuary, where he could get away from everything and everyone. And yet he hadn't hesitated at the thought of bringing Leo here.

That question from any other woman would have made him feel as if there was a hand around his neck, squeezing slowly. But this was different. *She* was different. Which was why he'd married her, he told himself now. Because she didn't induce that feeling of claustrophobia. The opposite, in fact.

Seeing the shock and awe on her face that first morning had been worth it alone. He was jaded, and the people around him were jaded. Yet Leo, even coming from the same world, was remarkably *un*-jaded.

He took her hand in his, slowing the vehicle as they veered off the road and onto a dirt track that ran deeper into the jungle. He looked at her. 'No, I've never brought anyone else here.'

She couldn't hide the relief on her face, even though she quickly masked it. And then she surprised him.

'Good,' she said. 'Because if I thought this was just some routine you've done a thousand times I think I'd have to kill you. And those other women.'

Gabriel threw his head back and laughed. Leo was grinning and his chest tightened. She was so beautiful. The sun had added a golden glow to her skin. Her hair tumbled over her shoulders, its normally sleek glossiness untamed in loose waves. And he wanted her with a hunger that only seemed to grow the more he had of her.

On that unsettling thought he let her hand go, ostensibly to put both his hands on the wheel in order to control the car on the rougher terrain. But it was also because he'd just realised how far under his skin she'd reached. All the way so that for the first time in his life work wasn't the first thought of his day. Or his last. It was *her*. And then, when he was sated, he thought about work again. As if he needed to take that edge off before he could think clearly.

He'd had to take a phone call with Lazaro Sanchez just now, and Sanchez had goaded him about using Leonora to score points in their rivalry. Just hearing her name on that man's lips had made Gabriel see red, even as his conscience had pricked when he'd recalled being very aware of how it would look to be photographed with her leaving the hotel the night of the failed engagement.

That felt like a long time ago now. He'd never envisaged then, that Leonora would become his wife.

He'd told Sanchez that Leonora was *where she belonged.* And he'd really meant it. He felt a possessiveness that he'd never felt before—for a woman or anything.

Gabriel shoved aside the niggling prickling sensation that felt like exposure. He was on his honeymoon. It was natural and expected to be captivated by one's wife. Possessive.

Leonora gasped out loud as they burst through the thick trees and onto the edge of the most pristine beach she'd ever seen in her life. Gabriel stopped driving and she stood up in the vehicle, scanning left and right. She could see nothing but sea, white sand and the line of trees bordering the beach. It was completely empty. The waves rolled in with a rhythmic *whoosh.*

Gabriel got out, picking up the wicker basket. Leonora got out too and stuck her sunhat on her head as she walked to the start of the beach. She slipped off her shoes and dug her toes into the soft warm sand.

It was beyond idyllic and there wasn't another human in sight. Just her and this charismatic man who had come into her life only a couple of short weeks ago and comprehensively turned it upside down and transformed her, inside and out.

Impulsively, she pulled off her caftan and threw her hat down on the sand. She started running backwards towards the sea. 'Last one in is a loser!'

Gabriel stood stock-still for a moment and then he put down the basket, kicked off his own shoes and started running after Leonora. She squealed and turned around, but it was no use. Gabriel caught her all too easily and lifted her up, over his shoulder, and carried her into the crashing surf of the glittering Pacific Ocean, dunking her mercilessly under the foaming waves until she begged for mercy.

He pulled her out, laughing and spluttering, and then she saw the intensity on his face, the way his eyes burned. She reached for him, seeking and finding his hot mouth, revelling in his whipcord body as he lifted her against him, wrapping her legs around him.

The waves crashed around them unnoticed as Gabriel pulled her swimsuit below her breasts, feasting on her wet flesh. The stark contrast of his hot mouth against her sea-cold skin made her head fall back...she was in paradise with the most exciting man she'd ever met and she never wanted it to end...

The knowledge that she'd never felt happier than in that moment was bittersweet. Because she knew it wasn't the same for Gabriel. What he was feeling was purely physical, evidenced by the way he couldn't take his hands off her, or she off him. But, weakly, she avoided thinking about that and gave herself up to the moment, like a miser with her gold.

A couple of hours later, after they'd made love under the shade of the trees on the edge of the beach, Leonora sat with her knees tucked up under her chin, her arms around them. She wore her caftan over her naked body while her swimsuit dried on a nearby rock, with Gabriel's shorts beside it. He wore a towel, tied precariously around his narrow waist.

The detritus of a delicious picnic lay around them. Fruit, bread, cheese, cold meats. Ice-cold water and sparkling wine. Of which Leonora had had a little.

The feeling of happiness lingered in her chest. It was unsettling, because she realised now how little she'd ever felt truly happy in her life. She'd always been so worried about her parents and Matías. And before they'd lost everything she'd always been far too reticent to let her emotions free rein.

'What are you thinking about?'

She glanced at Gabriel, who was sitting back, leaning on one elbow, watching her. He popped a piece of pineapple into his mouth. The thought of blurting out exactly what was on her mind made her break out in a sweat.

She shrugged lightly. 'Just about life...'

'Oh, just about *life*? Nothing much, then?' Gabriel mocked her easily.

Leonora smiled. 'I was thinking about how I used the *castillo* to hide away for a long time. I was so shy... I never felt as if I truly belonged in our world. Everyone else seemed so much more confident than I felt.' She looked at him almost accusingly. 'You even noticed it.'

He sat up too. 'Our perception of other people is usually wrong, you know. Some people just manage to put on a more convincing act. I don't think you're that shy, really. You didn't like being the centre of attention that evening in the hotel, but you did it because you felt you had to. For your family.'

Leonora absorbed that. She hadn't thought about it like that before. He was right—she hadn't liked it, but she hadn't been crippled by it. Maybe her shyness had dissipated over the years and she hadn't even noticed. And he was also right that when it came to doing something for her family she didn't hesitate.

Maybe it would be different if she felt she had a role. A reason to get up in front of people.

She looked at Gabriel and said grudgingly, 'You're very observant.'

He arched a brow. 'I'm observant because I have to be. If I can't read people and I don't see what's going on around me I lose my edge. And if I lose my edge I risk losing everything. My father lost his edge and I had to take over. Too many people depend on me. My family legacy depends on me.'

Leonora touched her belly under the caftan. 'And me too.'

He turned to her and she saw the seriousness of his expression. It cleared, and he smiled, but it was wicked.

'Yes. And you too, Señora Torres.'

He lay down again and pulled her with him, so she was sprawled across his chest. Her breasts were flattened against him and he funnelled his hands through her hair, pulling her head down to his.

'About that legacy... I think it still needs work...'

When his hands reached for her caftan, pulling it up and off her body, she helped, throwing it aside. He removed the barrier of the towel between them and she sat astride him and took him deep inside her on a gasp.

Afterwards, when the sun was setting and it was warm on her naked back, where she lay sprawled across Gabriel's bare chest, she knew she was in deep trouble. All the warnings in the world couldn't stop her falling for this man, because she was already deeply and irrevocably in love with him.

A couple of far too short days later they took off from San José airport. Leonora felt nervous at the thought of leaving behind the idyllic bubble they'd inhabited these past few days. Nervous at the thought of going back into the real world with a man who was still an enigma to her in so many ways—in spite of their physical intimacy, and in spite of her getting to know him in a little better.

They'd discovered similar interests in everything from art to books, movies and politics. But she couldn't afford to forget that the very urbane and seductive man she'd come to know hid a ruthless streak. How could he not be ruthless when he'd shouldered such responsibility for so long and when he was so successful? When he had a legacy to continue?

Physically, their obsession with each other didn't seem to be waning. Far from it. They'd been ready to leave for the airport, dressed and packed, and all it had taken was one burning look from Gabriel and they'd been back in the bedroom, on the bed, clothes ripped off in minutes.

Maybe Gabriel was right, Leonora told herself now. Maybe all they needed was this insane chemistry and mutual respect. And a willingness to commit to bringing up their children differently than they had been brought up in order to have a happy life?

But she couldn't shake the hollow feeling inside her that it wouldn't be enough.

In a bid to try and distract herself, she reached for the pile of newspapers and magazines left out by the plane's staff.

Almost immediately she noticed a picture on the front page of a tabloid magazine. It was Lazaro Sanchez and the red-haired woman who had crashed their engagement party. They were emerging from what looked like a town hall. She was wearing a cream dress and matching jacket, her bright red hair pulled back into a low ponytail, clutching a posy of flowers. He was in a suit and putting out a hand as if to ward off the paparazzi from getting too close. They'd just been married, clearly.

Leonora couldn't remember him ever looking as intense with her as he did in the photo. She could see the faintest outline of the woman's pregnancy bump. So he *was* the father. No wonder he'd married her so quickly. Her name was Skye O'Hara.

Leonora knew she should be feeling *something* at the sight of her recent almost-fiancé marrying another woman, but all she felt was relief. And a kind of terror to think that she might very well have not had that night with Gabriel which had led to their marriage.

'What's that?'

Leonora looked at Gabriel. She handed the magazine across and he took it, taking in the front cover.

He looked back at her, spearing her with those dark eyes. 'Does this bother you?'

She shook her head. 'No…actually, not at all.'

Gabriel crumpled up the magazine and tossed it in a nearby bin. Then he reached for Leonora, undoing her seat belt and tugging her all too easily out of her seat and into his lap. She blushed and looked around, but there were no staff.

'Sanchez's loss is my gain. He's a fool.'

Leonora looked down at Gabriel. There was a tone in his voice that made her want to ask if he knew Lazaro Sanchez personally, but before she could he was pulling her head down and pressing hot kisses along her jaw and neck. Her head fell back and every coherent thought was wiped out as the last, lingering effects of their magical honeymoon were continued in the luxurious bedroom of the private plane.

Almost a week after they'd returned from honeymoon they were having dinner in one of the *castillo*'s less formal dining rooms.

'How are you settling in?' Gabriel asked.

Leonora thought of the way he'd woken her this morning—the way he woke nearly every morning, actually—in a very sensual way that inevitably put her back into a satisfaction-induced coma for a couple of hours while he got up and went to work. She'd never behaved so decadently in her life.

He was watching her closely and she suspected he was even smirking slightly, which helped her not to blush.

Airily, she pretended not to be thinking about sex. 'Fine, thank you. Ernesto has been very kind. He's shown me every part of the *castillo*. Including the vaults where you store the wine that you don't drink and your family portraits.'

Gabriel took a sip of his sparkling water. 'The portraits are scary, aren't they?'

They were. And they were a sober reminder of the sheer weight and extent of Gabriel's family's legacy.

Unconsciously she put a hand to her belly, thinking that it would have to be miracle if she hadn't fallen pregnant on their honeymoon, given that they'd made love every night and every morning. She'd know in about ten days, anyway.

Now she did blush, which she deflected from by asking hurriedly, 'Why don't you drink—is it just because of your father?'

Gabriel put his glass down. 'That, and I don't like the sensation of not having my wits about me. I once got very drunk when I was a teenager and I never wanted to feel like that again.'

She could understand that. Even though she'd never really been drunk herself, she felt as if she lost her wits every time Gabriel looked at her.

Curious, she asked, 'Why did you get drunk?'

He looked as if he didn't want to say anything, but then reluctantly he said, 'My first lover. She was a bit older than me. I was besotted with her. Until I found her in bed with my best friend.'

Leonora felt her insides plummet. 'You were in love...once?'

He made a face. 'Was it love? It was more like an obsession. And even if it was love she merely confirmed for me that it doesn't exist.'

It was a sign, as if she'd needed one, not to look beyond the physical intimacy of their honeymoon.

She changed the subject and forced a neutral tone into her voice. 'I saw Matías today. He's so excited about the football match in a few weeks. Thank you for getting the tickets.'

Gabriel shrugged nonchalantly. 'I have a box at the stadium. He'll be treated like a king.'

Emotion caught in Leonora's chest. Gabriel really had no idea how a casual gesture could mean so much. 'He'll love it.'

Gabriel asked, 'How are renovations coming along at the Flores *castillo*?'

'Really well. They've done so much already. I think my parents have decided to keep doing the tours. They have plans to make them more dynamic—add in wine tastings, overnight stays, that kind of thing. The fact that they'll be able to hire staff makes all the difference. It's given them a new lease of life. Thank you.'

Gabriel inclined his head. 'It's all part of the agreement.'

That dented a little more of the hazy glow surrounding Leonora. Gabriel wasn't doing this out of the goodness of his heart. He was doing it because it was part of their prenuptial agreement. Laid out in black and white. Okay, so his relationship with Matías was something he *was* doing out of the goodness of his heart...but she needed to remember that this marriage was very much a transaction for him. Much as it would have been for Lazaro Sanchez.

She was a commodity who had value in her background, her

name, and in how she looked and could conduct herself. And she was lucky that Gabriel found her attractive or she wouldn't be here.

His hand came over hers and she felt that all too familiar tingle of electricity. She almost resented it for a second.

'Where did you go just then?' he asked.

She cursed the fact that she couldn't seem to hide her expressions around Gabriel, when for years she'd perfected the art of not showing anyone what was going on inside her.

She forced a smile. 'Nowhere.'

Gabriel lifted his hand off Leonora's. It was disconcerting to feel so attuned to another person. She'd retreated just then, closing herself off right in front of him. He'd immediately wanted to know why. Even though he was more used to people trying to read *him* for his reactions.

It was also disconcerting how quickly he'd adjusted to having Leonora here at the *castillo*. He almost couldn't remember a time when she hadn't been there. When he arrived home in the evening the first thing he noticed was her light scent. Floral, with musky undertones. Like her—serene on the surface but full of complexity and fire underneath.

The captivation he'd felt in Costa Rica didn't appear to be diminishing. During a board meeting earlier his mind had wandered all too easily to remembering how he'd woken her that morning. It had started slow and sensuous but had quickly become urgent and explosive.

She was addictive.

He assured himself that this was normal. He just hadn't expected that he would *want* his wife this much. He'd imagined a far more sedate arrangement, if and when he married, with sex turning into a function more than an indulgence. But this was a *good* thing, he assured himself now. He and Leonora had something to build on. A connection that went beyond what most couples in their world had.

* * *

Leonora said, 'Your assistant called me today—about a function in Paris at the weekend?'

'Yes. It's a gala in aid of a charity. It's on at the same time as Fashion Week, so it'll be pretty high-profile.'

Leonora immediately felt intimidated. Which was ridiculous. She'd been bred for this sort of thing.

'When do we leave?'

'We'll fly out Saturday afternoon, and come back on Monday. I have some meetings there on Monday morning.' He put his hand over hers again. 'You'll be fine.'

She looked at him. 'I don't want to let you down. I've never been the most gregarious person in a group.'

He shook his head. 'I don't want gregarious. I want you.'

The hazy glow was back. He interlinked their fingers and Leonora felt a pulse throb between her legs. It was as if her body had been made uniquely to respond to his. It was maddening—and utterly thrilling.

He stood up and held out a hand, the look in his eye very explicit. Unmistakable.

Her body reacted predictably, her blood growing hot, moving faster through her veins.

They'd just finished dinner. Leonora usually liked to relax, watching a boxset or reading a book before bed. But that had been before Gabriel had awoken this needy and insatiable side of her. And right then the thought of losing herself to his expert touch was a very enticing prospect. She really didn't want to think about their first official public outing together as a couple.

So she stood up and let him lead her up the stairs and into their bedroom. She tried to feel cynical about it and remind herself that this attention from Gabriel was in part to ensure a quick result for an heir, but when he touched her, or looked at her like he was doing now—as if, like her, he couldn't quite understand this *thing* between them—it was very hard to be cynical. It felt so pure. And raw. And necessary.

CHAPTER EIGHT

'YOU LOOK BEAUTIFUL, LEO.'

She tried to feel confident under Gabriel's approving gaze but a million butterflies were fluttering around her belly. No, buzzing. Fluttering was too gentle. She felt as nervous as she had the night of her engagement announcement.

She checked her reflection again. A styling team had come to get her ready and her hair was in a simple chignon. Her dress was a dark royal blue. Floor-length and fitted, it had three-quarter-length sleeves. It was modest at the front, with a high neckline, but it was backless at the back. A more risqué design than she would usually wear but the stylist had insisted.

Gabriel had surprised her with sapphire drop earrings and a matching bracelet and necklace. The jewels glittered against her skin. She knew she looked the part—she just didn't feel it.

She forced her gaze back to her husband's. 'Thank you. So you do.'

And he did. She'd seen him in a tuxedo before, but he still took her breath away. He wore a white bowtie this evening, and the white of the shirt and the tie made him look very dark.

'Shall we? My driver is ready downstairs.'

Leonora took a breath and slipped her arm through his, hating how much she liked it that he reached for her hand and held it in the lift on the way down. A little extra touch.

They were staying in a hotel not far from where the function was taking place. An exclusive hotel overlooking the Arc de Triomphe. Gabriel had an apartment in Paris, of course, but it was undergoing refurbishment. He'd taken Leonora there earlier to meet with the designer and get her input on the design. Another unexpectedly thoughtful gesture.

They were in the back of his sleek chauffeur-driven luxury car now, her hand still in his. She wanted to be able to pull away, tell him she was fine, but she wasn't. She saw the flashing of the paparazzi cameras in the distance. The sleek line of cars. The beautiful people getting out.

Bizarrely, at that moment she thought of the picture she'd seen on the magazine cover, of Lazaro Sanchez's new wife... Skye?...and of how terrified she'd looked. Leonora felt a spike of empathy for her.

It was time to get out.

Someone had obviously caught a glimpse of Gabriel inside the car and the camera flashes went crazy.

He looked at her. 'Ready?'

She nodded.

'Wait here. I'll get out first and come around and get you.'

He got out and the shouts were deafening.

'Gabriel! Over here!'

'Where's Leonora?'

'We want to see your wife!'

He came to her door and she sucked in a big breath and stuck on a smile—just as he opened the door and the world became one huge bright flash of light.

After about an hour of milling around the thronged ballroom, after the charity auction had taken place, Leonora's smile felt like a rictus grin on her face. Gabriel was deep in conversation with some very serious-looking individuals, and she'd spied some open doors leading out to a terrace that looked blessedly airy and empty.

She caught his attention and motioned that she was taking a little break, and then made her way through the crowd of well-known faces from film and politics. When she reached the doors she stepped outside, relief flooding her to find the space was indeed empty. Nothing but fresh air and the lights of Paris glittering as far as the eye could see.

She ventured further and then stopped suddenly—because there *was* someone else out here. A woman in a strapless black dress. Petite. Very pretty. With bright red hair. Looking at her with big blue eyes. Shocked eyes.

The woman said, *'You.'*

Recognition was swift. It was Skye O'Hara. Lazaro's pregnant wife.

Leonora looked down and saw the small bump. Inexplicably, she felt a spurt of something that felt like jealousy.

She spoke in English. 'Sorry, I didn't realise there was anyone here.'

She turned to leave, but she heard from behind her, *'No. Please, don't go.'*

Leonora stopped. Tension thrummed through her. She turned around again, schooling her expression to be as non-committal as possible.

Skye said, 'I just want to say how sorry I am... I never intended to ruin your engagement like that. I just... I'd tried to get in touch with Lazaro but it was impossible. I sneaked into that room and saw him... I had to let him know.'

The tortured look on her face and the sincerity of her words made Leonora do a double-take. She was used to a different breed of female. Like the ones who had been gossiping in the bathroom the night she'd met Gabriel. Clearly Skye was not in their league, and something in Leonora relaxed.

'I know. I get that now. You met before he proposed to me.'

'Yes!' The relief was evident on her face and she smiled rue-fully. 'I would have hated it if you'd been with him then.'

Leonora moved closer to Skye. 'No, that would not have been nice. But he would not have done that. These men…they have integrity, at least.'

'You mean Lazaro and…?'

'Gabriel—my husband.' Leonora couldn't stop her gaze from dropping again to Skye's pregnant belly. She looked up. 'Con-gratulations. I wish you all the best in your future with Lazaro.'

Skye put a small pale hand on her belly. She smiled shyly. 'Thank you…' Then she blurted out, 'I felt it move just now…a proper movement.'

The evidence of Skye's pregnancy only drove home the fact that no matter how in tune Leonora might feel with Gabriel, she really only had one function to fulfil as his wife. Bear him an heir. And she was in danger of forgetting it.

Skye must have seen something on her face. She looked anx-ious. 'I'm sorry—did I say something…?'

Leonora forced a smile. 'No, not at all. I really do wish you all the best in your future with Lazaro and the baby.'

She turned away to leave but Skye reached out and took her hand. 'I'm sorry again…and I wish you all the best too.'

Leonora was surprised at the surge of emotion she felt at the other woman's touch and sincerity. She squeezed Skye's hand and said, 'Thank you,' and turned away before she could notice the moisture springing into her eyes. Crazy. What was wrong with her? She'd never really had a close female friend, but she realised now that if she had, she would have wanted her to be someone like Skye.

She walked back into the room, her eyes searching out her husband. She didn't have to search for long because he was the tallest man in the room. Well, him and the man he was talk-ing to. Lazaro Sanchez. What on earth would he be talking to *him* for?

Suddenly concerned, Leonora made her way over, seeing the tension in Gabriel's body. And in Lazaro's. The grim looks on their faces. This was not a friendly chat. Far from it. They seemed to be locked in some private battle of wills.

She drew closer and they were still oblivious to her. She picked up their conversation.

Lazaro Sanchez was saying, 'Maybe this time you'll be surprised, Gabriel, and maybe the best bid will win—the one that has the good of the city at its heart, not just the insatiable Torres need for domination in all things.'

Gabriel took a step closer to Lazaro, his face etched in stark lines. 'I do remember you, you know. I remember that day when you confronted my father in the street and claimed to be his son. You have a chip on your shoulder, Sanchez, and it's time to get over it and stop telling yourself you've been hard done by.'

Leonora couldn't believe what she'd just heard. The two men obviously knew each other. Had history. The tension between them was palpable.

She took a step into their space, but even then they didn't notice her. She said, 'Hello, Lazaro, it's nice to see you.'

Lazaro Sanchez blinked and seemed to come out of his angry trance. So did Gabriel, and he immediately reached for Leonora, pulling her close with an arm around her waist.

Lazaro echoed what Skye had said. 'Leonora. I'm sorry for what happened. It was never my intention to do anything to hurt or embarrass you.'

She smiled tightly. 'I know. I just met your wife. Congratulations on the baby.'

'Thank you.'

Lazaro looked at Gabriel and Leonora could feel the tension in her husband's body. He was rigid with it. She'd never seen him react like this to anyone else.

'Till next time, Torres.'

Lazaro walked away.

Leonora looked up at Gabriel, who was staring after Lazaro with a hard expression. Almost bitter. She said, 'I didn't realise you knew each other.'

He looked at her, jaw tight. 'I'd prefer it if we didn't but, yes, we do.'

'You've known him since before the night of the engagement party?'

'Yes, for a few years now.'

Leonora felt sick as things slid into place in her mind. 'A few *years*?'

Instinctively she moved out of his embrace and stood apart. 'You know him and you didn't think it worth mentioning?'

'I didn't think it was relevant.'

Confusion and hurt and other emotions were swirling in Leonora's gut now. 'Not *relevant*? I slept with you on the night I was due to announce my engagement to him—the night you seduced me—and you didn't think it was relevant?'

Gabriel looked around and took Leonora's elbow, guiding her over to a corner of the room where a large plant shielded them a little. That only made her feel more incensed.

She pulled away again. 'Why didn't you tell me you knew him?'

'Because he's not someone I think about unless I have to.'

'You don't like him—that much is obvious.'

'No, I don't.'

The implications of this were huge. 'Why were you even at the engagement announcement if you don't like him?'

Gabriel's jaw clenched. 'Because I needed to know what he was up to.'

Leonora shook her head to try and understand. 'You came after me...after the interruption. I thought it was coincidental... but it wasn't, was it?'

'I came after you because I wanted you. You felt it too that night. And, I was concerned about you.'

But Leonora wasn't hearing him. She was reliving what had happened in slow motion. She looked at him, feeling the blood drain south through her body, leaving her cold all over. 'You seduced me just to get back at him. You seized an opportunity.'

Gabriel shook his head. 'No, I seduced you because I wanted you—for no other reason.'

Leonora was aware of a sharp pain near her heart. 'Are you telling me you weren't in any way aware of the fact that it might get to Lazaro if you were seen with me?'

Gabriel flushed. 'I admit I wasn't *un*aware that it might irritate him if he saw pictures of us together, leaving the hotel. But once we got back to my apartment Lazaro Sanchez was the last person on my mind.'

Leonora shook her head. 'You've used me from the very start—like a pawn. Is that why you proposed? Because it was another way to strike at your adversary?'

Leonora backed away from Gabriel. She had to leave before he saw how devastating this knowledge was to her. She turned and fled, apologising as she bumped into people in her bid to get out of the function room.

She emerged into a corridor and saw an elevator. The doors were closing and she ran, catching it just before they closed all the way. She stepped in, aware of people looking at her. Her heart was pounding. She felt wild. Undone.

She'd just been a pawn all along.

She saw Gabriel emerge from the room just as the doors closed. In that moment, when their eyes met for a split second, she hated him.

She didn't think when she got out on the ground floor. She went straight to the entrance and jumped into the first taxi she saw...

Gabriel cursed loudly and colourfully enough to make people stop and look at him at the entrance of the grand hotel. He'd just seen a flash of blue dress and bare back disappear into a taxi and the car was already merging into the heavy Paris traffic.

He tried calling Leo's phone but it went straight to voicemail. Gabriel was not unaware of the irony of his wife being pretty much the only woman who had ever consistently demonstrated that he wasn't as irresistible as people liked to make out.

He summoned his own car and got into the back, instructing the driver to go to his hotel. All he could do was hope that she had returned there.

But she hadn't.

He paced up and down, trying her phone again and again. Eventually he gave up. She'd run because she needed space. He couldn't blame her. His conscience stung hard. He *had* gone after her that first night because he'd wanted her, but he'd also seen an opportunity to stick the knife into Sanchez by letting them be photographed leaving the hotel together.

He just hadn't realised how much he would want her. Sanchez had become very much peripheral to everything once he'd slept with Leo and decided to ask her to marry him.

But could he convince her of that?

'Où allez-vous, madame?'

Leonora looked at the driver and blinked. Where *was* she going? Her instinct had been to get as far away as possible from Gabriel. But she had a limited amount of cash in her clutch bag and she was dressed in an evening gown. Hardly appropriate to roam the streets, even though she felt it would take miles to work off the anger she felt towards Gabriel.

Anger. *And hurt.*

She knew she had no choice but to go back to their hotel, so she gave the address reluctantly. The taxi did a U-turn in the road and went back the way it had come.

She felt sick. Bruised. And, worse, like a monumental fool. From the moment Gabriel had spoken to her he'd relished her strategic importance in scoring points against a rival.

Would he really be so petty?

Leonora ignored the question. Her anger was too fiery for her to try and be rational, to think this through. Lazaro had seen her as a pawn to use to get him accepted in a world closed to him. And Gabriel had seen her as a pawn to use to get back at Lazaro.

She knew she wasn't a helpless victim in all of this, but the revelation tainted every single interaction she'd had with Gabriel since they'd met. How he must have laughed at her the morning after that first night together when he'd realised that she hadn't even given her virginity to Lazaro. Another point scored.

For a moment she thought she might actually be sick, but she managed to control it. The hotel came into view, glittering in the distance. The taxi pulled up outside and Leonora paid the driver and got out.

As she ascended to their room in the elevator she nurtured her anger, feeling as if she needed some kind of armour against Gabriel's inevitable effect on her. When she reached the door she realised she didn't have a key, so she knocked on the heavy wood.

It opened almost immediately. Gabriel filled the doorway, jacket off, tie loose, top button undone. His hair was messy, as if he'd been running a hand through it. He held his mobile phone to his ear and he had the grimmest expression she'd ever seen on his face.

He said curtly, 'She's here. It's fine. Thank you, Marc.'

He stood aside and took his phone down from his ear. Ridiculously, Leonora felt like a rebellious teenager who'd been caught sneaking home from an illicit party. She refused to let Gabriel make her feel as if she was in the wrong, so she tipped her chin up and stalked past him into the suite.

She turned around to face him. He'd followed her and she could see the anger on his face.

'Don't *ever* do that again.'

Leonora was genuinely confused. 'What?'

'Run away and turn your phone off. We had no way of track-ing you or following you.'

'We?'

'My security team. The same security team that protects you without you even knowing it. You're a target, Leo, because *I'm* a target.'

To her surprise, although she could still see the anger, she could also see something else. Fear? And Gabriel looked slightly pale. Or was it just a trick of the light?

But his revelation just stoked her anger. She welcomed it. 'Well, if I had *known* that you had a security team I would have been more considerate. And I didn't turn off my phone when I left. It's been off since we arrived at the event.'

Gabriel ran a hand through his hair, mussing it up more. Le-onora hated how fascinated she was by this far less urbane in-carnation of Gabriel Torres.

Had he really been concerned?

She pushed that notion down, remembering seeing him go toe to toe with Lazaro Sanchez. The bristling tension between the men.

'Look,' he said, before she could say a word, throwing his phone down on a nearby chair, 'I'm sorry I didn't tell you that I knew Sanchez. I didn't realise how it would look. Or how it would make you feel when you discovered we did know each other.'

She asked tautly, 'What is it between you?'

Gabriel stuck his hands in his pockets. 'Ever since he ar-rived on the scene a few years ago he's made a beeline for me. Shadowing my every move, trying to disrupt deals I'm involved in. We're both currently involved in a bid to redevelop the old Madrid marketplace.'

Leonora had heard about that bid. It was huge. 'I had no idea you were involved in that.'

The hurt she was feeling intensified. While she'd been think-ing that she was growing closer to Gabriel, developing an intimacy that might one day extend beyond the bedroom, he had basically told her nothing about his day-to-day life. It was like a slap in the face.

He looked at her. 'I didn't think you'd be interested.'

'I'm your wife. I think I should know what you're involved in.'

Gabriel walked over to the window. He said, 'I've never had to answer to anyone. I've never had to explain myself.' He turned to face her. 'It didn't occur to me to let you know about these things.'

The anger in Leonora diminished slightly. She could appreciate how a lone wolf like Gabriel might find it hard to adjust to being in a relationship.

Still... 'That doesn't excuse you not telling me about Lazaro. It's too much of a coincidence that we ended up in bed together the same night my engagement was meant to be announced.'

Gabriel shook his head. He came closer, but Leonora backed away. He stopped.

'I went there that night because of Sanchez, yes. But as soon as I saw you I got distracted. It became about you, not him.'

Leonora cursed the fluttering in her belly. 'It was about him when you walked me out through the front door of the hotel.'

His mouth tightened. 'I was aware of how it would look, yes. But I was also conscious of wanting to get you out of there, and getting to know you.'

His straightforward honesty deflated her a little. Her heart beat fast as she recalled how she'd felt the pull between them that night. She'd felt guilty, standing next to her fiancé and being mesmerised by another man. And as soon as he'd asked if she wanted his help in leaving she hadn't hesitated.

As if sensing her weakening, Gabriel said, 'I swear to you, from the moment we got to my apartment Sanchez was not in my head or my thoughts or my motivations. I wanted *you*. Do you really think I would have seduced you into my bed just to get back at him?'

Pride oozed from every inch of the man in front of her. But she resisted the urge to let herself weaken too much.

She remembered something. 'You were saying something to Lazaro earlier...about meeting him in a street with your father. What was that?'

Gabriel's jaw clenched. 'He claims to be my half-brother on my father's side.'

Leonora sat down on the seat behind her. 'What?'

'He confronted us in the street years ago. It was my birthday. He accused my father of being *his* father...but then two of my father's men took him away and I never saw him again until a few years ago.'

'So...he *could* be your half-brother?'

'It's quite possible. My father could have sired any number of illegitimate children.' The bitterness was in Gabriel's voice was palpable.

'Who is his mother?'

Gabriel shook his head. 'I don't know...and I don't care.'

But Leonora saw something. A flicker of emotion. And the fact that Lazaro Sanchez could inspire emotion in Gabriel made her feel almost...jealous. Which was crazy. Jealous of a business rival!

'Did you marry me to get back at Lazaro?'

He took a step forward, a fierce look on his face. 'No. I married you because you were the first woman who made me even want to think about it.'

Suddenly she felt weary. She stood up abruptly. 'I'm quite tired now. I think I'll go to bed.'

She turned before he could see the emotion she was feeling. She suspected deep down that Gabriel wouldn't really have gone so far as to seduce her and marry her just to score points, but it still stung.

He called her name just as she reached the door. She stopped reluctantly but didn't turn around.

He said from behind her, 'You were never a pawn. I went to

the engagement announcement that night because of Sanchez, yes. But then I saw you, and I wanted you from that moment. I went after you because I wanted you. I seduced you because I wanted you. And I married you because I knew we'd be good together. Because I want you more than I've ever wanted another woman.'

Leonora's heart beat a little faster. Her hand tightened on the door handle. Gabriel had really hurt her this evening. And his power to hurt her only reminded her of how far she'd fallen. She had to protect herself.

She said, 'I'll take the spare room tonight.'

She walked out with her head held high and didn't look back. But it felt like a pyrrhic victory, because every instinct was urging her to go back and seek solace and oblivion in the arms of the man who had hurt her. Ironically, he was the only one who could help her to forget.

Leonora lay awake in the spare bed for a long time. It was the first night since she'd married Gabriel that she'd spent alone. And her body ached for him.

Dammit.

The hurt she'd been feeling had dissipated. She believed Gabriel. And she knew in her heart of hearts that if she was offered the choice of a sterile, emotionless marriage with Lazaro Sanchez over this...this sea of emotions with Gabriel, she would choose Gabriel again.

Something she'd been clinging to—a sense of injury—dissolved. She realised that her reaction would only reveal to Gabriel that she had feelings for him. Why else would she have been so affected? She thought of his anger because she'd disappeared. The expression of what had looked like fear on his face.

Impulsively, she got up from the bed and went outside the bedroom. The suite was dark. Quiet. She hovered uncertainly outside Gabriel's bedroom door, not even sure what she was going to do, but then she heard a sound coming from the living room so she went in that direction.

She found him sitting on the couch, watching a black and white movie on TV. One of her favourites. A classic. Her heart clenched. He was still wearing his tuxedo trousers and his white shirt was open at the neck by a couple of buttons, revealing the strong column of his throat. Stubble lined his jaw and her skin tingled with awareness.

Then he looked up and saw her. He stared at her for a long moment, almost as if he wasn't sure she was real. She was very aware of her flimsy silk negligée. Then he slowly sat forward and muted the movie.

He put out a hand and Leonora took a breath and moved towards him. He caught her hand and tugged her down onto the couch beside him. Electric heat flooded her body. Instantaneous. Addictive.

She opened her mouth but he put a finger to it, stopping her. He shook his head. And then he said, 'Let me show you how much I want you. *You*, Leo, no one else.'

Weakly she gave herself up to the temptation she'd denied herself earlier, and with every touch and kiss she blocked out the hurt and the fact that she would undoubtedly face more hurt in the future.

When Leonora woke the next morning the sun was up. She was disorientated, and then she realised where she was and remembered the previous evening. She looked around but the room was empty. She was naked and her body ached all over. They'd made love on the couch, like teenagers, and then Gabriel had taken her into the bedroom and they'd made love again. And then again, as dawn had been breaking. Each as insatiable as the other.

Leonora groaned and rolled over, burying her face in the pillow. She didn't recognise this wanton side of herself. In fact she barely recognised herself at all. Her emotions were so raw and all over the place.

The revelation that Gabriel had known Lazaro all along still had the power to hurt, in spite of his assurances. He wouldn't be human if he hadn't been aware that seducing Leonora might affect Lazaro's pride. But, having met Lazaro's pregnant wife, Leonora figured Lazaro had more important things to consider than hurt pride.

She put a hand on her flat belly. Could she and Gabriel have conceived a child? Last night? She had to be ovulating around now... Her pulse quickened. Even though everything logical told her that they weren't yet ready for the seismic reality of a baby—they were still getting to know one another!—nevertheless she had to admit that she'd felt a pang of jealousy when she'd seen evidence of Skye's pregnancy.

Leonora suddenly imagined Gabriel appearing and finding her dreaming of becoming pregnant with his baby. She scrambled out of the bed and grabbed a robe. She went into the opulent bathroom and took a shower, standing under the hot spray for a long time, relishing the jets of water on her pleasantly aching muscles.

When she soaped herself she saw the signs of Gabriel's lovemaking: stubble rash on the inside of her thighs. She blushed and quickly rinsed off and got out. She roughly dried her hair and pulled on the robe again.

She steeled herself before she left the bedroom, wishing she could feel blasé and nonchalant after a night like the one they'd shared. They were married, hardly illicit lovers, and yet she felt like a jittery teenager.

When she emerged into the living area she saw the dining table was set up for breakfast. A hotel staff member was there, pouring coffee for Gabriel, who stood up when he saw her.

'Good morning. I ordered a selection of everything. I wasn't sure what you'd prefer.'

Leonora smiled at the staff member as she poured her coffee

and then melted discreetly away. She took in the array of food laid out—fresh fruit, yoghurt, pastries, pancakes, bacon, eggs, toast—and to her mortification her stomach rumbled.

She sat down quickly, avoiding Gabriel's eye, putting some fruit pieces in a bowl and helping herself to some yoghurt.

'How are you feeling?'

Gabriel's question seemed innocuous enough and Leonora risked a glance at him, relieved to see him buttering some toast and not looking at her.

'Fine, thank you.'

Tired. She fought not to let the blush inside her rise to the surface when she thought of why she was so tired.

After a moment Gabriel said, 'I thought we'd spend a lazy day just wandering around the city. If you like?'

Leonora's heart thumped. She swallowed her food. 'You don't have to work?'

He shook his head. 'My meetings are tomorrow and everything is set up for them. It's Sunday—who works on Sundays?'

She'd used to. It had usually been quite a busy day for tourists visiting the *castillo*.

Gabriel said, 'You look surprised?'

Leonora felt self-conscious. 'I think I'd just assumed you'd be more of a workaholic.'

Something fleeting crossed his face, but it was gone before she could decipher what it was.

He said, 'I probably would have found an excuse to work today, but now I have a reason not to.'

It was ridiculous that she felt so excited and yet so trepidatious at the prospect of a day in Gabriel's company. Hadn't she spent a honeymoon alone with him for the best part of a week? But that had felt different—out of reality. It had all been so new. All-consuming. She hadn't been in love with him then.

She hid her trepidation and said lightly, 'Then I'd like that.' She thought of something, 'What if the paparazzi spot us?'

Gabriel was one of their favourite subjects to follow as he was usually so elusive. But there had been plenty of paparazzi out-side the hotel yesterday evening so they knew they were there.

Gabriel wiped his mouth with a napkin and stood up. He said with a wicked smile, 'I thought of that and I have a plan...'

CHAPTER NINE

GABRIEL'S PLAN HAD been to order up some casual clothes from the hotel's boutique, and now he and Leonora, dressed in jeans, shirts, light jackets and baseball hats, were ducking out of the hotel via a back entrance.

Leonora's hand was in Gabriel's as he led her around the side of the hotel. She could see the paparazzi waiting at the front, looking bored, checking their watches, and she couldn't help the small giggle rising as they made their escape. She felt as if she was playing truant from school. Giddy. And even giddier at this unexpected side of Gabriel.

To her surprise, he took her to the nearest Métro station saying, 'It's quicker than a taxi—do you mind?'

Leonora grinned up at him. 'Not at all.'

And that was the start of a magical and totally spontaneous day. They travelled around the city totally unnoticed, blending in with the crowds. Well, as discreetly as a six-foot-plus man *could* blend in with the crowds. Gabriel drew plenty of looks, but not necessarily looks of recognition. And if someone did do a double-take Gabriel and Leonora were usually gone before they realised who it was, having slipped down a side street.

Gabriel had left it to her to decide where to go, so they'd started at the Eiffel Tower and then wandered to the museums, going into the Rodin Museum, where his famous sculpture *The Kiss* had suddenly taken on a whole new significance for Leonora.

They'd stopped for delicious coffee and pastries on the Île de la Cité, near Notre-Dame, and now they were wandering through the leafy Jardin du Luxembourg, chatting easily about inconsequential things.

For the first time Leonora was acutely aware of families. Men carrying toddlers on their shoulders. Babies in prams. Her insides clenched. This could be them some day. And she appreciated more than ever Gabriel's desire for their children to have a different kind of upbringing.

On impulse, when they were standing by the lake in the park, Leonora turned to Gabriel and blurted out, 'I want to have a baby with you.'

He looked at her, a slightly nonplussed expression on his face, his firm mouth twitching. 'Well…that's…*good…*'

Leonora cursed her impetuosity. 'I mean, I know we have to have children, for so many reasons, but I actually…*want* to have a child with you.'

Her heart was pounding so fast. She tried to blame it on the coffee they'd just had. But she knew it wasn't the coffee.

Gabriel suddenly looked more serious. He twined his fingers with hers. 'I know,' he said. 'Me too.'

Leonora felt as if something intensely precious and delicate had been strung between them. And then she saw it: the heat in his eyes. The intent. It sparked the fire inside her and within seconds Gabriel was striding out of the park and flagging down a taxi.

He bundled Leonora in and she looked at him, taking the baseball cap off her head, half terrified and half exhilarated at the urgency suddenly beating between them.

'Where are we going?'

But she knew.

He gave directions to the driver to go back to the hotel, which wasn't far. They were there within minutes.

As they got out Leonora said, 'What about the paparazzi?'

But Gabriel just growled as he tugged her out. 'They don't matter.'

Within a short minute they were back in the hotel suite and Leonora's back was against the door, her mouth under Gabriel's and his hands roving over her body, removing her clothes with ruthless efficiency.

By the time they reached the bedroom, with a line of clothes strewn between the bed and the main door, they were naked.

They fell on the bed, limbs entwined. Leonora didn't know where she began and Gabriel ended. She'd never felt so primal in her life. When Gabriel joined their bodies in one cataclysmic thrust Leonora gasped. It was swallowed by Gabriel's mouth as he started to move in and out, taking them higher and higher, until they could go no further. After a taut moment, every muscle straining against the oncoming rush of pleasure, they fell into it, down and down...and Leonora wasn't even aware that she was crying as her emotions overflowed onto her cheeks.

It was early evening when Leonora woke in the bed alone. She realised her face and eyes were a little sticky and touched her cheeks, horror dawning on her as she realised she'd cried tears of pure emotion while making love to Gabriel.

She got up and dived under a steaming shower, as if that might wash away the signs of her weakness. She prayed that he hadn't seen her emotion. The thought of him realising he'd moved her to tears made her scrub herself even harder.

Eventually she got out, and only emerged into the living area once she'd put on some make-up and pulled back her damp hair. She dressed in casual dark trousers and a thin grey long-sleeved top. Clothes not remotely designed to entice.

Gabriel was standing looking out of the window, and for a moment before he heard her she drank in the tall, broad-shouldered magnificence of him. She wanted him. Again. Already. *Always.*

A sense of desperation mixed with panic gripped her and she felt like fleeing, as if she could escape the way he made her feel, but then he turned around and saw her.

She couldn't help the heat rising into her cheeks and was glad of the dusk outside and the low lighting hiding her reaction.

'I didn't want to disturb you,' Gabriel said.

Leonora's self-consciousness was acute. He hadn't wanted to disturb her—in case she started crying again?

She forced a bright smile. 'I'm awake now.'

He looked at his watch. 'I don't know about you, but I'm famished. We can eat here or go out. It's up to you.'

Leonora's relief that he wasn't making any reference to her tears was short-lived when she imagined sharing an intimate meal in this suite while she still felt so raw. And with the bedroom so near.

She said quickly, 'Let's go out.'

In the back of the chauffeur-driven car on the way to the restaurant, Gabriel found that he was ever so slightly piqued that Leonora seemed so eager to venture out to less intimate surroundings. Previous lovers would have been only too happy to capitalise on his undivided attention. But then, Leonora wasn't just a lover. She was his wife. And even as a lover...the lovemaking they shared was nothing like any kind he'd experienced before.

When he thought of this afternoon, and how desperate he'd been, his only consolation was that she'd been as hungry as him. He could still feel her nails digging into his buttocks and hear her rough entreaties. *'Please...don't stop...'*

Gabriel shifted in the seat, irritated. He was regressing. He was no more in control of his body now than he had been when he was a lusty teenager. *Por Dios.*

The car pulled to a stop and now Gabriel was the one who relished getting out of the intimate space. He went around and helped Leonora out.

She looked around her. 'Where are we?'

'Montmartre. There's a good place I know up here.'

He took her hand in his—a gesture that came to him as naturally as breathing air. A gesture he would never have allowed with previous lovers. Somehow it felt ridiculously intimate. But they were married, so that changed everything...didn't it?

They turned a corner and a beautiful square opened out before them, lined with trees and restaurants and bars, music drifting out into the warm evening air.

'Oh, this is lovely!'

Gabriel watched Leonora's face as she looked around, a rare kind of pleasure flowing through him at her reaction.

She caught him looking at her and she blushed.

He said, 'You're unbelievable—do you know that, Leo?'

She looked genuinely confused. 'Why?'

'You were born into one of Spain's oldest dynasties and yet you're not a snob, or spoilt—which, notwithstanding your father's fall from grace, you could very well be.'

Leonora wasn't sure how to respond to that, but she took it as a compliment.

Gabriel led her to a restaurant on the other side of the square. It looked discreetly expensive. The maître d' greeted them effusively and showed them to a table that was artfully screened off from the other diners, while giving them a view of the charming square.

They were seated and had been handed menus when Gabriel said, 'You could very well have sought out a suitable husband at a much younger age. Why didn't you?'

Leonora hadn't been expecting such a direct question. No one had ever asked her that before. But she'd certainly always been aware of people's looks and speculation whenever she'd appeared in public.

She took a breath. 'I think for a long time I was angry with my father for failing us like that. For being...fallible.'

A cynical expression flashed across Gabriel's face. 'I can attest to just how fallible fathers can be.'

'Once it became apparent that I was the only potential saviour of my family I resented it for a long time. I resented the structures that haven't changed much since medieval times. This notion of having to be married off for the good of the family name. I was made very aware of the fact that our—*my*—only real currency was our name and our lineage.'

'If it's any consolation, things weren't much different for me. I alone am responsible for carrying on the illustrious Cruz y Torres name. My sister doesn't bear that responsibility and I wouldn't put it on her.'

Leonora shook her head. 'And you never minded?'

Gabriel picked up an olive and put it in his mouth, chewing for a moment. 'I never said I didn't mind. When I was younger I contemplated running away many times. That day when Lazaro Sanchez confronted my father in the street and said he was his son... I actually felt slightly envious of him—that he wasn't burdened by the family name.'

Leonora looked at Gabriel. 'Maybe that's what's at the root of your issues with him. The fact that you're a little jealous of him.'

Gabriel leaned forward and took Leonora's hand. He brought it to his mouth and pressed a kiss to the back of it. He said, 'I was jealous of him that night when he announced your engagement.'

Leonora's heartrate picked up. All she could see were Gabriel's intense eyes, the gold flecks giving them a leonine quality.

There was a discreet cough and with a struggle she looked up at the waiter, for a moment feeling dizzy. Forgetting they were in public. Had they even ordered? She couldn't remember...

Gabriel let her hand go. Starters were placed down in front

of them. They ate in silence, and Leonora was glad of a moment to absorb what Gabriel had said, and to tell herself that his admission of jealousy didn't mean anything. He had decided he wanted her that night. That was all. He had an ongoing rivalry with Lazaro. That was all.

As if to reinforce that assertion in her head, their conversation didn't stray into personal territory again. But after the main course had been eaten and taken away Gabriel's gaze narrowed on Leonora.

'Did you enjoy today?'

Leonora was immediately rewarded with a flashback to when they'd arrived back at the suite earlier, ravenous for each other. She took a quick sip of wine—anything to cool her insides.

'It was lovely, thank you.'

He leaned forward. 'I want you to feel valued, Leo. You're not just a pawn. We both grew up knowing we bore a responsibility that most people don't. Our privilege isn't something we got to choose. But I'm glad that I bear this responsibility with you. I think we can be happy together.'

A chill breeze skated across Leonora's skin and she shivered slightly. Gabriel's words circled in her head sickeningly. *'I think we can be happy together'.* Lazaro had said almost exactly the same words just before the engagement announcement.

The truth was no matter what Gabriel said, or how many assurances he provided, she *was* just a pawn. But then, as he pointed out, so was he in many ways. They were both pawns. Somehow that didn't give her much comfort.

It was clear now that today hadn't really been born of a spontaneous desire to spend time with her. It had been a calculated move to make her feel valued. Wanted. Desired. Maybe he hadn't planned that explosive interlude back at the hotel, but all that confirmed was that they wanted each other.

Leonora cursed herself for being so sensitive. She had to develop a thicker skin if she was going to survive in Gabriel's world. The fact that she felt a growing intimacy with him beyond the bedroom—worse, a growing friendship—was all just an illusion. Gabriel was looking on her as an investment to nurture.

Leonora pasted on the brightest smile she could. 'I think we can be happy too.'

Gabriel smiled approvingly.

This was her life now and she had to come to terms with it. To want more... Well, that was just foolish.

In a bid to deflect Gabriel's attention, because he saw too much, Leonora said, 'So, tell me about this bid you're involved in...'

Ten days after they'd returned from Paris, Gabriel was at the public bid for the market space. A project he'd been working on for over a year.

For a man who wasn't used to being unsure of outcomes, he didn't like to admit that the bid might very well go Lazaro Sanchez's way. The man had come up with a decent plan. A plan that Gabriel could grudgingly respect even if he didn't agree with all of it.

But for the first time in his life the prospect of losing to someone else wasn't his main concern. Something else was distracting him and taking precedence over the bid. *Leonora.*

Things had been slightly *off* ever since Paris, and Gabriel couldn't figure it out.

That Sunday they'd spent together had been one of the most enjoyable days Gabriel could remember in a long time. He didn't have close confidantes. He'd always trodden his own path and had learnt very early on not to trust people. Women or business peers. Everyone wanted a piece of him or to best him.

But he trusted Leonora. Enjoyed spending time with her. *Wanted* to spend time with her. He never would have taken a day off like that before. It had been years since he'd taken the Métro or just wandered around a museum.

But when they'd returned to their suite after dinner on the Sunday night she'd been slightly withdrawn. He'd taken a call, and by the time he'd gone to bed she was asleep. The first night they hadn't made love since they were married.

And then, this week, he'd been busy preparing for the bid, and each night when he'd come back to the *castillo* she'd been in bed, asleep. So he'd hardly seen her. Or touched her. He could feel his hunger for her gnawing away inside him and she should be here by his side today, but she wasn't.

She'd been pale this morning—out of sorts. She'd said something about period pains and had assured him she just needed to rest. So he'd left her behind.

He'd found to his surprise that the evidence that she wasn't pregnant had made him feel conflicting things. Because, as much as he knew he had to have children, he was aware that it was too soon. He wanted more time with Leonora. Alone.

And yet they weren't using protection, so if she wasn't pregnant this month the likelihood was that it would happen very soon. Unless they made a decision to wait for a while, which would go against one of the reasons for this marriage: to have heirs. To continue the family legacy.

This revelation was disconcerting and it made him feel off-centre.

There was a movement in his peripheral vision and he saw Lazaro Sanchez walk over to where his wife had just arrived. Her bright red hair was distinctive. And the small bump of her pregnant belly.

He had to concede that she was not the kind of woman he would have expected Sanchez to go for. She looked...*nice*. Kind. She was smiling, and he could see from here that it was genuine. Warm. Leonora had a similar quality but she was more reserved.

Leonora.

He took out his phone and sent her a quick text, asking how she was.

She replied almost instantly.

Feeling okay, thanks. Good luck with the bid. Sorry I'm not there with you. x

To his surprise, that small 'x' impacted him in his gut, taking his breath for a moment.

Someone approached him. 'Señor Torres? It's time.'

Gabriel saw Sanchez moving towards the stage and knew he couldn't afford to lose focus now. Sanchez was married, having a baby. Gabriel was also married, and even if Leonora wasn't pregnant now, she would be soon.

There was a lot riding on every decision Gabriel made now. His responsibilities and his legacy were growing exponentially and he wasn't going to let anything distract from that. Not now, not ever.

When Gabriel returned home from the public bid he was met by Ernesto, who looked anxious. 'It's Leonora, sir, she hasn't left the bedroom. She tells me she's all right, but I'm concerned.'

Immediately all thoughts of the bid and the brief altercation he'd had with Lazaro Sanchez afterwards left Gabriel's mind. He looked at his watch. It was early evening. That meant she'd been in bed all day with these pains. Surely this was not a usual menstrual problem?

He took the stairs two at a time to their bedroom and opened the door. Leonora was just a shape under the covers and he went over, his gut clenching with concern. She turned over and he could see even before he reached her that she was pale.

He sat down and automatically put a hand to her brow. It was clammy. 'What is it? Is this a regular occurrence?'

She shook her head, dark hair slipping over one shoulder. Her cheekbones stood out starkly. She was clearly in pain.

'Not every month. Some are worse than others. I have a history of bad cramps. They usually pass within a couple of days. How did the bid go?'

He waved a hand, dismissing that and asked, 'Have you ever seen a doctor about this?'

She nodded. 'When I was younger. He told me it was mild endometriosis.'

She tried to sit up and winced, sucking in a breath.

Gabriel made a split-second decision, pulling out his phone.

Leonora heard him, and went even more ashen. When he'd terminated the call she said, 'Hospital really isn't necessary, Gabriel. I just need to take some more painkillers and I'll be feeling much better by morning.'

Gabriel stood up and said tautly, 'We're not debating this, Leo. You need to get checked.'

Leonora was in too much pain to argue with Gabriel, much as she'd have liked to. She couldn't deny that she was a little freaked out herself, because this month her cramps seemed even more acute than normal.

She got out of bed slowly, trying not to show how much of an effort it took. Gabriel found some shoes and laid them by the bed. As she stood up a wave of dizziness hit her.

Immediately Gabriel was scooping her up into his arms and Leonora realised she was too weak to argue. Most likely from not having eaten all day.

She tried to protest, but he was already out of the room and down the stairs, walking into the main hall, saying something to Ernesto, who leapt to attention, opening the passenger door of Gabriel's car.

Gabriel put her in as carefully as if she was made of fine bone china.

She said, 'Really, there's no need for this...' But he didn't listen to her, strapping her in and closing the door.

Leonora kept her mouth shut as Gabriel drove into the city

and stopped on the forecourt of a hospital. People were there to greet them and Leonora was embarrassed—until a wave of pain from her abdomen made her grit her teeth.

An orderly appeared at her door with a wheelchair for her to sit in, and suddenly she was glad that they were there. Because this was definitely not normal any more.

The following few hours became a blur as she underwent a series of tests. There was a lull while they waited for the doctor to return with some results. Wanting to divert her mind from all sorts of scary possibilities, she asked Gabriel about the bid again.

He turned around from where he was standing at the window, hands in his pockets. His tie was pulled loose, the top button of his shirt open, jacket off and thrown on a chair. His hair was mussed because he'd been running a hand through it.

He said, 'We won't know for at least another month. The two bids have gone on public display at City Hall and the public now has a chance to see both sets of plans and to vote for their favourite. Their vote, together with the city councillors, will decide who gets the commission.'

'Was Lazaro there?'

Gabriel's expression darkened. He nodded. 'Yes—and his wife.'

Leonora plucked at the sheet, feeling guilty. 'I'm sorry again that I wasn't there.'

After all, wasn't that her role now? To be by her husband's side to show support? Lazaro's wife might not have the right name or lineage, but she appeared to be fulfilling her brief far better than Leonora was—on every level.

Gabriel shook his head and came and sat on the end of the bed. 'Don't be silly. It really wasn't that important.'

'But you've been working on it for a year and you hate Lazaro.'

Gabriel stood up, hands dug deep in his pockets again. His

jaw was tense. 'I don't *hate* Sanchez...but he winds me up like no one else.'

Leonora squinted at him. 'Are you *sure* you're not related?'

Gabriel made a face, but before he could respond the doctor arrived in the room.

He looked at Gabriel. 'You should go home for the night, Señor Torres. I'm afraid we'll have to do more tests in the morning before we'll be able to give you any conclusive results.'

A sense of dread filled Leonora and she forced herself to ask, 'What do you think it is?'

The doctor looked at her, and she could see the gravity of his expression. 'I'm sorry to say, my dear, that your endometriosis is no longer mild, and probably hasn't been for some time. It appears to be extensive and acute. The fact that your symptoms haven't necessarily been severe up until now is atypical. But every woman with this condition is different. We'll know more tomorrow, when we conclude the tests. I'm sorry I can't tell you more right now.'

A week later

A kindly voice came from a great distance. 'How are you feeling, Leonora?'

She knew it wasn't Gabriel. It was too kindly and he called her Leo.

She struggled to open her eyes, feeling the huge effort it took. When she opened them she shut them again quickly. It was too bright. She was aware of pain...dull, down low...in her abdomen.

There was something pressing on her mind—something urgent—but she knew she didn't want to think about it.

She managed to croak out, 'Thirsty...'

Whoever was there held her head up and pressed something to her lips. A straw.

The kind voice said, 'Drink, Leonora, you'll be feeling better soon.'

But she knew she wouldn't be.

Before she could figure out why, she slipped back down into the dark, comforting place.

'How are you feeling, Leo?'

Gabriel. She knew it was him because she'd been feigning sleep since he'd come into the room, like a coward. But she couldn't keep hiding.

She opened her eyes and blinked in the light.

He looked huge, standing at the end of the bed. Worried. There was stubble on his jaw. For a moment emotion threatened to overwhelm her but she pushed it down. She remembered everything now. She had done as soon as she'd woken properly from the anaesthetic, two days ago.

He said, 'The doctor said you can come home today. But there's no rush. As soon as you're feeling up to dressing.'

She opened her mouth. 'We should…we need to talk about—'

Gabriel shook his head. 'Not now, Leo. We can talk about it when you're feeling better.'

Leonora might have laughed if she'd been able to. Right at that moment she couldn't imagine ever feeling better. But she forced herself to push back the covers and swing her legs over the side of the bed.

Immediately Gabriel was there, but she put up a hand, terrified of what his touch would do to her in her emotionally brittle state. 'I'm fine. I'll have a shower and pack. You should go… have a coffee… I'll be ready when you come back.'

He left the room and she let out a shuddering breath. She felt hollow. Aching. A kaleidoscope of images and memories from the past few days came back into her head before she could stop them.

A doctor standing by the bed, saying, *I'm so sorry, Señora Torres, but tests have confirmed that your fallopian tubes are*

*beyond saving. The endometriosis has caused too much dam-
age...surgical removal of the fallopian tubes...you'll still have
your uterus and ovaries...'*

She was infertile. At the age of twenty-four.

Unbeknownst to her, because her symptoms hadn't been
severe, the endometriosis had been quietly and devastatingly
wreaking havoc on her insides, cruelly targeting her fallopian
tubes, rendering them useless. Beyond saving.

She knew she was still in shock. It hadn't sunk in fully. Nor
had the ramifications. She hadn't been able to deal with seeing
her parents, though she knew they were worried. Too afraid
of what she'd see on their faces. Their terror that this might
change everything.

Leonora pushed herself up from the bed and walked over
to the private bathroom, locking herself inside. Physically, the
doctor had said she should be fully recovered within a couple
of weeks. Emotionally, however...

She turned on the spray of the shower and stripped off, stepping into the small cubicle. She used the shower head to clean
herself, careful to keep the wound dressing dry.

When she was finished she wrapped herself in a towel and
washed her face, brushed her teeth, avoiding looking at her face
in the mirror. But then she caught her reflection and stopped.
Her eyes looked like two huge pools of pain. Her skin was white,
stretched taut, her cheekbones standing out starkly.

All of a sudden she couldn't contain it any more. The emotion rose up and came out of her in great, shuddering sobs.

Gabriel came back into the hospital room carrying coffee for
Leonora. He stopped when he heard the sobs coming from the
bathroom. His blood ran cold. He'd never heard such a raw outpouring of emotion before, and every instinct in him told him
to go to her...but he knew she wouldn't welcome it. This was
a very private pain, and for the first time in his life he knew
what it was to be helpless.

A week later

Leonora was sitting on a chair on the back terrace of the *castillo*. The late-summer early evening still held lots of warmth, but nevertheless Ernesto had insisted on putting a rug over Leonora's legs.

The spectacular grounds of the *castillo* soothed Leonora's ragged emotions, so she'd taken to sitting here every day, while her body healed on the outside. She was still numb on the inside, though. Still trying to compute the catastrophic loss of her fertility. Every time she tried to dwell on it her mind skittered away.

Her parents had come to visit and her mother had been pale. She'd said, '*Por Dios,* Leo...he'll have to divorce you if you can't give him an heir. What will happen to us?'

Leonora's father had taken her mother away after that, telling Leonora not to listen to her. But her mother was right. And it was something Leonora knew she'd have to discuss with Gabriel sooner or later. The fact that she was no longer capable of providing her husband with an heir.

At that moment she heard footsteps and her skin prickled with awareness. Still. Even after what had happened.

Gabriel came into her field of vision, tall and broad. Dressed in a three-piece suit. His long fingers were tugging at his tie, opening it and the top button of his shirt.

'How are you today?'

Leonora nodded. 'Feeling much better, thank you.'

Gabriel sat down on the lounger beside her, his dark gaze roving over her face. Leonora knew she must look pale and wan.

'The doctor came to see you today?'

She nodded. 'He was here earlier. I'm healing well.'

Physically.

Gabriel nodded. 'That's good.'

Leonora forced herself to look at him. 'We should talk about—'

He held up a hand. 'We're not talking about anything until

you're back on your feet. All you need to think about now is recuperating.'

Leonora swallowed her words.

Gabriel stood up. 'Dinner will be ready shortly. I'm just going to take a shower and change and then I'll come back down.'

Leonora watched him walk away, athletic grace in every move he made. She turned her head, eyes stinging suddenly. She pulled her glasses down over her eyes in case anyone saw her emotion.

Dealing with this diagnosis would be massively disrupting to the best of relationships, founded on love, so what hope could they possibly have? Gabriel could delay the conversation for as long as he wanted, but ultimately Leonora knew this spelled the end of their marriage.

CHAPTER TEN

GABRIEL WAS IN his office, staring out of the window, which took in a spectacular view of Madrid. Sunlight bathed the city in a golden glow. But he didn't see any of that. His thoughts were inward.

It had been two weeks now since Leonora's operation, and physically she seemed to be fine. But emotionally…

Gabriel couldn't begin to fathom what she was going through, and the feeling of helplessness he'd felt that day in the hospital when he'd heard her crying was still there.

Helplessness was totally alien to Gabriel. He was used to being able to influence things, events. And yet even he had to concede that this was entirely out of his control.

There was no amount of money he could throw at the situation to make it better. To restore Leonora to full health.

Unsurprisingly, she'd been withdrawn for the past two weeks. She'd been sleeping in one of the guest suites, in spite of Gabriel's insistence that he would move rooms.

He hadn't liked not having her in his bed. Not at all. It made him feel even more helpless as he watched her retreat further and further to some place he couldn't reach.

There was a knock on his door and he turned around, irritated at the interruption. It was his secretary.

'Sorry, I know you don't want to be disturbed…but it's Lazaro Sanchez.'

Literally the last person Gabriel wanted to see right now. But to his surprise, instead of issuing an immediate rejection, he heard himself say, 'Send him in.'

Sanchez walked in. Familiar tension and something much more ambiguous mixed in Gabriel's gut.

Leonora's words came into his head. *Are you sure you're not related?'*

He said, 'To what do I owe this pleasure?'

Lazaro walked over to the desk, and as he did so Gabriel noticed that he looked a little less cocky than normal. As if some of the stuffing had been knocked out of him. He almost felt compelled to say something, but then he noticed a padded envelope in Lazaro's hand.

Lazaro put it down on the desk and tapped it lightly. He looked at Gabriel. 'There is all you need in there to prove that we are related. Which we are. Again, I don't want anything from you or your family—simply an acknowledgement that I am of your blood. It's the least I'm due, I think. Also, I've decided to pull out of the bid for the market. I still think my bid was the better one, but it's not my priority any more. And, yes, you're right. A big part of my motivation *was* in going up against you. You're a worthy adversary, Gabriel, but I've lost the appetite for battling with you.'

Lazaro was almost at the door before Gabriel had recovered enough to say, 'What's changed?'

Lazaro turned around and smiled. 'I've just realised what's truly important in life…that's all.'

He walked out before Gabriel could get his wits back together. Very few people surprised him. But Lazaro Sanchez had just blindsided him. Rapidly, Gabriel tried to assess what Lazaro's agenda might be…but he couldn't come up with anything.

He walked over and picked up the padded envelope. Inside

was a piece of paper with the information for a doctor who had a sample of Lazaro's DNA in storage. All Gabriel had to do was provide his own sample of DNA for comparison and they would know if they were related.

But Gabriel didn't need to do the test. He knew in his gut what the result would be. He'd known that day in the street, when he'd first seen Lazaro, that the possibility that he was his kin was very real. In fact, on the other side of the animosity that had played out between the two men, there had been a sense of affinity that he'd never wanted to acknowledge.

It was an unsettling revelation.

Gabriel put down the piece of paper and walked back over to the window. He should be feeling triumphant because he was going to be awarded the bid for the market. But he wasn't feeling triumphant. He was feeling deflated. As if something had been taken out of his grasp.

He realised that he'd relished the fight with Lazaro. The chance to prove himself. Because it happened so rarely.

And then an insidious suspicion came into his mind. Had Lazaro found out about Leo's diagnosis, somehow? Was this why he'd gone a step further in his claim to be of Cruz y Torres blood? Because he knew that if Gabriel didn't have an heir, then any child of Lazaro's would therefore have a claim on the Torres inheritance?

Gabriel shook his head. He was being paranoid. There was no way Lazaro could have found out. It was just coincidence...

But, the fact remained that without an heir, the family name would die out. Even if Lazaro *was* his half-brother, he might not want anything to do with the Cruz y Torres name. Especially after the way he'd been treated...

Gabriel thought of how only a couple of weeks ago he'd been almost hoping that Leo wouldn't be pregnant, so they could have more time alone together. Fate was laughing in his face. Because now they had all the time in the world.

* * *

Leonora sensed Gabriel before she saw him, but she kept on reading aloud to Matías, who had come to the *castillo* to visit her. He'd always loved being read to, and she still did it on occasion. It was like a security blanket, and he'd obviously sensed that something wasn't quite right with his big sister. She hadn't told him about her operation, he'd be too upset.

But Matías had spotted Gabriel and he jumped up from the seat they were sharing and went over, throwing his arms around Gabriel's neck. Gabriel looked at her over Matías's shoulder and she could see it in his eyes.

Now he was ready to discuss things with her.

She'd been feeling perfectly well again for a few days now. Apart from the small scar on her abdomen it would be hard to know that anything had happened. But it had. And it had had catastrophic repercussions.

They both had dinner with Matías, and then he was taken back to his school by one of Gabriel's staff.

Gabriel turned to her at the door, from where they'd waved him off. 'Come and have a nightcap on the terrace?'

Leonora's hand gripped the door for a moment, and then she let go and nodded. 'Sure.'

She followed him out to the terrace, peaceful and fragrant with blooming flowers and plants. Candles flickered gently in the light breeze. Leonora sat down in a chair and tucked her legs underneath her. She watched Gabriel pour himself a coffee and then he looked around.

'What would you like?'

'A little port, please.'

He poured some into a delicate glass and brought it over. Amazingly, considering how battered and bruised her insides were, Leonora felt a flicker of response. She took a sip of the sweet alcohol.

Gabriel came over and sat down on a chair at right angles to hers. His shirt was unbuttoned at the top, revealing the strong bronzed column of his throat and a glimpse of curling chest hair. His sleeves were rolled up and the muscles of his arms were a distraction that sent further tendrils of awareness to Leonora's core.

To her surprise he said, 'I had a visit from Lazaro Sanchez today.'

'Oh?'

'He told me he was pulling out of the bid...that he no longer cares about it.'

'That's...strange.'

From what Leonora had learnt about Lazaro during their short and very chaste relationship, he was ruthlessly ambitious. He'd been willing to marry a woman he hardly knew, after all.

As had Gabriel, pointed out a small voice.

'Yes...it is,' Gabriel said, and took a sip of coffee.

They sat in silence for a while, and then Gabriel put his cup down and sat forward.

Leonora tensed. He looked at her and she saw compassion in his eyes.

He said, 'I'm so sorry, Leo, for what's happened to you. If there was some way I could reverse the diagnosis or offer you a solution then I would.'

He stood up and she realised how agitated he was when he ran a hand through his hair. He cursed and walked over to the wall, placing his hands down on it.

Leonora untucked her legs and sat up, putting down the glass. She wasn't sure what to say.

He turned around and there was a bleak expression on his face. 'I've never felt so helpless in my life. And it's not a nice feeling. To know that there was literally nothing I could do. You were at the mercy of the doctors.'

A little of the ice that had been like a block in her chest for two weeks started melting slightly. She hadn't really thought of this impacting on Gabriel, but of course it must have.

'I know…and thank you for wanting to do something. But nothing could have been done.'

He came back over and sat down. 'It's not fair, Leo… I see you with Matías and know that you'd be a wonderful mother. Loving, caring, compassionate…'

Leonora had been trying not to give in to anger after her diagnosis, so hearing Gabriel articulate it for her was like a balm to her jagged edges.

'Thank you.'

But suddenly he was too close. Emotions were threatening to crack her open from the inside out—emotions she'd been clamping down on for fear of what would be unleashed. Like that day in the hospital, when the storm of grief had left her weak and spent.

She stood up and went to take his place at the terrace wall. She looked out at the view for a long moment, as if hoping it might give her strength, and then she turned, wrapping her arms around her midriff.

'This changes everything, Gabriel. I'm not the woman you married. I can't give you what you need. The sooner we file for divorce, the sooner you'll be free to move on.'

Gabriel stood up. 'Divorce?'

Leonora's arms tightened around herself, as if that might help her contain the rising emotion. 'Yes. Of course.'

He shook his head and came over to where she was standing. 'We don't need to divorce.'

'I can't give you what you need. An heir. Heirs. You're the last in your line and I'm infertile.'

He looked at her for a long moment as the word *infertile* hung starkly in the air between them. Then abruptly he turned away to look out over the gardens.

Eventually he said, 'The doctor assured us that all was not lost. We have options—IVF, adoption…'

'An adopted child wouldn't be of your blood. And IVF is a long and arduous process that may never work. I worked with an

IVF charity for a while and I saw the devastation it can wreak on couples, families. Even when it works it takes a toll on the strongest of relationships.'

Gabriel's jaw clenched. 'You don't think *we* have a strong relationship?'

Leonora swallowed, thinking of how rocked she'd been by the revelation that Gabriel knew Lazaro. How hurt.

'I think, like you said, we have a lot going for us... But this was one of the fundamental requirements, and I can't deliver.'

He looked at her. 'Do you want to divorce?'

Leonora couldn't escape that dark gaze. *No.* The word beat through her blood. She'd imagined a life with this man; a life beyond anything she had believed she could have with someone like him. But those fragile dreams had died two weeks ago.

'I think it's the only option.' They'd been married for almost three months, the legal requirement for granting divorce.

Gabriel looked away. His jaw was tight. Leonora knew that for a man like him it was difficult to admit defeat. As he'd said himself, he hadn't liked feeling helpless. But they were both helpless here.

He said, 'I have a full social schedule coming up. Now would not be a good time to draw adverse press attention. We will discuss this again when you are feeling stronger. A lot has happened in the past two weeks.'

Leonora desperately wanted to say, *What is there to discuss?* But she knew she didn't have the energy to deal with that conversation. So maybe he was right.

'Of course. Goodnight, Gabriel.'

Gabriel watched as Leonora walked back into the *castillo*, effortlessly graceful in a long flowing maxi-dress, her hair loose and slightly more unruly than its usual sleek perfection. Her face was bare of make-up but no less hauntingly beautiful.

'Do you want to divorce?'

'I think it's the only option.'

He still felt slightly winded by the punch to his gut at her suggestion of divorce. Not once since her diagnosis had that possibility even entered his head. But evidently it was the first thing she'd thought of.

He had thought they were building a solid basis for a long and enduring marriage. Solid enough to weather this storm.

Gabriel felt disorientated as he took in the full meaning of the fact that Leonora's diagnosis of infertility hadn't impinged upon him in the same way it had her. She'd been looking for the first opportunity to leave this marriage. And he hadn't.

Fool.

All sorts of insidious suspicions came into his mind. Maybe she'd played him from the start? Just looking for a way to save her family and ensure their security before seeking her freedom via divorce? Even if they'd had children? Maybe she'd just told him what he wanted to hear?

He cursed himself. He more than anyone knew they hadn't married for love. They'd married for myriad reasons—one of which, as she'd pointed out, was to procreate. Have heirs. Continue the line. The legacy.

Now that had been ripped away from them. Leaving...what? The reality that chemistry and mutual respect and friendship weren't enough? He'd mentioned the options that the doctor had given them—IVF, adoption... Gabriel didn't know much about IVF, but he knew enough to agree with Leonora. It was a hugely invasive and precarious method of having children, and she would be the one to bear the brunt of the pain and the procedures.

If she wanted out of the marriage she was hardly going to put herself through those procedures.

An emotion Gabriel had never felt before burned down low in his gut. It felt a lot like hurt.

He slammed his hand down on the terrace wall. No woman had the power to hurt Gabriel. She had made a commitment to him and she would honour it.

He wouldn't accept anything less.

* * *

It took hours for Leonora to fall asleep that night. The pain in her heart was almost physical. She couldn't believe how far she'd let herself fall for Gabriel. How far she'd let herself dream that even without his love they could have a good life together. She'd imagined that when the desire burned out they'd have a family to care for, to unite them.

She considered the fact that he'd mentioned IVF. Adoption. Maybe she owed it to him to give it a shot? But then maybe he'd only mentioned it because he felt duty-bound?

She thought of the families she'd met through that charity. She knew what a toll it took, and how it caused huge fissures in relationships and families.

Of course it could be successful, and many people went on to have children, but people who underwent IVF ached to have children and had exhausted every other possibility. They did it for love. And that was not what this relationship was about.

Even if she did agree to undergo IVF and they had children, she realised now that it wouldn't be enough for her to have children without Gabriel's love. It would kill her. She wanted the dream.

Gabriel would move on. He would find another suitable wife and have children. Of that she was sure. He deserved that.

He'd never made her any promises. She would do her duty as his wife for the next few weeks and then they would file for divorce. There was no other discussion to be had. Her infertility wouldn't have magically healed itself in a few weeks.

'You must be very proud, Torres, your wife is stunning.'

Gabriel looked at where Leonora was standing a few feet away. She was a vision in a long ballgown with a fitted sleeveless bodice and chiffon skirts falling to the floor. The gown was ice-blue. Her hair was pulled back and long diamond earrings glittered when she moved her head.

She was indeed stunning. Without a doubt the most beautiful woman in the room. She had an effortless kind of beauty that he could see people noticing and envying. What they didn't know was that her beauty wasn't just skin-deep. Or that she hid a very painful and devastating secret.

He glanced at the man beside him. A business acquaintance who was looking at Leonora far too covetously for Gabriel's liking.

He made his excuses and walked over to her, slipping an arm around her waist.

He felt the tension come into her body at his touch and everything inside him rejected it. It was a over a month now since they'd had that conversation about divorce. They'd been existing since then in a kind of sterile civil environment that was driving Gabriel slowly around the bend.

They were still in separate bedrooms—and Gabriel fully respected the space that Leonora had needed since the operation. But sexual frustration was a constant gnawing ache, exacerbated by the fact that she had retreated to some icy, closed-off place that he couldn't seem to reach.

She was always in bed when he came home from work. She busied herself at weekends at her parents *castillo*, helping with renovations and plans for the business. Or she spent time with Matías.

For someone like Gabriel, who had never envisaged marriage being anything but a means to an end, to find himself *missing* his wife was not a welcome revelation.

The closest they got to any kind of intimacy was at moments like this, when they were amongst hundreds of people. And everything in Gabriel rejected it. Rejected her closing herself off and retreating to a place he couldn't reach. Rejected the notion of divorce.

Leonora was holding herself so stiffly she could hardly breathe. Gabriel's arm was around her waist, and the urge to melt into his side, let him take her weight, was almost overwhelming.

The urge to touch him, kiss him…make love to him was even more overwhelming.

But she couldn't.

The only thing keeping her upright and able to function for the past few weeks was the block of ice in her chest. Keeping her emotions in a kind of deep freeze.

Gabriel represented heat and pain. She couldn't go there. Not when the time was approaching when they would file for divorce. Surely in a matter of days. Once that had happened, and she could maintain her distance from him, she would allow herself to breathe again. To feel the pain she knew she was avoiding.

But it was getting harder and harder. And tonight was worse than any other night.

It was as if he knew how tenuous her self-control was. At every opportunity he was touching her—her back, her arm— taking her hand, massaging her neck.

His touch was like a hot brand through her clothes. As if her body was conspiring with him to just melt and give in.

It would be so easy, whispered a little voice.

But she couldn't. She knew Gabriel wanted her. It was in his eyes every time he looked at her. Or maybe that was just her desire projected onto him?

She was going crazy.

After the operation she'd thought she'd never *feel* again. Feel desire. Hope. Sensation. But the human body was a fickle traitor. Her body seemed disinclined to remember those painful days. It was as if normal operations had resumed in spite of Leonora's emotional trauma.

'Are you ready to go?'

Leonora blinked. As much as she dreaded Gabriel's touch, because of what it did to her, she realised now that on some level she craved these fleeting moments for a few hours every week.

She moved out of his embrace and saw how his jaw tightened. 'Yes, I'm ready to go.'

He put a hand on her elbow and led her out through the crowd. She could feel the tension in his body, reminding her of that night when she'd seen him and Lazaro together.

The function this evening had taken place in the same hotel where her engagement to Lazaro had almost been announced. She'd been so distracted that she only really noticed when they walked outside and there was a barrage of flashes and questions from the paparazzi.

'Leonora! Gabriel! Over here!'

And then there was one voice which seemed to be elevated over all the rest.

'Are you pregnant yet, Señora Torres?'

Gabriel bundled her into the car and Leonora was tight-lipped as he sat into the driver's seat beside her. She was desperately trying to stem the hurt blooming inside her.

He was looking at her. She could feel his gaze on her. Concerned.

'Are you okay? I'm sorry about that—they're idiots.'

Leonora looked straight ahead. 'Just drive. Please.'

Her tenuous hold on her emotions was breaking. Like taut wires finally snapping under the pressure.

Leonora wasn't even aware of where they were going until Gabriel pulled into the underground car park of his city centre apartment. A sense of *déjà vu* slammed into her, further diminishing her sense of control. The memories here—

'Why have we come here?' she asked Gabriel.

He turned off the car engine and looked at her. 'I have an early meeting in town in the morning. There's a fully stocked closet here—it's not a problem, is it?'

Leonora shook her head quickly, in case he might see something. 'No, not at all.'

There was a touch of weariness in his tone, 'There's a spare bedroom here too, Leo. Don't worry, I'm not trying to seduce you again.'

He got out.

For some reason his words felt like a slap in the face. Even though she'd been the one putting distance between them.

He opened her door and put out a hand. Leonora recalled that first night, when she'd been afraid to touch him. She'd been right to be afraid. And she was afraid again now. But she couldn't avoid it.

She put her hand into his and let him help her out.

He let her go again almost immediately, and Leonora curled her fingers over her palm as if to keep the sensation of his skin on hers a little longer. But it wasn't enough.

In the elevator on the way up she could feel the tension pulsing between them. Like a heart. Beating. A live thing. She studiously avoided looking at Gabriel but she could smell him. Sense him. *Imagine him.* Touching her, removing her clothes, devouring her...transporting her to a place where the pain didn't exist.

The bell chimed, signalling the elevator's arrival at the apartment, and Leonora flushed at her wayward mind.

She stepped out and was acutely conscious of Gabriel behind her. His sheer size and bulk.

This was her first time back in the apartment since that night. She stopped at the entrance to the living area, almost as if she could see in her mind's eye how events that night had unfolded, like a movie. He'd seduced her from the moment their eyes had locked that night at the hotel. Even though she had been about to be betrothed to another.

She turned around and saw him yanking at his bowtie, opening the top button of his shirt. Their eyes met and his movements slowed to a stop.

The words *Goodnight, Gabriel* were stuck in Leonora's throat. She'd said them after every other event. Every night. As she'd made her escape. But tonight...she couldn't say them.

Gabriel frowned. 'Leo...?'

She was breaking apart inside. All the ice was melting and flowing into the whirlpool of emotion she'd been holding back.

She struggled to say something. Anything. 'I can't... I don't know...'

He moved towards her, taking her arms in his hands. His touch burned.

'Leo...what is it? What do you want?'

She couldn't speak.

He came closer. 'Shall I tell you what *I* want?'

Weakly, she nodded, needing him to articulate the turmoil inside her.

He said roughly, 'I want *you*, Leo. I want you so much it hurts.'

He lifted a hand and cupped her jaw. It took every ounce of strength she possessed to try and hold firm. Resist. Not to turn her face into his palm and taste his skin.

'But what's the point?' she asked.

He took his hand away from her face. Something flickered in his expression. Hurt?

'Does there need to be a point? I want you and you want me. That hasn't changed.'

After a long moment of silence he stepped back, and immediately she felt bereft.

He said, 'Go to bed, Leo. It's late.'

He was walking around her and into the apartment and suddenly everything in her rejected him moving away from her. Even though she knew she was the one who had caused him to do it.

She turned around. 'Wait...stop.'

He had taken off his jacket and thrown it aside. She could see the powerful muscles of his back through his shirt.

He turned around.

'You're right,' Leonora said. 'There doesn't need to be a point... I want you, Gabriel.'

For a long moment Gabriel said nothing. It looked as if he was wrestling with something. But then he said, 'Are you sure?'

No.

Yes. She wanted him too much and the floodgates had

opened. She needed him to set fire to the emotional turmoil inside her so it would be transformed into something other than this...pain.

She nodded.

He held out a hand. 'Come here.'

She walked forward, her eyes never leaving his face, as if he was a port in the storm. He drew her close and after a torturous moment lowered his head and settled his mouth over hers.

She'd expected instant conflagration. But it was far more subtle than that. His kiss was like a benediction. And it soothed her as much as it frustrated her.

She pressed closer, hands finding his shirt, gripping it tightly. Her tongue sought his, and that first contact was like a match being thrown onto dry tinder. The kiss went from gentle to carnal in seconds and Leonora relished it, seized it.

Gabriel pulled back his head, breathing fast. 'You... Is this what you want?'

Leonora nodded jerkily. 'Please don't be gentle with me. Not now.'

He looked at her as if trying to figure her out, but then he took her hand and led her into the bedroom. He undid her hair, letting it fall loose around her shoulders. Then he pulled down the zip at the back of her dress. It fell to the floor in a swathe of silk and chiffon. She kicked off her shoes and stepped out of it and turned around to face Gabriel, lifting her hands to his shirt.

She tried not to think of that first night when he'd brought her to life. It was too cruel when they couldn't create life.

She almost faltered at that point, but Gabriel took her ineffectual hands from his shirt and undid his buttons, opening the shirt and pulling it off. Then his trousers. Everything until he was naked. And her mind was wiped clean of anything but *this*. Perfection.

Her inner muscles clenched with anticipation. It had only been a few weeks but it felt like a lifetime. Suddenly she was the one who wanted to go slow. She reached out and touched him reverently. Trailing her fingertips over his chest, tracing his muscles.

Then he caught her hand and lifted it to his mouth, pressing a kiss to her palm. Her heart ached. She pulled away and lay down on the bed, slipping off her panties. She hadn't been wearing a bra.

He looked at her for such a long moment that she almost begged him to stop. But then he moved towards her, kneeling on the bed between her legs, pushing them apart so he could come down between them, pressing kisses to her inner thighs.

Leonora caught his hair in her hand, lifting his head. He looked at her, sultry and sexy. Her heart broke.

She said, 'No. I want you...now. Please, Gabriel...'

Because in that moment she knew this was it.

The last time.

He moved up between her legs, taking himself in his hand to guide himself into her.

At the last moment she said, 'Wait, let me...'

He took his hand away and she put her hand on him, around his length, savouring the sheer majesty of his body.

She stroked him until he said, 'Leo...'

And then she took him and guided him home. He seated himself inside her, as deep as he could go. And then, with slow and remorseless precision, he moved in and out.

Leonora could feel the storm building, gathering pace inside her. She desperately clung on, wanting to record every tiny second onto her brain so she could take it out and remember what it felt like. But she knew her memory would be cold comfort...

The point came when she couldn't hold back any longer. With a sob, she let the energy rush through her, incinerating everything in its wake, and waves of pulsing pleasure made a lie of the pain in her heart...

When Gabriel woke at dawn he knew immediately that he was alone in the apartment. A sense of *déjà vu* mocked him. He opened his eyes. He could still smell Leo's scent. He could still feel her nails scoring his back as her body clamped down on his, so tightly that he'd not been able to hold on, falling over the edge and down into an abyss of pleasure so intense he was still wrung out.

He got up and pulled on jeans. As he'd intuited, the apartment was empty. Like last time, he almost had a moment of wondering if he'd imagined it—but, no. There was a note on the table in an envelope.

Gabriel.

He went over and opened it. There was a card inside. A short note.

Dear Gabriel,
I'm so sorry. I can't do this.
Leonora

His first instinct was to leave immediately and find Leo, track her down and make her say that to his face while that sensual satisfaction still lingered in her blood.

He walked over to the window and looked out at the view. A view he'd always taken for granted until Leo had come into his life and made him see things with new eyes. Unjaded eyes.

That unwelcome sense of helplessness was back. He'd broken through the ice last night but now he was being punished for it. He'd known Leo had been fighting some internal battle when they'd arrived back at the apartment. She'd wanted him but hadn't wanted to articulate it. So he'd walked away. And then she'd said, *'I want you.'*

And he'd wanted to resist. Not to give in. To demand if she was just making the most of the arrangement she wanted to be set free from. But there had been something so raw on her face, in her eyes. And his need for her had been too great.

So he hadn't resisted, even though he'd suspected that he would pay the price. And the price was this.

He looked at the note in his hand again and then crumpled it up.

She just needed space. She'd been through a lot. He would give her a few days and then he would go to her and tell her—

Tell her what? interjected an inner voice.

Gabriel knew what he had to tell her. He'd known for some time now. But he wasn't sure if she wanted to hear it.

A few days later, after no contact with Leonora, who had gone back to her family *castillo*, Gabriel's assistant came in with a package from a courier. Gabriel opened it and took out a sheaf of papers.

Divorce papers from Leonora.

Something snapped inside Gabriel.

Enough.

He pulled out his cell phone and made a call, standing up and walking over to the window as he waited for the person at the other end to pick up.

If he didn't answer—

But he did.

He heard Lazaro Sanchez drawl, 'Gabriel Torres, to what do I owe the pleasure?'

Gabriel took a deep breath. 'Can we meet, please?'

CHAPTER ELEVEN

'AND THIS PART of the *castillo* was built in the twelfth century—'

Leonora was used to gasps of awe at this point, but not gasps that loud, followed by excited whispers.

She turned around to see that a new visitor had joined the group. *Gabriel*. She put a hand on the wall beside her to steady herself. Maybe it was a hallucination.

But then he spoke. 'Sorry I'm late. Please carry on.'

How on earth did he expect her to just 'carry on'? But then she saw the far too innocent look on his face and a far steelier look in his eyes.

The divorce.

Leonora turned around again quickly, struggling to find her way back into the spiel which she could narrate in her sleep in three different languages.

Somehow she managed to conduct the rest of the tour without making eye contact with Gabriel or tripping over her words.

After the small group of visitors had dispersed and left, she faced him reluctantly. 'Did you get the papers?'

'Yes. Can we talk somewhere private?'

No.

She could see he was angry. Leonora led him into one of the reception rooms and he closed the door behind them.

She moved away from him and folded her arms. 'I don't know why you're here. We've discussed divorcing.'

He came into the room, pacing fast. 'No,' he said, 'Actually we didn't discuss it. You brought it up, I asked if you wanted a divorce, and you said you thought it was the best option. I then said we'd discuss it at a later date. Sending me papers is not a discussion, Leo.'

'I left you a note. I thought that made it pretty clear where I stood. I didn't hear from you.'

He arched a brow. 'Oh, so you're taking that as a signal of my acquiescence? I was giving you space, Leo. Space to think things over. Clearly that was a mistake.'

Leonora's heart thumped. It was heaven and hell to see him again. 'Okay, well here's the discussion—I want a divorce.'

'I don't.'

Leonora looked at him. 'That's crazy. We both know that I can't have children and you need heirs.'

'There are options. IVF. Adoption.'

Leonora turned around to face the window, afraid of her emotions. Damn him. Ever since she'd slept with him they'd been impossible to close off.

'I already told you—they're not viable options.'

'I thought you were better than this, Leo.'

She whirled around, hurt. 'I'm just not—'

He cut in. 'Willing to give us a chance?'

'It's not that.'

'What is it, then? I know IVF is a hard process, Leo, but I know you're strong. And I'd be with you every step of the way.' He continued. 'Did our vows mean nothing to you? For better or worse? In sickness and in health?'

Leonora could feel her blood draining south. 'That's not fair.'

'Isn't it?' He moved closer. 'Why don't you want to try, Leo?'

'It's not that I don't want to…'

'Then *why?* Are you just looking for an excuse to get out? Now that your family are provided for?'

She was horrified. *'No.'*

He was a lot closer than she'd realised. His scent wound around her and she fought against his pull. She stepped back. She had to be strong. Gabriel was just doing what he always did—not taking no for answer. Refusing to see Leonora's infertility as something that couldn't be surmounted.

'No, Gabriel—just *no*. Can't you understand that one little word?'

He was grim. 'I can understand it. What I can't understand is why my wife doesn't think our marriage is worth fighting for.'

He turned away as if to leave and his expression was so stony that Leonora couldn't bear it.

She said brokenly, to his departing back, 'I *would* fight for it. I would do everything in my power to give us a family if I thought for one second that you loved me. But I won't put us through a process that might never work for anything less than love. You deserve a family, Gabriel, and you can have that with another wife. Just not with me. I wouldn't survive it. If it worked we'd have a family, yes, but I don't want to bring a child into the world just to act as the glue in our marriage. And if it didn't work you'd resent me—' She broke off and turned away, trying to stem the sobs working their way up her chest and into her throat.

She expected to hear the door closing behind Gabriel as he made his hasty escape now she'd uttered the word *love*, so she wasn't prepared when she felt his hands on her and he swung her around to face him, his eyes more intense that she'd ever seen them.

'What did you just say?'

She hiccupped.

Gabriel took her over to a couch and sat down, pulling her with him. He took her hands in his. 'What did you say, Leo?'

Her vision was blurry. 'I said, I won't do it for anything less than love.'

He gripped her hands tight. 'Are you saying that you love me?'

She debated denying it for a second. But how could she? She'd just exposed herself spectacularly. She nodded.

Gabriel let her hands go and rubbed the tears she'd shed from her cheeks with his thumbs. She couldn't read his expression. It was something she'd never seen before. A kind of emotional nakedness.

He looked at her. 'I love you, Leo.'

At first his words didn't impact, and then they did. She pulled back instinctively, disbelieving. 'You don't. You're just saying that.'

He shook his head. 'I'm not lying. I would never lie to you.'

'But you don't believe in love. You never wanted it.'

'I didn't. Until a dark-haired temptress captivated me and ruined me for any other woman. I think I fell in love with you the moment I saw you that night in the hotel. I've never had such a visceral reaction to anyone. I had to know you, follow you. *Have you.* And the next morning I knew that this was different. I wanted more.'

Leonora looked at him, searching his eyes, his face. Searching out insincerity. But she couldn't see it. She could only see *him.*

'Why didn't you say something?'

'Why didn't you?' he countered.

She flushed. 'I was scared.'

He said, 'I was in denial. I kept thinking my feelings for you were strong just because you were my wife. It was natural. Expected. I only realised what they truly were when you suggested a divorce... I was so angry. I suspected you of marrying me solely to secure your family's fortune. But mostly I was hurt, and I had to acknowledge that you only had the power to hurt me because I'd fallen for you. And then afterwards...when you closed yourself off...'

'I'm sorry... It was too hard. I was afraid of what would spill out if you touched me. I was barely holding it together. But that night... I couldn't not touch you.'

'And then you left.'

She took his hand. 'Because I knew that I wouldn't survive a loveless marriage. That's my weakness.'

He shook his head. 'It's not weak. It was self-preservation. I was the one who was weak. I was prepared to bully you into staying married to me in the hope that if you agreed to try for a family you'd learn to love me.'

Leonora took her hand from his. 'There's a very strong possibility that we won't ever have children, Gabriel, no matter what we try. If that happens…how do you know I'll be enough for you? What will you do about having no heirs?'

Gabriel took her hand back, lacing his fingers with hers. 'You *are* enough for me. If we never have a family but I have you that's all I need. I've met with my board and we've drawn up a document that details what will happen in the event of my having no heirs. The Cruz y Torres name won't die out. It's a brand now, and brands last far longer and far more effectively than mere humans. And I've also been in touch with Lazaro Sanchez.'

Leonora instinctively held tighter to Gabriel's hand. 'And?'

He smiled a rueful smile. 'He *is* my half-brother. I did the DNA test. He wants nothing to do with the family name or any inheritance. It's a point of pride with him. Even when I told him our situation, and that any children he has might be the only heirs to the Cruz y Torres name. We've also teamed up for a bid on the marketplace. We're going to work *together.*'

Leonora shook her head, as if that might help her to understand everything Gabriel had just told her. 'You did all of that… before you knew…?'

'That you loved me? Yes, I did. I'm not as selfless as you. I wasn't prepared to let you walk away. Ever. You're mine.'

Leonora's vision was blurring again.

Gabriel said, 'You haven't actually said it yet.'

'What?' Leonora could hardly speak over the way her heart was expanding in her chest.

'That you love me.'

Leonora moved so that she was straddling Gabriel's lap. She cupped his face with both hands and pressed a kiss to his mouth. The she pulled back. 'I love you, Gabriel Ortega Cruz y Torres. With all my heart. Is that good enough?'

His hands cupped her buttocks and he expertly manoeuvred her so that she was under him on the couch. He smiled down at her and she could see the sheer love and joy in his eyes, on his face.

He said, 'I want for ever, Leo, is that good enough?'

Leonora looked up at him and saw the intensity blazing from his face and in his eyes. But a tendril of doubt and fear made her say, 'What if we don't—?'

But Gabriel cut her off with his mouth. With a kiss. He pulled back. 'For ever, Leo. No matter what. You are all I need. Anything else will be a bonus.'

She looked up at Gabriel. She saw love and commitment in his gaze. It had been there for weeks, but she hadn't wanted to believe in it. She'd shut it out.

She smiled up at him and wound her arms around his neck as tears pricked her eyes. 'For ever it is, then.'

EPILOGUE

Three years later
Lazaro Sanchez Torres's hacienda in Andalusia

'GETTING YOU TO agree to take on the Torres name was the most difficult negotiation I've ever conducted.'

Lazaro grinned at his half-brother and clinked his beer bottle against Gabriel's glass of water. 'You didn't think I was going to make it easy, did you?'

Gabriel smiled back. 'God, no. That would have been far too predictable. All I can say is that I'm glad we're on the same side now. It makes life so much easier.'

A moment passed between them. Deeply felt emotion. And then a baby's gurgle made them both turn back to the tableau in front of them.

Dragged out onto the back lawn of Lazaro's *hacienda* was a couch, overlaid with colourful throws. On the couch sat Lazaro and Skye's almost three-year-old son Max. He was looking very serious, because lying in each of his arms, propped up by cushions either side, was a baby, the two of them blinking contentedly and kicking their arms and legs in the shade under a huge tree. They were three months old.

'Okay, Max, you're doing so well—just another few seconds.'

Leonora chuckled beside Skye, who had become a good friend. Her sister-in-law was moving around, getting lots of pictures from different angles with her camera.

Leonora said, 'Poor Max looks terrified.'

Skye groaned and stood up. 'He does, doesn't he?'

She was wearing faded loose dungarees and a bright yellow T-shirt that should have clashed with her red hair but didn't. The swell of her second baby was evident under her clothes, at nearly eight months along.

'Max, smile, sweetie! It's okay—you won't drop them. Honestly.'

Tentatively Max smiled, his blond, slightly reddish hair blowing in the breeze. His blue-green eyes were full of pride at his responsibility as the older cousin.

After another few shots Skye straightened up. 'Okay, that should be loads to work with.'

Skye, who had built up a name for herself as a talented portrait artist, was going to do a painting of Max and his baby cousins, Sofia and Pablo.

After Leonora and Gabriel had made the decision to try IVF, it had taken two years and three painful miscarriages before it had worked, on their last attempt. Gabriel hadn't wanted to put Leonora through even another attempt but she'd insisted. And, happily, that last round had brought them a successful pregnancy and the twins, and every time Leonora looked at them her heart was so full of awe and love that she almost couldn't breathe.

An arm snaked around her waist now and she turned to look up at her husband. Her life.

'Okay?' he asked.

She nodded, feeling emotional. She had a family now, and more fulfilment than anything she'd ever imagined or fantasised about. And a love that she knew would last for ever.

'I'm fine. You?'

Gabriel looked at her and she saw all her thoughts and feelings reflected in his eyes.

'I'm fine too. More than fine. I love you, Leo.'

'I love you too.'

She reached up and pressed a kiss to Gabriel's mouth, and he caught the back of her head, not letting her pull away, deepening the kiss.

'Ugh, kissy-kissy.'

They broke apart, laughing at Max's disgusted pronouncement, and went to rescue their babies, taking one each.

Lazaro said, all too innocently, as he scooped up his own son, 'Honestly, I don't know where he gets that from.'

Skye rolled her eyes and came over to her husband putting her arms around his waist. 'He gets it from seeing his mother being kissed by his father on a regular basis.'

'Oh, and you're a passive partner in that, are you? As I recall, this morning...'

Gabriel and Leonora watched as Lazaro and Skye walked back into the *hacienda*, with Max perched on Lazaro's shoulders. Their voices faded and Gabriel tugged Leonora over to the couch. The sun was setting, bathing everything in a golden and red glow.

Leonora's breasts were heavy with milk. Just as she became aware of that Sofia made a mewling sound. She deftly undid her sundress and placed Sofia on her breast. The small baby suckled hungrily, dark eyes gazing up at her mother.

Pablo snuggled against his father's chest, eyes closed. Leonora and Gabriel shared a look and smiled, not needing words to articulate the love flowing through them and their babies...

* * * * *

The Secret He Must Claim

Chantelle Shaw

Books by Chantelle Shaw

Harlequin Modern

Acquired by Her Greek Boss
To Wear His Ring Again
A Night in the Prince's Bed
Captive in His Castle
The Ultimate Risk
Ruthless Russian, Lost Innocence

Wedlocked!

Trapped by Vialli's Vows

Bought by the Brazilian

Mistress of His Revenge
Master of Her Innocence

The Howard Sisters

Sheikh's Forbidden Conquest
A Bride Worth Millions

The Chatsfield

Billionaire's Secret

The Bond of Brothers

His Unexpected Legacy
Secrets of a Powerful Man

Visit the Author Profile page at millsandboon.com.au for
more titles.

Chantelle Shaw lives on the Kent coast and thinks up her stories while walking on the beach. She has been married for over thirty years and has six children. Her love affair with reading and writing Harlequin stories began as a teenager, and her first book was published in 2006. She likes strong-willed, slightly unusual characters. Chantelle also loves gardening, walking and wine!

For Arpita who loves reading romance books as much as I enjoy writing them. Thank you for being such a dedicated fan. With love, Chantelle

CHAPTER ONE

THE ROOM WAS SPINNING. Bright lights flashed in front of her eyes, forming colourful patterns as if she were looking through the lens of a kaleidoscope. Elin blinked and found she was staring up at the chandelier in the drawing room. She had never noticed before how the crystal prisms sparkled like diamonds.

'Can I get you another drink?' A voice sounded over the pounding beat of rock music. She felt disorientated and strangely disembodied, as if she were floating and looking down at herself. She tried to focus on the guy who had spoken to her, and vaguely recognised he was one of Virginia's friends who had been at the nightclub earlier in the evening. Elin didn't know half the people who had come back to her family's London residence in Kensington to continue her birthday celebrations.

'You can't be on your own tonight,' Virginia had insisted when the nightclub where they'd planned to spend the evening had closed early. 'You'll only feel miserable, remembering your mother. I'll put the word around that the party is carrying on back at your place.'

Elin hadn't argued because Virginia was right; she couldn't bear to be alone with the memories of her adoptive mother's shocking death six months ago. She'd told Ralph she was spending her birthday with friends in Scotland, but freezing fog had caused travel disruption at Gatwick and her flight had been cancelled. The person she most wanted to spend her birthday with was her brother, but Jarek was in Japan on business for Saunderson's Bank. His trip was unavoidable he'd said, but Elin had a feeling that Jarek was avoiding her because he blamed himself for Mama's death.

'Elin?'

She jerked her mind back to the guy—Tom, she thought he'd said was his name. He was standing too close and looking at her in a way that made her wish she hadn't worn the daringly low-cut dress Virginia had persuaded her to buy. The dress was little more than a wisp of scarlet silk and chiffon and the shoe-string shoulder straps meant she couldn't wear a bra.

Tom plucked her empty glass out of her hand. 'Do you want the same again?'

'I'd better not. I think I've had too much to drink.' This strange feeling must be because she was drunk. It was odd because usually alcohol made her sleepy but she felt wildly energetic and euphoric. The exhausting grief of the past months seemed distant, as if she were detached from her emotions. Maybe the answer was to drink herself into oblivion, the way her brother had done too often lately, Elin thought bleakly. For a split second, misery ripped through her. But she couldn't cope with it tonight. She was desperate to forget for a few hours the image of her mother collapsed on the floor and lying so still. Too still.

'What was in the last cocktail you made me?' she asked Tom. 'It tasted different from a usual Manhattan.'

He gave her an odd look. 'I might have added a dash too much Angostura bitters.' He slid his arm around her waist and Elin repressed a shudder when she felt his hot breath on her cheek. He was good-looking and she guessed a lot of women would find him attractive, but there was something about him that repelled her and she stiffened when he murmured, 'Let's go somewhere where we can be alone, baby.'

'Actually, I would like another drink,' she said quickly. 'I'm really thirsty.' It wasn't a lie. She had a raging thirst, and for some reason her heart was beating unnaturally fast. She watched Tom push his way across the crowded room to the sideboard which was being used as a drinks bar and hurried away before he returned.

In the lounge, someone had rolled up the Wilton rug so that people could dance. The music was even louder in here and the heavy bass throbbed through Elin's body. Someone grabbed her hand and started dancing with her. The pounding beat was irresistible and she shook back her long hair and danced like she'd never danced before, wild and abandoned. Laughter bubbled up inside her. It was a long time since she'd laughed and it felt good.

Many times in the past months she'd tagged along to nightclubs with her brother so she could try to stop him drinking too much. She'd learned that the best way to distract the paparazzi's attention away from Jarek was to grab the limelight herself, and so she'd thrown herself into partying and made sure it was her the press photographed falling out of a club in the early hours rather than her brother.

The tabloids had dubbed her an It Girl and said she was a spoiled socialite. She had been accused by some of the media of bringing shame to Lord Saunderson and to the memory of his wife.

What a way to repay the philanthropic couple who adopted Elin from an orphanage in war-torn Bosnia when she was four years old and gave her and her older brother a privileged upbringing!

That was what one journalist had written. Elin didn't care what the tabloids said about her as long as Jarek's name stayed out of the headlines and he did not earn even more of Ralph's disapproval.

But tonight she wasn't pretending to be having fun. Tonight

she felt super-confident and carefree and if it was because she'd had too much alcohol, so what? It was her twenty-fifth birthday and she could do what she liked on her birthday. And so she carried on dancing and laughing because she was scared that if she stopped she would plunge back into that dark place of heartache and grief that had consumed her for six long months.

She had no shortage of dance partners. Men crowded around her and she flirted with them because for this one night she was a siren wearing a sexy red dress. At midnight Virginia brought out a cake covered with candles. 'Don't forget to make a wish,' she reminded Elin.

A birthday wish was supposed to come true if you blew out all your candles with one breath. But a million wishes could not bring Mama back. Elin looked around at the party guests. Some were friends she'd known since her childhood after her adoptive parents had brought her to England. Others she'd never met before, but she guessed they belonged to Virginia's wide circle of friends. Everyone was waiting for her to blow out her candles but she didn't know what to wish for.

And then she saw him.

He was standing apart from the crowd. A lone wolf. The thought came into Elin's mind and was immediately followed by the certainty that he was a dangerous predator. She stared across the room at him…and time simply stopped. The music and voices disappeared and there was nothing but him. The most beautiful man she had ever seen.

Taller than everyone else in the room and darkly handsome, there was something Byronic and brooding about him that made her think of Heathcliff from Emily Brontë's classic novel *Wuthering Heights*. On one level her brain registered surprise that she hadn't noticed him all evening until now, but her rational thought process was overtaken by a more primitive reaction to his raw maleness.

He was dressed in black jeans and a fine-knit black sweater that clung to his broad chest. Over it he wore a brown leather jacket which was scuffed in several places and furthered the impression that he lived life on his terms and didn't give a damn what others thought of him. His black hair was thick and tousled, as if he had a habit of raking his fingers through it, and the black stubble on his jaw and above his top lip added to his smouldering sex appeal.

Something visceral knotted in the pit of Elin's stomach. So this was what desire felt like. This fire in her blood. Her breasts felt heavy and there was a dragging ache between her legs. She *wasn't* a freak, as she'd assumed when her friends had talked about their love lives and she'd had nothing to say.

'Maybe you're gay, but you can't face up to the truth about your sexuality,' Virginia had suggested when Elin had admitted that she was still a virgin.

'The truth is I'm not interested in having sex with anyone. I've dated a few guys but I've never wanted to take things further.' Elin suspected that a psychologist might blame the traumatic first four years of her life spent at an orphanage in the middle of a war zone for her trust issues. Or maybe she *was* frigid, as one ex-boyfriend had told her when he'd failed to persuade her to sleep with him.

Her friend had refused to write her off. 'I reckon you just haven't met the right man yet. One day you'll meet a guy who will flick your switch.'

Was this what Virginia had meant? As Elin stared at this modern-day Heathcliff she felt light and heat and energy explode inside her and suddenly she knew what to wish for when she blew out the candles on her cake.

Someone turned up the volume on the stereo and music pounded in the room, echoing the pounding of Elin's blood in her veins as the crowd around her dispersed and she discovered the man was watching her. He was leaning against the mantelpiece, one foot casually crossed over his other ankle. He gave the appearance of being relaxed but his stillness reminded Elin of a jungle cat preparing to pounce. He did not move his gaze from her when she walked towards him, and it was as if he had taken control of her mind and she could not turn away from him even if she'd wanted to.

His eyes were the colour of sable flecked with gold, she discovered when she halted in front of him. Set beneath heavy black brows that drew together in a faint frown when she smiled at him.

'You're supposed to wish me a happy birthday.' She did not recognise the teasing, flirtatious voice as hers, but then she didn't recognise anything about herself tonight, especially the heat that blazed inside her and made her yearn for something she could not even explain.

Something flickered in his dark eyes but his stern mouth did not soften. 'Happy birthday, Blondie.'

'That's not my name.' She hated the nickname the tabloids had given her, with its implication that because she was pretty and blonde she must also be a brainless bimbo. 'My name is Elin.'

'I know.'

She tilted her head and studied him. The dimmed lighting in the room cast shadows over the hard angles and planes of his face and emphasised his austere beauty, making Elin long to explore the chiselled perfection of his jaw with her fingertips. As for his mouth… Her heart thudded as she imagined his sensual mouth covering hers. The knot in her belly tightened and every nerve-ending in her body felt fiercely alive.

'How do you know my name?' She was certain they'd never met before. Dear God, she would have remembered him.

She wondered if she'd imagined that he hesitated infinitesimally before he shrugged his wide shoulders. 'I'm here at your birthday party and of course I know your name. There can't be many people who haven't heard of Elin Saunderson. Photographs of you falling out of nightclubs are a regular feature in the British popular press.'

Inexplicably she felt hurt by his cynicism, and she was

tempted to explain that she'd deliberately courted scandal to turn the media's attention away from her brother. But it would mean betraying Jarek and she would never do that, especially to a stranger. Even if he was the most gorgeous man she'd ever set eyes on. Her gaze locked with his and she saw his gold-flecked eyes blaze with a heat that burned her.

Every one of her heightened senses quivered with the realisation that he desired her. He might not want to want her, but he had no more control over the electricity that crackled between them than she did. He clearly believed she was the goodtime girl portrayed by the press so why shouldn't she live up to her reputation for one night? Elin asked herself.

Some part of her recognised that this wild, reckless feeling wasn't *her*. She shouldn't want a complete stranger to cover her mouth with his and kiss her with the savage passion that she sensed he was capable of. She shouldn't want him, but she did.

'It would be good manners to introduce yourself.'

His mouth quirked then, not exactly a smile but it was enough to send scalding heat flooding through her. 'There's nothing good about me,' he warned her in his deep, dark voice with a faint undercurrent of a Mediterranean accent. Once again he hesitated before he drawled, 'My name is Cortez.'

'You're Spanish?' His dark olive complexion and that raven-black hair indicated that he spent a lot of time in the hot sun. His name—Cor-*tez*... She silently repeated it the way he had pronounced it, emphasising the second syllable. It reminded her of a history book she'd read about the Spanish conquistadors who had invaded the Aztec and Inca civilisations in the sixteenth century. The conquistadors were reputed to have been utterly ruthless and she would be happy to bet that he was a descendent of those infamous adventurers.

'Half-Spanish,' he said after another pause, as if he had been about to say something else but had changed his mind.

She deliberately trailed her eyes over his chest and continued lower, down to his flat abdomen and lean hips, hugged by his black jeans. 'Which half?' she asked innocently.

He looked startled for a few seconds and then laughed. The sound was warm and golden, like liquid honey, Elin thought. '*You* are wicked,' he told her. The bright flecks in his eyes gleamed and something almost feral flickered across his hard features. 'And very, very beautiful.'

He stretched out his hand and wound a lock of her pale gold hair around his fingers. Elin could feel the frantic thud of her heart, and her breath caught in her throat. He must have heard the faint sound, and although he did not appear to move she sensed a sudden tension in him, as if he truly was a predator stalking its prey. He exuded danger and she should run for the hills, but the reckless feeling that had swept over her tonight made her ignore the voice of caution in her head.

The heavy bass music pounding in the room stirred her blood with its sensual rhythm. 'Will you dance with me? You can't refuse,' she said when his eyes narrowed, 'because it's my birthday and I can have whatever I want on my birthday.'

He did not laugh now and the liquid honey in his voice was replaced by a harsh tone that sounded like rusty metal dragged across gravel. 'What *do* you want, Elin?'

'You,' she heard herself say in a husky voice she did not recognise as her own. Once again she felt a peculiar sensation that she was floating outside her body and none of this was real. Perhaps it wasn't, perhaps it was a dream, but it was a much better dream than her usual nightmare about her mother's death.

Cortez swore softly. The gold flecks in his eyes glittered and he seemed to be waging an internal battle with himself before he shrugged. 'So be it then,' he muttered as he moved towards her. He put his hands on her waist and pulled her against him so that they were hip to hip.

The effect on Elin was electrifying. The brush of his thighs against hers as they moved with the beat of the music turned the heat inside her into an inferno. Cortez danced with a fluid grace that was entirely sensual, and she gasped when he slid one hand down to the small of her back and exerted pressure to bring her pelvis into closer contact with his.

Her senses went into meltdown as he clamped her against his whipcord body. He smelled divine, a mixture of spicy cologne and the dry heat of his body that had its own unique scent. She wanted to press her face into his neck and breathe in the essence of him, lick his olive skin and taste him. Her hands were lying flat on his chest and she felt his heartbeat accelerate beneath her fingertips. Startled, she tilted her head to look at his face, and saw a stark hunger in his eyes that made her tremble.

She'd never felt like this before and she'd certainly never behaved so impetuously. She felt crazily out of control. For the first time in six months she felt alive instead of numb. Life, she'd learned, could be taken away in an instant, in the release of a trigger and a bullet fired from a gun.

She wanted to grab hold of life with both hands, and more than anything she wanted to be even closer to this dangerously beautiful man who made her feel like no other man ever had. And so she slid her hands up to his shoulders and stretched herself up against him, pressing her breasts with their pebble-hard nipples into his chest. She heard him mutter something in Spanish as he sank his hand into her hair and lowered his face towards hers. His mouth was tantalisingly close and with a low moan she closed the tiny gap between them and pressed her lips to his.

The world exploded in a firestorm of heat and colour. Cortez hesitated for a fraction of a second but then a shudder went through him and he took control of the kiss and plundered her mouth like a conquistador claiming the spoils of his conquest. It was hotter and wilder than anything Elin had ever experienced before. She felt consumed by his kiss, by him as he moved his hand to cup her jaw and angled her mouth to his satisfaction before he pushed his tongue between her lips and tasted her.

The kiss went on and on, becoming deeper and ever more

erotic, a ravishment of her senses, and Elin hoped it would never end. When Cortez eventually tore his mouth from hers to allow them to snatch air into their starved lungs, he stared at her as if he was trying to figure her out.

'This is madness,' he grated. 'I should tell you...' He broke off when one of the other guests who was dancing wildly stumbled into them. *'Dios!'* Cortez tightened his arms around Elin and his protective gesture made her melt even more. 'Is there somewhere we can go to talk?'

Over Cortez's shoulder, Elin saw Tom, the guy who had been plying her with drinks earlier, walk into the room. Keen to avoid him, she led Cortez through a different door to the narrow hallway and staircase at the back of the house, which had once been used by servants. Even here there were people sitting on the stairs playing a raucous drinking game, and so she continued up to the second floor and along the corridor to her bedroom.

'We won't be disturbed in here,' she told him as she ushered him inside and closed the door. After the loud music downstairs the room was quiet, with just the distant thud of heavy bass audible through the floorboards. On some level Elin knew she must be crazy to have invited a stranger into her bedroom. Except that he wasn't a complete stranger, she reassured herself. She knew his name and she assumed Virginia knew him. Why else would he have come to the party unless her friend had invited him?

Even so, a tiny, sane part of her realised she was acting a little bit crazy tonight. She couldn't explain the buzz of exhilaration that felt as if she were riding on a big dipper at a theme park, but she didn't want the feeling to end. She stared at Cortez and thought how unbelievably gorgeous he was. No wonder Virginia had kept quiet about him. But he had kissed *her.*

In the mirror she could see her mouth was swollen from when he had crushed her lips beneath his. She hardly recognised herself in a sexy scarlet dress, with her hair dishevelled and her mouth reddened...and inviting. She looked back at Cortez and watched his eyes narrow as she moistened her lips with the tip of her tongue.

'You said you wanted to tell me something. Are you married?'

'*What?*' He looked startled. 'No, of course not. I would not have kissed you if I were married.'

'Why *did* you kiss me?'

'Why the hell do you think?' he said roughly.

'I'm not sure. Perhaps you should kiss me again and I might work out the reason.' There it was again, that teasing, flirty voice that she didn't recognise as her own. But the truth was she wanted him to kiss her, and she wanted more. She wanted... Her eyes flicked to the huge double bed that she'd only ever slept in alone. She heard Cortez mutter something incomprehensible as he followed her gaze.

'You are an irresistible temptation.' He made it sound like an accusation as he closed the gap between them in a couple of strides. Her bedroom seemed to shrink and she could not tear her gaze from him. The golden gleam in his eyes promised he would make her birthday wish come true.

'Are you going to resist me?' she murmured when he stood in front of her and cupped her cheek in his big hand. The skin on his palm felt rough and she wondered briefly what he did for a living.

'Not a chance,' he growled as he pulled her against him, into his heat and strength and intoxicating maleness, and claimed her mouth in a kiss that plundered her soul.

'Do you want this?' he demanded, lifting his head and staring into her eyes as if he was trying to read her thoughts.

'Do you have to ask?' replied the voice she didn't recognise that belonged to the bold creature who had taken over her body. It was *that* woman who wound her arms around his neck and pulled his mouth down to hers—a scarlet-clad temptress who murmured words of encouragement when he lifted her up and placed her on the bed before he stretched out on top of her.

His weight pinned her to the mattress and his muscular body felt alien and hard against her softness. He kissed her mouth, demanding a response she gave willingly. She wanted everything he could give her, and her urgency increased when he trailed his lips down her throat.

Their clothes were a frustrating barrier and she pushed his jacket over his shoulders while he tugged the straps of her dress down her arms. There was the sound of material ripping and then the feel of cool air on her bare breasts.

She moaned when he bent his dark head to her breast and took her nipple into his mouth. The sensation of him sucking her was exquisite, and flames shot down from her breasts to the molten place between her legs as he transferred his mouth to her other nipple and tugged on the taut crest.

'Please...' she choked. Instinct took over and she lifted her hips towards him as he thrust a hand beneath her skirt and skimmed his palm over the sensitive skin of her inner thigh. He dragged her panties down her legs, and then his fingers were there where she was desperate for him to touch her, probing her slick heat before he slid one digit, two, into her and moved them expertly so that within moments she was trembling on the brink.

'I want...' she gasped. She had never felt desire like this before, so fierce and urgent, making her shake with need.

'I know.' His voice was like rough velvet. He kissed her mouth again and in between hungry kisses he pulled his sweater over his head. His skin felt like satin overlaid with wiry chest hairs that scraped her palms as she moved her hands down to the zip of his jeans.

Everything was colour and heat and fierce, frantic need that built in intensity as he swirled his fingers inside her. Somehow Cortez was naked and the sight of his erection made Elin draw a swift breath. He was awesome—so beautiful, so *big*. But her faint doubt was obliterated when he twisted his fingers inside her and she shattered, her orgasm so overwhelming that she gave a keening cry.

'I don't have a condom.' His harsh voice broke through the haze of sexual excitement fogging her brain and she heard him swear as he lifted himself off her. *She didn't want him to stop.* Frantically she clutched his shoulders and remembered the packet of condoms which had been given out for free when she had been a fresher at university. She had shoved them into the bedside drawer, wondering if she would ever need them.

'In the top drawer,' she muttered.

It took him mere moments to locate the packet and don a protective sheath before he positioned himself over her and nudged her legs apart with his thigh. And then he entered her with a hard thrust that made her gasp. The slight discomfort was over almost immediately. She felt him hesitate, but the sensation of being stretched by him and filled by his steel-hard length was so incredible that she arched her hips and urged him to possess her utterly.

The intense pleasure of her first orgasm made her greedy for more and she dug her fingers into his shoulders, anchoring herself to his powerful body as he drove into her again and again, taking her higher and making her sob with need, until finally the world exploded and she heard him groan as together they fell over the edge of the abyss.

Elin stirred and the light hurt her eyes before she'd even opened them. Cautiously, she lifted her lashes and winced as a shaft of bright sunshine fell across her face. Her head felt strangely woolly and it took several minutes to register that she was in her bedroom at the house in Kensington. She pushed back the sheet and discovered she'd fallen into bed wearing her dress. The top half was pushed down around her waist, leaving her breasts bare, and when she moved her hand lower she discovered that her knickers were missing.

Dear God! Vague memories swirled in her mind. There had been a party, loud music, candles on a cake. She remembered dancing with various men—with one man in particular. A savagely handsome man with jet-black hair and gold-flecked eyes who had said his name was Cortez.

She jerked upright and the room spun. Her stomach churned but her symptoms didn't feel like a hangover. Patches of her memory of the previous night were blank but others were shudderingly vivid. She remembered that she'd danced with Cortez and they had kissed. Embarrassed heat flooded her cheeks when she recalled that *she* had initiated the kiss before she'd invited him up to her room.

What else had she done?

She spied her knickers on the floor and the answer hit her in a tidal wave of shame. She'd had sex for the first time in her life with a man she'd never met before, and the fact that she had woken alone at—the clock showed it was midday—suggested that Cortez had long since gone.

'Elin, are you in there?' Virginia's voice sounded from outside the door.

'Just a minute.' She grabbed her robe and pulled it on over her crumpled dress, desperate to hide the evidence of her night of shame. Virginia was her best friend but Elin did not want to tell anyone what she'd done, how she'd behaved like a slut. She wanted to crawl away and hide in a hole, but she forced herself to smile when she opened her bedroom door.

'Are you alone?' Virginia sounded surprised. 'I saw you disappear from the party with a gorgeous guy and thought maybe you'd spent the night with him. Who was he?'

'He said his name was Cortez.' Elin swallowed. 'I didn't get round to asking his surname. But I thought he was a friend of yours. Didn't you invite him to the party?'

'I'd never seen him before he turned up here last night.' Virginia frowned. 'It's a bit odd. I haven't spoken to anyone who was at the party who knows him.'

Virginia dismissed the mystery of Cortez's identity with an airy shrug that Elin envied. 'You missed all the drama last night. A guy called Tom Wilson was arrested on suspicion of spiking my friend Lisa's drink. Apparently she felt strange after drinking a cocktail Tom had made her but she assumed she was drunk. A while later he tried to get Lisa to leave the party with him, but someone else warned her that they'd seen Tom slip something into her drink. The police were called, and when they tested the dregs of drink in the bottom of Lisa's glass they found evidence of a substance which is a well-known date-rape drug.'

Something clicked in Elin's mind and she sank down onto the bed. 'Do you know what the effects of taking the drug are?'

'Lisa said she felt dizzy and out of control and she described feeling detached from reality. Oh, my God,' Virginia said in a horrified voice as she noticed Elin's white face. 'Do you think your drink was spiked too?'

'Tom made me a cocktail and I felt strange after drinking it. But, like Lisa, I thought I was drunk.'

'You had better inform the police that it's possible you were another of Tom's victims. Some so-called date-rape drugs can cause blackouts and amnesia and if you unwittingly took the drug it would explain why you've been asleep for half the day.'

If her drink had been spiked it would explain her bizarre, out-of-character behaviour last night. But it was a cold comfort, Elin thought grimly. Cortez would have been unaware that she'd been drugged. However, he'd mentioned her reputation as an It Girl—how she detested the label—and he had clearly believed she made a habit of sleeping with men she'd just met. The fact that he had disappeared after they'd had sex, without waking her, made her feel like a tramp.

As soon as Virginia had gone, Elin stripped off the scarlet dress that had become her badge of shame and shoved it into the bin. She felt soiled, but when she took a shower no amount of hot water and soap could scrub away her self-loathing or the marks on her body left by Cortez. Padding from the en suite bathroom back into her bedroom, she stood in front of the mirror and allowed the towel she'd wrapped around her to fall.

The evidence of her guilt was branded on her body. There

were red patches on her breasts where Cortez's rough jaw had scraped her delicate skin, and although there were no visible signs of the ache between her legs, the dull throb was an uncomfortable reminder that she had lost her virginity having casual sex with a stranger.

Thank God he had used a condom. Elin held her hands to her hot cheeks and wished she *did* have amnesia. But memories of her wanton behaviour were painfully clear in her mind. Cortez hadn't forced her or coerced her to have sex with him, and even discovering that her drink might have been spiked by another of the party guests did not make her feel any better about herself. She'd behaved like a whore, and her only consolation was that she was unlikely to meet the Spanish conquistador who had taken her self-respect along with her virginity ever again.

CHAPTER TWO

One year later

AN ICY BLAST of air swept into the church and the ancient oak door creaked on its hinges, heralding the arrival of a latecomer to Ralph Saunderson's funeral. Sitting in a front pew beside her brother, Elin felt the cold draught curl around her ankles and wished she'd worn her boots. But her black patent four-inch stilettos looked better with her nineteen-fifties style coat and matching black pillbox hat with a net veil that the milliner had said made her look like Grace Kelly, and Elin had learned when she was four years old that looks were everything.

A faint frown creased between her perfectly arched brows as she listened to footsteps ring out on the stone floor of the nave. When she and Jarek had followed their adoptive father's coffin into the church she'd noted that every pew was filled. It seemed as though the entire population of Little Bardley had turned out to bid farewell to the squire of the pretty Sussex village on the South Downs. Elin had made a mental note of the many familiar faces in the congregation so that she could thank each person who had attended the funeral.

Who had arrived halfway through the service? She felt a prickling sensation between her shoulder blades and although she tried to concentrate on the minister while he gave the eulogy, she could not dismiss an inexplicable sense of unease. When the congregation stood to sing a hymn, she glanced over her shoulder and her heart collided with her ribs when she thought she recognised the man standing at the back of the church.

Cortez!

It couldn't be him. Elin drew a shaky breath. Her brain must be playing a cruel trick on her. It was over a year since her fateful birthday party when she'd had sex with a stranger who she'd known only as Cortez. There was no reason in the world why he would have turned up at her father's funeral.

She jerked her head round to the front and stared down at the hymn book that shook uncontrollably between her fingers. Her brother swore softly as he slid his hand beneath her arm.

'You're not going to faint, are you?' Jarek muttered. 'The press pack who are slavering outside the church would love to snap you being carried unconscious from a venue for the second time this week. Of course there would be speculation in the tabloids that you were drunk or high at your dear papa's funeral.'

'You know I'm neither,' Elin said in a low voice, while the congregation sang the second verse of the hymn. 'I explained that I fainted at Virginia's hen party two nights ago because it was so hot and stuffy in the nightclub.'

'A more likely explanation is that you are still not fully recovered from Harry's traumatic birth. I know he is three months old, but you lost God knows how many pints of blood when you haemorrhaged after giving birth,' her brother said grimly. 'I told you before you went to London that I didn't think you were fit enough to return to your frenetic social life.'

Elin was stung by the faint censure in his words. The only reason she had become a familiar face on the London club scene a year ago had been so that she could try and keep Jarek out of trouble and out of the tabloids' headlines. At least she no longer had to worry that Ralph would lose patience with her brother. Their adoptive father had died a week ago, a month after being diagnosed with a brain tumour. Jarek was destined to take over as head of Saunderson's Bank and even though many of the bank's board members were concerned by his reputation as a risk-taker, no one could prevent Ralph Saunderson's heir from becoming chairman.

Elin bowed her head while the minister intoned a prayer, but her mind was on the man she'd seen in the church. She'd only caught a glimpse of him, and of course he couldn't be Cortez, she reassured herself. Although he had known her name and London address, he had never tried to contact her in the past year and, as she did not know his surname, she'd been unable to find him to tell him about Harry.

She thought of her baby son, who had been asleep when she'd left him with his nanny in the nursery at Cuckmere Hall. Harry was innocently unaware that he had been conceived as a result of a few moments of lust between two strangers. But when he was older he was bound to be curious about his father, and Elin planned to make up a story that Harry's father was dead. It would be better to tell her son a white lie than for him to learn that his father had abandoned him before his birth, she reasoned.

She and her brother had been abandoned by their own parents when she was a baby. Jarek had been six and he had a few vague memories of their mother and father. But Elin's earliest memories were of looking through the bars of a cot. Jarek had told her that at the orphanage the younger children had been left in their cots, often for days. She hadn't learned to walk until she was over two years old, and only then because her brother had sneaked into her dormitory and held her hand while she took her first steps.

Her own son had been conceived as a result of her night of shame with a stranger, but she was determined to love Harry twice as much to make up for the fact that he would never know his father.

The ceremony finished and she walked with Jarek behind Ralph's coffin as it was carried out of the chapel. She looked

closely at the people in the congregation but did not see anyone who resembled Cortez. Her imagination must have played a
trick on her, she told herself, yet her sense of unease remained.

The procession of mourners filed into the graveyard and
gathered around a freshly dug grave next to Lorna Saunderson's headstone. Tears welled in Elin's eyes. It was eighteen
months since Mama had died and she still felt a deep sense
of loss. Willing herself not to cry in public, she stared across
the graveyard, and her heart lurched when she glimpsed a tall
figure half-hidden behind the thick trunk of an old yew tree.
She could not see the man's features clearly from a distance,
but something about his proud bearing and the breadth of his
shoulders were familiar.

She blinked away her tears and refocused but the figure had
disappeared. A flock of crows flew out of the tree, cawing
loudly as if something had disturbed them. Had she imagined
that she'd seen someone? Elin forced herself to concentrate on
the minister reciting a final prayer, and when he finished she
stepped forwards and dropped a white rose into her father's
grave.

'You look like you've seen a ghost,' her brother told her later
when they arrived back at Cuckmere Hall. 'The old man is
more likely to come back to haunt me than you. He did at least
feel some affection for you,' he added drily. 'Ralph wanted to
adopt a pretty little daughter but he was less keen to take on a
ten-year-old boy with issues.' Jarek strode into the house and
took a glass of sherry from the butler, who was waiting in the
entrance hall to greet them.

'Ralph cared for both of us,' Elin murmured, telling herself
it was true. Admittedly she had not felt the close bond with her
adoptive father that she'd had with Lorna Saunderson, but she'd
been fond of the man who had been the only father she'd ever
known. However, Jarek had struggled to settle into his new life
in England and to accept Ralph's authority.

'We were his social experiment. Take a couple of kids from

the lowest tier of society and see if he could mould them to fit in with the gentility.' Jarek gave a sardonic smile. 'It's fair to say that Ralph had more success with you than with me.'

'That's not true. I'm sure he thought highly of you, and he respected your financial flair, which is why he appointed you in a senior position at Saunderson's Bank.'

Elin took off her hat and coat and smoothed a crease from her black pencil dress. She declined the glass of sherry the butler offered her. 'Baines, I noticed there is a car parked on the driveway. I presume that my father's solicitor is here?' She had hoped to run up to the nursery and spend five minutes with Harry, but she would have to wait until after the formal reading of Ralph's will.

'Mr Carstairs and his associate arrived ten minutes ago and I showed the gentlemen into the library.'

'Business must be doing well for old Carstairs to drive an Aston Martin,' Jarek commented. 'I suppose he's brought a trainee from the law firm with him, but there wasn't much point. Ralph had no other family apart from us and his will must be straightforward. At least the reading of the will shouldn't take long,' he said, glancing at his watch. 'I'm racing later this afternoon.'

'I wish you wouldn't race that damned motorbike,' Elin muttered as she followed her brother across the hallway. 'It's such a risky sport.'

'Everything carries an element of risk.' A nerve jumped in Jarek's jaw. 'No one could have predicted that a trip to a jewellers would cost Mama her life.'

Elin was saved from answering as she entered the library and Peter Carstairs immediately got up from an armchair. 'Elin, Jarek, I am sure this is a difficult day for you and I will endeavour not to take up too much of your time.'

'Thank you.' Elin wondered why the normally affable solicitor seemed tense. 'Would you like a drink?'

'No, thank you. I think we should proceed.' Mr Carstairs

moved to the chair behind the desk and Elin followed her brother over to the sofa. She suddenly remembered that Baines had said he had shown two men into the library, but before she could suggest that they wait until the solicitor's clerk returned—presumably he was visiting the cloakroom—Mr Carstairs picked up a document and began to read from it.

He began by announcing several small bequests that Ralph Saunderson had made to members of the household staff. 'Next we come to the Saunderson's estate winery.' The solicitor cleared his throat. 'I leave a fifty per cent share of the vineyards and winery to my adopted daughter Elin Dvorska Saunderson.'

Elin felt a jolt of surprise. She had assumed that Ralph would hand the entire ownership of the estate winery to her. She'd worked as production manager for the past eighteen months and was committed to fulfilling Lorna Saunderson's vision of producing world class English sparkling wine. Jarek had never shown any interest in the vineyards and winery, but perhaps Ralph had hoped his heir would become more involved in developing Saunderson's Wines, she reasoned.

She was vaguely aware of the library door opening and heard a faint click as it closed again, but her attention was on Mr Carstairs and she did not look round to see who had entered the room. The solicitor gave another nervous cough. 'There is a stipulation attached to the bequest, Elin. Mr Saunderson decreed that you must marry within one year and provide your son with a father before you can claim your inheritance. If you choose not to fulfil the obligation, your share of Saunderson's Wines will revert to your adoptive father's main heir.'

Shock rendered Elin speechless. She knew her adoptive father had disapproved of her being a single mother but once Harry had been born he'd seemed delighted with the baby. 'I can't believe Ralph would really have expected me to meet the terms of his will,' she said at last in a shaky voice. 'Or that a judge would uphold such an outrageous stipulation if I contested the will.'

'Mr Saunderson was completely within his rights to distribute his assets in any manner he saw fit,' the solicitor murmured. 'I have to advise you that there are no grounds on which you could contest your father's wishes.'

Her brother reached over and squeezed Elin's hand. 'You know Ralph liked to play his little games,' he said sardonically. 'This is just his way of trying to maintain control from beyond the grave. Don't worry, Ellie. Your share of the wine business will come to me if you haven't married in a year and I'll sign the whole of Saunderson's Wines over to you. I have no desire to toil in the vineyards.' Jarek glanced at the solicitor. 'Do you mind getting on with it? I have other things to do today.'

Mr Carstairs cleared his throat again. 'There are only two further items.' He continued to read the will. 'I leave two properties, Rose Cottage and Ivy Cottage, to my adopted children, Jarek and Elin, to live in or dispose of according to their wishes.'

Why had Ralph made the odd bequest? Elin's feeling of unease grew. It did not make sense. Her brother was Ralph's heir and would inherit the entire Cuckmere estate, which included Cuckmere Hall, two thousand acres of Sussex farmland, woodland and vineyards, plus thirty-five cottages and the pub in Little Bardley. She knotted her fingers together in her lap while Mr Carstairs continued.

'Finally, I give everything I own at my death, excluding the aforementioned bequests, all monies and properties and also the position of chairman of Saunderson's Bank, of which it is my right to appoint my successor, to my only natural son, Cortez Ramos.'

Silence. Lasting for what felt like a lifetime. Elin pressed her hand to her chest to try and ease the violent thud of her heart as the solicitor's words reverberated around her head.

Cortez.

It couldn't be the Cortez she'd had sex with a year ago. It must be a ghastly coincidence, she frantically told herself. But her sense of dread intensified when she remembered the dark figure she'd caught sight of in the graveyard. What did Ralph's astonishing will mean for her and Jarek? For her son? Her heart felt as if it would jump out of her chest. Fear, she realised. The certainty of the future that she had taken for granted had just been blown apart.

She was aware that her brother had stiffened but as always he kept tight control over his emotions. 'Is this some kind of joke, Carstairs?' Jarek drawled. 'You know full well that Ralph and Lorna Saunderson were unable to have children and so they adopted my sister and I. Ralph did not have a natural son and this Cortez Ramos, whoever he is, cannot have any legal claim to my adoptive father's estate.'

Before Mr Carstairs could reply, a voice spoke from the back of the room. A deep voice with a husky accent that Elin had heard too often in her dreams in the past year. 'Ralph did not have a *legitimate* natural son, but he had a bastard.' The voice became harsh. 'I am Ralph Saunderson's biological son and heir.'

Elin felt her stomach twist. *This can't be happening*, she thought, prayed. *If I turn my head, he won't be there and this whole nightmare will have been a dream.* She jerked her head round and her heart juddered to a standstill. At her birthday party a year ago she'd thought him the most beautiful man she'd ever seen, but Cortez was even more stunning than her memories of him.

'So it *was* you I saw in the church,' she choked. 'I thought I'd recognised you, but there was no reason why you should be there…or so I believed.' Her voice dropped to a whisper as the shock of seeing him stole her breath from her lungs.

Jarek had leapt up from the sofa. He looked at Cortez and back to Elin. 'Do you know this man?'

She swallowed, desperately trying to block out the images in her mind of Cortez's naked, powerfully muscular body poised above her as she lay sprawled on her bed at the house in Kensington. His dark olive skin a stark contrast to her paleness as he pushed her dress up around her waist and nudged her thighs apart. A bold conquistador laying claim to his prize. At least all that sleek, hard beauty was clothed today, but the formality of his charcoal-grey suit that he wore with a black shirt and tie did not lessen the impact of his raw masculinity.

'We...we met once,' she managed. The gold flecks in Cortez's dark eyes gleamed with what Elin furiously recognised was amusement. Never had she been more grateful for her reserved English upbringing with its emphasis on controlling her emotions. 'It was an unmemorable event,' she said coolly.

Her brother frowned. 'Did you know of his alleged relationship to Ralph?'

'Of course not.' The faint suspicion in Jarek's eyes felt like a knife in her heart. She owed her life to her brother. If it hadn't been for him, God knew what would have happened to her when Sarajevo had been attacked and a bomb had landed on the orphanage. 'If I'd had any inkling I would have told you.'

Elin bit her lip as her brother strode across the library and flung open the door. 'Jarek—where are you going?' She carefully did not look at Cortez as she hurried past him, but she was conscious of his tall, brooding presence and the evocative spicy scent of his aftershave tugged on her senses.

'You know why Ralph has done this, don't you?' Jarek said bitterly when Elin caught up with him in the entrance hall. 'He blamed me for Mama's death. And he was right. I should have saved her.'

'There was nothing you could have done against an armed raider. It wasn't your fault. Jarek...' Elin's hand fell from her brother's arm as he spun away from her and grabbed his motorbike helmet from the hall table.

'If I hadn't tried to be a hero, Lorna would still be here. I took a gamble when I tackled the gunman, but the gamble failed. I understand why Ralph excluded me from his will but he had no reason to cut you out.' Jarek opened the front door and turned to face her. 'Do you know what I wish?' he said rawly. 'I wish that when we were held hostage in the raid on the jewellers the goddamned gunman had shot me instead of Mama. It's obvious that's what Ralph wished.'

'Oh, please be careful.' Elin wanted to go after her brother when he ran down the front steps and leapt onto his motorbike parked on the drive, but Peter Carstairs came out of the library and spoke to her.

'Mr Ramos was kind enough to give me a lift here and I arranged for a taxi to collect me,' he said as a car turned onto the driveway. 'I'm sorry to have been the harbinger of bad news, my dear. This must all be a great shock.'

The solicitor was the master of the understatement, Elin thought with a flash of macabre humour. 'My father died from a brain tumour. Is it possible that he was not of sound mind when he made Cortez Ramos his heir? Do we even know for sure that Mr Ramos is Ralph's son?'

She tensed when she saw Cortez standing in the doorway of the library and realised he must have overheard her. Too bad, she thought grimly. She was fighting for her and her brother's inheritance and, more importantly, for her son's future.

Harry was Cortez's son.

Oh, God, she couldn't think about the implications now, or how she was going to break the news to the granite-faced stranger she'd had sex with one time that he had fathered a child. She heard Jarek's motorbike roar off down the drive and a knot of fear for his safety tightened in her stomach.

The solicitor shook his head. 'Mr Saunderson was definitely of sound mind when he asked me to draw up a new will for him six months or so after his wife's death. I believe he had suspected for some time that Mr Ramos could be his son and when a DNA test proved it, he invited his son here to Cuckmere Hall. He asked me to draw up the new will on the same day that Mr Ramos visited, on the third of March a year ago.'

'The third of March is my birthday,' Elin said faintly. The realisation that her adoptive father had written his extraordinary will, which effectively left her penniless, on her birthday, felt like a devastating betrayal. There was no possibility of her marrying within a year so that she could claim a fifty per cent share of Saunderson's Wines.

She felt bombarded by one shock after another, and on top of the worry about her future she was terrified that her brother would risk his life riding his motorbike dangerously fast. She felt the same sensation of being unable to breathe that she'd experienced two nights ago in a crowded nightclub. Her legs buckled beneath her, and as if from a long way off she heard Cortez swear.

CHAPTER THREE

ELIN WEIGHED NEXT to nothing, Cortez discovered as he sprang forwards and caught her before she hit the floor. Her fragility was the first thing that had struck him when he'd seen her standing at the front of the church. Was her slender figure the result of dieting to be fashionably thin, or was there a more sinister reason? he wondered as he strode into the library with her in his arms.

Two days ago, pictures of her being carried out of a London nightclub had been plastered over the front pages of the tabloids. There had been speculation that she'd taken cocaine or another recreational drug, popular on the club scene. *Is this proof that Elin has resumed her party lifestyle?* had been one headline.

Cortez had been annoyed with himself for pandering to his curiosity and buying the newspaper to read the full story. The references to Elin's party girl reputation of a year ago, before she had mysteriously dropped off the paparazzi's radar for a few months, had made him shove the paper into the rubbish bin in disgust.

What the hell had possessed him to have sex with her when he'd unwittingly gatecrashed her party? The answer felt like a punch in his gut. The same punch that had made him catch his breath when he'd watched her dancing at her party. *Desire*.

Uncontrollable, ferocious desire had shot through him like a lightning bolt.

Unbidden memories pushed into his mind of Elin wearing a low-cut red dress that barely covered her pert breasts. Her pale blonde hair fell in a silken curtain around her shoulders, framing her exquisite face with its elfin features and a wide mouth that was entirely sensual. The moment he'd seen her he'd been unable to take his eyes off her. Even knowing what she was—a spoilt little rich girl who cared about nothing other than where the next party was being held and—if the press stories about her were true—where she could get her next fix—hadn't lessened his hunger for her.

It was a little over twelve months ago when he had come to England after he'd received the result of a DNA test which confirmed he was Ralph Saunderson's son. Ralph had invited him to Cuckmere Hall, and Cortez had gone because he could not deny he was curious to meet his biological father, who had abandoned his mother when she was pregnant. He had already discovered that Ralph was wealthy and the Saundersons were an old aristocratic family.

Driving through the vast Cuckmere estate on his way up to the mansion, Cortez had felt bitter remembering how his mother had worked herself literally into an early grave. Thirty-five years ago, Marisol Ramos had been pregnant and alone, abandoned by her lover and shunned by her family in Spain. She had managed to establish a small vineyard in Andalucía and from almost as soon as Cortez could walk he had helped his mother tend the vines and harvest the grapes. The bodega had produced a fine sherry, but it couldn't compete with the big sherry producers in the sherry triangle in south-west Spain. Life had been hard, and when his mother had died at the age of forty-two Cortez had been convinced that she'd simply felt too exhausted to carry on living.

When he had finally met Ralph Saunderson the only emotion he'd felt was anger that his father had consigned his mother to a life of poverty and hardship. At the time of his visit to Cuckmere Hall the English press had been full of stories about Ralph's adopted son and daughter's jet set lifestyle, in particular Elin's wild partying. But the pictures of her in the newspapers and her photo on Ralph's desk that had caught Cortez's attention had not prepared him for the impact she had on him when he saw her dancing at her birthday party.

He jerked his mind from the past as Elin's eyelashes fluttered open. For a few seconds she stared at him with her dark blue eyes that had reminded him of sapphires when he'd danced with her a year ago. He recalled how she had pressed her body up close to his. As close as she was now, except that then she had been soft and pliant in his arms and she'd parted her lush mouth in an invitation he had been unable to resist.

That should have been a warning, he thought grimly. He never had a problem resisting women. He was always in control and when he took a mistress it was always on his terms, with rules and boundaries established first. Falling into bed with Elin had broken every rule he'd imposed on himself since he'd fallen in love with Alandra in his early twenties and she had shattered his illusions about love and his own judgement.

'What are you doing? Put me down.'

Cortez heard panic in Elin's voice and he felt a stab of irritation when he lowered her onto the sofa and she immediately recoiled from him as if he were infected with a contagious disease. She hadn't behaved like that a year ago, he brooded. She'd been all over him then. He walked across to the desk, where the butler had left a tray of drinks, and tried to dismiss the memory of Elin sprawled on a bed with her red dress rucked up around her waist and her pale thighs spread wide open.

'Here,' he said curtly, returning to hand her a glass of brandy.

She shook her head. 'I never touch spirits and in fact I rarely drink alcohol at all.'

How could she look so damned *innocent* when he had irrefutable proof that she was far from it? He remembered how she had flirted with him at her birthday party and he had been blown away by her sexual allure.

Cortez's anger with himself increased when he found he could not tear his eyes away from Elin. She was even more beautiful than he remembered. The black dress she was wearing was a classic style reminiscent of a previous era when women had looked effortlessly elegant. Her pale blonde hair was swept up into a chignon that emphasised the incredible bone structure of her face, with those high cheekbones and perfectly arched brows above the bluest eyes he'd ever seen. He felt a sudden tightness in his chest and to his fury he was powerless to control the almost painful throb of his sexual arousal.

'If you were not drunk when you had to be carried out of a nightclub the other night, then perhaps the recent lurid tabloid headlines alleging that you have a drug habit are true,' he drawled.

Colour stained her porcelain cheeks. 'The press print a lot of lies about me, but the truth is that I fainted in the nightclub because I've been unwell recently. I felt wobbly just now because it was a huge shock to learn that my father had excluded me and my brother from his will, and named you—his illegitimate son that no one knew existed—as his heir.' Elin's voice was icy but her eyes flashed with fury as she got up from the sofa and faced him.

'Did you go to the house in Kensington and gatecrash my party so you could gloat? Ralph must have told you a year ago that he intended to make you his heir. Wasn't it enough to know you would inherit Cuckmere Hall, the house in London and the chairmanship of Saunderson's Bank, and you decided you would take me too?'

Cortez gave a hard smile, because here at last was proof that she might look like an angel, with her golden beauty and that ridiculous air of innocence that made his gut twist, but she was just another blonde who had satisfied his libido for a few hours, and she was no different to all the other blondes who regarded sex as a bartering tool. No doubt if he had stuck around after they'd slept together, Elin would have issued demands the way all women did.

'As a matter of fact I did not know about the will,' he told her. 'After I met my father for the first time at Cuckmere Hall I had planned to spend the night at a hotel in London, but Ralph suggested I could stay at his house in Kensington and gave me a key. He said that you and your brother were both abroad and the house would be empty. When I walked into your party I had every intention of leaving, but you begged me to dance with you.'

Cortez was fascinated by the tide of scarlet that swept along her high cheekbones. 'I did not take anything that was not offered freely,' he said harshly. 'You invited me into your bedroom and made it clear that you wanted sex.' He shrugged. 'Knowing of your reputation, I don't flatter myself that I was your first or last one-night stand.'

The colour receded from her face. 'You really *are* a bastard, aren't you? That night I was under the influence of a drug which impaired my judgement and caused me to behave in a way I would never normally have done. As for my reputation—' she gave a short laugh '—you know nothing about me.'

There was a strained note of what he could almost believe was *hurt* in her voice that made Cortez feel uncomfortable. He had no reason to feel guilty, he assured himself. Elin had just admitted that she'd taken drugs at her party and implied that she'd had sex with him because she had been high. But he'd been unaware she'd taken any kind of substance or that her behaviour was out of character. Everything he'd read about her in the press suggested she'd had many previous sex partners.

Memories of that night were crystal-clear in his mind, despite the distance of a year. He remembered that when he had pulled her beneath him and thrust himself into her with a desperation he'd never felt before, she had tensed and caught her breath. *Dios*, she had been so tight and so goddamned hot that he'd almost come instantly. But then she'd wrapped her legs around his hips and matched his pace when he began to move. Passion had blazed between them and he'd dismissed the unlikely notion that she was sexually inexperienced.

Maybe it was an act she put on with other men, Cortez thought darkly. He had proof that he could not have been her first lover.

'I know you have a child.' He wondered why he felt a simmering rage at the thought of her slender body wrapped around another man. He had been shocked when he'd heard during the reading of Ralph's will that Elin had a son. It was odd the media had not reported that she had a child.

'Ralph stated in his will that he wished for you to marry and provide your son with a father. Are you in contact with your child's father, and do you intend to marry him in order to claim your inheritance?'

He did not know why he had asked her when he really wasn't interested in her private life. But he stared at her because he couldn't help himself and waited tensely for her answer. He realised he was bracing himself for her to reply, but when she did he was unprepared for the shockwave that ripped through him.

'*You* are my son's father,' she said in her soft voice that had haunted him for the past year.

For a split second he wondered if it was possible, but... 'No.' He dismissed the idea. 'You can't pin the blame on me. Although I can see why it would be convenient if I was the father of your child,' he said sardonically. 'I would feel duty-bound to marry you, and you need a husband in order to meet the terms of Ralph's will. Marriage to me would give you not only a share of Saunderson's Wines but also everything you had expected to inherit from my father. As my wife, you could continue to live here at Cuckmere Hall and enjoy the affluent lifestyle Ralph provided, until he named me as his heir.'

He smiled cynically when she shook her head. 'I'm not a fool, *querida*. I always practice safe sex. Perhaps you were out of your mind from whatever substance you had taken at your birthday party, but I'll prompt your memory and remind you that I used a condom. I'm afraid you will have to look elsewhere for a husband and a father for your child.'

Elin swayed on her feet, whether for dramatic effect or because she hadn't fully recovered from fainting a few minutes ago, Cortez did not know and he told himself he didn't care. She swallowed before she spoke. 'Only a fool would believe that contraception is one hundred per cent effective, and in our case it failed.'

She lifted her chin and met his gaze, and for some reason he was compelled to look away from her intense blue stare. 'Believe me, hell will freeze over before I'd ever want to marry you,' she said coldly. 'Harry is yours, but I might have known you would shirk your responsibility for your son when you scuttled off without even having the decency to say goodbye after you'd had sex with me.'

'You were in a deep sleep and I did not think you would appreciate me waking you,' he bit out, incensed by her scathing tone and her insistence on continuing with what was undoubtedly a lie. He did not believe for a minute that he was the father of her child. *Dios*, after what had happened with Alandra he had taken care never to have unprotected sex.

Even so, he disliked the image Elin had presented of him hurrying out of her bedroom while she slept because he could not deny that was exactly what he'd done. He'd been rattled that she had made him lose control and he had left before he'd given in to the temptation to kiss her awake and make love to her again, slowly, taking his time to explore her beautiful body so that she gasped and moaned while he pleasured her.

Cortez swore silently as his body reacted predictably to his erotic thoughts, and he forced himself to focus on the present situation. He wasn't surprised that Elin had played the oldest trick in the book to try to secure financial security for herself, after she'd learned that she and her brother had been excluded almost entirely from their adoptive father's will. He could not imagine that 'the party princess'—as one of the tabloids had nicknamed her—had ever held down a job. She needed a source of income, but what was surprising was how quickly she conceded defeat.

'I've done my duty and informed you that you have a son,' she said crisply. 'I neither want nor expect anything from you, except for a few days' grace while I arrange to move out of Cuckmere Hall.' Her voice bore the faintest tremor and she pressed her lips together before she continued. 'You are aware that Ralph left my brother and I each a property on the estate. But the cottages have been empty for several years and I don't know what state they are in. I may need to have some renovation work done before I can take a baby to live there.'

He reminded himself that she did not deserve his compassion. She had enjoyed a privileged lifestyle, which had been denied to his mother and him when he was a child. But Ralph's vile treatment of his mother was nothing to do with Elin, Cortez conceded. Nor was it her fault that she had grown up in the gracious surroundings of Cuckmere Hall, while he had spent his boyhood working in the vineyards in the blazing Spanish sun, helping his mother to eke out a living.

'I'm going back to London to meet the board of Saunderson's Bank this afternoon,' he told her. 'I have no plans to return to Sussex for a week or so. You and your brother can remain at Cuckmere Hall while you make arrangements to move into the cottages Ralph left you.'

'I doubt Jarek will want to live in a cottage. He has his own home in London.' She hesitated. 'My brother had anticipated that he would become chairman of the bank. What will happen now? Will he continue in his current job?'

'For the immediate future the situation will remain unchanged, until I have met the board of directors. When I have assessed all aspects of the bank's business portfolio there are likely to be changes,' he warned. 'Ralph's will was as much of a surprise to me as it was to you. I was informed of his death by Mr Carstairs and I attended the funeral to pay my respects to my father, even though he had never given my mother the respect she deserved.'

Cortez did not try to disguise his bitterness. His mother had been an angel and his greatest regret was that she had died before he'd become rich and successful and he hadn't had the chance to make her life more comfortable.

'It was a great shock to discover that my adoptive father had a secret son,' Elin said quietly. 'How did your mother meet Ralph?'

'She worked as a maid here at Cuckmere Hall. My mother never spoke of my father or revealed his identity and I had no idea that I was Ralph's son until I received a request for a DNA test. When I met Ralph he explained that he'd had an affair with my mother at the same time as he became engaged to Lorna Amhurst. He said his marriage was an arrangement to merge two banking families.'

Cortez frowned. 'Ralph insisted that he gave my mother money when she told him she was pregnant. He assumed she returned to her family in Spain. But her family threw her out for having an illegitimate child and she brought me up on her own, with no money other than the small income she earned from growing grapes used for making sherry.

'I don't know why Ralph made me his heir, but I think it is unlikely that he wanted to make amends for abandoning me before I was born,' he said cynically. 'A more obvious reason is that, having ignored me—his biological son—for most of my life, Ralph was faced with leaving his personal fortune and Saunderson's Bank to the mercy of his two adopted children who, despite the privileges of wealth and excellent education, have become spoiled brats in adulthood.'

Elin jerked her head back as if he had slapped her. *Dios*, how did this woman manage to make him feel as if he were a monster? Cortez thought frustratedly.

'You know nothing about me or my brother,' she said in a clipped voice that made him want to ruffle her cool composure and reveal the fire that he knew simmered beneath her air of refinement. 'Jarek is a thousand times a better man than you could ever be.'

Finally he glimpsed a flicker of emotion on her face that up until now had been a serene mask. It was interesting that her brother was her weak spot, he mused. Everyone had an Achilles heel and he had made it his particular line of expertise to detect weaknesses in an opponent which he could ruthlessly use to his advantage. Although he was unlikely to ever need to use boardroom tactics with Elin. She did not have anything he wanted—apart from the face of an angel and a body that would tempt the most devout saint to sin, he thought with grim humour.

But she was off limits. He'd had his share of one-night stands and saw nothing wrong for two consenting adults to enjoy sex without the complication of emotions. What he found intolerable was that Elin was the only woman he had been unable to forget. And yes, he'd tried the obvious method of having sex with other women, but after a few unsatisfactory encounters he hadn't had a mistress for months.

The dull ache in his groin mocked his belief that he'd lost interest in sex but, far from feeling relieved at the proof that his libido was functioning normally, he was consumed with equal measures of rage and a terrible hunger that he feared would be his doom. That *she* would be his doom.

Santa Madre. Cortez cursed beneath his breath and jerked his eyes from her lovely face and that soft mouth that he longed to taste. He glanced at his watch and realised he had already wasted too much time. Elin was a dangerous distraction. 'My meeting with the board of Saunderson's Bank is scheduled for three o'clock, and I need to leave now if I am to make it on time.'

He walked over to the door and paused to glance back at her. 'I will make arrangements for a representative from a hotel design company to visit Cuckmere Hall next week. They should not inconvenience you while you are packing to move out.'

'Hotel?' she said sharply. 'You...you're not thinking of turning the house into a hotel?'

'It's one option I am considering. I have no desire to live in an ugly Gothic monstrosity.' He strode into the hall and Elin followed him.

'Cuckmere isn't ugly. Admittedly the house is a quirky mix of architectural styles, but most of the main house was built or renovated in the early nineteenth century. There has been a house on this site since Tudor times and the Saunderson family have lived here since then. You are a Saunderson. Cuckmere Hall is your heritage...and...it is also your son's.'

Cortez could not control the fierce emotions that ripped through him at Elin's words. His mind flew back to when he had been in his early twenties and had moved to Madrid to start his career with Hernandez Bank. Life in the big city had been exciting, and when he'd met a stunning model, Alandra Ruiz, he'd fallen hard for her exotic looks.

He pictured himself in the bathroom of Alandra's apartment, staring at a pregnancy test he'd found on the vanity unit. He'd picked up the test and carried it into the bedroom.

'When were you going to tell me you are pregnant, *carina*?'

Her reaction had surprised him. She had frowned and then given a careless shrug. 'I meant to throw the test away before you saw it.'

'So it's true—you're going to have my baby?' He'd never felt so happy in his life. The woman he loved was pregnant with his child, and he was filled with excitement and pride.

But Alandra had pushed him away when he'd tried to take her in his arms. 'Don't be ridiculous. I can't go through with the pregnancy,' she'd snapped. 'For one thing, getting fat will ruin my career. But, more importantly, Emilio will know it is not his child because he has been abroad for months.'

Cortez had felt as though a lead weight had dropped into his stomach. 'Who the hell is Emilio?'

'He's my fiancé.' Alandra gave another shrug. 'He has moved to Canada, where he has a good job, and I'm waiting for a visa so that I can join him in Toronto. I was bored and you were a little light entertainment,' she'd told Cortez. 'But it has to end now.'

He had tried to persuade her to keep the baby. 'Marry me and I'll take care of you and our child,' he'd begged.

At first she had laughed at him. 'You don't earn half as much as Emilio, and I don't want his baby, so why would I want yours?' Eventually she had agreed, and he had been overjoyed, but days later Alandra had called him and said she had never been serious about accepting his proposal and she had got rid of his baby before flying to Canada to be with her fiancé.

Cortez snapped his thoughts back to the present. Elin had to be lying because if she'd really had his child why wouldn't she have told him before now and demanded money? Alandra had ripped his heart out when she'd got rid of his baby, and he re-fused to give credence to the idea that he could be the father of Elin's child when the chances were frankly negligible.

'I don't have a son,' he snapped. He swung away from her and moved towards the front door, but she came after him and put her hand on his arm.

'Please, Cortez…'

Please, Cortez. He pictured her sprawled on a bed with her scarlet dress awry. He heard her soft voice urging him on, incit-ing his hunger, his desperation to sink between her soft white thighs. She had made him feel out of control a year ago and she was threatening his self-control now. He wanted to haul her back to the sofa in the library and slide her elegant black dress up to her waist to bare her to his hungry gaze. He wanted her more than he'd ever wanted any other woman, and his need infuriated him and at a deeper level it shamed him. Cortez Ramos did not *need* anyone. Certainly not a social butterfly who, if only half the press stories about her were true, was a trollop.

He stared at her hand on his arm while the silence in the hall simmered with tension. She was standing so close that he breathed in her perfume, a light floral fragrance with underlying sensual notes of jasmine, and the beast inside him roared. He brought his other hand up and snapped his fingers around her wrist to jerk it away from his arm.

'If you ever repeat your unfounded accusation that I am the father of your child I will sue you for slander,' he said grimly. 'We had protected sex on one occasion. It would be *too* convenient from your point of view if you had conceived my child, but I don't believe you did.'

He pulled open the front door and the cold March air stung his nostrils as he dragged in a breath. 'It is not wise to play games with me, Elin. Unlike you, I did not enjoy a privileged upbringing. When I was a boy my mother often could not afford to buy food for us, but the hunger in my belly fired my determination to succeed and escape the poverty of my childhood. I've heard that Ralph Saunderson had a reputation for being ruthless and, I warn you, in that respect I take after my father.'

CHAPTER FOUR

ELIN WATCHED CORTEZ ease his tall frame into the low-slung sports car parked on the drive and slammed the front door shut as if she were shutting out the devil. She released her breath on a shuddering sigh and leaned against the solid wooden door for support while she replayed the unbelievable scene in the library over in her mind.

She did not know what was most shocking: Ralph's will which stipulated that she must marry before she could claim her inheritance, or that Ralph's natural son and heir was Cortez Ramos—the father of her baby son, who had been conceived as a result of her night of shame.

Harry was the innocent one in all of this. With a low cry, she ran across the hall and up the sweeping staircase. Her suite of rooms, including the nursery, were in the east wing of the house. Cuckmere Hall had been her home since she was four years old and the possibility that Cortez might turn it into a hotel felt like another stab of a knife into her already mortally wounded heart.

The sound of her son's cries drove every other thought from her mind as she flew across the nursery and lifted him out of his cot. 'It's all right, sweetheart. Mummy's here,' she crooned softly, feeling a familiar clench of emotion when Harry buried his face in her neck and his cries subsided to little snuffles.

'I was just preparing his next feed,' the nanny explained, hurrying into the room from the private kitchen. 'Do you want me to give it to him?'

'No, I will.' Elin held out her hand for the bottle of formula and quashed a flicker of jealousy of the nanny. Barbara Lennox had proved to be invaluable and she had also become a trusted friend.

Elin had not planned to hire a nanny. But she had been desperately ill after giving birth to Harry and when she had finally left hospital and returned to Cuckmere Hall with her newborn son, Jarek had told her that he had employed Barbara temporarily while Elin regained her strength. Suffering a life-threatening haemorrhage moments after the birth had been a terrifying ordeal and, despite having been given two blood transfusions, she'd still felt weak and exhausted. To make matters worse, she'd then developed a serious kidney infection and had been too ill to be able to take care of her baby.

Barbara had turned down another job offer to stay and help look after Harry. It occurred to Elin that she would no longer be able to afford to employ a nanny now that Ralph had left her nothing in his will. She hadn't felt a sense of entitlement, as Cortez had implied, but for twenty-two years she had regarded Ralph as her father and she was deeply hurt by the evidence that he had not cared about her.

She settled herself in a chair and felt a pang of guilt when Harry nuzzled his face against her breast and tried to suckle. 'Here you are,' she murmured, offering him the teat of the bottle. It was a lasting sadness that she had been unable to breastfeed him because of the strong antibiotics she'd had to take to fight the kidney infection, but Barbara had assured her that Harry was thriving on formula milk.

He was now just over three months old and he had a surprisingly strong grip when he curled his chubby fist around her finger. She couldn't resist kissing his downy cheek and silky black hair. He stared up at her with his big eyes that were already changing from dark blue to an even darker brown flecked with gold that reminded her of Cortez's eyes.

She could insist on a DNA test to prove that Cortez was Harry's father, but what would be the point? she thought wearily. Cortez did not want his son and she would not demean herself by pursuing him through the courts for a maintenance pay-out. Harry was her responsibility and she was prepared to bring him up on her own. At least she would have somewhere for them to live. Rose and Ivy Cottages were tucked away on a remote part of the Cuckmere estate. She knew Jarek would insist she took ownership of whichever cottage was in the best condition. He rarely came to east Sussex and when he was in England he stayed at his London penthouse apartment, but most of the time he lived in Japan, where he worked as head derivatives trader for Saunderson's Bank.

She would have to look for another job. Elin chewed on her lower lip as the harsh reality of her situation sank in. Marriage was not an option. She did not have a prospective husband handily available and, even if she could bear to force herself onto the dating scene, she was a single parent with no money or prospects and she was hardly a great catch. But it meant that under the terms of Ralph's will Cortez would inherit one hundred per cent of Saunderson's Wines.

The pain that had lodged beneath her breastbone following her mother's death gave a sharp tug with the realisation that she would not be able to fulfil Lorna Saunderson's dream of producing a top quality English wine from Cuckmere's vineyards that Lorna herself had planted.

It was conceivable that Cortez would allow her to continue in her role as production manager of the winery, but she did not relish the thought of working for him. Not if there was a chance she might see him regularly. She could not risk it when he had such a powerful effect on her. She pictured his handsome face: the chiselled cheekbones and square jaw, those dark, almost black eyes with their golden flecks and his wickedly sensual mouth that promised heaven—and delivered. Oh, boy, did it deliver.

Memories she'd blanked out for over a year filled her mind. His lips on hers, the way he had plundered her soul and ravished her senses with his devastating kiss. Until today she'd convinced herself that her outrageous behaviour on the night of her birthday party had been the result of her drink being spiked with a date-rape drug by one of the other guests. But when she had seen Cortez in the library at the reading of Ralph's will, her body had betrayed her and forced her to acknowledge the shameful truth. She had fallen into bed with him a year ago because she'd seen him across a crowded room and she'd wanted him so badly it had *hurt*.

She had ignored the voice in her head which warned her that a man as lethally attractive as him was way out of her league. He had stolen her breath and her sanity and all that had been left of her was a burning need to feel his arms around her, his mouth against her mouth, his body on her body. Damning memories of having sex with Cortez came storming back and her treacherous body betrayed her all over again. Her nipples tightened and the quiver she felt low in her stomach was a shameful reminder that she had behaved like a slut at her birthday party.

But her night of shame had resulted in her son. Harry finished his bottle and Elin held him against her shoulder while she winded him. Her heart turned over when he gave her a gummy smile. She would never regret having him even though she regretted the circumstances of his conception. She loved him so much and she vowed that as he grew up she would protect her son from the painful truth that his father had refused to acknowledge him.

She told herself it would be best if she forgot that Cortez Ramos existed but, after she had changed Harry's nappy and settled him in his cot, she found herself in front of her computer searching for Cortez's profile on social media sites. His biography revealed that he had spent his childhood living with his mother on a small vineyard in Andalucía. After graduating from university with a first-class business degree he had worked for one of Spain's largest banks and quickly proved he was a brilliant financier. His rise through the ranks to the position of CEO of Hernandez Bank had been meteoric.

It was no wonder that Ralph had chosen his illegitimate son to be chairman of Saunderson's Bank over his adopted son, Elin thought heavily. Ralph had been concerned that Jarek was too much of a risk-taker and it was an opinion shared by many of the board of directors, who would no doubt be very happy to have Cortez as the head of the bank.

His success was not confined to banking. He had earned a reputation as a skilled viticulturist, and at his vineyards and bodega near the town of Jerez de la Frontera he specialised in producing exceptionally fine sherry. Five years ago, Cortez had formed a partnership with an international sherry company to produce and export specialist sherries around the world. The business, Felipe & Cortez, had become so successful that he was reputedly a multimillionaire.

Elin was deep in thought as she switched off the computer. Her mind went blank for a moment when her phone rang and she answered a call from a catering company who wanted to discuss arrangements for the party that was to take place at Cuckmere Hall.

'Oh, yes, the event is definitely going ahead,' she confirmed to the caterers. The party was to raise funds for a charity organisation that she, Jarek and Ralph had established after Lorna Saunderson's death. Lorna's Gift aimed to support children living in orphanages around the world, and the many celebrities who had been invited to the party were likely to make huge donations to the charity.

Elin was sure her adoptive father would have wanted her to hold the party. But Cortez was now the owner of Cuckmere Hall and she did not have time to find another suitable venue. He had told her before he'd left for his business meeting in London that he did not plan to return to Sussex for some time. There was a good chance he would never find out that the party had taken place. Her conscience felt uncomfortable, but she reminded herself that the charity was already making a difference to the lives of orphaned children and it might be her last chance to hold a major fund-raising event before she had to leave Cuckmere Hall.

What if Elin had told him the truth?

The question had haunted Cortez when he'd driven away from Cuckmere Hall, and uncertainty had continued to plague him for the past two days while he'd had meetings with the board and management team of Saunderson's Bank. He had dismissed Elin's claim that he was the father of her child because he was ninety-nine per cent certain she was lying. But that left a one per cent possibility that it was true.

His conscience pricked that he had rejected her claim outright and rushed away from Cuckmere because he hadn't trusted himself around her. She unsettled him in a way no other woman had ever done and he resented the effect she had on him. But he needed to rule out the slim chance he had a son, which was why, instead of spending a relaxing evening at the house in Kensington, he had driven down the motorway back to Sussex in the pouring rain that at times had turned to sleet.

Cuckmere Hall was a beacon of blazing lights against the black sky. When Cortez turned the car through the gates of the estate he was surprised to see dozens of vehicles parked on the driveway in front of the house. He was tired, which was perhaps understandable after the bizarre last few days, when he'd learned that the man he struggled to think of as his father had bequeathed him the chairmanship of the UK's most prestigious private bank. The role came with a huge amount of responsibility and the expectation of the board that the bank would flourish under his leadership. But he felt no loyalty to Ralph Saunderson, who had ignored him for thirty-four years and had only made Cortez his heir because Ralph's adopted son was not up to the job of running Saunderson's Bank.

The journey from London and the foul English weather had darkened Cortez's mood even more, and his temper simmered when he walked into Cuckmere Hall and found a party going on. He threaded his way through the crowd of people in the central hall and shook his head at the waiter who offered him a tray of canapés. In one of the reception rooms there was a champagne bar, and in the ballroom music blared from the speakers and people were dancing.

He saw Elin immediately, and the punch in his gut made him catch his breath. It was history repeating itself, he thought furiously. She was even wearing a red dress like she had done at her birthday party a year ago. But, instead of a scrap of scarlet silk, her dress tonight was a burgundy velvet floor-length gown with a side split up to her mid-thigh. The top of the dress was strapless, leaving her shoulders bare, and the laced bodice pushed her breasts up so that they looked like ripe, round peaches that he longed to taste. Her pale blonde hair reached to halfway down her back and shimmered like raw silk.

He wanted her. *Dios*, he could feel the thunder of his pulse, and the fire in his blood mocked his belief that his desire for her a year ago had been an aberration. What was it about Elin that tested his self-control to its limits? She was not the only beautiful woman he had known, not even the most beautiful—her eyes were too big in her heart-shaped face and her mouth was too wide. She was elfin and ethereal and too petite for his six feet four frame.

The rage inside him turned darker and more dangerous as he watched her dancing with a man he vaguely recognised was a television chat show host. The guy's hands were all over Elin, but she seemed to be enjoying the attention, and her lilting laughter audible above the music caused acid to fizz in Cortez's gut. He snapped his teeth together and strode across the ballroom, driven to distraction by an unfamiliar emotion that he grimly realised was jealousy.

'My turn, I think you'll find,' he growled to Elin's dance partner. The other man obviously valued his doubtless exorbitantly expensive dental work and quickly dropped his hand from her waist.

'That was incredibly rude.' Elin threw Cortez a furious glare before she spun round and began to walk away, but he snaked his arm around her waist and jerked her towards him.

'I'm sure you don't want to cause a scene, so I suggest you dance with me.'

'*I'm* not the one causing a scene,' she snapped. 'Do you know who that man is? He is Clint Cooper, one of the highest paid people on television, and he was about to promise me a lot of money before you barged him out of the way.'

'*Santa Madre*, you would barter yourself like a whore on a street corner?' Cortez made no effort to hide his disgust, but to his fury he realised that he still wanted her and he didn't care that she had lived up to her reputation in the tabloids as a goodtime girl.

'*How dare you?*' She reacted instantly and swung her hand up, but his reactions were quicker and he seized her wrist before she could slap his cheek.

'Careful,' he warned her softly. 'If you hit me, I'll retaliate. Right here in front of your guests, I will put you across my knee and spank you as befits the spoiled brat you are. And, believe me, I would dare, Elin.'

The pink flush on her cheeks deepened to scarlet and she breathed jerkily, causing her breasts to quiver above the low-cut neckline of her dress. Her eyes flashed with temper, but Cortez sensed the scorching sexual chemistry beneath her anger and he felt an answering lick of fire along his manhood.

'You are an odious man,' she hissed. 'Why are you even here? You said you would be staying in London.'

'Is that why you decided to throw a party while I was conveniently out of the way? I'm sure I don't have to remind you that Ralph left me Cuckmere Hall. The house and estate are mine by right of birth—even though my father failed to acknowledge me for most of my life.' He could not hide his bitterness. 'I suppose you are angry because your adoptive father excluded you from his will, but I find it distasteful that you arranged a party two days after Ralph's funeral. You might as well have danced on his grave.'

She stiffened when he moved his hand to the small of her back and held her tightly against him so that she was forced to dance with him. 'As a matter of fact, Ralph helped to organise the party before he died,' she snapped. 'The charity, Lorna's Gift, was my brother's idea and all the funds raised go to helping children living in orphanages around the world.'

She pointed to a banner on the wall that he had not noticed because his attention had been riveted on Elin. The banner had the slogan *Lorna's Gift* and a photograph of a sweet-faced woman who he guessed was Lorna Saunderson. Cortez was aware that Ralph's wife had died eighteen months ago.

'Clint Cooper was telling me of his intention to make a donation to the charity,' Elin continued furiously. 'He was not offering me money for sex. What gives you the right to judge me?' Her mouth trembled and Cortez sensed she was struggling to control her emotions. 'Do you think I don't judge myself?' she said in a low voice. 'My birthday party a year ago was the most shameful night of my life. You have no idea how bitterly I regret that I had sex with you.'

Cortez told himself she was a good actress. He *knew* her air of innocence was fake. He focused his thoughts on the reason he had driven from London to Sussex on a filthy night. 'I need to talk to you, but not in here with this deafening music.' He had noticed there was a conservatory next to the ballroom and he steered her over to it. The glass room was empty and he closed the door to muffle the sound of the disco.

Elin immediately stepped away from him and put her hands

on her hips. 'What now?' she demanded belligerently. 'After we spoke two days ago I got the impression that you had nothing more to say to me, and I certainly have nothing to say to you.'

He pushed away the infuriating thought that she looked magnificent when she was angry. Her blue eyes gleamed with the fiery brilliance of sapphires and her breasts heaved beneath her velvet gown. 'When was your son born?' he said abruptly.

'The sixth of October.' She did not drop her gaze from his, and Cortez narrowed his eyes to hide his inexplicable feeling of disappointment.

'So he is five months old. You could at least have worked out the maths. You must have conceived in January last year, but we had sex in March.' His lip curled in disgust as another thought occurred to him. '*Dios.* You must have been pregnant when you slept with me, but you told me I was responsible. Surely you had the sense to realise I would not accept a paternity claim without a DNA test?'

She shrugged. 'It was worth a try.'

Dark and dangerous emotions swirled inside him and he felt the same savage wrench in his gut that he'd felt years ago when Alandra had informed him that she had terminated her pregnancy. He had wanted his baby but he hadn't been given a chance to be a father. Tonight he had come to Cuckmere Hall because he'd realised there was a chance he was the father of Elin's son. But she had lied and made a clumsy attempt to foist another man's child on him.

His jaw clenched as he struggled to control his anger. He was furious, not only with Elin but with himself because, despite the proof that she was a lying bitch, he was trapped in her spell and the shaming hunger he felt for her was a weakness he found intolerable.

'I warned you not to play games with me.' He resisted the urge to shake some sense into her. If he touched her he feared he would be lost. 'Maybe your whole life is a game of endless parties and various sexual partners, but you have a child to consider. I know what it is like to grow up without a father. What will you tell your son when he asks why he doesn't have a father?'

She paled, and that made him even angrier. How dare she look so *tragic*, as if he had wounded her, when he knew—when everyone who read the English tabloids knew about her wild sex-and-drugs party girl reputation?

'I'll tell Harry the truth,' she said quietly, 'which is that his father did not want him.' Her voice hardened. 'You're such a hypocrite. You think that it's fine for you to sleep around, but you judge the women you sleep with. That's blatant double standards. Equality between the sexes means nothing. It's still women who are left with the babies when they are abandoned by their lovers.'

Elin stalked out of the conservatory without giving Cortez a chance to reply. She was incensed by his arrogance and re-assured herself that she had done the right thing by mislead-ing him about Harry's date of birth. Cortez had made it clear he did not want a child, and after hearing his insulting opinion of her it was impossible to see how they could both have a role in Harry's life.

It was equally impossible to understand why she allowed herself to be affected by Cortez. But she did not allow it, she thought bitterly. She was kidding herself if she believed she had any control over her reaction to his dangerous good looks, and that *thing* that smouldered between them, that intense heat that licked through her veins every time she met his gaze and saw the gold flecks in his dark eyes blaze. She did not know what she found more unsettling—her uncontrollable fascina-tion with him, or the realisation that he desired her, and de-spised himself for it.

The din in the ballroom, of guests talking loudly in compe-tition with the blaring disco music, had given Elin a headache and after her run-in with Cortez she felt an urgent need to be with her baby. But as she exited the ballroom and was about to run upstairs to the nursery, someone called her name.

'Nat!' She smiled at the young man who hurried over to her. Nat Davies drove a tractor at the vineyard and he also worked in the winery where his father, Stan, was head winemaker for Saunderson's Wines. 'Are you enjoying the party?'

'Yeah, it's great. But Dad's just called me and said there's a problem at the vineyard.'

Elin frowned as Nat went on to explain that the latest weather forecast predicted an overnight frost. 'There are already buds on the vines after that unusually warm spell we had at the beginning of March,' he reminded her. 'Frost damage now could ruin the entire crop.'

It could mean the end of Lorna Saunderson's dream of producing a top quality sparkling wine in England that was on a par with wines from across the Channel. Elin remembered how ten years ago Mama had been inspired to establish a vineyard in Sussex after visiting the Champagne region of France. Ralph had initially been enthusiastic but, as was his way, he had quickly lost interest in the project. It had been Lorna and Elin, aided by a small team of estate workers, who had planted fifteen acres of Chardonnay and Pinot Noir vines in the chalky soil.

The winery had been producing wine for seven years, and the previous year's vintage had been the best yet. Following Lorna's death, it had been important to Elin to keep her mother's dream alive, but the terms of Ralph's will meant that her involvement with Saunderson's Wines would soon be over. The vines were Cortez's responsibility now, she reminded herself. But she couldn't bear the idea that all the years of Mama's hard work could be wiped out by a frost.

'We'll have to light the frost candles,' she told Nat. She glanced at her watch. 'It's almost midnight. We need to hurry before the temperature drops to below freezing. Go and round up any of the estate workers from the party who are sober enough to help.'

Twenty minutes later, Elin drove the farm truck through the grounds of the Cuckmere estate up to the vineyard. It was a clear night and the full moon cast a silver gleam over the rolling Sussex Downs. She briefly wondered what Cortez would make of her if he saw her as she was dressed now. She had changed out of her glamorous ball gown, into jeans and as many jumpers as she could fit beneath her duffel coat.

The air was icy when she climbed out of the truck and walked through the vineyard, but remembering her last conversation with Cortez made her burn with anger. She had not noticed his car on the drive, and hoped he had returned to London and she would never see him again. It was imperative that she moved out of Cuckmere Hall as soon as possible so that she could avoid him. Although it would break her heart to leave the only home she had ever known, she thought bleakly.

She forced her mind away from Cortez Ramos and concentrated on the task of lighting eight hundred *bougies*—or frost candles. They were the size of big paint tins, filled with paraffin wax and a wick, and were placed at intervals between the rows of vines. When the *bougies* were lit they warmed the air temperature enough to prevent frost from damaging the tender new shoots on the plants.

It was laborious work walking along the endless rows of vines and stooping every few yards to light the candles, and Elin was grateful to Nat and his father and a couple of estate workers who had come to help. When they had finished, the sight of acres of vineyards glowing with golden lights was spectacular, but Elin knew that in a few hours all the candles would have to be extinguished when the sun rose and the temperature lifted a few degrees. She sent Nat and the other workers home, but Stan stayed with her to keep a watch on the *bougies*. It was nearly seven a.m. by the time they had put all the candles out and she was able to return to the house.

Harry was awake in his cot and greeted her with a winsome smile that melted her heart. While she fed him she had to force her eyes to remain open, until Barbara gently lifted the baby out of her arms. 'Go to bed for a couple of hours,' the nanny told her. 'I'll put Harry in his pram and take him for a walk. You won't be able to take care of him while you're exhausted from lack of sleep.'

Elin was too tired to argue but, when she crawled into bed, worries about the future circled in her mind. How would she manage to hold down a job and take care of her son without Barbara's help? What job was she likely to find when her only qualifications were in viticulture and oenology? Wine production was a growing industry in England but most vineyards were small, family run businesses.

There was also the question of where she was going to live. She had checked out the two cottages that Ralph had left her and her brother and found that both properties had a problem with damp, which would not be a healthy environment for a baby.

She had not heard from Jarek and he hadn't answered any of her calls. She hoped he hadn't been drinking too much. It was vital Cortez did not find out that her brother had developed a reliance on vodka to help him cope with his feelings of guilt and grief about Mama's death.

Elin's head felt as if it would explode, and when she did eventually fall asleep her shamefully erotic dreams were fuelled by memories of Cortez's naked, powerfully muscular body pressing down on her and the bold thrust of his manhood pushing between her thighs.

CHAPTER FIVE

THE GRAVEL CRUNCHED beneath Cortez's feet as he strode down the driveway. When he passed the ornamental pool he noticed there was a layer of ice on the surface of the water, despite the fact that it was officially the first day of spring. He missed the warmth and sunshine of southern Spain, and he'd told Elin the truth when he'd said he had no desire to live in the draughty monstrosity Cuckmere Hall which Ralph Saunderson had bequeathed to him.

He had left his car next to the gatehouse the previous night. There had been nowhere to park in front of the house because Elin's party guests had parked their cars there. This morning the only other vehicle on the driveway was an old truck that he assumed belonged to one of the estate workers. It was unlikely that the party princess would drive a mud-spattered farm vehicle, Cortez thought cynically.

He recalled his sleepless night in the master bedroom which the staff had prepared for him. The past few days had been hectic, and he'd been unable to face driving back to London late at night. But it had felt strange to be in the room that had once been Ralph Saunderson's. He'd wondered if his father had invited his mother into the bedroom when she had been employed at the house as a maid. It had occurred to Cortez that in all probability he had been conceived at Cuckmere Hall, but when his mother had revealed she was pregnant Ralph had sent her back to Spain. He frowned as he remembered the remark Elin had made that women were in a vulnerable position if they were abandoned by their lover and left to bring up a baby alone. It was why he had visited Elin again, to establish if there was any chance he could be her baby's father.

Now he knew what a lying bitch she was, he thought savagely. He unlocked his car and threw his bag into the boot. The sound of a baby crying caught his attention and he looked up to see a woman dressed in a beige nurse's uniform pushing a pram down the driveway. He guessed she was the nanny and the crying infant must be Elin's son. Despite himself, Cortez was curious.

'Good morning.' He smiled at the woman. 'Your charge does not sound happy.'

She halted beside the car and gave a rueful laugh. 'I think Harry wants his mother but Miss Saunderson is sleeping in this morning.'

Cortez glanced into the pram and shock jolted through him when he saw that the baby had a mass of jet-black hair. He visualised Elin's pale blonde hair and doubt flickered in his mind. There was no way the child could be his because the date of conception did not tally with when he'd slept with Elin, he assured himself.

'At the party last night Elin mentioned that her son is five months old,' he said casually to the nanny.

'As a matter of fact he is three months.' The nanny reached into the pram and folded the blanket away from the baby's face. 'Although he is growing so fast that he could be mistaken as being older.'

'I must have misheard Elin. I thought she said her son was born in October,' Cortez murmured. He stared into the pram and was aware of the painful thud of his heart. The baby had ceased crying and stared back at him with unblinking dark eyes flecked with gold.

'Harry's birthday is the sixth of December,' the nanny told him. 'Elin says he was an early Christmas present.' She gave Cortez a polite nod before she continued to walk down the drive, pushing the pram in front of her. She did not appear to hear the choked sound he made as his acute sense of shock turned to anger.

Why had Elin lied about her baby's date of birth? *Could* black-haired, dark-eyed little Harry be his son? He would get the truth from Elin if he had to drag it out of her, Cortez vowed grimly.

The butler greeted him deferentially when he returned to the house. The staff had been informed that he was Ralph Saunderson's son and heir and no doubt they hoped to keep their jobs at Cuckmere Hall. He elicited from Baines that Elin's suite of rooms were in the east wing. He took the stairs two at a time and strode down the corridor, but when he hammered on the door there was no answer. Without hesitating he turned the handle and walked into a large sitting room.

The elegantly furnished room was filled with light that poured in through the tall windows overlooking the gardens at the back of the house. Cortez thought of the rundown farmhouse where he had lived with his mother when he was a boy. The house had only had two rooms and he'd slept on the couch in the living room. Many nights he had lain awake watching his mother sewing traditional flamenco dresses which she sold to tourists at the market as a way of earning a little more money.

Once again bitterness surged through him as he recalled the poverty he and his mother had endured while his father's adopted daughter had grown up in the luxurious surroundings of an English mansion. According to the nanny, Elin was still in bed at ten o'clock in the morning. No doubt she had enjoyed being the lady of the manor since Lorna Saunderson's death and had expected that her affluent lifestyle would continue. It must have been a great shock when she'd learned that Ralph had left her virtually nothing, Cortez thought cynically.

He prowled through the private suite of rooms and discovered a small kitchen and a nursery painted a sunny yellow. Something on the wall of the nursery caught Cortez's eye and he walked over to take a closer look at a framed photo of a newborn baby wearing a hospital tag on his wrist. The baby's birth weight and date of birth were printed beneath the photo, stating that Harry had entered the world on the sixth of December, weighing seven pounds and two ounces.

Cortez's jaw was rigid with tension as he knocked on the door next to the nursery. There was no reply and, unable to contain his impatience, he let himself into what was obviously Elin's bedroom. As he glanced around at the pastel pink décor a door at the far end of the room opened and Elin walked into her bedroom from the en suite bathroom.

She was naked and Cortez's breath rushed from his lungs as he was transfixed by the sight of her. The pale spring sunshine streaming through the window bathed her body in a pearlescent light so that she looked ethereal and so beautiful that he felt blinded, as if he had looked directly at the sun. Her fair hair cascaded down her back like a river of gold. She reminded him of a painting of the goddess Aphrodite with her alabaster skin and perfect, small round breasts tipped with rose. He moved his gaze over her flat stomach and narrow hips to the neat cluster of pale gold curls between her thighs, and he was so hard that his arousal was almost painful.

Time seemed to be suspended, but in reality only a few seconds could have passed before Elin snatched up her robe from the bed and wrapped it around her. 'What are you doing in here?' she demanded. 'You have no right to barge into my private rooms.'

Her face was flushed and Cortez had noticed before she'd covered her body with her robe that a pink stain had spread down her throat and over her breasts. The ability to blush at will was no doubt a useful tool in her armoury of feminine wiles, he thought cynically.

'Actually, I have the right to enter any room in *my* house,' he corrected her, struggling to bring his raging libido under control. 'I knocked but you can't have heard me.'

She crossed her arms over her chest, but not before he'd noticed the prominent outline of her nipples beneath her silk robe. The knowledge that she was as much at the mercy of their mutual desire as he was did not appease his grim mood.

'You said I could stay at Cuckmere Hall while I arrange to move into other accommodation,' she said stiffly. 'What do you want?'

'Why did you lie about your baby's date of birth? The nanny told me your son was born in December, not October as you told me.'

She shrugged. 'Why do you care?'

He crossed the room in a couple of strides to stand in front of her, and felt an unholy satisfaction when she shrank from him. Good, he wanted to rattle her. 'Tell me the truth, damn you.'

'How can I tell you the truth when you threatened to sue me for slander?' she snapped. 'Harry was born in December, nine months after we slept together. Work the maths out for yourself.'

'But that does not necessarily mean I am his father.' He refused to believe her claim without proof. 'You might have slept with other men at around the same time that you had sex with me. Statistically, the chance of a condom failing to be effective is very small.'

'You are the *only* man I've ever had sex with,' she said in a taut voice with an underlying note of hurt that Cortez dismissed with a sardonic laugh.

'Your pretence of innocence is ridiculous when details of your love-life are frequently reported by the gutter press.'

Elin drew a sharp breath as if he had struck her. But she quickly controlled the tremble of her soft mouth, and her blue eyes were clear and perhaps a little too bright when she lifted her head and met his gaze. 'Believe what you like. I don't give a damn what you think of me. But I'd appreciate it if you would get out of my room and at least have the decency to respect my privacy. I assure you I won't remain at Cuckmere for any longer than it takes me to find somewhere for me and Harry to live.'

'The only way to resolve the issue of the child's paternity is to have a DNA test. And if he *is* my son, you won't be taking him anywhere.'

'You can't stop me,' she flared. 'I'll deny you are his father. You made it clear that you don't want a child. It will be better for Harry to grow up knowing nothing about you than for him to discover that you didn't want him.'

'If you refuse to allow a DNA test I will apply to the court for the right to discover if I have a child.' He could not hide his frustration as he raked his hair off his brow and despised the hard clench his body gave when he breathed in her scent: sensual jasmine perfume and a fresh lemon fragrance in her hair. 'I never said I would not want my son,' he said gruffly. 'But I am suspicious that you are now backtracking your claim, perhaps because a paternity test will prove you are a liar.'

Cortez's anger simmered. He told himself it was because he wanted Elin to give him a straight answer, but deep down he acknowledged the far simpler truth was that he wanted *her*. He couldn't dismiss the image of her naked body from his mind, and knowing that her dove-grey silk robe was all that hid her slender beauty from his gaze was sending him quietly mad.

'If Harry is mine, why didn't you name me as his father when he was born?' he said abruptly.

She laughed, but it was not a happy laugh, it was cold and bitter, and the sound of it made something twist in his gut. 'How *could* I name you? I didn't know your full name, or anything about you.' She took him by surprise when she pushed past him. He followed her out of the bedroom and into the sitting room and watched her open a drawer in the bureau.

'This is Harry's birth certificate.' She handed him the document and he noticed that a blank space had been left under the section headed 'Name and Surname of Father'. 'Do you have any idea how humiliated I felt when I registered his birth and I didn't know the name of my baby's father? All I knew was that I'd had sex with someone called Cortez, but how could I know you were in fact my adoptive father's real son? And as you didn't stick around the next morning I had no way of contacting you when I found out I was pregnant.'

Temper had turned her eyes to the deep, dark blue of an ocean. 'You blamed Ralph for treating your mother badly by abandoning her when she was pregnant, but your behaviour was even worse than your father's. You knew who I was, and you could easily have got in contact with me. But you didn't because I was just a one-night stand and you did not care about how I might be feeling, even though you must have realised when we had sex that it was my first time.'

Her words dropped into the room like a pebble thrown into a pool, shattering the calm surface and creating ripples. For a few seconds the effect on Cortez was just as shattering, before he remembered all those goddamned press stories about her busy love-life.

'What I have realised is that you are a fantasist,' he said grimly. 'You are also delusional if you think I'd believe you were a virgin after you had invited me into your bedroom and told me with that pretty mouth of yours that you wanted me. I can't deny it was convenient that you kept contraceptives in the bedside drawer, but the fact that you were prepared for sex suggests you'd had previous lovers.'

He shrugged. 'I don't judge you for being sexually active and I do not hold double standards, as you accused me. But I deplore lying, which is why I insist on a DNA test, which will prove if I am your baby's father or if your claim is another lie.'

Elin had turned so pale that he wondered if she was going to faint. Or was it another ploy designed to gain his sympathy? Cortez thought cynically.

'I've already explained that on the night of my birthday party my behaviour was affected by a drug that I was unaware I had taken,' she said with a quiet dignity that disturbed him more than it should have done. 'My drink had been spiked with a date-rape drug that made me unable to control my thoughts and reactions.'

Anger growled in his voice. 'Are you suggesting I slipped you a drug with the intention of sexually assaulting you?'

'No, I know it wasn't you who spiked my drink. But, all the same, it was the effects of the drug that led me to have sex with you.'

'Really?' He disguised his fury behind a mocking smile. 'So you're saying that if you hadn't been drugged you would not have wanted me to kiss you? I assume you are not under the influence of any kind of behaviour-altering drug now?'

She looked puzzled. 'Of course not.'

'Then let us put your theory to the test.' He reached for her and watched her eyes widen as she realised his intention. But, curiously, she did not try to evade him, or perhaps he was simply too quick as he pulled her into his arms and bent his head.

Her mouth was a sweet promise that had driven him to distraction and a sensual memory that had disturbed his dreams for too long. He covered her lips with his and kissed her with a hunger and need that should have appalled him if he had been able to think. But he was lost the instant she opened her mouth beneath his and allowed him to probe his tongue into her sweetness. Triumph surged through Cortez as he felt the tension ease from her body and she melted into him, soft against his hardness, her surrender a delicious victory that he was determined to savour.

It had been so long. That was the only thought in Elin's mind as Cortez claimed her mouth with bold confidence and kissed her with devastating passion. It was more than a year since she had been in his arms, but it felt like a lifetime of loneliness, waiting for him, dreaming of him, secretly yearning for him. Now he was here, as dark and dangerously attractive as she remembered him, and she was incapable of resisting his mastery. Her traitorous body melted with the first brush of his lips against hers, and when he deepened the kiss and demanded her response the fire inside her became an inferno.

He drew her closer to him, crushing her against his whipcord body and making her aware of his strength and his desire. His arousal jabbed between her thighs, and with a low moan she stood on tiptoe so that she could press her pelvis against the hard bulge outlined beneath his jeans. He muttered something incomprehensible as he clamped his hand on her bottom, and when he kissed her again he thrust his tongue into her mouth in an erotic mimicry of sex.

The kiss went on and on and she never wanted it to end. There was nothing but heat and flame and searing need. Hers. His. Whatever Cortez might think of her, the potent force of his arousal betrayed his hunger.

She was stunned when he released her and dropped his hands to his sides. Nothing made sense, not the thunder of her pulse, or the grim fury on his beautiful face, or the voice from the doorway.

'I do beg your pardon,' the nanny murmured, sounding embarrassed, before she stepped back into the corridor and closed the sitting room door behind her.

Barbara's timely interruption had been a godsend, Elin told herself as her memory stormed back and brought with it the humiliating knowledge that Cortez had kissed her to prove a point. She stared at him because she could not help herself. Because he was a sorcerer and she was trapped in his spell. She braced herself for his taunts. Dear heaven, after the way she'd responded to his kiss he probably thought she was a nymphomaniac. But, to her surprise, he broke eye contact first and she had an odd feeling that he was as shocked as she was by the tumultuous intensity of that kiss.

'We will take Harry to London today to have the DNA test carried out at a clinic which provides an express paternity testing service,' he said abruptly. 'I've booked us an appointment, and they promise to have the result within eight hours of the test. How soon can you be ready to leave?'

Elin realised it would be pointless to refuse the paternity test when Cortez had stated he would go to court to force her to agree. But she was infuriated by his arrogant belief that if he ordered her to jump she would ask how high. She had dozed for an hour this morning and woken with a headache, the result, no doubt, of her sleepless night. It was likely her shivery feeling was due to her getting so cold in the vineyard last night, she assured herself. The frost candles might have protected the vines but it had taken hours for her to warm up after her moonlit vigil. She dismissed her concern that she could be developing another kidney infection, which had been a recurrent problem since she'd given birth to Harry.

'Why are you in such a rush for the test? Three days ago you refused to consider the possibility that you could be Harry's father. I've told you I won't make any financial demands on you and you can just walk away and forget about the night we spent together, as I had pretty much done until you turned up at Cuckmere Hall.'

'You did not appear to have forgotten me when I kissed you just now,' he said sardonically.

She felt heat bloom on her face and silently cursed her fair skin that blushed so easily.

Cortez swung his gaze to the bureau where she kept Harry's birth certificate. He picked up the two passports that were lying in the drawer and studied them. 'Were you planning to take Harry abroad as you have a passport for him?'

'I've been invited to my friend's wedding in Rhodes and I had to apply for a passport for Harry so that I can take him abroad.' She frowned. 'When I met you at my birthday party I assumed you were one of Virginia's friends.'

He slipped both passports into his pocket. 'We'll take these to London with us. The DNA clinic might need to see them for identity verification. Do you know your brother's whereabouts?'

Elin had been about to demand that he give her the passports, but she was distracted by his question.

'Jarek should have returned to Saunderson's Bank in Japan,' Cortez continued. 'But I have been informed by the bank's manager that he failed to turn up for work.'

'I'm sure there's a good reason,' she said quickly. 'Perhaps his flight from England was delayed.' Elin silently acknowledged a more likely explanation was that Jarek had been on a drinking binge and was holed up in his London apartment in one of his black moods. But she was certainly not going to tell Cortez of her suspicion. However, it was vital that she went to London to try and talk some sense into her brother before he was sacked from his job.

'I suppose it makes sense to have the DNA test as soon as possible,' she said. 'I can be ready to leave in an hour.'

Cortez gave her a speculative look but fortunately he did not ask why she had suddenly changed her mind. 'Make it half an hour,' was all he said as he walked over to the door.

Truly he was the most self-centred man she'd ever met. She was tempted to wipe that smug look from his face before she remembered his threat last night when she had been goaded beyond endurance and had tried to slap him. To her eternal shame, an image came into her mind of being held across his knee while he administered a spanking, and the warmth that flared on her face was almost as hot as the molten sensation pooling between her legs.

Elin was shocked by the intensity of her sexual arousal. It had taken her body many weeks to recover from giving birth, and the effort of looking after a baby, the night feeds, lack of sleep and a fog of hormones clouding her brain meant that sex simply had not been on her radar. But one look at Cortez and it was all she could think about. She realised he was giving her an odd look and prayed he could not read her mind.

'You've obviously never had anything to do with babies,' she muttered. 'Taking a small child anywhere with all the paraphernalia they need is like a military operation.'

His dark eyes bored into her. 'I haven't witnessed you taking care of your son on either of my visits to Cuckmere Hall. Maybe you find motherhood boring compared to your exciting social life. It seems to me that you leave Harry with his nanny most of the time.'

Forty-five minutes later, Elin was still seething over Cortez's comments when he drove them to London in his car. During the journey she maintained a frosty silence and he seemed preoccupied with his own thoughts. The nanny, who was sitting in the back of the car next to Harry in his baby seat, made a couple of attempts at conversation but soon gave up.

Elin had asked Barbara to accompany them to London, thinking she might need the nanny to look after Harry while she searched for her brother in the bars near to his home in Notting Hill, where he was a regular customer. She was relieved when she received a text message from Jarek saying he was on a flight to Japan. It was one thing less to worry about. She suggested that Barbara might like to take the afternoon off to visit her daughter who lived in Greenwich. Cortez pulled over outside a Tube station to drop Barbara off, before driving on to the private clinic in central London.

It did not take long for the samples to be collected which would be analysed for the DNA test, and afterwards they drove to the townhouse in Kensington. Cortez had decreed that they would stay in London overnight while they waited for the result of the paternity test.

Walking into the house, Elin was swamped by memories of when she had slept with Cortez on her birthday a year ago. She was agonisingly aware of him as he carried Harry in his baby seat from the car. Her lips felt tender from where he had kissed her earlier, and when she flicked her tongue over them she could still taste him.

She was glad when he opened his laptop and told her that he intended to get on with some work. Her head was pounding, and although Harry was usually a placid baby he was fretful all afternoon and she couldn't settle him. As she paced up and down the nursery with the inconsolable baby in her arms she decided that she must be a bad mother, as Cortez had implied.

'Why does he keep crying?' Cortez asked when he walked into the kitchen and found her struggling to make up a bottle of baby formula with one hand while she jiggled Harry on her hip. 'Could he be ill?'

'He's just a bit colicky. Babies cry because it's their only way of communicating,' she said shortly. She felt her tension ratchet up another notch as she tried to feed Harry and he refused to take the teat into his mouth.

'You don't feed him from your breast?' Cortez commented.

'I wasn't able to.' It was another failure that weighed on her conscience but she was in no mood to explain that she had been fighting for her life immediately after Harry's birth. Although she had tried to breastfeed him when she'd come out of Intensive Care, her body hadn't produced enough milk.

'I didn't realise you were an expert in childcare,' she said to Cortez sarcastically. 'It's a pity you weren't around when Harry was born and you could have helped to look after him.'

To her relief Harry finally stopped crying and took his feed. When he finished his bottle she carried him up to the nursery and placed him in his cot. Her headache was worse and she had developed a severe pain in her lower back as well as a high temperature. A phone call to her GP in Sussex confirmed her suspicion that she had all the symptoms of another kidney infection, and she was advised to start the course of antibiotics which she'd been prescribed to treat a recurring infection.

Thankfully, she had brought the antibiotics with her. She

swallowed one of the pills and a strong painkiller before she called the nanny's mobile number and explained that she was feeling unwell.

'Do what the doctor said and start the course of antibiotics immediately,' Barbara instructed. 'I'll leave my daughter's right away and I should be in Kensington by the time Harry wakes up from his afternoon nap.'

Elin was shivering, but when she glanced in the mirror she saw that her face was flushed and her hair was damp with sweat. Hopefully, the high-strength medication would halt the infection before it got too bad, she thought, as she climbed into bed fully dressed and burrowed beneath the duvet in an attempt to get warm. When she'd suffered previous kidney infections the antibiotics had made her feel as unwell as the illness.

She fell into a fitful, feverish sleep. One minute she was hot and the next freezing cold and, as she tossed and turned, her mind was taken over by terrifying hallucinations. Distantly she was aware of Harry crying, and she knew she must go to him, but her limbs felt heavy and uncoordinated. She thought she heard a man's deep voice talking to her but she couldn't make sense of what he said. Some time later she felt herself being lifted and carried in a pair of strong arms, but maybe she dreamed it. After that she remembered nothing.

CHAPTER SIX

CORTEZ GAVE UP trying to concentrate on a financial report for Saunderson's Bank after he'd read it three times and still had no idea what it said. Business had been his life since he'd graduated from university with a first class degree and a determination to succeed. His new role as chairman of the prestigious private bank was more proof that he had come a long way from picking grapes at his mother's small vineyard in Jerez. But waiting to learn if he was the father of Elin's child dominated his thoughts and he drummed his fingertips on the coffee table and glanced at his watch for the hundredth time.

When his phone rang and he recognised the number of the paternity test clinic on the screen he took a deep breath before he answered the call. Moments later he ran an unsteady hand across his face.

Santa Madre! He had a son.

Conflicting emotions stormed through him. A fierce joy and pride in his beautiful son, but anger when he thought of the child's mother. Elin had lied about Harry's date of birth and Cortez was furious, knowing that if he had not insisted on a DNA test she might have disappeared with the baby and he would never have known he was a father.

He lurched to his feet. He felt drunk although he had not

had a drop of alcohol. He was in shock, he realised. When he'd seen Harry's black hair and dark eyes he had wondered if the baby could be his. But he was unprepared for the overwhelming emotions that poured through him. Driven by a need to see his child, he strode out of the room and quickly climbed the stairs. He heard Harry crying and a feeling he could not begin to describe welled inside him, a fundamental desire to protect his son.

Following the sound of Harry's cries, he located the nursery and was surprised that Elin was not already there to comfort the baby. He stood next to the cot and felt as if his heart was being squeezed in a vice as he stared down at the screaming, red-faced infant. It was incredible that a small baby could make such a loud noise. Yet still Harry's mother did not appear.

Cortez opened a door to an adjoining room and recognised he was in the bedroom where he had spent the night with Elin just over a year ago. Memories assailed him of her wearing a scarlet silk dress and not a lot else besides, he'd soon discovered. Their passion had been electrifying and she had been with him every step of the way. He did not know what to make of her assertion that she'd had sex with him that night because her drink had been spiked with a date-rape drug. The sexual chemistry that had ignited between them when he had kissed her earlier today had been undeniable.

The room was dimly lit by the bedside lamp. He switched on the overhead light and frowned when he saw the top of her blonde head poking above the duvet. 'Elin?' She did not answer, and when Cortez pulled back the covers her eyes flickered open and she stared at him vacantly. Her skin was pale and beaded with sweat. 'Your baby needs you,' he told her. She muttered something incomprehensible and huddled beneath the duvet. Cortez's concern for his son was paramount. 'Does Harry want to be fed?' His jaw tightened. 'For pity's sake, you can't leave him to cry.'

She either did not hear what he said or did not care, and she closed her eyes again. Cortez frowned as he remembered the recent speculation by the media that Elin used recreational drugs. There had been a photo in some of the tabloids of her being carried out of a nightclub in a semi-conscious state. Had she taken an illegal substance this afternoon which had rendered her unable to care for her baby? *His* baby.

He returned to the nursery and hesitated. His heart was pounding and for the only time in his life he felt terrified. He had never held a small baby before, and Harry looked so *breakable*. Taking a deep breath, he reached into the cot and picked Harry up. The baby's cries immediately subsided to little whimpers that tore on Cortez's heart.

'Hey, little man,' he murmured as he held the baby against his shoulder. Harry stared at him with big, dark eyes fringed with long black lashes. He was more beautiful than anything Cortez had ever seen. The baby's Cupid's bow mouth curved into a smile and Cortez felt a constriction in his throat. 'My son,' he said thickly, wonderingly. He was Harry's father and he would *never* abandon his child like his own father had abandoned him. He was instantly smitten with his baby boy, and his heart felt as if it had swelled to twice its size and was filled to overflowing with love for his child. 'I would give my life to protect you,' he whispered to Harry.

He heard a noise and looked round, expecting to see Elin, but it was the nanny standing in the doorway. 'Ah, Miss Lennox.'

'I would have been back from my daughter's earlier, but there was a delay on the Tube,' she explained.

Cortez looked down at the baby he was cradling so carefully in his arms. 'I am Harry's father.'

'Oh, I guessed that,' she said cheerfully. 'He has inherited your colouring rather than his mother's.'

'Elin is asleep and didn't hear the baby crying. She seems... spaced out,' he said tersely.

The nanny nodded and seemed unsurprised. 'She has these

episodes quite frequently. Hopefully, she'll be back to herself in a day or two.'

Cortez instinctively held Harry a little tighter. The nanny's words seemed to confirm the suggestion in the tabloids that Elin was a drug user and he resolved to protect his son from his mother, who was obviously unfit to take care of a child. One of the first things he intended to do was arrange for his name to be added to Harry's English birth certificate under the section for father's details. Even more importantly, he wanted to register his son's birth in Spain, which would be Harry's country of residence from now on. But, to do so, he would need Elin's agreement.

He handed Harry over to the nanny so that she could change his nappy. The procedure was one of many things he would have to learn how to do, Cortez mused.

'Miss Lennox...' he smiled at the nanny and turned on the full force of his charm '...may I call you Barbara? You guessed that I am Harry's father and you might also have realised when you saw Elin and I together at Cuckmere Hall that we are reunited.'

The nanny looked embarrassed by his reminder of when she had caught him and Elin kissing. 'I'm very glad for the two of you,' she murmured, 'and for Harry to have both his parents.'

Cortez did not disabuse Barbara of the idea that he and Elin were going to play happy families. 'We have decided to take our son to Spain, and before we left Cuckmere Hall Elin gave me her and Harry's passports.' It was not a lie, more an elaboration of the truth, he assured his conscience.

'Certain reasons make it necessary for me to return to Spain earlier than I'd planned,' he told the nanny. 'In fact, I need to leave tonight to deal with an urgent business matter. As I am sure you will appreciate, I am reluctant to leave my son and Elin behind in England, especially when we have just got back together.' He shamelessly pushed the idea that their relationship was the romance of the year.

'I know it is short notice,' he continued, giving Barbara another dazzling smile. 'Would you be prepared to accompany us to Spain on my private jet? Elin will be able to rest during the flight, and I'll need you to take charge of Harry because I am a new and inexperienced father.' He thought of a possible problem. 'You will need your passport.'

'As a matter of fact I always carry it with me. Of course I'll be happy to help in any way that I can,' Barbara told him. 'Elin came up to London only last week to shop for clothes to take on a holiday she'd booked to Greece. Would you like me to pack some things for her and Harry, Mr Ramos?'

'Thank you. And Barbara, please call me Cortez, as all my friends do,' he murmured. The nanny could be a useful ally in his bid to win custody of his son, he decided. He was a master strategist and he knew the benefits of making a friend in the enemy's camp.

'Harry.' Elin sat bolt upright and took a shuddering breath when she realised she'd been having a nightmare. In her dream she had been running down a long corridor and at the end of it was Harry's pram. But when she finally reached the pram and looked inside, it was empty and she had no idea where her son was.

She looked around her bedroom still with a sense of shock. Yesterday, or was it the day before?—she'd lost track of time—her fever had abated and her head no longer felt as if someone was boring into her skull with a pneumatic drill. But her relief had turned to astonishment when she'd found herself in unfamiliar surroundings and Barbara had told her that they were in Cortez's home in Andalucía.

The nanny had explained that Cortez had arranged for them to fly to Spain on his private jet. He had carried Elin into the plane's bedroom and she had been in a deep sleep for the entire journey. A car had collected them from the airport at Jerez and brought them to his mansion, La Casa Jazmín.

'Cortez had to return to Spain urgently, but he did not want

to be separated from you and Harry,' Barbara had told Elin.
'I think it is so romantic that the two of you have got back together. Cortez is devoted to his son. He insists on giving Harry
his bottle and he has learned how to change nappies.'

Elin had masked her anger because she did not want Barbara
to feel guilty that she had been tricked by Cortez into helping
him in effect kidnap her and Harry. She hadn't yet seen him to
demand an explanation. Barbara said he had visited her room a
few times, but on each occasion she had been feverish and she
hadn't recognised him.

Worry gnawed in the pit of Elin's stomach as she slid out
of bed and went into an adjoining room which Barbara had
explained had formerly been a dressing room. Cortez had instructed his staff to transform it into a nursery. Apparently no
expense had been spared to equip the nursery and Harry slept
in a magnificent hand-carved cot. She walked past the latest
addition to the nursery, an enormous wooden rocking horse,
and hurried over to the cot.

Her heart missed a beat when she found it empty. For a few
seconds she was back in her nightmare, searching desperately
for her baby who had disappeared. She spun round at the sound
of footsteps and stared frantically at the nanny, who walked
into the room carrying a pile of baby clothes. 'Where's Harry?'

'Cortez took him downstairs.' Barbara seemed unaware of
Elin's tension. 'He keeps the pram in his study so that he can be
near to Harry while he is working.' She looked closely at Elin.
'I told Cortez that you were feeling much better this morning
and he asked me to give you a message that he wants you to
meet him in his study at eleven o'clock.'

Elin was desperate to immediately go and find her son. She
had been ill for a week but it felt like a lifetime since she had
held Harry in her arms and smelled his delicious baby scent.
But she acknowledged that she could not walk around Cortez's
house wearing her nightdress. When she met him in an hour
from now she was determined to appear calm and in control,

even though her insides were churning as she wondered what, if any, input he intended to have in his son's life now he must have proof from the paternity test clinic that he was Harry's father.

Although she was feeling better, the effort of showering and getting dressed sapped her energy. She was grateful to Barbara for packing some clothes for her before they'd left London. It was unfortunate that the new outfits she'd bought to take to Rhodes for Virginia's wedding were designed to be worn at beach or pool parties, and the short skirts and skimpy tops were more daring than she usually wore.

She chose a pale blue chiffon dress that did at least have sleeves, but when she checked her appearance in the mirror she was dismayed that the floaty skirt was almost see-through. There was no time to change her outfit when a maid came to her room to escort her to Cortez's study, but Elin reminded herself that he would not be interested in how she looked. He'd had sex with her once and had disappeared immediately afterwards. She was just another notch on his bedpost.

As she followed the maid downstairs she could not help but admire the design and décor of the house. The white marble floors and neutral-coloured walls could have made the rooms feel cold, but patterned rugs and brightly coloured cushions and artwork lent interest and a homely feel to the elegant villa. She walked into the study and her eyes were immediately drawn to the large and very regal-looking pram. With a low cry she sped across the room. Her arms were literally aching to hold her baby.

'Harry has just dropped off to sleep and it would be best if you did not disturb him.'

Cortez's peremptory voice made her halt, and she turned her head to see him leaning against his desk. He was wearing a superbly tailored grey suit, a crisp white shirt and dark grey tie and the formality of his clothes made Elin conscious of her insubstantial summer dress. She lifted her eyes up to his face and felt her heart crash against her ribs as she absorbed the perfection of his sculpted features. His lips were curved in a cynical expression but nothing could detract from the sensual impact of his mouth, and she hated herself for the quiver that ran through her.

Anger was her only defence against her awareness of him. 'You had no right to *abduct* me and my son. It's outrageous that you brought us to Spain without my agreement,' she said heatedly.

'You were not in a fit state to agree or disagree to coming here,' he responded coolly. 'And you are forgetting that Harry is my son too.'

Elin cast a yearning look at her baby sleeping peacefully in the pram before she marched over to the desk, determined to show that she was not intimidated by Cortez. 'I have never forgotten that Harry was conceived as a result of the most shameful night of my life.'

Her attention had been riveted on Cortez, but she was suddenly aware that there was someone else in the room and a frisson of unease ran down her spine as she saw an older man with grey hair and a stern face standing by the window.

'This is Señor Fernandez,' Cortez introduced the man. 'He is a lawyer specialising in family law, particularly in cases when there is a dispute between parents over custody of a child.'

Custody! Elin's legs almost gave way but she fought against the dizzy sensation that swept over her, determined she wouldn't faint. 'There is no dispute.' She was pleased she sounded forceful rather than scared. 'I am going to take Harry back home to England as soon as possible. I've already told you that I don't intend to ask you for financial help towards the cost of his upbringing.'

'Harry does not have a home with you in England. If you think I would allow you to take him to live in a partly derelict cottage which, under the terms of Ralph Saunderson's will, is your only asset, think again,' Cortez said in a hard tone.

'You can't keep me a prisoner here.' Panic gripped her as

she remembered that he was in possession of her and Harry's passports.

'I prefer the term guest to prisoner,' he drawled. '*You* can leave whenever you wish.' His meaning was sickeningly clear; she could leave, but he would not allow her to take her baby. Elin was tempted to grab Harry and run out of the study with him, but her common sense reminded her that she had nowhere to run to.

'Sit down,' Cortez ordered.

Tension coiled in her stomach as she sank down onto the chair he pulled out for her. Cortez waited until the lawyer was also seated, before he took his place behind his desk. 'Señor Fernandez has prepared a document for you to read.'

The chill in his voice sent an ice cube slithering down Elin's spine. She picked up the piece of paper Cortez pushed across the desk and as she read down the printed page her heart thudded painfully fast in her chest.

'What the hell is this?' she said thickly when she had finished reading.

His dark brows lifted. 'I believe it is self-explanatory. I am offering to give you Cuckmere Hall: the house and entire estate, including the vineyards and winery. The current value of the Cuckmere estate is twenty-five million pounds, and I am prepared to offer you an additional ten million pounds which you could invest and use the interest to pay for the running costs of the house and estate. Alternatively, if you decide to sell Cuckmere for its market value, you will still receive the additional ten million pounds, which will be transferred directly into your bank account.

'In return,' he continued smoothly, 'you will sign sole custody of Harry over to me with a legally binding guarantee that you will not seek to change or reverse this decision at any future date.' He ignored her sharply indrawn breath. 'The agreement will take effect immediately when you have signed the document that you have in your hand. My private jet will be available to take you to England, and you will leave here with the deeds of the Cuckmere estate in your possession.'

'This is a joke, right?' Elin moistened her dry lips with the tip of her tongue and saw Cortez's eyes narrow on her mouth. He couldn't be serious, she assured herself. Obviously he had a warped sense of humour. 'You can't really think I would agree to your disgusting offer.'

The lawyer spoke. 'Señor Ramos's offer is extremely generous. I am certain that you would not receive any more from a court judgement.'

Cortez leaned back in his chair and gave her a hard stare. 'Is there something more that you want?'

'Yes, there is.' She was proud that her voice sounded calm while inside she was a seething cauldron of emotions ranging from anger through to a deep sense of hurt that was inexplicable. Why should she care that Cortez believed she would *sell* her son in a deal that would shame the devil? 'I want you to rot in hell.'

Her control was hanging by a thread. Tears stung her eyes but she would not give him the satisfaction of seeing her cry. Carefully she tore the piece of paper she was holding in half and then tore the two halves into quarters and then eighths, her movements jerky with suppressed violence.

'There is nothing you could offer me. All the riches in the world would not tempt me for a nanosecond to give my son away. And especially—*especially*—' her voice rose, sharp with revulsion '—to a man such as you, who treats women like objects, like dirt. If Ralph had not made you his heir you would not have gone to Cuckmere Hall and discovered that you have a son. Harry would have grown up never knowing who his father was.'

She stood up and dragged in a ragged breath. 'You left after you'd had sex with me because I was nothing, just a means of sexual gratification. You treated me like a whore, but what does that make you? How can you be a good and decent father when you did not even bother to find out if I had conceived your child?'

'*Bastante!* Enough.' Cortez jumped to his feet and glared at her across the desk. He turned his head and spoke in Spanish to the lawyer, who immediately got up and hurried out of the room.

'How can you have the audacity to question my suitability to be a father when you are patently unsuitable to be Harry's mother?' Disgust was stamped on Cortez's patrician features. 'If you refuse my offer, which I believe is a fair one, I will seek to be granted custody of my son through legal channels.'

'No court would take a three-month-old baby away from his mother,' Elin said vehemently, but her heart was thumping with fear. Cortez was a rich man and could hire the best lawyers, but she had nothing to her name, apart from a rundown cottage that she could not afford to have repaired.

'A court would not leave a baby with a known drug-user.' He took no notice when she gasped. 'Perhaps you are an addict, or maybe you are in control of your drug habit—for now. But the risk of addiction is high and I do not believe any judge would risk leaving Harry in your care. I certainly will not.'

'*I'm not a drug addict.*' Elin heard the hysteria in her voice and fought to bring herself under control, aware that Cortez was likely to suggest she was emotionally unbalanced. But she was astounded by his accusation. 'I have never taken any kind of substance, legal or illegal, in my life, apart from the one time that my drink was spiked at my birthday party.'

'I was led to understand from a reliable source that you are a drug-user,' he said coldly. 'Stories of your wild lifestyle have often been reported by the press.'

'*Stories* is right. Half the things the tabloids print are made up.'

He gave her a cynical look. 'Are you saying that photographs of you staggering out of nightclubs on numerous occasions when you were clearly either drunk or high were fake?'

'No, but...'

'If the reports of your affairs with football stars and other minor celebrities weren't true, why did you not demand that the newspapers retracted the stories?'

'I...' Elin trailed to a halt and bit her lip. She couldn't admit that she had deliberately played up for the paparazzi to keep the media's interest away from her brother. Jarek's addiction to vodka, gambling and women—so many women—made *her* supposed wild lifestyle seem tame in comparison. If Cortez learned that Jarek had been going off the rails since Lorna Saunderson's death, he might sack him from Saunderson's Bank.

'Presumably you could not threaten to take legal action against the tabloids because the stories they printed about you were true,' Cortez said grimly. His eyes were chips of obsidian. 'I have been advised by a child psychologist that Harry is too young to have formed a meaningful bond with you, and he will not be adversely affected by a clean break from you when he is only a few months old.'

'Of course he has formed a bond with me,' she choked. 'I am his *mother*. For God's sake, I carried him inside me for nine months, but where were you, his father, then?' Elin's anger turned to despair and she struggled to swallow past the lump that had formed in her throat.

'I was shocked when I realised that my night of shame had resulted in pregnancy,' she admitted. 'And terrified that I had to face my pregnancy alone. All the other women at the childbirth classes had their husbands or partners with them, and I pretended that my baby's father was working abroad because I was too embarrassed to admit I didn't even know his identity.

'I never knew my parents,' she told Cortez huskily. 'They died when I was a baby and my brother was six, and we were placed in an orphanage. I was luckier than other children in the orphanage because at least I had my brother, who took care of me as well as he was able to. My earliest memories are of feeling fear and confusion. I am Bosnian by birth, and the orphanage was in Sarajevo. When the city was bombed during the Bosnian war, many of the orphanage staff were killed or ran away and abandoned the children.'

She was breathing hard, as if she had run a marathon. 'I know what it is like to be abandoned. I will never, ever leave my son. Your vile accusations—especially that I use drugs—are untrue. I love Harry more than life and I would never do anything that might harm him or put him at risk.'

From the pram came a faint cry as Harry stirred. Elin shot across the room. Her heart felt as if it would burst with love as she lifted her baby into her arms and pressed tender kisses to his satin-soft cheek. 'Hello, my angel,' she murmured and was rewarded with a sleepy smile from her little son that filled her with the sweetest joy.

She turned to find that Cortez had followed her over to the pram and he was standing next to her with a tense expression on his face, as if he feared she might drop Harry, she thought furiously. His next words shocked her more than anything else he had said.

'When you discovered you were pregnant, why did you decide to go through with it?'

Elin was counting Harry's eyelashes and only half paying attention to Cortez. 'What do you mean?'

His breath hissed between his teeth. 'Did you consider not having your child?'

She jerked her eyes to his face as his meaning sank into her stunned brain and she felt sick. 'Oh, my God! You think I could have done that? What have I done to deserve your foul accusations? I thought when you suggested I could give away my baby for financial gain that you could not be any more insulting. But I was wrong.'

Something indecipherable glittered in Cortez's eyes. 'It was not an unreasonable question. You said you felt scared when you found out you were pregnant and faced being a single mother.'

Elin shook her head. 'I loved my baby from the minute I knew that a miracle was happening inside me,' she told him fiercely. 'At my ultrasound scan when I was told I was expecting a boy, I felt sad that he wouldn't have a father because I know from my own childhood that a child needs to have security provided ideally by both its parents. A child needs to feel loved. Nothing else is as important.'

She whirled around and walked over to the door with Harry held tightly in her arms. 'I know something else,' she said, turning back to stare at Cortez with disgust in her eyes.

He looked…stunned was the only way she could describe the expression on his face. His skin appeared to be drawn tight over his razor-sharp cheekbones. The first time she had seen him at her party a year ago he had reminded her of a wolf, and she should have followed her instincts and fled from him while she'd had the chance, she thought grimly.

'I know that your wealth does not mean you will be a good father. You can't *buy* your son. What Harry needs is a father who will always be there for him, but you weren't around when I was in Intensive Care after his birth.' Her voice shook. 'Thankfully my brother spent hours in the hospital nursery with my son. And of course Harry was looked after by the nurses, but he did not have either of his parents with him, just like I didn't have my parents when I lived at the orphanage.'

Cortez frowned 'Why were you in Intensive Care?'

'I bled heavily soon after giving birth.' Elin swallowed hard. It was only three and a half months since Harry had been born and the memories of what had happened in the delivery room— when the euphoria of her son's birth had rapidly turned into a scene from a horror film—were vivid in her mind.

'The medical term is a postpartum haemorrhage. I was terrified I would bleed to death,' she admitted. 'I was rushed into Theatre and given a general anaesthetic, and I don't remember anything after that. But I was told afterwards that I had emergency surgery and a blood transfusion. If the crash team had not been able to stop the bleeding they would have had to perform a hysterectomy, which you probably know is an operation to remove the womb. But luckily the doctors were able to save my life without ending my chances of one day having another child.'

She looked down at her infant son and blinked away her tears that always welled up whenever she thought of how close Harry had been to being motherless and fatherless. 'I'm grateful to my brother for saying he would have adopted my baby if I had died. But at the crucial time when Harry needed his father, you weren't around. So don't preach to me that I am not a suitable mother, because I fought to stay alive for my son and I will fight to the death to keep him.'

CHAPTER SEVEN

FROM THE WINDOW Cortez watched Elin walk across the lawn holding Harry in her arms. She had swept out of the study, leaving him reeling from what she had told him. He went cold at the thought that she could have bled to death following Harry's birth, and guilt knotted in his stomach as he acknowledged the damning truth that if Elin had died he would never have known about his son.

The gazebo next to the swimming pool offered shade from the midday sun, which was strong even in March. Elin sat down on a garden chair and held the baby against her shoulder. Even from a distance Cortez could see the gentle expression on her face as she cradled her son.

A lioness protecting her cub.

The vehement words she'd flung at him a few minutes ago echoed inside his head. *'I fought to stay alive for my son and I will fight to the death to keep him.'* Cortez thought of another woman who had been fiercely protective of her child. His mother had brought him up without any support from his father. Marisol Ramos had been shunned by her family and by many of the villagers, who had judged her for being an unmarried mother. She had worked day in, day out at her small vineyard to earn money to feed and clothe him.

He remembered the recent discovery he had made while he'd been at Cuckmere Hall and had sorted through some of Ralph Saunderson's private papers. He had found an old bank statement which proved that his father *had* given his mother money when she'd told him she was pregnant. But Marisol had not spent the money to make her life easier, and the only explanation Cortez could think of was that she had saved the money to pay for him to go to university.

A good education had given him the means to escape the poverty of his childhood, and it could be argued that he owed his success partly to Ralph's financial contribution. He had been shocked to discover that his father had not completely abandoned him. *Like he had abandoned Elin.* The knot of guilt in his stomach tightened.

But if Elin loved Harry as much as she insisted, why was she a drug-user? She had furiously denied that she was a drug addict and Cortez conceded it was possible that the tabloid stories about her having a drug habit were exaggerated. But in London the nanny had not been unduly surprised when Elin had been incapable of caring for Harry. He had assumed that Elin had been semi-conscious on the flight to Spain as a result of something she had taken, but could there be a different explanation? For his baby son's sake he had to find out the truth about Elin, and his first step would be to talk to the nanny.

Barbara was in the nursery, unpacking the latest delivery of baby clothes and toys that Cortez had ordered for his son. 'Harry will have to be dressed in two new outfits a day if he is going to wear all these lovely clothes before he grows out of them,' she said as she folded a cute sailor suit and placed it in a drawer.

'I'm sorry to give you extra work,' Cortez murmured, glancing at the boxes strewn across the floor. He spied a wooden train set and wondered how old Harry would be before he became interested in toys. He was looking forward to watching his son grow up and he was determined that he would be around when Harry took his first steps and spoke his first words. There had been many times when he was a boy that he'd wished he had a father like the other boys at school. *His* son would never doubt that his father loved him, Cortez vowed.

'To be honest, I like having something to do,' Barbara told him. 'I often feel guilty that I am paid to do very little.'

'Caring for a baby must be a full-time job.'

'Yes, but Elin has always insisted on doing everything for Harry. Even when he went through a period of waking several times in the night, she kept his crib next to her bed so that she could see to him. Of course she couldn't do very much just after she'd given birth and she was weak from losing so much blood. That was why her brother hired me. And then, when Elin was getting her strength back, she developed a serious kidney infection. I do hope that this latest bout of a recurring infection which made her so unwell for the past few days will be the last,' Barbara said. 'The drugs she took to fight the infection are very powerful and, as you noticed, the side-effects absolutely knocked her out.'

Cortez stiffened but he managed to keep his tone casual as he asked, 'What exactly are the drugs Elin took?'

'She was prescribed a powerful penicillin antibiotic to destroy the bacteria that causes the infection. But, as I said, the drug has unpleasant side-effects, which meant that Elin was unable to breastfeed Harry when she developed a kidney infection soon after he was born.'

Cortez stared at the nanny. 'To your knowledge does Elin use recreational drugs, for instance cocaine? There have been reports in some of the more lurid English newspapers that she is involved in the drug culture which is popular in nightclubs,' he persisted when Barbara looked astonished.

'Good heavens, you don't want to believe anything you read in those kinds of papers. They are called the gutter press for a good reason. There was even a story printed last year which stated that Elin was having an affair with a married actor simply because they were photographed leaving a club at the same time. But she'd never even spoken to the man. As for her taking recreational drugs—' the nanny shook her head '—I've never seen any evidence of that, and I simply don't believe it. Elin is the most devoted mother I have ever met and I am absolutely convinced that she would not do anything that could be detrimental to Harry.'

'I see,' Cortez said slowly. The uncomfortable realisation was dawning on him that he might have misjudged Elin. And it was not the first time, his conscience reminded him. When he had gone to Cuckmere Hall for the reading of Ralph Saunderson's will, Elin had told him that he was her baby's father but he had refused to believe her until a DNA test had proved she was telling the truth.

But if she was not a drug-user, and according to the nanny Elin was a good mother, then he was unlikely to win custody of his son in a court battle. And he could not forget that Elin had turned down the chance to own Cuckmere Hall. He knew she loved the house. The value of the estate plus the additional money he'd offered her amounted to thirty-five million pounds. It was a sizeable fortune and he had believed that she might be tempted, but she had unhesitatingly rejected his offer and scathingly told him that he could not buy his son.

Even so, could he trust that her apparent devotion to Harry was real? Cortez's jaw hardened. After Alandra he had vowed never to trust any woman. But Elin was the mother of his child and somehow they were going to have to come to an agreement on how they could both be parents to their son.

Elin had fled from the acrimonious atmosphere in the study and sought refuge in the garden. But when Harry became fretful for his next feed she took him back to the house and her heart sank when she met Cortez in the entrance hall. Revulsion swept through her as in her mind she heard his cold voice offering her Cuckmere Hall if she gave up all rights to her baby. It had been even worse than his accusation that she was a drug addict and she tensed as he strode towards her, fearful of what he was going to say to her, what new insult he might throw at her now. Her wariness must have shown on her face and he frowned when she clutched Harry tightly to her chest.

'*Dios*, you do not need to look so terrified,' he said roughly. 'I am not going to hurt you.'

'Really?' Her voice was brittle, her emotions balanced on a knife-edge. 'You don't think I might have found your disgusting attempt to bribe me to give up my baby hurtful?'

He did not answer but something flashed in his dark eyes that she might have believed was regret if she did not know that Cortez Ramos had a lump of granite where his heart should be.

'I have to go to Madrid on business and I will be away for one night, at the most two,' he said abruptly. 'The trip was planned before I knew about Harry but when I return we will talk about what we are going to do with regard to our son.'

Elin tried to ignore the tug her heart gave when Cortez said *our* son. It gave an impression of unity between them that did not exist, she reminded herself.

'What am I supposed to do while you are able to get on with your life, but I am a prisoner in your house? I demand that you give back my and Harry's passports.'

'If I did give them back would you promise to remain at La Casa Jazmín?' He gave her a sardonic look when she stayed silent. 'If you took Harry away from here I would not rest until I'd tracked you down,' he warned her. 'But to save us both time and effort and spare Harry unnecessary upheaval if you decide to try and disappear with him, I will keep the passports in my possession for now.'

'You have no right...' Elin broke off when she realised that Cortez was not paying her attention and was watching his son avidly. Harry was staring at his father and gave a winsome smile that was guaranteed to melt the stoniest heart. The effect on Cortez was startling. His hard features softened and he murmured something in Spanish as he leaned closer and kissed the top of the baby's head.

Elin's senses stirred as she breathed in the musky scent of Cortez's aftershave. The sight of his dark head against Harry's downy black hair evoked a curious ache in her heart. For a moment she allowed herself to imagine that they were a happy family. In her daydream Cortez kissed his baby son before he moved to cover her mouth with his and kissed her with bone-shaking tenderness and the promise of passion later, when they were alone in each other's arms.

But the reality was that they were at loggerheads and set to fight a custody battle over their son, she reminded herself. It was a battle that she could lose, for Cortez's wealth and power meant he had access to the best lawyers. The idea that she might be ordered by a court to hand over her baby caused icy fingers of fear to wrap around her heart.

She realised that Cortez was looking at her with an odd expression, as if he also wished that the situation between them was different. But that was too much of a stretch for her imagination, she told herself sharply. Cortez had kidnapped her and was keeping her a prisoner. Never mind that La Casa Jazmín was a beautiful house, it was a gilded jail. Cortez had said some vile things to her, and his promise that they would talk when he returned from Madrid had sounded more like a threat. She jerked away from him and whatever it was that had flickered between them disappeared.

He picked up his briefcase and walked across the hall. 'I will be back as soon as I can.'

'Don't rush back on my account,' Elin said coldly. But, absurdly, when he strode out of the house and she heard his car roar off down the drive she immediately missed him. She wondered if he had a mistress in Madrid who he was planning to spend the night with. He was a virile man and he was bound to have a lover. The thought bothered her more than it should have done and she despised herself for feeling jealous as she visualised him having sex with another woman.

In fact Cortez was only away for one night and returned to La Casa Jazmín late the following afternoon. Elin was pushing Harry in his pram around the garden, hoping that the rocking movement would send him off to sleep. Her heart gave an annoying leap when the gates swung smoothly open to allow Cortez to drive through them. He parked his rampantly masculine black sports car in front of the house and leaned against the bonnet, watching her from behind his designer shades as she walked towards him.

The top few buttons on his shirt were undone, revealing a vee of his darkly tanned chest and a sprinkling of black hairs that Elin remembered from a year ago arrowed down over his flat abdomen. She felt heat spread over her face and hoped he would think she was flushed from the warm sun, and not because she was overwhelmingly aware of him.

'I suppose you have a secret code to unlock the gates,' she said as she drew nearer to him. 'Beautiful though the garden is, I am bored of walking around it and I'd hoped to take Harry on a longer walk, perhaps to a village if there is one nearby. But the perimeter gates are locked.' Frustration edged into her voice. 'You have no right to keep me imprisoned.'

Cortez looked unconcerned by her outburst. 'The main gates are activated by car number plate recognition and they are kept locked for security reasons. The village is five miles away but it has no shops and there's little there to excite you.'

'You don't know what excites me,' Elin snapped, irritated by his arrogance.

He threw back his head and laughed, and she was riveted by the sheer beauty of his face, alight with merriment. The rich sound of his amusement reached down to something deep inside her. Laughter made him even more attractive, and he was already too gorgeous for his own good, she thought ruefully.

'Actually, I have vivid memories of what excited you when you lured me into your bed, *querida*,' he murmured.

She pressed her lips together to stop herself from responding to his baiting. She did not want to be reminded of her night of shame a year ago.

'La Casa Jazmín is surrounded by vineyards,' Cortez told her. 'If you like I will show you where you can walk among the vines.'

Despite herself, Elin was curious to see the vineyards that produced the grapes which were used to make the famous Felipe & Cortez brand of award-winning sherry. Cortez led the way across the garden and held open a gate in the wall so that she could push the pram through it.

'I suppose you grow Palomino grapes here,' she said, recognising the dark green leaves on the vines. 'The *albariza* soil type has a high chalk content, perfect for retaining moisture, which is vital during the hot, dry summers you have in this region of Spain. It's interesting that the soil on the South Downs is also chalky, similar to soil in the Champagne region of France. But of course English summers are cooler than here, allowing us to grow Chardonnay and Pinot Noir grape varieties at Cuckmere. At least—' Elin broke off and grimaced '—we grow those grape varieties currently at Saunderson's estate winery, and we have concentrated on producing a sparkling white wine. But you, or whoever buys the estate if you decide to sell it, might decide to grow something else.'

She glanced at Cortez and found him staring at her with evident surprise. 'I did not realise that you took a genuine interest in the winery,' he said.

'It was my adoptive mother's dream to produce an English sparkling wine on a par with Champagne. When Mama died I was determined to continue her work and fulfil her dream, which is why I have a Master's degree in viticulture and oenology. You look shocked,' she said wryly. 'Did you think I was the brainless bimbo that I am portrayed by the tabloids?'

He shrugged. 'You cannot entirely blame the media for your reputation. The paparazzi did not have to look hard to find evidence of your wild lifestyle. Admittedly, it was months ago that you were regularly seen at the coolest London nightclubs and scandal was never far from you.' He looked at her speculatively. 'What makes me curious is why you seemed to deliberately seek notoriety and the attention of the press.'

Cortez's insight made Elin uneasy. She did not want him to guess that she had sought to keep the paparazzi away from her brother when Jarek's life was in freefall. She looked down the long rows of vines that stretched into the distance. 'How many hectares of vineyards do you have?' she asked in a blatant effort to change the subject.

'Two hundred.' Cortez's voice was drier than the finest Manzanilla sherry and Elin dropped her eyes from his sardonic gaze.

'There are only six hectares of vineyards at Cuckmere. It's lucky you don't have winter frosts this far south,' she told him. 'It would take an army of workers to light frost candles to protect all your vines.'

He helped her to steer the pram around the deep tractor tyre grooves on the path. 'I have heard of the practice of lighting candles to raise the air temperature around the vines to above freezing but I've never seen it done.'

'If you had looked out of the window the night you stayed at Cuckmere Hall you would have seen the vineyards glowing with golden candle lights,' Elin told him. 'There was a frost, but luckily a few of the estate workers stayed up all night to help me light the *bougies*. It would have been a catastrophe if the new shoots on the vines had been frost damaged.'

'So that's why you were still in bed at ten o'clock the next morning,' Cortez murmured in an odd voice. 'I thought you lazed around every morning and left Harry to be cared for by the nanny.'

'Lack of sleep was probably a contributing factor when I developed a kidney infection,' Elin confided. 'Harry had been restless for a few nights before the fund-raising party for Lorna's Gift. When I'm tired my immune system seems to shut down.'

Cortez was still holding the pram handle and Elin caught her breath when his fingers brushed against hers. She looked down at his darkly tanned fingers next to her much paler ones, and memories flooded her mind of his hands roaming over her body, caressing her breasts and slipping between her legs. She was appalled when she felt a molten sensation *there*, where a year ago his skilful touch had given her unbelievable pleasure.

'We should go back to the house before Harry wakes up for a feed,' she said stiltedly, praying that Cortez did not notice her flushed face. She felt hot with shame and a helpless longing that made her angry with herself. How could she want him after the way he had treated her? Where was her self-respect?

'Another time I will give you a tour of the bodega,' Cortez offered. To Elin's relief, he seemed unaware that her hormones were in meltdown. 'Not all the grapes from these vineyards are used to make Felipe & Cortez sherry. About a third of the crop is sold to other wineries.' They had reached the gate in the wall, and he held it open to allow Elin to push the pram through to the garden before he continued speaking. 'Tomorrow evening I am hosting a party for F&C's shareholders and clients. A few media representatives have also been invited. At the party I intend to give a press statement announcing that Harry is my son.'

Elin's heart dropped like a stone. 'Why now? I mean…there is no rush, especially as nothing has been decided yet about who will have custody of him.'

'Whatever happens in the future with regard to arrangements for where Harry will spend his childhood, and with whom, I want to publicly recognise that he is my son.' Cortez frowned when he saw her dismayed expression. 'I'm not going to drop out of his life, however much you might wish that I would,' he said in a hard voice. 'I want to be a full-time parent to him while he is growing up.'

'So do I,' she cried emotionally. 'But you want to take Harry away from me.'

'That's not true. I accept that he needs you, certainly while he is so young. At the party I will introduce you as the mother of my child.'

Her brows rose. 'Aren't you worried I'll turn up in a drug-fuelled haze, out of my head on whatever substance you think I snort up my nose, or inject into my veins?'

To Elin's surprise Cortez looked uncomfortable as he raked a hand through his hair. 'I have realised that I was wrong about you, and you are not in fact a drug-user,' he said gruffly. 'The stories about you in the tabloids seemed to prove that you had a drug habit. But it is now clear to me that you take mother-hood seriously.'

'My commitment to Harry has never been in doubt,' she said furiously. 'But you refused to believe he was your son when I first told you.'

His jaw hardened but his response was controlled, as if he was forcing himself to remain calm in the face of her angry condemnation. 'I now have proof that Harry is mine, and to-morrow evening I will make it public knowledge that I am his father. You do not need to worry that I am one hundred per cent committed to my son.'

Cortez smiled at the CEO of a brandy production company which was an important client of Felipe & Cortez Vineyards, and realised that he had no recollection of the conversation he'd had with the other man for the past ten minutes. Over Señor Santana's shoulder he watched Elin chatting to another client, and he gritted his teeth when he noted that the guy looked dazzled by Elin. Cortez understood how that felt.

Desire had jack-knifed through him when he had knocked on her bedroom door fifteen minutes before the guests were due to arrive to escort her downstairs. The day before, he had suggested that he could order an evening gown for her from an exclusive boutique in Jerez, but she had declined his offer, saying she'd brought a dress with her from London that was suitable to wear to the party.

Elin's idea of suitable was not the same as his, Cortez brooded as his eyes followed her obsessively when she moved around the room, stopping frequently to speak to guests. Her long sapphire-blue dress was a deceptively simple silk sheath with a diamanté belt that showed off her tiny waist. The halter-neck style left her shoulders and back bare and her blonde hair was swept up into a chignon, revealing the slender column of her white throat. In truth, the gown was elegant and sensual rather than overtly sexy, but Cortez hated the fact that every man in the room was looking at her and no doubt fantasising about her. He would feel happier if she were wearing a shroud. This possessive feeling was new and unwelcome and he felt irritated that she was the only woman who had such an effect on him.

When she had opened her bedroom door and given him one of those cool smiles of hers that never failed to set his teeth on edge, he had come worryingly close to sweeping her into his arms and carrying her over to the bed. He had wanted to strip her dress from her body and kiss her mouth and her breasts until he heated her up and she turned into the sensual siren who a year ago had begged him in a throaty whisper, that still haunted his dreams, to make love to her.

He forced his mind to the present when his PA came over and told him that everything was ready for him to make a statement to the press. He had asked the nanny to bring Harry downstairs when the baby woke for his ten p.m. feed. Barbara walked into the ballroom and Cortez strode over and took his son from her. As he lifted Harry into his arms, Elin materialised at his side. Her tension was almost tangible.

'Let me hold him,' she muttered. 'He hasn't long been fed, and he might be sick on your tuxedo.'

'I don't give a damn about my jacket.' He stared at his son and Harry stared right back with his big, dark eyes flecked with gold. The baby's rosebud mouth curved into a smile of recognition and Cortez silently repeated his vow that he would willingly sacrifice his life to protect his little boy.

The room fell silent as he made his way to one end of the ballroom, where a group of journalists were assembled in front of a microphone. There was a ripple of interest from the audience as he stepped onto the podium holding the baby in his arms. He held out his hand to Elin and she hesitated before she walked up to stand beside him.

He had given prior instruction that the press conference would be conducted in English for Elin's benefit. 'Ladies and gentlemen, the continued success of Felipe & Cortez, which is reflected in the latest rise in profits, makes me very proud. But I am even prouder to introduce my son, Harry Ramos.'

The news was met with murmurs of surprise and interest from the guests. Cortez's PR team had arranged that the press could ask a few pre-arranged questions, but as the session drew to an end a journalist stood up and asked an unplanned question.

'Do you have any plans to marry your son's mother? And, if so, when will the wedding be?'

Cortez smiled to hide his irritation with the journalist. 'Miss Saunderson and I are not prepared to make a statement with regard to our personal situation yet,' he said smoothly.

'Miss Saunderson is English, and I am sure that your shareholders would like to know if you will continue to live in Spain, Señor Ramos, or if you plan to move to England to be with your son and his mother.'

'Felipe & Cortez's shareholders can be assured that I will continue to be based in Spain and my commitment to the company and also to my role as CEO of Hernandez Bank is unchanged.'

'Will your son also live in Spain?'

'Of course. Harry is my heir and when he is older I hope he will develop the same passion that I have to grow the best grapes and produce the best sherry for which F&C is renowned.'

'But you do not intend to get married and your son will remain illegitimate?' the journalist persisted.

'As I have already stated, I do not intend to make any further announcement about my private life right now,' Cortez said tersely. 'All I will say is that the current situation regarding my son's legitimacy will be resolved in the very near future.'

He signalled to his PA that the press conference was over and stepped down from the podium. As he carried Harry out of the ballroom Elin hurried after him, and he guessed from the staccato beat of her stiletto heels on the marble floor that her temper was simmering.

'What did you mean by that last vague reply you gave to the journalist?' she demanded after Cortez handed Harry to the nanny so that she could take him back upstairs to the nursery. The entrance hall was full of guests who were preparing to leave now that the party was over, and he led Elin into his study and locked the door to ensure their privacy. She put her hands on her hips. 'How can Harry's legitimacy be resolved?'

He waited a heartbeat. 'By us getting married.'

'Very funny,' she snapped. 'But I'm not in the mood for jokes.'

'It wasn't a joke. I'm serious.' In his mind Cortez heard the journalist say that Harry was illegitimate, and he was hurtled back in time to when he had been taunted by other boys in the village where he had lived with his mother. *'Malparido!'* they had shouted at him. The word meant bastard in English. Worse had been when they had called his mother a *puta*—a whore. Cortez had retaliated to the boys' insults with his fists. He hadn't cared what they called him, but he had fought to defend his mother's honour. Working in the vineyard from an early age had made him physically strong, and after a while the boys had stopped calling him names to his face because they knew he would retaliate with punches.

Attitudes had changed in the thirty-four years since he had grown up among villagers who had held traditional values and sneered at him because his mother was unmarried. But the journalist's comments showed that there was still a stigma attached to being illegitimate. He would not allow his son to be called a *malparido*.

He looked at Elin's mutinous expression and knew he would have a battle on his hands to persuade her to marry him. But she wanted Harry as much as he did and Cortez was prepared to play dirty to get *everything* he desired.

CHAPTER EIGHT

'WHAT MAKES YOU think I'd marry you after you have kidnapped me, insulted me and accused me among other things of being a drug addict?'

Elin's chest heaved as she struggled to control her overwrought emotions. When Cortez had announced to his party guests and the press that Harry was his son, she had felt a sense of being trapped and powerless. 'This ridiculous situation has gone on long enough,' she said forcefully. 'I don't know why you told the journalist that Harry will live in Spain. His home is in England with me.'

Instead of replying, Cortez picked up a crystal decanter and poured a generous measure of pale gold liquid into a glass. 'Do you want a drink?' he asked her. 'This is F&C's finest fifteen-year-old cask-aged sherry.' When Elin shook her head he lifted the glass to his lips and swallowed half its contents in one gulp, almost as if he had needed the hit of alcohol. He looked at her with an unfathomable expression in his eyes. 'So how do you think it will work if we share custody of Harry?'

'What do you mean?'

'Will we each have him living with us for a week or a month at a time? That might work while he is a baby, but when he's older don't you think he will find it unsettling to be shipped between England and Spain like he is a parcel? Is that what you want for our son?'

'Of course not.' A memory flashed into Elin's mind of herself as a little girl, walking up the front steps of Cuckmere Hall for the first time after Ralph and Lorna Saunderson had adopted her and taken her to England. She had only known the orphanage in war-torn Sarajevo, but even though it had not been a happy place she had been scared to leave. Moving away from familiar surroundings was unnerving for a child. She remembered how she had clung to her brother's hand for reassurance. How would Harry feel when he was a bit older and he was separated from one of his parents and taken to live with his other parent in a different country every few weeks? Not having a permanent home would be unsettling for him.

'What about Christmases and birthdays?' Cortez went on relentlessly. 'How much do you think he will enjoy those special occasions if he has to choose which of his parents to spend them with?'

'Plenty of parents manage to lead separate lives and successfully share custody of their children,' Elin argued. 'We don't have to get married for Harry's sake.'

'No, we don't *have* to,' Cortez agreed flatly. 'But why *wouldn't* we choose to give our son stability, security and the consistency of growing up with both his parents? Harry needs to be part of a family and surely his needs are paramount?'

'This is crazy!' Elin's frustration bubbled over. Everything Cortez had said made sense, but marry him...*really*? 'You are the last man on earth I'd choose to marry.'

'Yet, if I am to believe what you told me, I am the first and possibly only man you've had sex with,' he drawled.

She flushed. 'I explained why I slept with you on my birthday night. I certainly wasn't tempted to sleep with anyone else after I'd found out that I was pregnant by a stranger who had gatecrashed my party.'

Cortez finished his drink and set his glass down on the desk.

'I hired a private investigator in England, who checked police records and confirmed that a male guest at your birthday party was accused of tampering with several of the women's drinks. Tom Wilson was charged with administering a substance which is a well-known date-rape drug.'

Elin gave a deep sigh. 'There is the proof that I behaved out of character when I went to bed with you. The drug that had been slipped into my drink without my knowledge had the effect of lowering my inhibitions.' Deep down, she knew she could not only blame the date-rape drug for the way she had responded to Cortez's smouldering sensuality. She had taken one look at him and been blown away by his handsome looks, but she wasn't about to admit that to him.

She became aware that he had moved closer to her without her noticing him doing so. He possessed the stealth and predatory instincts of a wolf stalking its prey. The thought unnerved her even as her body reacted to the evocative scent of his cologne. He was always impossibly handsome, but tonight, wearing an impeccably tailored black dinner suit, he took her breath away. It hurt her to look at him and she wanted to turn her head away, but he trapped her gaze and the sultry heat in his gold-flecked eyes sent a sizzle of electricity through her.

'You can tell yourself that it was a drugged drink that made you desire me a year ago, but it doesn't explain your response when I kissed you at Cuckmere Hall,' he drawled.

'You took me by surprise.' She was quick to defend her actions but she flushed guiltily as she remembered how she had melted in his arms. She held up her hand to ward Cortez off when he stepped even closer to her. He was so tall that she had to tilt her head to look at his face and the implacable expression stamped on his chiselled features caused her heart to miss a beat.

'What are you doing? Leave me alone.' Her panicky plea was muffled against his mouth as his head swooped down and he crushed her lips beneath his in a kiss designed to prove that he was her master.

She must not succumb to his sensual magic, Elin told herself frantically. But she felt boneless as Cortez pulled her into the heat and strength of his big body, making her aware of his powerful abdominal muscles and, lower down, the shockingly hard ridge of his arousal that pressed insistently against her pelvis.

He deepened the kiss, exploring the moist interior of her mouth with his tongue while he slid one hand into her hair and clamped her skull so that escape was impossible. His other hand skimmed down her bare back, his touch setting her skin alight before he spread his fingers over the swell of her buttocks. Her silk dress was a frustrating barrier and Elin longed to feel his hands on her naked bottom. Heat coursed through her veins, evoking a carnal craving that mocked her belief that she was not a sensual person.

He continued his exploration of her feminine curves and stroked his way up her body to her breasts. She caught her breath when he pushed the top of her dress aside and played with one nipple, rolling the hard peak between his fingers. Pleasure arced down to the sweet spot between her legs and multiplied a thousand times when he unfastened the halter straps on her dress and bared her breasts to the mercy of his mouth. She felt his warm breath on her skin before he took her nipple into his mouth and sucked hard until she whimpered with pleasure and he transferred his lips to her other breast.

The last vestiges of Elin's resistance crumbled and she gave a low moan of surrender as she wound her arms around his neck. He lifted his head to plunder her mouth with his wicked tongue. In a distant recess of her mind she acknowledged that Cortez had given a masterclass in domination which had rendered her helpless against the onslaught of his passion. A warning voice in her head whispered that she would pay a heavy price in humiliation for these moments of pleasure.

She was right. He suddenly released her and she swayed

on her feet, feeling utterly bereft. She lifted her fingers to her mouth and touched its swollen contours. God knew what she looked like. She could feel that her hair had half fallen out of its chignon, and her hands shook as she pulled the top of her dress up over her breasts to hide her swollen, reddened nipples that were still damp from Cortez's tongue. She might as well have shouted from the rooftop that she was his for the taking, she thought in self-disgust.

'Our marriage will provide our son with the security of growing up with both his parents, which is something we know from our childhood experiences is important.' Cortez's voice was coolly unemotional and Elin's stomach gave a sickening lurch as she realised that he was unaffected by what had just happened. Why didn't she learn? A year ago he had left her after they'd had sex, and he had only kissed her now to prove that she couldn't resist him.

'You can't possibly want me for your wife,' she said desperately.

'I have just demonstrated what I want.' He dropped his gaze to the betraying hard peaks of her breasts and smiled cynically. 'What we both want. And there will be other compensations to our marriage of expediency in addition to our sexual compatibility.'

He made it sound so clinical, Elin thought bleakly. 'Your knowledge of viticulture and your ability to walk into a room and instantly charm every person present will be useful when you act as my hostess at social and business functions. My shareholders will love you,' Cortez said drily.

'I don't actually care what your shareholders think of me. What concerns me is how could we possibly create a happy home and family life for Harry when there is so much antipathy between us?' She bit her lip. 'We hardly know each other.'

'Then we had better go on a crash course to learn about each other, hadn't we, *querida*?' His softer tone was unexpected and made Elin wish that the situation was different. If only Cortez loved her.

Shock jolted through her and she told herself not to be stupid. It was bad enough that he made her body feel out of control, and she was not going to lose control of her heart too. She stiffened when he lifted his hand and traced his thumb across her kiss-stung lips.

'Our son was conceived by mistake,' he said quietly, 'but although we may not know each other very well yet, I am confident we agree on one thing. Neither of us regrets for one second that we have been blessed with Harry. For his sake, let us endeavour not to make any more mistakes.'

Perhaps her doubts showed in her expression because he stepped away from her and said coolly, 'Don't forget that by marrying me you'll fulfil the terms of Ralph's will, which stipulates that you can only inherit fifty per cent of Saunderson's Wines if you marry within a year. I have decided not to sell the Cuckmere estate because, as you pointed out, it is Harry's heritage. If you marry me you will be able to continue the work your adoptive mother started when she planted the vineyards, and hopefully produce a top quality English sparkling wine.'

Owning a share of the winery would give her financial security and independence, Elin brooded. Cortez had played his trump card. He knew how much Saunderson's Wines meant to her, and her desire to fulfil Mama's dream. It made sense to agree to marry him to secure her position as Harry's mother and also to take part-ownership of the winery that she had invested so much of her time and energy in.

'All right,' she said abruptly, before she could change her mind. 'I'll marry you for the reasons you have mentioned. I agree that it will be better for our son if we bring him up together. And I am determined to make Saunderson's Wines a successful business.'

Cortez nodded and poured himself another drink, which he swallowed in one gulp. 'I'll make the necessary arrangements for us to marry as soon as possible,' he told her in a crisp tone which indicated that he regarded their marriage as purely a matter of convenience, which of course it was for her too, Elin assured herself.

The bureaucratic process of applying to marry in Spain was fairly long-winded, and it was three weeks later before Cortez was able to book the wedding ceremony at the local Town Hall.

Although he was impatient at the delay in becoming his son's legal parent, he had nevertheless found it fascinating to watch Harry develop. It was astonishing how much the baby had grown and changed in a few short weeks, he said to Elin at Harry's bathtime one evening. The hours they spent together with their son had given Cortez an opportunity to prove his desire to be a good father and he had noticed a gradual thaw in Elin's attitude towards him. He knew he had hurt her with his accusations, and it would take time to win her trust, but he was determined to do so, and show her that they could have a successful marriage.

Now it was the day before their wedding and they were on their way to Seville to have lunch with his married friends, Nicolás and Teresa García. The couple had a one-year-old son, and Cortez hoped that Elin would enjoy spending time with other parents after she'd complained that she felt cut off from her friends in Sussex while she was living in Spain.

He briefly took his eyes from the road and glanced at her sitting beside him in the front of the car. 'What kind of man was Ralph Saunderson?' he asked her. 'It feels strange that I know nothing about my father.' He thought of the man he had met once a year ago. He had not seen Ralph Saunderson after that first visit to Cuckmere Hall and Ralph had not been in contact again before his death. 'You were his adopted daughter and you must have known him well.'

Cortez focused back on the highway, which was bordered on both sides by acres of vineyards stretching to the horizon, and tried unsuccessfully to ignore his fierce awareness of Elin. The light floral perfume she wore stirred his senses, and the expanse of slender thigh exposed by her skirt, that had ridden up when she'd climbed into the car, made him wish that he could pull over by the side of the road and make love to her. But relieving his sexual frustration was not possible for many reasons, not least because Harry was asleep in his baby seat in the back of the car.

Their wedding could not come soon enough, he brooded. Sometimes he had caught Elin looking at him in a way that made him wonder if she was as desperate as he was for them to share a bed. He certainly hoped she was. But he'd heard genuine concern in her voice when she had said that they hardly knew one another, and for that reason he had forced himself to suppress his desire while he concentrated on making her feel at ease with him. He'd never taken as many cold showers as he had recently, he thought wryly.

Elin shifted in her seat and the pretty, floral-patterned dress she was wearing rode a little further up her thighs. She had lost the gaunt look she'd had when Cortez had brought her to Spain, and her unhealthy pallor had been replaced with a light golden tan. Her long hair was tied in a braid that fell over one shoulder and she looked utterly lovely and wholesome and at the same time incredibly sexy. His fingers itched to undo the buttons running down the front of her dress and discover if she was wearing a bra.

'I didn't really know Ralph very well,' she said. 'I wasn't close to him like I was to my adoptive mother. He had a tendency to start many projects with plenty of enthusiasm but he became bored quickly. I think he only agreed to adopt me and my brother because Mama wanted us. She couldn't have children of her own, and when she saw news coverage of the devastation in Sarajevo she was keen to give a home to orphaned children.' Elin grimaced. 'Jarek said that we were another of Ralph's projects and he soon lost interest in us.'

She turned her head to look over her shoulder and check on Harry and Cortez breathed in the lemony scent of her hair. 'On the surface we appeared to be the perfect family, but the truth was that Ralph had affairs with other women,' Elin said flatly. 'I'm sure Mama chose to ignore his infidelities because she did not want Jarek and me to suffer more upheaval if she and Ralph divorced.'

Elin fell silent when they reached the centre of Seville and Cortez needed to concentrate on driving in heavy traffic. Finally he turned the car onto a driveway in front of the Garcías' elegant villa.

'Don't be nervous,' he said softly when he saw her tense expression. 'This is an informal occasion, and Teresa and Nic are charming people.' He climbed out of the car and carried Harry in his baby seat up the front steps of the house. A maid opened the door and Cortez slipped his arm around Elin's waist as they stepped out of the bright sunshine into the cool hallway. 'Our wedding is tomorrow, and we need to put on a convincing act in front of people that we are a happily engaged couple,' he murmured when she stiffened.

'Why does it matter what other people think about our relationship?' she muttered.

'I don't want rumours to spread that we are marrying for practicality so that we can both bring up our son. Harry is only a baby now, but when he is older he might be teased by other kids at school. How do you think he would feel if he learned that his parents had only married for his sake?' Memories of when he had been taunted by the other boys at school because he did not have a father made Cortez determined that his son would never have reason to feel embarrassed about his parentage.

The maid showed them into a large salon with glass doors that opened onto an attractive courtyard garden. A man and woman came towards them, smiling warmly, and Cortez introduced Elin to Teresa and Nicolás before proudly showing off his son. Harry looked adorable in his blue and white striped outfit and seemed quite happy to be the centre of attention when the other guests crowded around to make a fuss of him. Elin visibly relaxed after a few minutes as she chatted to Teresa and admired the Garcías' son Luiz, who had recently learned to walk.

'*Hola, cariño,*' a woman's seductive voice murmured close to Cortez.

'Sancha.' He greeted his ex-mistress with a cool smile and tried to suppress his irritation when she linked her arm possessively through his. 'I did not realise you would be here today.'

'I wouldn't have missed my sister's party for the world when Teresa told me that *you* would be coming,' she assured him softly. She leaned forwards so that her breasts were in danger of spilling out of her low-cut dress. 'I was surprised you did not mention that you had accepted an invitation to the party when we met in Madrid a few weeks ago.'

Fortunately, Nic came over to ask Cortez what he and Elin would like to drink, and Sancha sashayed across the room back to her latest lover, who, Cortez happened to know, was some twenty years older than her and a multimillionaire. He almost felt sorry for the guy.

Would Sancha have turned down a mansion and estate worth thirty-five million pounds? It was unlikely, he thought cynically. He turned his head towards Elin and watched her carefully lift Harry out of the baby carrier. Her face was soft with love for her baby. She glanced over and returned Cortez's smile and he felt his heart kick in his chest.

In twenty-four hours she would be his wife and he was surprised by how relaxed he felt at the prospect. He had not planned to marry, certainly not at this stage of his life. But discovering that he had a child had changed everything. He would not allow his son to be illegitimate. Elin had shown herself to be a devoted mother, and perhaps it was time that he let go of the past, and Alandra's terrible betrayal, and learned to trust his soon-to-be wife.

* * *

The Garcías' party was the first occasion that Elin had taken Harry out in public. She had hidden away at Cuckmere Hall after his birth, partly because she had needed to recover her strength following the postpartum haemorrhage, but mainly because she could not bear the idea of the tabloids branding her an irresponsible single mother and all the speculation there was bound to be about the identity of her baby's father.

Cortez looked shocked when she admitted that she had kept Harry's birth a secret. 'Are you ashamed of our son?'

'Of course not.' She looked over to where Teresa was holding Harry while she and Cortez helped themselves to lunch from the buffet table. 'I am ashamed of myself,' she said in a low tone, 'and my behaviour when I met you at my birthday party. You probably don't believe me, but I had never slept with any man before that night.'

Cortez speared a king prawn viciously with a fork and transferred it to his plate. 'I wish I had realised you were a virgin,' he said in a taut voice that Elin had never heard him use before. She could almost believe he cared about her feelings until she reminded herself that he was being attentive to her at the party because they were pretending to be in love. She should not read anything into the way he smiled whenever their eyes met, as if she were the only woman in the room.

She glanced down at the sparkling engagement ring on her finger, a square-cut sapphire surrounded by white diamonds. It was the most exquisite ring Elin had ever seen and she could only guess how much it was worth. When Cortez had slipped it onto her finger a few days after she'd agreed to marry him she had protested that she could not accept a valuable piece of jewellery from him. He'd replied that the engagement ring would prove to people that their relationship was genuine, but then he had made her heart leap when he'd said he had chosen the sapphire because it matched the colour of her eyes.

The party was a relaxed affair and Elin found she was enjoying the good food and wine and the chance to socialise with Cortez's friends. A few other couples had young children, and she began to think that living at La Casa Jazmín would not be as isolating as she'd feared. Although she would have to learn to speak Spanish quickly, Elin decided. The other guests all spoke to her in English but they slipped back into speaking Spanish among themselves. She and Cortez had already agreed that Harry would be brought up to be bilingual but she was worried that if she did not master Spanish she would feel alienated from her son and husband.

Husband! Her heart lurched when she thought of her wedding tomorrow. Since she had woken up at La Casa Jazmín nearly a month ago and discovered that Cortez had brought her to Spain while she'd been ill with a kidney infection, her life had seemed unreal. And her sense of unreality had increased over the past weeks as Cortez's attitude towards her had changed radically.

He was no longer cold and stern, and it was hard to believe he had made those horrible accusations that she was a drug-user and an unfit mother. It was as if he was now determined to charm her, and he did not have to try very hard, she acknowledged ruefully as she looked across the room to where he was standing by the glass doors that opened onto the garden. Late afternoon sunshine filled the courtyard garden and danced over his hair so that it gleamed as black as a raven's wing. His black jeans moulded his powerful thighs, and his cream shirt was open at the throat, showing his tanned skin and a sprinkling of black hairs that Elin knew, from when she had watched him swimming in the pool at home, grew thickly over his chest.

She realised with a jolt that she had mentally thought of La Casa Jazmín as home. Tomorrow night would she and Cortez consummate their marriage in the master bedroom? Anticipation coiled in the pit of her stomach. They had not discussed the terms of their marriage, but the hungry gleam in his gold-flecked eyes told her that he desired her, and she had decided that she wasn't going to hide behind her pride and deny that she craved physical intimacy with him. He was her only lover. But he was more than that, for his charm offensive these past weeks had captured her heart and deep down she knew she was falling in love with him.

Harry behaved beautifully for the entire afternoon, but by early evening he became fractious and Elin took him into a small sitting room away from everyone so that she could feed him in peace. She changed his nappy and had just placed him in his baby carrier, ready for Cortez to put him in the car for the drive home, when the door opened and a woman walked into the sitting room.

Elin had met Teresa's sister Sancha earlier in the day. She smiled, trying to ignore a little flicker of feminine jealousy of the Spanish woman's stunning looks. It was no surprise that Sancha worked as a presenter for a national television station in Madrid, she mused. Sancha's gorgeous figure looked as if it had been poured into her tight-fitting white dress, and the co-lour was a perfect foil for her smooth olive-gold skin. Her jet black hair had been cut into an asymmetric bob that showed off her high cheekbones and flashing dark eyes.

Sancha closed the door and strolled over to sit down on a chair opposite Elin. 'I'm glad to have a few moments alone with you,' she murmured. 'I must congratulate you.'

Despite the other woman's apparently friendly tone, Elin was aware of undercurrents swirling in the room. She looked at Harry, who had fallen asleep in the baby carrier. 'Thank you. I feel very lucky to have a beautiful son and so does Cortez.'

'Mmm...' Sancha did not glance at the baby. 'It was clever of you to turn up and present Cortez with his son. I suppose you had guessed that, having suffered the stigma of being born to an unmarried mother himself, he would not allow his child to be illegitimate. That is the reason he is marrying you, isn't it?'

'I really think that is between me and Cortez,' Elin said po-litely, but her insides were knotted with tension as she waited for Sancha to get to the point. She did not have to wait long.

'It's all right; he explained it all to me.' The Spanish woman gave a little feigned laugh when she saw Elin's expression. 'Oh, didn't you know that Cortez and I were lovers?'

She hadn't known for sure, but Elin had suspected. Several times during the afternoon she had noticed Sancha and Cortez standing apart from the other guests, their dark heads bent close as they spoke intently. There had been an incident when Sancha had asked Cortez to get her a drink and he hadn't had to ask what she wanted; he'd simply brought her a glass of white wine. The seemingly insignificant event had revealed an intimacy to their relationship that went far beyond that of casual acquaintances. But Elin was not going to let Sancha know that she felt as if she had been stabbed through her heart.

'Cortez is a very attractive man, and I'd be surprised if he hadn't had other lovers in his past.'

Sancha gave her a speculative look. 'It's good that you have a sensible attitude to his relationship with me. He often has business in Madrid and he always stays at the apartment he bought for us. Would you like to see a picture of it?' She took her mobile phone from her purse and held it out. Elin didn't want to look at the photo on the screen but her eyes were drawn to the image of a bare-chested Cortez lying on a bed with a sheet draped over his hips.

'The apartment only has one bedroom, but it has a very big bed,' Sancha said coyly, twisting the knife into Elin's heart. 'I took this photo the last time Cortez was in Madrid three weeks ago.'

Elin almost choked on the bile that rose in her throat. Three weeks ago, Cortez had told her he was going to Madrid for business, and he'd stayed away for the night. When he had returned to La Casa Jazmín he had suggested that they get married so that they could both be full-time parents to Harry. But he must have told Sancha of his intention to marry the mother of his child. How else would the Spanish woman have known that it was a marriage of convenience? Elin thought grimly.

She stood up and busied herself with packing Harry's bottle, bib and other paraphernalia into the changing bag while she stifled the hurt that ripped through her. Pride came to her aid and she gave Sancha a bland smile.

'I can guarantee that in future if Cortez has business in Madrid he will come home the same day because he won't want to be apart from his wife and son for even one night.' She held out her hand to Sancha and took a small triumph from the Spanish woman's look of surprise. 'It was nice to meet you,' she murmured before she picked up Harry in the baby carrier and forced herself to walk unhurriedly out of the room.

But Sancha's poison drip-fed into Elin's mind on the journey back to La Casa Jazmín. Cortez seemed convinced by her explanation that she was tired after he'd remarked that she was very quiet. She closed her eyes to shut out his handsome profile while her thoughts went round and round in her head.

She accepted that he must have had countless affairs with beautiful women in his past. Elin could even accept that Sancha had been his mistress. But three weeks ago he had vowed to fight for custody of his son and he had even offered her Cuckmere Hall if she signed custody of Harry over to him. Despite being desperately hurt by his accusation that she was a drug addict, in a strange way she had felt reassured by Cortez's determination to take care of his son. But now she knew that on the same day he had vowed to fight to keep Harry he had visited Sancha in Madrid and spent the night with her. So much for Cortez's promise that he would be a devoted father. He hadn't given Harry a thought when he'd rushed off to have sex with his lover, Elin thought bitterly.

She recalled their conversation when they had been driving to the Garcías' house and Cortez had asked her what kind of man his father had been. Ralph Saunderson had had a low boredom threshold, which presumably was the reason why he'd had numerous extra-marital affairs and why he had lost interest in his adopted children. Elin remembered how, as a child, she had studied hard at school, hoping to impress her adoptive father, but his disinterest had decimated her self-confidence and left her feeling worthless.

What if Cortez grew bored of fatherhood? She couldn't bear to think of Harry when he was older, trying to please his father and make him proud, but then feeling a failure if Cortez rejected him. Cortez had never had a chance to know Ralph but it was likely that he had inherited some of his father's traits. And perhaps, like his father, he did not consider fidelity important in marriage. Elin had a sudden flash of insight to a future where she was tormented by jealousy and suspicion every time they attended a social event and she wondered which beautiful woman was her husband's latest mistress.

She couldn't do it. She couldn't go through with the wedding when she knew that Cortez was only marrying her out of duty. He had stated that marriage was the best option to give Harry a settled upbringing. But how could a childhood marred by his parents' rows and recriminations be good for Harry?

Cortez's phone rang as they walked into La Casa Jazmín. He frowned when he checked the name of the caller. 'I need to speak to the head of the Japanese branch of Saunderson's Bank,' he told Elin. 'Can you manage Harry on your own?'

'Of course I can.' Was he implying that he didn't think she had been capable of looking after her baby before he'd arrived on the scene like some knight on a white charger to take up his role as Harry's father? she thought irritably. She had managed perfectly well for the past couple of days while the nanny had taken annual leave to do some sightseeing in nearby Cadiz.

She took Harry up to the nursery. He was fast asleep and looked so comfortable in the baby carrier that she decided not to risk waking him by moving him into his cot. But there was another reason to leave him in the baby seat. A crazy plan was forming in her mind, which, the more she thought about it, seemed to be her only option. She did not want to marry Cortez tomorrow. Too much was at stake, not least her heart. But if she refused he had threatened to fight her in court for custody of Harry.

In her bedroom she opened the bedside drawer and took out her and Harry's passports, which Cortez had returned to her a week ago. She had regarded the gesture as a sign that he trusted her not to take their son away. But perhaps he believed that she had fallen under his spell and was too besotted with him to consider leaving, she thought grimly.

She knotted her fingers together, wishing she knew what to do. As far back as she could remember she had been able to ask her brother for advice, but when she had phoned him in Japan to tell him that Cortez was Harry's father and she was going to marry him, Jarek had sounded terse and distracted and had said she should do whatever was best for her and her baby.

Would a loveless marriage to Cortez be best for her and for their son? An image flashed into Elin's mind of stunning Sancha, and she wondered how she could have believed that Cortez desired *her* when he had an exotic mistress in Madrid, and quite possibly several other mistresses dotted around Europe. She had spent her childhood trying, and failing, to please her adoptive father and she was not going to spend her adult life feeling a failure as Cortez's convenient wife.

CHAPTER NINE

ELIN'S ESCAPE PLAN had seemed easy in theory. But in practice she struggled to strap Harry's baby seat into the car when her hands were shaking. She consoled herself with the thought that she would not have to drive Cortez's powerful sports car that roared like a savage beast and would no doubt have woken the entire household. Recently he had bought a family estate car for her to use, but she'd never driven on the right-hand side of the road and she had been glad when he'd sat beside her to give her confidence on her first outing to a nearby village. Now she was planning to drive some twenty kilometres to the airport in Jerez de la Frontera in the dark, and her stomach was knotted with nervous tension.

She waited until midnight before she took Harry in the baby carrier downstairs and collected the car keys from the utility room. The car's engine purred quietly as she drove out of the garage. The main gates at the bottom of the driveway were activated by number plate recognition and should have swung open as the car approached them, but Elin's heart sank when they remained shut.

'Open, damn you,' she muttered. She had spent hours of soul-searching before she'd made the decision to leave Cortez and take Harry back to England, and now that she had got this far with her plan she did not want any delay. She was not going to deny Cortez a role in Harry's life, but it could not only be on his terms.

She switched off the engine and checked that Harry was still asleep before she got out of the car and walked up to the gates with little hope that she would be able to open them manually. To her surprise, when she leaned against one of the gates, it moved. She pushed both gates fully open and stood on the road outside the grounds of the house. Above her the moon was a silver disc in the black sky. She stared up at the stars that glittered as brilliantly as the diamonds on her engagement ring that she had left in Cortez's study with a note explaining her reasons for leaving.

There was nothing to stop her getting into the car and driving away from La Casa Jazmín—except for her conscience. She tried to imagine how Cortez would feel when he discovered that she had taken his son. He would be devastated because he loved Harry. The truth struck her like a lightning bolt. From the moment Cortez had received proof that Harry was his, he had constantly shown that he adored his baby son. With brutal honesty, Elin acknowledged that she'd felt a little bit jealous of the attention Cortez paid to Harry and his love for his son that was so obvious.

Behind her she heard a faint click and she spun round to find that the gates had smoothly and silently closed and she was locked outside Casa Jazmín's grounds, while the car with Harry inside was on the other side of the gates. Frantically, she tugged the gates but they would not budge. Her heart thudded painfully in her chest. The moon had disappeared behind a cloud and the darkness seemed menacing as the horror of her situation sank in.

She could not understand how the electronic gates had started working again. But when the moon reappeared and cast a ghostly gleam along the driveway, the answer stood before her in the form of a six foot four, furiously angry man.

'*Cortez.*' Elin swallowed as she waited for him to speak. The moonlight slanted over his harsh features and his anger was evident in the rigid set of his jaw. But he said nothing as he lifted the baby seat out of the car and walked back towards the house with Harry.

She rattled the metal gates, fear cramping in her stomach. '*Cortez*, please let me in.' He carried on walking as if she hadn't spoken, as if she did not exist. '*Please...*' A sob tore through her. 'You can't take my baby.'

'You were going to take him away from me.' Finally he halted and turned around. His voice was as dark and menacing as the night. 'By chance I went into my study to look for some paperwork, and when I found your note I deactivated the electronic gates. But if I hadn't been in time you would have driven off with Harry. *Dios*, I trusted you, Elin. Something I vowed never to do with any woman,' he said bitterly. His temper exploded. 'How *dare* you repay my trust by attempting to steal my son? How *dare* you try to separate me from him and deprive Harry of a father who loves him more than anything on this earth?'

'I wasn't going to go.' Desperation made her voice unsteady. 'I swear I'd changed my mind and I was going to turn the car around.'

He gave a grim laugh. 'There's no chance I'd believe a word you say. And there is even less chance that a court will award you custody of Harry after you were willing to risk his safety by taking him in the car when you are inexperienced at driving on roads in Spain.'

Cortez's voice was icy with disdain. 'My first opinion of you was correct and you are unfit to be his mother. The best place for Harry to be right now is in his nursery, safely asleep in his cot, and that is where I am going to take him.'

Elin beat her fists against the gates. She was crying so hard that she could barely speak. 'You seem to love Harry, but for how long will you love him?' she choked. 'When the novelty of fatherhood wears off will you lose interest in your child, the same as my adoptive father grew bored of me?'

She watched Cortez walk into the house and collapsed onto her knees in despair. Every ragged breath she dragged into her lungs hurt. 'If you take my son away from me you might as well cut my heart out,' she cried after him. 'He is all I have. *Please.*'

Violent rage coursed through Cortez. Elin should consider herself lucky that she was on the other side of the locked gates because if he could get his hands on her he'd be tempted to shake some sense into her.

But he would be tempted to do much more than shake her, he acknowledged with furious self-derision. Even though he had proof that she was an untrustworthy, deceitful bitch he still wanted her. She was a fever in his blood and a constant clamouring hunger in his gut. He thought about her all the time and there had been many nights in the past month when he'd resorted to using his hand to alleviate the throbbing ache of his arousal.

He resented the power she had over him. After Alandra he had assured himself that he would never allow a woman to affect him. But Elin had fooled him with her sweet smile, while all the time she had been plotting to steal his son. Ten years ago Alandra had told him that she did not want his baby and had ended her pregnancy. Sometimes when Cortez saw a child of roughly the same age as his child would have been he was still haunted by a deep sense of loss and regret. Now he had a son and he was fiercely determined that Elin would not deprive him of his right to be Harry's father.

In the nursery he carefully transferred Harry from the baby carrier to the cot. *'Te amo, mi hijo,'* he whispered as he leaned over the cot rail and kissed the baby's velvety soft cheek. Cortez hadn't known he could feel like this—so fiercely protective that he would kill anyone who tried to hurt his child. Harry needed his father, but he was not yet five months old and the inescapable truth was that he needed his mother too.

Cortez's jaw clenched when he walked over to the window that overlooked the driveway and saw Elin was where he had left her, slumped on her knees behind the locked gates. How long would she remain there? The answer felt like a punch in his gut. She would never abandon her son. Over and over again he had seen evidence of Elin's love for Harry. Her words echoed inside his head.

When the novelty of fatherhood wears off will you lose interest in your child, the same as my adoptive father grew bored of me?

Both he and Elin had suffered from Ralph Saunderson's failures as a father, Cortez brooded. Elin had not known her real parents, and although Ralph had adopted her and given her a home he had not given her the attention and love she had desperately needed. It was not hard to understand why Elin had trust issues. And he had not helped in that respect, Cortez acknowledged. *Dios*, he had taken her innocence and then turned his back on her. Cursing beneath his breath, he abruptly swung away from the window and took the device that operated the driveway gates from his pocket.

At first Elin couldn't understand what was happening when she suddenly fell forwards and landed on her face on the gravel driveway before she had a chance to put her hand out to save herself. The realisation that the gates had swung open sent relief flooding through her, and her legs trembled as she stumbled to her feet and ran towards the house. The front door was ajar and she tore across the hall and up the stairs to the nursery.

Her baby was fast asleep and blissfully unaware of the drama of the past half an hour. She clung to the side of the cot and forced herself to breathe deeply. Harry's long black lashes curled against his cheeks and his rosebud mouth was pursed in an adorable expression that brought more tears to Elin's eyes. If she had to crawl over broken glass to Cortez and plead with him not to seek custody of their son she would do whatever he demanded. She had better start by apologising, she thought ruefully.

His private suite was along the corridor. Her heart was thudding as she knocked on the door, and when there was no answer she cautiously stepped into the sitting room. Cortez wasn't there, nor in the adjoining master bedroom. Elin turned to leave, thinking he might be downstairs in his study. She froze when he emerged from the en suite bathroom.

He did not seem surprised to find her in his room and flicked his cold gaze over her while Elin stared at him uncertainly, waiting for him to speak. His simmering silence ratcheted up her tension, but the shameful longing that the sight of Cortez always evoked in her licked fiery heat through her body and pooled, hot and molten, *there,* between her thighs, where only he had ever touched her.

He was naked apart from the towel wrapped around his hips, and droplets of water clung to his black chest hairs. She visualised the photo of him on Sancha's phone and all her feelings of hurt and anger exploded.

'How dare you say I am unfit to be Harry's mother? *I* have never left him to go off and spend a night with a lover.'

He frowned. 'Neither have I.'

'You went to Madrid, supposedly on business, and stayed with Sancha at the apartment you bought for her. She showed me a photo of you, naked in bed at your love nest. Sancha is your mistress, isn't she?'

Cortez did not deny it, and Elin felt sick. He walked past her into the sitting room and opened his briefcase that was on the table, returning to the bedroom moments later and handing her a piece of paper.

'What is this?' she muttered.

'The hotel receipt for the night that I stayed in Madrid.' He shrugged, and Elin could not help but notice the way his powerful shoulder muscles rippled beneath his bronzed satin skin. 'Sancha and I were lovers for a brief time but I ended my affair with her three months before I went to Cuckmere Hall for Ralph's funeral. My property portfolio includes an apartment block in Madrid and Teresa García asked me if I would rent a flat to her sister when Sancha was looking for a place to live.'

Elin noted that the date on the receipt tallied with the night when Cortez had stayed away. 'You could still have visited Sancha at her apartment.' And had sex with her, she thought, but did not voice her suspicion.

'I happened to run into her at a restaurant where I was having lunch with a client, but that's all,' he said calmly. 'I crammed two days of meetings into one day and worked until late so that I could come home, rather than have to spend another night away from you and Harry.'

It was scary how desperately she wanted to believe him. 'Then why did Sancha say that the photo of you on her phone was taken three weeks ago?'

'To cause trouble and make you jealous, I imagine. I broke up with her because she made it plain that she hoped I would marry her.'

'I am not *jealous*,' Elin denied, flushing hotly. Cortez sounded so matter-of-fact that she found she believed him. Sancha must have been bitter that he had dumped her, and Elin knew she had been too ready to believe the Spanish woman's spite because she was unsure of her own relationship with Cortez.

'You threatened to fight for custody of Harry,' she said in a low voice. 'But I don't want us to be embroiled in a court battle over our son. You were right to say that he needs both his parents, and so I... I want to go ahead with our wedding tomorrow.' In fact they were due to marry later today, she realised when she glanced at the clock and saw it was almost one a.m.

Elin didn't know how she'd expected Cortez to react. Not with a loud cheer, obviously, but she'd thought he would say *something.* He flicked his dark gaze over her once more and his implacable expression caused her heart to jolt against her ribs.

'You'll have to do better than that if you want to convince me that I should make you my wife,' he finally drawled.

'I don't understand.' She was fascinated by the glittering gold flecks in his eyes.

'If I hadn't caught you trying to sneak out of La Casa Jazmín, you would have stolen my son,' he said harshly. Elin's heart sank as she realised that he was still furious with her. 'You need to give me a good reason why I should marry you.'

She stared at him and wished he would put some clothes on because the sight of his near naked body was making it difficult for her to think straight. 'I don't know how to convince you,' she said helplessly.

He strolled over to the bed and sat down on the edge of the mattress. Elin's eyes were drawn to the towel he wore that rode up his thighs and barely concealed the bulge of his arousal. Angry and aroused were a dangerous combination, and she swallowed when her eyes crashed with his and she saw the speculative gleam in his unforgiving gaze.

'You can start by proving to me that you will be an obedient wife. Get undressed,' he commanded softly.

She was outraged by his arrogance, but at the same time she could not control the searing heat that swept through her and made every nerve ending in her body quiver. The truth was that she had secretly yearned for him to make love to her ever since he had brought her to Spain. When they had been out in public together he had acted the role of a loving and attentive fiancé, but when they were alone he had not made any attempt to seduce her after she'd agreed to marry him. She had believed Sancha because Cortez was such a virile man and surely he must have wanted sex in the weeks that they had been at La Casa Jazmín.

She wanted sex too, but not like this, with resentment and mistrust simmering between them. She could tell him to go to hell and retain her pride but risk the very real likelihood of losing custody of her baby. It wasn't a risk Elin was prepared to take.

Before she had attempted her ill-thought-out escape plan she'd changed into clothes that would be comfortable for travelling in with a small baby in tow. But her jeans were difficult to peel off when her hands were trembling. She felt the blush that stained her cheeks spread all the way down to her toes as she tugged her T-shirt over her head while Cortez watched her with an intent look in his eyes that made her stomach muscles contract.

If she had hoped for a reprieve she was disappointed. 'Why have you stopped?' he growled. 'Your plain underwear does not send me wild with desire. *If* I decide to marry you I will expect you to wear lingerie that excites me, not bores me.'

Once again she controlled the urge to tell him to go to hell. Only now did she realise how much damage she had done by betraying Cortez's trust. But she was not going to allow him to humiliate her, Elin decided as she reached behind her and unclipped her bra. She lifted her chin and held his gaze as she slid the straps down her arms, allowing the bra to fall to the floor.

She felt a little spurt of feminine triumph when dull colour flared on his magnificent cheekbones, and she was glad that her body had regained its pre-pregnancy shape with the help of regular sessions in the gym. Her stomach was flat, and although she'd always wished that her breasts were bigger, they were firm, and she saw Cortez's eyes focus on the hard points of her nipples that jutted provocatively forwards.

But he did not move; he just sat there waiting for her to finish unveiling her body to him. Elin wished she was wearing a sexy thong instead of her distinctly unglamorous underwear. No doubt he was used to seeing his mistresses in silk and lace. Temper made her movements jerky as she tugged her knickers down her legs and stepped out of them. She pushed her long hair over her shoulder and stared right back at him.

'I was a pretty child,' she told him. 'When a news crew filmed a piece about abandoned children at the bomb-damaged orphanage in Sarajevo, they turned the cameras on me because I

was blonde and cute. I was lucky to be adopted by the Saundersons but there were many other children they could have chosen. Even at four years old I understood that I had been given
a chance in life because of the way I looked.'

Cortez said nothing and his hard-boned features gave no clue
to his thoughts. Elin felt a nervous flutter in the pit of her stomach when he lifted his hand and crooked his finger, beckoning
her to him. She wanted to refuse him but she reminded herself
that she wanted to keep her son. 'You only wanted my body,'
she said flatly. 'And after you'd had me you walked away and
did not give me another thought. You made me feel worthless.'

She caught her breath when he placed his hand on her stomach. His touch burned her and she knew he must have felt her
muscles contract as awareness of his smouldering sensuality
ripped through her.

'I wish I had seen you when your belly was swollen with our
child,' he finally said and his voice was deeper than she had
ever heard it, as if he felt as raw as she did. But that was impossible, Elin told herself. Cortez had demonstrated how unimport-
ant she was to him when he'd failed to contact her for a year.

'You *should* have been around when Harry was born and I
nearly died. I was terrified he would not have either of his parents,' she said thickly.

To her surprise he nodded. 'You're right; I should have been
there for both of you.'

Something in his voice made Elin believe that his remorse
was genuine and the tight bands around her heart loosened a
little.

He lifted his other hand and shaped the curve of her hips and
the indent of her waist before he moved his hands higher and
splayed his fingers over her ribcage, tantalisingly close to the
undersides of her breasts. She knew he could feel her erratic
heartbeat and at that moment she hated him for the ease with
which he could make her mindless with desire.

'Is there a purpose to this exercise?' she said grittily. 'Are you planning to throw me down on the bed and demonstrate your power over me by forcing me to have sex with you?'

He looked amused. 'Is that what you want me to do?'

'Of course not.' She silently cursed when she heard the huskiness in her voice. He was tying her in knots and he damned well knew it. Her stomach muscles clenched when he trailed his hand down her body and slid his fingers through the blonde curls at the junction between her thighs.

'Why did you try to run away with Harry?'

'I was worried you might grow bored of fatherhood and abandon him.' *Like you abandoned me.* The unspoken words hung in the air between them.

He shook his head. 'I don't believe you. I've told you how much I wished I had a father when I was growing up, and I will always love and protect my son.'

Cortez slipped his hand between her legs, and Elin caught her breath when he eased his finger inside her and discovered her molten heat. He gave a little tug of his hand to propel her forwards so that she was standing between his open legs.

'Our marriage cannot succeed without honesty. Tell me the truth, Elin.'

The truth! She gave a pained laugh and suddenly she was tired of fighting him, of fighting herself. 'The truth is that I'm scared of how you make me feel,' she muttered.

'How do I make you feel?' he demanded relentlessly. He eased a second finger inside her and moved his hand in a devastating dance that left her incapable of concentrating on anything but the blissful sensations he was creating.

She stared at his face, at his dark eyes flecked with gold and his beautiful mouth that could look stern or sensual depending on his mood. The smile that tugged the corners of his lips stole her heart and she had to remind herself that this was the man who had threatened to take her baby from her if she failed to persuade him to marry her.

'I told myself that the reason I slept with you at my birthday party was because I wasn't in control of my behaviour after my drink had been spiked with a date-rape drug. But the truth,' she whispered, 'is that I danced with many men that night and I didn't invite any of them into my bedroom. Only you. I saw you and you blew me away. But the next morning, when I woke and you had gone, I felt ashamed. When Virginia told me that her friend Tom had been charged with tampering with women's drinks, I pretended to myself that what had happened hadn't been my fault.'

She trembled as Cortez continued his erotic exploration of her body with his clever fingers. The way he was watching her intently while he pleasured her was shockingly intimate, and she closed her eyes as she moved against his hand.

'It was the same for me,' he growled. 'I took one look at you and I wanted you more than I'd wanted any other woman.'

Elin's eyelashes flew open and she gave him a startled look. 'In that case, why did you leave without waking me the next morning?'

'I was angry with myself. I'd read the tabloid stories about you and I couldn't understand why I had succumbed to your obvious charms. You were even more beautiful than the photos I'd seen of you, and you drove me out of my mind that night. But in the morning I was furious that you had made me lose control.'

Elin had seen evidence of how Cortez kept a tight control on his emotions and she could imagine he had felt horrified by what he would have regarded as his weakness.

'Is that why you have kept your distance from me?' She wanted nothing more than to surrender to the mastery of his wickedly inventive fingers, but she fought against the tide of pleasure that she could feel building low in her pelvis.

He gave a husky laugh as he swirled his fingers inside her and she trembled. 'I'm not keeping my distance from you now, *querida.*'

'Because you're trying to teach me a lesson,' she choked. 'You don't want me.'

Cortez moved so fast that Elin couldn't have said how she came to be lying flat on her back on the bed with him on top of her. He had whipped off the towel from around his hips and she could feel the rock-hard length of his arousal between her legs. 'Does this feel like I don't want you?' he demanded hoarsely. 'You needed time to adjust. I will always be Harry's father and I'm not going to abandon you or him, ever.'

Of course everything Cortez did was for his son, Elin reminded herself. But she was finding it impossible to think clearly when she was trapped beneath him. And she'd been wrong in one respect, because the evidence that he desired her was unmistakable.

'I thought...' she began.

'Don't think, just feel,' he muttered as he bent his head to her breast and flicked his tongue across her nipple. He drew the swollen peak into his mouth and sucked hard until she writhed beneath him and he moved across to her other breast to mete out the same devastating punishment.

Elin ran her fingers through his hair, as she had longed to do often over the past few weeks. It felt like warm silk against her skin and when she explored the sculpted shape of his face the rough stubble on his jaw scraped her palm. Cortez lifted his head and stared down at her, the flecks in his dark eyes gleaming pure gold before he claimed her mouth in a kiss that plundered her soul.

Could he believe Elin? Cortez asked himself. Or was her admission that she'd tried to leave him because of the way he made her feel a lie to persuade him not to seek custody of their son? She had told him she would do anything to keep her baby, and perhaps this was all a lie—the soft gasps she gave when he twisted his fingers inside her, and the way she arched her slender body beneath him when he tasted her cherry-red nipples. But he found that he didn't care. All he cared about was that Elin was beneath him, and he pressed himself into the sweet contours of her body so that her breasts were crushed against his chest and her smooth thighs offered a tempting haven for his painfully hard erection.

But he forced himself to wait and ignore his primal instinct to drive his shaft deep inside her. He could not forget that if he hadn't happened to go into his study earlier, she might be carrying Harry onto a plane bound for England now. She'd said she had changed her mind and had been about to return to the house, but he did not know if he believed her and he was even less sure that he could trust her.

He'd played on Elin's fear that he might seek legal custody of Harry and told her she would have to convince him to marry her. But in truth he would never try to separate mother and child, and *he* needed to persuade *her* that marriage was not only in their son's best interest, but it would be good for her too.

She was not interested in his money. *Dios*, she had turned down thirty-five million pounds without hesitation. No, his trump card was Elin's obvious desire for him, Cortez brooded. Sexual chemistry had simmered between them since he had brought her to La Casa Jazmín, and he could see a double advantage to seducing her with sex. He would use every skill he possessed as a lover to bind her to him so that she would never want to leave and take their son, and at the same time he would sate himself on her exquisite body until the damnable hold she had over him was broken.

He stretched out next to her on the bed and propped himself up on one elbow while he skimmed his other hand over her delectable curves and felt a tremor run through her when he cupped her breast. Her body betrayed her beautifully. Her nipples were flushed and damp from where he had sucked them, and the musky feminine fragrance of her desire stirred his senses when he nudged her thighs apart with his shoulders and placed his mouth over the delicate nub of her clitoris.

She gave a startled cry. 'You can't...'

'Oh, but I can,' he assured her softly and bent his head to

continue his task of exploring her with his tongue. He loved that she was shocked by the intimate caress and at the same time he was appalled by the fierce possessiveness he felt. She had told him she'd been a virgin when they had slept together at her birthday party, and he believed her despite the stories about her supposed torrid love-life reported in the tabloids. Her innocent delight in what he was doing to her was coupled with surprised gasps that could only be genuine.

'Cortez.' She breathed his name like a prayer, a plea, and her guttural voice told him what her body was already signalling to him as she bucked and writhed and sobbed beneath his merciless onslaught. He considered making her come with his mouth, but his own need was too great. He was shocked to realise that his control was slipping and his plan to enslave Elin with sex could go spectacularly wrong.

Somehow he held back long enough to slide a protective sheath over his erection, and then he thrust his way inside her and heard above the thunderous pounding of his heart the harsh groan he made when he sank into her velvet heat and discovered heaven. Somewhere along the path to nirvana the seducer had become the seduced and the slave master was now the slave. And the most astonishing thing was Cortez did not care that the point of making love to Elin was to trap her in his sensual web. He simply wanted to worship her and glory in the knowledge that she was his.

He set a rhythm and drove into her with steady strokes that quickly took them both to the edge. She filled up his senses with the fragrance of her skin when he pressed his lips to her throat, and the sweet taste of her lips when he kissed her mouth. He captured her cry as she suddenly arched beneath him and her body trembled like a slender bow under intolerable tension, seconds before she climaxed around him. And when he thrust deep into her for a final time and felt the unstoppable force of his own release thunder through him, she filled up his heart utterly and exclusively. *His.*

CHAPTER TEN

IT FELT AS if she were watching a replay of a bad film, Elin thought when she opened her eyes and discovered that her room was filled with bright sunshine and she was alone in bed. Just like the morning after her birthday party in London over a year ago, she ached *everywhere*. Erotic memories of Cortez's hands and mouth—dear God, his wicked mouth—caressing every inch of her body, flooded her mind, and pain filled her heart.

Last night they had made love endlessly in his big bed, until the sky outside the window had turned the palest pink as the sun edged above the horizon. She had fallen into an exhausted sleep in Cortez's arms but, although she had no recollection of him doing so, he must have carried her back to her bedroom before he'd left her—again.

Her heart leapt when the door opened, but plummeted when a maid entered the room. Rosa was followed by another housemaid, Maria, and the two girls were giggling as they carried a large flat box and deposited it on the bed.

'Your wedding dress,' Rosa told Elin in reply to her puzzled look. 'From Señor Ramos,' the maid added helpfully.

Elin hastily pulled her robe around her naked body that bore the marks of Cortez's lovemaking. The rough stubble on his jaw had grazed her breasts and her inner thighs. She determinedly shut off her wayward thoughts as she opened the box and lifted a dress out from the layers of tissue. It was an exquisitely simple sheath made of pure white silk, exactly the style of wedding dress she would have chosen if she'd been a real bride. But for her sham marriage to Cortez she had bought a pale blue skirt and jacket that could best be described as functional. Did he hope she would wear the unashamedly romantic dress?

Her heart was beating fast as she turned her attention to the other boxes the maids had brought to her room. One box contained a pair of pretty, strappy white shoes. She took the lid off another to reveal delicate lingerie as fine as gossamer. Maria opened the final box and held up a bouquet of white roses, each half-opened flower so perfect and pure that tears filled Elin's eyes.

Her phone rang and Cortez greeted her, his voice as dark and indulgent as the finest bittersweet chocolate. 'Good morning, *querida*. I don't want to panic you but we are due to get married in one hour.'

'I…' She broke off as she glanced down at her hand and saw her engagement ring that she had left in his study before she'd planned to leave La Casa Jazmín the previous night twinkling on her finger. 'When did you return my ring?'

'I slipped it back onto your finger before I left you to sleep for a couple of hours, having kept you awake for most of the night,' he said drily. 'It is meant to be bad luck for the bride and groom to see each other before the wedding.' He paused and then said softly, 'I would like the omens for our marriage to be good. The maids will help you to get ready, and the nanny is back from her trip and has taken charge of Harry.'

With a stab of guilt, Elin realised that she had not thought of her son until that moment. But when she hurried into the nursery Barbara shooed her back to her room after she'd given Harry a cuddle. There was just enough time for her to shower, blow-dry her hair and apply minimal make-up before the maids slipped the wedding dress over her head. It was a perfect fit, and the cool silk felt deliciously sensual against her skin.

She'd assumed Cortez would be waiting for her and they would travel to the Town Hall in Jerez together for the civil ceremony. But when she went downstairs she was met by the butler, who told her that Señor Ramos had already departed for the wedding venue and had taken Harry with him. Reality cast a shadow over Elin's excitement with the realisation that he did not trust her. Last night he had made love to her with passion coupled with unexpected tenderness that had given her hope for their relationship. But this morning his message was clear. He had laid claim to his son. Cortez would not force her to marry him, and it was her decision whether or not she met him at the Town Hall.

It was a stark choice. Marry a man who did not love her, or lose custody of her baby and be denied her chance to own a share of Saunderson's Wines. If the marriage failed she would at least have a means of supporting herself and Harry with the winery business. Her footsteps did not falter as she walked out of La Casa Jazmín and climbed into the car that was waiting to take her to her wedding.

She supposed Cortez had arranged for her to wear a wedding dress and carry a bouquet of flowers to convince the wedding guests that their marriage was real. But when she stepped out of the limousine and walked into the Town Hall he was waiting to escort her into the marriage room, and she noticed a nerve jump in his cheek that almost made her think he was as nervous as she was. He looked devastatingly handsome in a light grey suit and blue silk tie, and the expression in his eyes when he saw her made Elin's heart miss a beat.

'You look just as I imagined you would do in that dress,' he said huskily. 'Pure and innocent and incomparably beautiful.'

Some of her tension lifted and she dimpled at him. 'I'm not quite so innocent after last night, but I very much enjoyed being corrupted by you.' Amazing sex was a good start for their marriage, she thought prosaically, and perhaps in time Cortez would grow to care for her.

The gold flecks in his dark eyes gleamed. 'You say this to me now, moments before I will have to stand in front of the celebrant and our guests and pray they cannot tell that I have an erection as hard as a rock? I will take my retribution tonight, *querida*,' he warned her softly, sending a shiver of anticipation through her.

'I'm counting on it,' she murmured and hid a smile when he swore beneath his breath as he placed his arm possessively around her waist and led her towards the marriage celebrant.

It had been an unexpectedly joyous day, Elin thought much later, after she had made her vows in a voice that shook a little, and Cortez had made his in an oddly fierce tone that echoed the intent expression in his eyes when the celebrant had told him he could kiss his bride.

Harry was the centre of attention at the reception lunch which was held at La Casa Jazmín for the twenty or so wedding guests, who included Nic and Teresa García, but not Teresa's sister Sancha. The only thing that slightly marred Elin's happiness was the absence of her brother. Jarek had been adamant that he was too busy with his job at Saunderson's Bank in Japan to be able to take time off to attend the wedding, even though she had told him how much she wanted him to be there.

Elin hated the distance that had grown between them. She understood her brother's bitterness towards Ralph Saunderson's heir, and she was worried that Jarek believed she had betrayed him by marrying Cortez. The last few times she had phoned him, he had sounded as if he was drunk, and she feared he was sliding deeper into the dark place in his mind where she knew he was haunted by memories of the past.

She pushed her concerns about Jarek to the back of her mind as she watched Cortez proudly showing off his son. After Harry's birth, when she had haemorrhaged badly, her terrible fear had been that if she died, her baby would be placed in an orphanage. Now her son had his father and she knew that Cortez would be a million times a better father than Ralph Saunderson had been.

Harry's future was secure, and as for her own future—she looked over at her husband and found him watching her. The glint in Cortez's gaze made her wish they were alone so that he could make love to her. When she was in his arms his fierce passion made her forget that their marriage was a practical arrangement and she could pretend that he loved her as deeply as she now accepted that she loved him.

After lunch Cortez drove Elin, Harry and the nanny to the airport, where his private jet was waiting. 'If you had told me we were going abroad, I would have changed out of my wedding dress,' she muttered, feeling self-conscious when she had to walk through the busy airport terminal in her wedding gown.

'I have spent all day anticipating undressing my beautiful bride,' he drawled. 'Allow me to enjoy my fantasy for a few more hours until we reach our destination.'

He refused to tell Elin where they were heading, but by early evening, when the plane prepared to land at a small airport in West Sussex, she gave him a half hopeful, half disbelieving look. 'Are we going to spend our honeymoon at Cuckmere Hall? I thought you hated the house? You called it an ugly Gothic monstrosity.'

'I'm willing to re-evaluate my opinion of it, for your sake. I know how much you love the place.' He shrugged. 'I think perhaps I hated Cuckmere because it represented everything that Ralph had denied my mother. If she'd had an easier life maybe she would not have died far too young. Harry is Ralph's grandson and I have a responsibility to care for the estate and provide good leadership at the bank so that one day our son can take over from me. Which reminds me,' he added. 'Now we are married you will have to re-register Harry's birth so that I can be declared his natural father on the birth record.'

The infant heir to Cuckmere Hall seemed unimpressed when

the car drew up outside the house and Cortez carried his son into the house. Harry wanted to be fed and demonstrated his excellent lung capacity by yelling loudly until the nanny took him upstairs to the nursery. Meanwhile, Elin explored the familiar rooms that had been updated with a fresh décor by an interior designer company that Cortez had hired.

'I have resigned from my position as CEO of Hernandez Bank in Spain,' he told Elin. 'I've also appointed an operations manager to oversee Felipe & Cortez, to give me time to concentrate on running Saunderson's Bank. It means that we can alternate between living here at Cuckmere Hall and at La Casa Jazmín. When Harry is school age we'll decide then whether to make our home in England or Spain.'

The housekeeper had laid out a light supper for them in the conservatory overlooking the garden, and Baines served a vintage Saunderson's sparkling wine before he retired and left them alone.

'Home,' Elin said softly. 'Cuckmere represents safety,' she explained to Cortez. 'Before I was adopted and came to live here, I remember feeling scared when the orphanage was bombed. But at least I had Jarek to take care of me.' She sighed. 'My brother refuses to discuss the past. I wish he was able to talk about what happened when Sarajevo was attacked. He let slip once that he used to earn money by taking food to the Bosnian soldiers on the front line, and then he would buy food for the children who had been abandoned in the wreckage of the orphanage. I know he has nightmares about the things he saw when he was a boy, and also about when Mama was killed.'

'What exactly happened to Lorna Saunderson?'

'She was shot dead by an armed raider during a bungled robbery at a jewellers.' Elin's voice wobbled as memories of that devastating day flooded her mind. 'Jarek and I had taken Mama to choose a present for her birthday. The raider said in court that he hadn't meant to fire the gun, but he panicked and when the gun went off Mama was killed instantly. My brother blames himself for not saving her life. He can't accept that there was nothing he could have done.'

She bit her lip, wondering how much she could reveal to Cortez without betraying her brother. 'Jarek really struggled afterwards, and there was a period when he drank a little too much and spent more time than was good for him in casinos and nightclubs. His relationship with Ralph had always been difficult and it got a lot worse. I pretended to be an out of control party girl to distract the paparazzi's attention away from my brother because I was afraid Ralph might sack him from Saunderson's Bank.'

She took a sip of wine and felt a pang of sadness that Mama would never taste the wine produced from the vines she had planted. To her surprise, Cortez reached across the table and took her hand in his.

'I understand how much you must miss Lorna,' he said gently. 'After my mother died, my grief made me a little crazy for a while.'

She gave him a startled look. 'I can't imagine you ever losing control of your emotions.'

'I did once, and paid a heavy price for my weakness.' Cortez's voice was suddenly harsh and Elin sensed that he had revealed more about himself to her than he'd intended.

He took a sip from his glass. 'This is an excellent wine,' he said, making an obvious attempt to steer the conversation away from his personal life. 'By marrying me you have fulfilled the terms of Ralph's will and you own fifty per cent of Saunderson's Wines. I am keen to work in partnership with you to develop the winery. Do you want to tell me your plans for the business?'

'For a start, I'd like to expand the vineyard and plant another four or five hectares of vines.' Elin jumped up and walked to the door of the conservatory. 'Come with me and I'll show you what I'm thinking of. What's wrong?' she asked when he looked amused.

'I can't imagine many *vigneronnes* inspect their vines wearing a wedding dress.'

She shrugged. 'I could go and change, but I thought you have been fantasising about taking my dress off later.'

His eyes gleamed with wicked intent. 'Not a lot later,' he warned. 'I can't wait much longer to fulfil several of my fantasies, including the one where...' He bent his head close to her ear and whispered what he would like to do to her.

Elin's cheeks were still pink when she led Cortez across the garden. They walked through the Cuckmere estate to the vineyards that she had helped her adoptive mother to plant on the chalky slopes of the South Downs. The vines were covered in green leaves and clusters of grape berries which would continue to grow over the summer until the ripened fruit was harvested in September.

Now, in late May, the summer equinox was only a few weeks away and dusk fell late as the days lengthened. In the gloaming the white flowers on the hawthorn bushes looked like tiny stars and their perfume mingled with the sweet scent of wild honeysuckle. The air was soft and still, disturbed only by the bleating of the sheep that grazed on the Downs, and by Elin's voice as she outlined her vision for the estate winery.

She slipped her shoes off, enjoying the feel of the soft grass beneath her feet as she strolled with Cortez among the rows of vines. He listened intently to her ideas, occasionally asking a question or making a suggestion. When she finally ran out of breath and words, he smiled. 'I'm impressed by your enthusiasm to expand the business. We'll do it.'

'It will require significant financial investment,' she said cautiously. 'This is my dream, Cortez. Do you really believe we could make Saunderson's Wines into a major UK wine producer?'

'I believe in you,' he murmured. 'With your extensive knowledge of viticulture and your drive and determination, I don't see how you can fail.'

Elin was tempted to point out that growing grapes in England's unpredictable climate did not have the guaranteed success that Cortez was used to in the near-perfect conditions of dry, warm southern Spain. But she was overwhelmed by his confidence in her. After Mama had died, Ralph had lost all interest in the estate winery and had refused to take Elin's ideas for expanding the business seriously. But she was convinced that with Cortez's support Saunderson's Wines could produce a world-class wine.

She halted halfway along a row of vines and turned to face him. 'I like the idea of us working together in partnership. I was wondering whether you see yourself as a sleeping partner, or if you will take an active role?' she said innocently.

His soft growl of laughter curled around her and desire coiled tight and urgent in her belly as he slid his hand beneath the weight of her hair and drew her towards him. 'I envisage that my participation will be *very* active,' he told her. His warm breath grazed her lips before he claimed her mouth and kissed her with a fierce hunger that made her melt against him. 'Naturally, I will welcome any input you might like to make to our partnership.'

'Is this the sort of input you mean?' she whispered, dipping her tongue into his mouth.

'Exactly like that, *querida*.' Cortez's tone was no longer teasing, but raw with sexual need. Elin ran her hands over his chest and felt the erratic thud of his heart. She continued her exploration and brushed her fingers along the hard ridge of his arousal she could feel beneath his trousers, making him groan.

It thrilled her to know that she did this to him. She undid his zip and he muttered something in Spanish, but he did not try to stop her when she freed his thickened length from his clothes and stretched her hand around him. Steel encased in velvet. So powerful and yet so sensitive, she discovered when she gripped him harder and he shuddered.

She had been afraid that Cortez might try to undermine her

once she was his wife, but instead he had brought her back to the home she loved and offered her a business partnership. Now it was her turn to prove that she wanted to be an equal partner in all areas of their relationship, Elin thought as she knelt in front of him. She did not have the courage to tell him she loved him, but she could show him.

If this was a dream, Cortez never wanted to wake up. The moon had risen in the night sky, and it cast a silvery gleam over Elin's upturned face as she sank gracefully to her knees before him and rested her cheek on his thigh. Her long hair poured like a golden river down her back and felt like silk against his fingers when he placed his hand at the back of her head. He couldn't believe she actually intended to fulfil his hottest fantasy. Just the sight of her in her white silk dress that became semi-transparent in the moonlight was better than any erotic dream he'd had about her—and he'd had plenty.

She flicked her tongue over his swollen tip and he rocked back on his heels while his heart tried to claw its way out of his chest. *Dios*, this must be a dream and he would rather die than wake up before it reached its climax.

'Elin,' he growled, trying to fight his longing for her to lick him again. He swallowed convulsively and ordered himself to take control of the situation. After Alandra he had promised himself that he would never give a woman power over him. But here he was, in the most vulnerable position a man could be, at Elin's mercy, and the mercy of her tongue that she was using with such devastating effect.

She lifted her head away from him and he did not know whether to be relieved or disappointed. She looked like an angel kneeling there, and her soft smile shattered his resolve to end this madness. Maybe it was a dream, he consoled himself when she closed her lips around his shaft and her hair fell around her face like a golden veil.

The feel of her mouth on him drove him to the edge of reason. But, more than his physical response to her, he was moved by her generosity and eagerness to please him after he had blackmailed her to marry him by threatening to seek custody of their son. He hoped their marriage would be a true partnership and what he wanted more than anything was to make love to his wife.

He drew her to her feet and kissed her mouth, slow and sweet beneath the stars and the silver moon. She kissed him back with that generosity of hers that made him ache right down to his soul. If this was a dream, he never wanted it to end, he thought as he finally did what he had dreamed of doing all day and slid the white silk wedding dress over her shoulders to reveal her slender body. He removed the wisps of silk and lace lingerie and bared her small, perfect breasts with their rosy tips.

The dew-damp grass was cool on his back when he lay down and held her against his chest. He heard her catch her breath when he guided her down onto him, and she paused for a moment while her body adjusted to the thrust of his hard length inside her. He wrapped his hands in her hair and kissed her rose-tipped breasts as she moved above him—a pale nymph, ethereal and lovely in the moonlight. And when they soared to the stars together and she cried out his name, he dared to believe that the dream would last for ever.

He should have known dreams were ephemeral. Reality caught up with Cortez four weeks later, and it started with an earthquake in Japan.

CHAPTER ELEVEN

'ARE WE STILL on our honeymoon, or is this real life?' Elin asked Cortez one morning, midway through the fourth week of their marriage.

He placed the tray he had carried up to their room on the bedside table and sat down on the bed, bending his head to kiss her. It was a long kiss and Elin was breathless when he finally, and with obvious reluctance, lifted his mouth from hers. 'Does there have to be a difference?' he murmured.

The aroma of freshly brewed coffee rose from the cafetière. Elin picked up the pale pink rose that was lying on the tray and inhaled its sensual fragrance. 'I only ask because you have brought me a rose from the garden every morning since we came to Cuckmere Hall. I've decided that I like being married,' she confessed, feeling inexplicably shy. Inexplicable, because he knew every centimetre of her body and had revealed a sensual side to her nature that delighted both of them.

Being married to Cortez was nothing short of wonderful. Bringing her a rose every day was just one of so many ways he made her feel cherished. Their relationship might have had a rocky start, but these past weeks had been the happiest of her life and it was hard to remember that theirs was a marriage of convenience to allow them to both be full-time parents to their son.

Maybe the reason why they had married didn't matter, Elin mused. She felt that she and Cortez were growing closer every day. She loved spending time with him and Harry as a family, but she also loved the times when they were alone together, working in the vineyard and winery, chatting over dinner or relaxing in the evening and watching a film before they went to bed. She especially loved being in bed with him and they could lose themselves in their private world of passion that was stronger than ever.

'Tell me what in particular you like about our marriage,' he said in his molten chocolate voice that she found as irresistible as the rest of him. She cupped his face in her hands and whispered in his ear all the things she liked him to do to her, and all the things that she liked doing to him.

'You have a wicked mind, Señora Ramos,' he growled. 'Hold on to the thought about the whipped cream until I come home.'

Elin finally registered the fact that he was dressed in a suit instead of jeans and a polo shirt that she'd grown used to seeing him wearing at Cuckmere.

'I need to go to work occasionally,' he said, kissing away her frown. 'I'll stay up in London for the rest of the week. I haven't been as involved at Saunderson's Bank as I should have been because you are a dangerous distraction. Fortunately, the bank has a good management team, but Andrew Fowler, the COO, called me early this morning and requested an urgent meeting at the London head office.'

'Is there a problem at the bank?'

'Andrew didn't say much.' It was Cortez's turn to frown. 'Your brother seems to have gone AWOL from the Japanese office again. Have you spoken to Jarek recently?'

Elin shook her head. 'I haven't heard from him since before our wedding.' She unconsciously chewed on her lower lip. 'It's unusual for him not to call me, and he hasn't responded to any of my calls or text messages. I'm worried about him,' she admitted.

'Hey,' he said softly, 'I'm sure your brother is fine.' Cortez slid his hand beneath her chin and tilted her face up to his. He dropped a light kiss on the tip of her nose before taking his phone from his jacket pocket.

'In answer to your question of whether we are still on our honeymoon. The answer is yes, and this is where we will spend the next two weeks.' A picture of a French château came onto his phone screen. 'Château Giraud is in the Dordogne region of France and has well established vineyards and a winery. I thought we could explore the ancient caves nearby, and the heated pool in the château's grounds will be perfect to introduce Harry to swimming.'

He stood up and walked across the room to the bureau. 'I'd actually arranged a couple of meetings at the bank before Andrew Fowler called me. Knowing that I would be in London, I made an appointment at the passport office to get a replacement passport for Harry under his new name. I'll need to take our marriage certificate and his birth certificate with me.'

Cortez lifted a document out of a drawer in the bureau and frowned as he looked at it. 'You said you would re-register Harry's birth and name me as his natural father on the birth record, as the law requires. But this is his original birth certificate, which states that his name is Saunderson and does not include my details.'

Elin sat up and pushed her hair out of her eyes. The accusatory tone of Cortez's voice made her flush guiltily. 'I forgot all about it,' she admitted. 'I meant to download the necessary form and take it to the register office, but it completely slipped my mind.'

'Are you sure that is the reason?' Cortez stood at the foot of the bed and subjected her to a hard stare that made her feel like a naughty child.'

'Of course.' She heard the defensive note in her voice. 'What other reason do you think there could be?'

His dark eyes bored into her, cold and hard without the golden flecks that usually gleamed with warmth. 'You know it is important to me that I am recognised as Harry's father on a legal document. Only you can re-register his birth to include my details. But maybe it suits you if I am not named as his father on the birth record,' he suggested tersely.

'I'm human and I forget things occasionally,' Elin snapped, her temper stirring in response to Cortez's clipped voice. But she felt uncomfortable as she acknowledged there was a grain of truth in what he had said. She hadn't got round to changing the details on Harry's birth certificate because subconsciously she'd thought that if her marriage to Cortez failed she would automatically be granted custody of her son.

She glanced at the rose that Cortez had brought from the garden for her and her guilty feeling intensified. 'I'll sort out the paperwork to have your name added to Harry's birth record today,' she promised.

He nodded but although he returned her smile the expression in his eyes was still guarded. Elin sensed his tension when she knelt up on the bed and placed her hands on his shoulders so that she could cover his mouth with hers. The incident made her realise that the contentment they had both discovered in their marriage was fragile.

She missed him as soon as she heard his car roar away down the drive. Trust needed to be on both sides, she acknowledged. Cortez had shown her over the past weeks since their wedding that she could trust him. Why, he had even brought her to Cuckmere Hall, which he had once described as a Gothic monstrosity.

The argument was the first time that they had fallen out during their marriage, and it was her fault, Elin thought dismally. She was determined to make it up to him, and when Harry had settled down for his afternoon nap she switched on the computer in Cortez's study and filled out an online form, and then made an appointment at the local register office to arrange for both of Harry's parents' details to be included on his birth certificate.

Her phone rang and relief swept through her when she heard her brother's voice. 'I've been trying to contact you ever since you missed my wedding,' she told him. 'Where are you? Cortez said you haven't been seen at the Japanese office for a few days.'

'I'm not in Japan… I'm in London. Elin…' Jarek sounded tense '…have you heard about the earthquake in Japan?'

'Oh, my God! I haven't seen any news reports today. Are you all right?'

'I'm fine. I actually flew back to London two days ago, so I wasn't affected by the earthquake. At least, not physically.'

Something about her brother's tone made Elin uneasy. 'What do you mean?'

'I can't explain now. Is Cortez there? I need to speak to him.'

'He went to Saunderson's Bank in London this morning. The COO asked to see him urgently. Jarek, what has happened?' she asked worriedly when her brother swore. 'Are you in some kind of trouble?'

'That's one way of putting it.' His tone was grim.

'Why can't you tell me? We have always confided in each other.' It hurt her to realise that a chasm had opened up between her and her brother since she had married Cortez. When they were children in Sarajevo Jarek had risked his life for her many times, and she owed him her loyalty.

'You can't help me, *ijubljen*,' Jarek said flatly. His use of the Bosnian endearment that he had often used when she was a little girl tugged on Elin's emotions.

'I'll support you, no matter what the problem is,' she assured him fiercely. 'Are you at your apartment? I'll come now.' She remembered that the nanny was away visiting relatives. 'I'll put Harry in the car and drive up to town to meet you. Cortez is going to be in London for a couple of days and he doesn't need to know that I've spoken to you.'

She heard a sound behind her and glanced across the room. Her heart missed a beat when she saw Cortez standing in the doorway, and she wondered if he had realised that she was talking to her brother. 'I have to go,' she muttered to Jarek before quickly ending the call.

'I didn't expect you back so soon.' She smiled at Cortez but his expression was unreadable.

'Evidently.' He stepped into the study and closed the door behind him. 'I take it that was Jarek you were speaking to?'

'I…yes.' Elin realised there was no point denying it.

His lip curled cynically. 'How curious that your brother, who you told me you hadn't heard from for weeks, was in contact with you once I had left Cuckmere Hall.' A nerve jumped in his cheek. 'I heard you say that you are going to meet Jarek and take Harry with you.' He stalked towards her, his dark eyes glinting with fury that made Elin back away from him. 'Over my dead body,' he snarled. 'I won't allow you to take my son from me.'

'I wasn't…' she began.

He cut off the rest of her words with a bitter laugh. 'Even now you look and sound like an innocent angel, and it proves that I am a fool for wanting to believe in you. 'Tell me, *querida*—' he made the endearment sound like a curse '—were you planning to help your brother escape abroad? The three of you would disappear some place where I couldn't find you? It makes sense now why you did not include me on Harry's birth certificate or change the details on his passport.'

'I told you I simply forgot to add your name on his birth record,' she insisted, but Cortez ignored her.

'I rushed back here when I heard news reports of an earthquake in Japan. No one had been able to get hold of your brother, and I guessed you would be worried about him. But you must have known he had returned to England, just as you knew all along what he was doing at the bank in Japan.'

'You're not making any sense.' Elin's spine was jammed against the desk, but when she tried to step around Cortez he grabbed hold of her wrist. 'Ow! You're hurting me. Why would Jarek need to escape abroad?'

'*Dios!* Stop pretending you don't know what your brother has been doing for the last few months.' His explosion of temper made Elin flinch. 'You are in Jarek's confidence and you must have been aware of his irregular trading practices at Saunderson's Bank. Technically, he did not do anything illegal, but he took unacceptable risks with the bank's funds by using his position as a derivatives broker to speculate on the future direction of the Japanese markets.'

Cortez raked his hair off his brow and glared at Elin. 'A few months ago Jarek's unhedged losses began to accumulate, but he might still have pulled off his gamble if there hadn't been a large earthquake in Japan this morning. The effect on the Asian financial markets was catastrophic and, as a safeguard, trading on the Nikkei was temporarily stopped. The value of Jarek's investments plummeted. So far he has lost Saunderson's Bank one hundred million pounds and the situation is likely to get worse over the next few days.'

Elin swallowed. No wonder Jarek had sounded strained on the phone.

'If I had been more involved at the bank these past weeks I might have noticed discrepancies in Jarek's daily trading reports. But you cleverly held my attention here at Cuckmere,' Cortez said bitterly. He let go of her wrist as if he could not bear to touch her. 'You used all your feminine wiles to keep me hooked on you and distract my attention away from what your brother was up to.'

She felt sick when she realised he was deadly serious. 'I don't have any feminine wiles,' she said shakily.

He gave another mirthless laugh that sliced through her heart like a rapier. 'You went down on your knees in front of me and gifted me such sweet pleasure that you made me think...' He broke off and stared at her with bitter contempt. There was no flicker of emotion on his granite-hard face as he watched her tears slide down her cheeks.

'I swear I had no idea what my brother was doing, and I certainly did not make love to you with an ulterior motive. I don't know how you could believe I would do that,' Elin choked. She was devastated by Cortez's accusations and horrified by what her brother had done. But she was not only agonisingly hurt, she was as angry as hell.

'We seem to have come full circle,' she told Cortez bitterly. 'On the day of Ralph's funeral you refused to believe that Harry was your son. And you accused me of being a drug-user without any real evidence. I thought I had finally earned your trust but you are still determined to think the worst of me. I can only repeat that I did not know about Jarek's risky trading strategy at the bank.'

'Do you deny that you were planning to take Harry and go and meet your brother?'

'No... I don't deny it. I wanted to find out what was wrong with Jarek. I was going to take Harry with me because Barbara is on annual leave, but I would have returned to Cuckmere Hall. I have already emailed the form to effect the changes to Harry's birth record and include you as his father. You can check my email account if you don't believe me,' she said, pointing to the computer. But Cortez swung away from her and strode over to the door.

'I don't believe a word in your pretty, lying head,' he said savagely. 'Years ago I was denied my child by a woman who lied to me repeatedly, and I swore I would never be so stupid to trust any woman again. I almost broke my vow with you, Elin, but I won't be a fool again.'

She was stunned by his revelation about his past and only when she heard a door slam shut did she run out into the hall. By the time she had opened the front door Cortez was climbing into his car. 'Where are you going?'

'To deal with your brother,' he replied ominously. 'Don't even think of leaving Cuckmere and taking Harry because I swear I will find you—and you'll wish I hadn't.'

He fired the engine and as the car began to roll down the drive Elin ran alongside it, clinging on to the open window. 'I don't know what Jarek has done but I'm sure there will be an explanation. He hasn't been in a good place since Mama died, and I admit I should have told you about his issues,' she panted as she tried to keep up with the moving car. 'Why would I plan to go away with my brother when you have given me everything I could possibly want?'

'I forced you into marriage by threatening to try and take your baby away from you.' There was a hollowness in Cortez's voice that made her heart ache.

'I don't remember you dragging me to our wedding. I chose to marry you, not because of Harry, or because it allowed me to claim my inheritance...'

They had almost reached the bottom of the driveway and Elin's hand fell away from the car.

'What possible other reason could you have for marrying me?' he demanded.

Nothing but her complete honesty would do, and she was afraid she had left it too late. *'I love you.'*

The car came to an abrupt halt and he stared at her for what seemed like eternity before his mouth twisted in a cynical smile. 'That is the biggest lie of all,' he said harshly before he accelerated away so fast that the tyres screeched.

Cortez was glad that the traffic heading into London was busy because it meant he had to concentrate on driving and not allow his thoughts to stray to Elin. A pack of reporters were gathered outside Saunderson's Bank's headquarters. The news of huge financial losses to the bank and speculation about the future of Saunderson's was already in the media. He gave a short statement which contained few facts, but most journalists did not care about facts and no doubt the papers tomorrow would carry dramatic headlines about the bank that bore little in the way of truth, he thought sardonically.

Truth and lies. Right from the start, his opinion of Elin had been formed by what he had read about her in the tabloids. But she had proved over and over again that she was nothing like the selfish, self-absorbed It Girl she was portrayed by the paparazzi. He had accused her of lying to him—but what if he had misjudged her *again*?

He chaired a crisis meeting with the board and put out a statement to the shareholders that all steps were being taken to limit the damage to Saunderson's Bank. But, although he was facing the greatest professional crisis of his career, Cortez realised that he didn't give a damn about anything but Elin and the abominable way he had treated her. How the hell could she love him? he asked himself grimly. Surely she must have lied about that.

When his office door opened he thought it probable that the only person who looked more haggard than he did was Elin's brother. He had planned exactly what he would say to Jarek before he sacked him and called Security to escort him from Saunderson's Bank. But Cortez had finally got his priorities in order.

'Elin explained that she suffered a near fatal blood loss after giving birth, and while she was in Intensive Care you stayed with Harry and refused to leave him.' He swallowed hard as he acknowledged his guilt that he should have been with Elin throughout her pregnancy and their son's birth. He could never forgive himself for abandoning her. 'I am in your debt,' he told Jarek, 'for being there for my son and for Elin.'

A flicker of surprise and grudging respect flared in Jarek's ice-blue eyes that rarely showed any emotion. 'My sister means the world to me,' he said curtly. 'She had nothing to do with the bloody mess I've caused. If she'd had any clue about the financial risks I was taking at the bank she would have tried to persuade me to tell you. Elin is the most honest, loyal person in the world.'

It was what Cortez had been afraid of. He had chosen to believe the worst about Elin because then he could assure himself that all he felt for her was sexual attraction. Her brother had confirmed what he had known deep down for a long time, and the realisation that he was a coward made him feel even worse about himself, if that were possible.

He looked intently at his brother-in-law. 'The only reason I'm prepared to give you a second chance is because Elin adores you. What are you going to do about the goddamned mess you've created at the bank?'

'I give you my word that I'll sort the problem out,' Jarek said with his trademark cool arrogance. 'I'll repay the bank every penny of the money I lost.'

'No more taking risks.'

'I can't promise that.' Elin's brother pushed his long dirty-blond hair out of his eyes. 'Sometimes risk is necessary if you want to reap the richest reward.'

There was only one reward he wanted, Cortez thought with sudden, blinding insight. He was prepared to risk everything he owned, including his heart, for a chance of a lifetime of happiness.

He shot to his feet so fast that Jarek looked startled. 'I too have something to sort out,' Cortez said gruffly. 'I only hope I haven't left it too late.'

It was raining. Hard. The heatwave had come to an abrupt end with a violent thunderstorm, and Elin, who had been in the vineyard without a jacket, was drenched. She could have run back to the house to get out of the rain, but she simply did not have the energy and she trudged up the driveway with her head bowed against the downpour.

The previous afternoon she'd watched Cortez drive away from Cuckmere Hall. She'd felt furious that he had accused her unjustly *again*, and she'd lugged her clothes out of the master suite that she'd shared with him, back to her old bedroom. She had ordered herself not to cry. Surely she'd shed enough tears over a man who had proved time and again that he had a heart of stone. She'd definitely wasted enough time loving a man who would never return her love.

But, lying in her lonely bed, memories had crept into her mind of Cortez greeting her every morning with a rose he had picked from the garden, and she'd wept so hard that her heart might have broken if it hasn't already been shattered into a million pieces.

'Was it all a dream?' she'd asked Harry when she'd scooped him out of his cot this morning and his cheery smile had brought more tears to her eyes. Had the past weeks of blissfully happy marriage to Cortez been in her imagination? He'd made love to her with exquisite passion every night, but maybe for him it had only ever been sex, she thought bleakly. Without trust, passion was meaningless, a cruel parody of the marriage she yearned for.

She walked into the house and hurried upstairs to her old room to change out of her wet clothes. But, to her shock, she found the wardrobe empty. As she stared at the empty rails in disbelief, a gravelly voice came from behind her.

'I took the liberty of moving your things back to our bedroom.'

Elin spun round, and the sight of Cortez leaning nonchalantly against the doorframe released her from the terrible lethargy that had dulled her spirit and set her temper alight. It did not help that he looked as gorgeous as he always did in black jeans and a shirt, while the mirror over the dressing table revealed that she resembled a drowned rat.

'You have taken too many liberties,' she said in a hard voice, because pride was all she had left. 'I don't want to do this any more, Cortez.' It was the truth, she thought wearily. Loving him was destroying her.

He moved then, and as he came closer she was shocked by his grim expression. The gold flecks in his eyes were dulled and his skin was drawn tight over his slashing cheekbones so that he looked austere and beautiful, as if he'd spent the past twenty-four hours in hell, she realised with a jolt.

'Elin, I'm sorry,' he said roughly.

She closed her eyes to blot out his haggard face that made a fool of her because it gave her hope that he cared after all.

'I'm sorry too,' she whispered. 'For ever thinking that our crazy marriage could work.'

He flinched. 'It can work. It *did* work, until I screwed up.'

She shivered as the cold from her wet clothes seeped down to her bones, and heard him swear.

'You need a hot shower.'

'I'll have one when you've gone.' She gave a startled cry when he lifted her off her feet.

'Don't you get it? I'm not going anywhere, *querida*,' he told her fiercely as he carried her down the corridor to the master suite and strode straight into the bathroom. Elin tried to push his hands away when he set her on her feet and began to peel her sodden T-shirt over her head. But her body was trembling from the sweet pleasure of being in close proximity to him, and she did not have the strength of will to fight him when he tugged off her jeans and unfastened her bra. The hard peaks of her nipples betrayed her and she could not look at him, certain she would see mockery stamped on his hard features.

'How can you not know that I love you?' he said in an unsteady voice that *ached* with emotion.

Elin's eyes flew to his face and she felt her heart slam into her ribs when she saw the fierce intensity in his gaze. But she was afraid to believe.

'Don't make a joke of me,' she choked, hating the wretched tears that filled her eyes and clogged her throat. 'You drove away and left me.' She swallowed as he placed his thumb pads beneath her eyes and gently, oh, so gently wiped away the betraying moisture from her cheeks.

'Ah, Elin, *mi amor*,' he said huskily. 'How can you not know that I adore you, my innocent angel, *mi corazón*, when I told you every time I made love to you? With every kiss of my lips on yours and every caress with my hands and mouth I worshipped your body.'

She shook her head. 'That's just sex.' Her voice broke. 'You don't trust me.'

'I trust you with my life.' He turned on the shower taps, scooped her up and stood her beneath the spray, before he stripped off his clothes and joined her in the cubicle. Elin put her hand out to ward him off, but she had never been able to resist him, she thought with a flash of despair when he tugged her against him and held her so tight she could feel his heart-beat echo the pounding of hers.

'Tell me, my angel,' he said against her lips. 'Is this sex or love?' He kissed her mouth, her throat and paid homage to her breasts before he dropped to his knees and hooked her leg over his shoulder so that he could bestow the most intimate caress of all, while she sank against the shower wall and fell apart utterly with each stroke of his tongue.

He held her upright when her legs would have buckled with the intensity of her orgasm. And afterwards he soaped every inch of her body and washed her hair, gently kneading his fingers into her skull so that a simple hair-wash became erotic foreplay. He dried her with a soft towel and carried her through to the bedroom. When he laid her on the bed as if she was infinitely precious, Elin reached for him, needing him inside her as much as she needed to breathe oxygen.

But he lifted her hands from him and swiftly kissed her to reassure her when he saw the betraying wobble of her mouth.

'My mother never got over her bitterness that my father had abandoned both of us before I was born,' he said sombrely. 'I grew up believing that trust was a fool's game. I was a hot-headed teenager and I frequently sought to defend my mother's honour with my fists. When another boy called my mother a whore, I went too far and one of my punches put him in hospital. I might have killed him, and rightly I would have spent the rest of my life in prison. Fortunately he recovered, but I'd learned that I must suppress my emotions and rely on my brain to secure a better life for my mother and myself.'

He stretched out beside her on the bed and drew her close so that her cheek was resting on his shoulder. 'My mother died the year I graduated from university and I moved to Madrid to work for Hernandez Bank. I was young, naïve—' he shrugged '—still grieving for the only person who had ever loved me. Whatever the reason, I fell hard for Alandra.'

Elin moved restively and he stroked her hair back from her face with a tenderness that made her tremble anew.

'When I discovered that Alandra had conceived my baby I wanted to marry her, but she told me she was engaged to a man who was richer than I was ever likely to be. I pleaded with her, and eventually she agreed to continue with the pregnancy and to be my wife.' His face darkened. 'I believed her when she said she was going home to break the news to her parents. Three days later she called me from Toronto. Her visa had come through, and she informed me that she had got rid of the baby before flying out to join her fiancé.'

'Oh, Cortez,' Elin said softly. 'No wonder you were so angry when you caught me trying to drive away from La Casa Jazmín with Harry. I swear I had decided not to leave because I knew you loved him and I couldn't take him away from you.'

'I was angrier with myself. I'd done everything wrong with you. It's no defence but, a month before I met you, Alandra turned up at my office. I hadn't seen her for ten years. She told me that the guy she'd married hadn't made as much money as she'd hoped, while I had become a millionaire. She had left her husband and she suggested we could get back together. She would even have my child if I was still "hooked on fatherhood"—her words, not mine,' he said grimly. 'Needless to say, I turned down her offer, but the episode made me wonder why I'd been so stupid to fall in love with her, and I was determined never to allow another woman to have power over me.'

He slid a finger beneath Elin's chin and tipped her face towards his. 'After Alandra, I vowed that I would never give my trust so easily again. But I took one look at you and I was lost. I didn't want to fall in love with you,' he said rawly. 'It was convenient to believe the stories in the tabloids and convince

myself that you could not have been as innocent as my heart insisted you were.'

Cortez lifted himself on top of her and trapped her gaze with his, and the wealth of emotion, of *love* reflected in his eyes caused Elin to catch her breath. 'When I found out that Harry was mine, I was overwhelmed with guilt that I had abandoned you, like Ralph Saunderson abandoned my mother. I didn't know how you could forgive me, let alone love me,' he said roughly.

In that instant everything that had seemed so complicated and hopeless became blindingly simple. So simple that Elin wondered how it had taken them so long to realise what had happened on her birthday night over a year ago. Some people said that love at first sight couldn't happen, but she knew for certain it could. It had. For both of them.

'There is nothing to forgive,' she said softly. 'You are a wonderful father to Harry and everything you have done has been for him.'

'That's not quite true, *querida*. I coerced and threatened you into marrying me because you are the only woman I will ever love.' Cortez swallowed convulsively and Elin blinked back her tears when she saw the betraying glitter in his eyes. 'Do you love me?' he muttered, revealing a vulnerability that made her love him all the more.

'With all my heart. I will love you for ever.' Taking him by surprise, she pushed him onto his back and straddled him, loving the way his eyes gleamed with golden flames when he guided her down onto his erection. 'Is this love or sex?' she whispered against his mouth.

'Ask me again after a lifetime,' he murmured. 'I want to share love and laughter, friendship and trust with you for the rest of our lives, my angel.'

And Elin thought the future sounded blissful.

* * * * *

Keep reading for an excerpt of
Twilight At Wild Springs
by Delores Fossen.
Find it in the
Twilight At Wild Springs anthology,
out now!

CHAPTER ONE

LILY PARKMAN HIT the brakes when she turned into her driveway and spotted Sherlock Holmes and the *Hunger Games*' Katniss Everdeen in her front yard. Well, they were people dressed like those characters, anyway.

And Sherlock and Katniss weren't alone.

There were at least two dozen other people milling around the yard as if such milling around in that particular area was perfectly normal. It wasn't.

"What the heck?" Lily muttered, automatically going with the milder profanity that she'd trained herself to use because her fourteen-year-old daughter, Hayden, was seated right next to her in the truck. But there were some much harsher curse words going through Lily's head.

Some mountain-sized questions, too.

Despite the clothes and getups, Lily recognized every single one of the folks doing the milling around. Not hard to do since she'd lived her entire life in Last Ride, Texas, and knew all the residents. However, to the best of her knowledge, many of these folks had never paid a visit to her Wild Springs Ranch.

"What's going on?" Hayden asked.

Lily thumbed back through her memory to recall if today was her birthday and if this was some sort of surprise party. An unwanted one. But her birthday was months off. Ditto for Hayden's. And months off, too, for her ranch foreman, Jonas Buchanan, and his stepson, Eli, who lived on the ranch grounds just a quarter of a mile from her own house.

Nope. No birthdays. No anniversaries. So, either she'd won the lottery, unknowingly become a celebrity or... Lily stopped and mentally thumbed back through another date.

Since it was the first of August and just past 7:00 p.m., this crowd could have something to do with the Last Ride Society—aka a group of her Parkman kin who had way too much time on their hands, more time than she did, anyway. But many of her kin would say the Last Ride Society was the ultimate tribute to their ancestor and town founder, Hezzie Parkman.

Lily knew the spiel as well as the faces of those in her yard and on her porch. Hezzie had formed the Last Ride Society before her death in 1950 as a way for her descendants to preserve the area's history. The woman hoped to accomplish that by having a quarterly drawing so that a Parkman would then in turn draw the name of a local tombstone to research. Research that required the Parkman who'd drawn the name to dig into the deceased person's history, take a photo of the tombstone and write a report for all the town to read.

The date fit for the Last Ride Society meeting since the quarterly drawing was done on the first of the months of February, May, August and November. The timing fit, too,

since the drawing was usually done around 6:00 p.m. So, maybe her guests were all there to tell her that she was this quarter's drawer and to give her the name of the drawee since Lily hadn't attended the meeting.

Her stomach tightened.

Oh, heck. She hoped she hadn't drawn Maddie Buchanan's name. The woman had been married to Jonas and had died two years earlier from cancer. He was still grieving for her, and researching Maddie would only take jabs at that grief.

At least the name couldn't be one that would jab at her own grief. Griff Buchanan. He'd died years ago and had not only been Jonas's brother, but he'd also been the love of Lily's life.

Well, maybe he had been.

Since Griff had died when they were teenagers, maybe that love would have faded by now. Still, Lily wouldn't have to take that particular trip down memory lane because her own twin sister, Nola, had drawn Griff's name a year ago, and those jabs of grief had had some time to fade.

Lily took her foot off the brake and inched closer to the house. The sound of her approaching truck obviously got the attention of, well, everyone since they all stopped milling around and turned in her direction. Some of them cheered, and others came rushing toward her.

Crap.

This couldn't be good. Now that she'd gotten a better look at the expressions of her visitors, Lily could see the downright giddiness coming off them in gleeful waves. She saw something else, too. Glancing in her rearview mirror, she spotted her sisters, Nola and Lorelei, pull up in Lorelei's car. They came to a stop behind her and proceeded to barrel out. Yes, barrel. They were obviously in a hurry.

Alarmed they were there, Lily got out as well and turned toward them, ignoring the shouts of welcome and congrats from the others. "Is everything okay?" Lily couldn't ask her sisters fast enough. "Are the kids all right?"

It was a reasonable question since Nola had a three-month-old son and Lorelei had a nearly two-year-old daughter, but her sisters just seemed puzzled that she'd gone there with her response. *Welcome to the club.* Lily felt like a poster child for puzzlement right now.

And she got another gut punch of concern.

Even though Lorelei and Nola were heading toward her and the crowd of visitors were converging on her from behind, Lily glanced at her phone that she'd silenced while Hayden and she had been doing some errands and having an early dinner in nearby San Antonio. She goggled at the sheer number of texts and calls she'd missed. They probably equaled the number of visitors she had right now, but none was from her mother, Evangeline. So, all was probably well with her.

"It's Hezzie," Nola said, causing Lily's attention to snap to her twin sister.

Before she could grasp the unlikelihood of what she was doing, Lily glanced around as if expecting to see her great-great-great grandmother's ghost since the woman had been dead for over seventy years.

"Hezzie," someone in the crowd verified while others kept doling out congratulations to Lily.

And Lily got it then.

"I'm the drawer, and Hezzie's the drawee," Lily grumbled, trying to wrap her mind around that.

Many verbally confirmed it, and some patted her on the back. Others did little bouncy dances around the grass. Katniss, aka Frankie Parkman, the owner of the town's costume shop and tat salon, shouted, "I volunteer as tribute."

That got some laughs, and the president of the Last Ride Society, Alma Parkman, stepped through the crowd to reach Lily. She took hold of Lily's hand and gave it a few enthusiastic pumps and pats.

"Congratulations, congratulations, congratulations," Alma gushed. The woman was in her eighties, but clearly had a lot of energy since she was bobbling around in glee as well.

Lily couldn't muster up the matching enthusiasm or glee, but she did have some questions. "In the past seventy-odd years of the Last Ride Society, no one has ever drawn Hezzie's name?"

"Nope," Alma confirmed. "Her name was one of the first in the drawing bowl, and over the decades, hundreds of names have been added. Now you'll get to do the highest honor a Parkman can have by researching her."

Others joined in on that *highest honor*, and one of the Sherlocks, Derwin Parkman, threaded his way to her. "Of course, the Sherlock's Snoops will help you in any way we can."

This was a little out of the realm of the Sherlock's Snoops, a club formed to investigate mysteries. Lily suspected there were no mysteries left in Hezzie's life, but she gave a polite thanks to Derwin anyway.

"I'm sure you'll do Hezzie proud," Alma went on, and while she slid her arm around Lily's waist, she turned to the others. "Now, why don't y'all head home so Lily here can get started? I need to go over the research rules with her so she can dive right into doing the report."

That brought on some mumbled groans from those who clearly wanted to stretch out this moment a little or a lot longer, but the crowd started moseying toward their vehicles. Alma waved at each one, smiled and kept waving and smiling until they'd all driven away. Then the woman released a long, weary breath, and both her smile and enthusiasm went south.

"Let me get the research packet from my car, and then we'll have a little chat," Alma muttered on a sigh and headed toward her vintage VW that she'd had painted to resemble a turtle.

The sudden change in the woman's mood baffled Lily, but she supposed this might be a situation of catching the biggest fish in the proverbial pond. Everything else after this would be a small haul, and some Parkmans might lose interest in the drawings.

"Oh, there's Eli riding one of the new mares," Hayden said, and her daughter immediately headed in the direction of the pasture where Eli was astride an Andalusian horse that Lily knew had been delivered to the ranch earlier that day.

"A lot of people will bug the crap out of you about drawing Hezzie's name," Nola remarked, speaking what Lily knew was the God's honest truth. As Nola was prone to do. "That's why Lorelei and I came right over."

"We'll try to run some interference for you so you don't have a constant flood of people showing up to ask you about the research," Lorelei added.

"I appreciate that," Lily told them.

And she did. That was the God's honest truth, too, and

since both her sisters had gone through this, they had some experience in research pitfalls of the Last Ride Society. Still, Lorelei and Nola had busy lives, what with their babies and businesses. Nola was a glass artist, and Lorelei owned the shop that sold Nola's pieces and other glass art.

"But don't worry if you don't have the time," Lily added. "I suspect I won't have much to do since Hezzie's life is probably an open book..."

Her words trailed off. So did her attention on the subject of Hezzie. Her sisters' attention shifted as well, and the reason for that was the hot, hunky guy who walked out of the barn.

Jonas.

He'd stripped off his shirt, baring a muscled chest that was toned, tanned and perfect for being bared. Mercy, the man could give hot cowboy cover models an inferiority complex with that body and the rest of the package that went with it. The midnight black hair, sizzling green eyes and a face that had to be a benchmark for "hot guy" faces.

"So can't believe you haven't tapped that," Nola muttered.

Lily automatically frowned. "So can't believe you'd think I'd *tap* my ranch foreman. A man who works for me and lives just a stone's throw away."

But since Lily wasn't blind and had normal urges, she had fantasized about such things. Then again, probably every woman in Last Ride had had some smutty fantasies about Jonas. About his brothers, too, who had those same dreamy looks and bodies.

"You're lusting over your own brother-in-law," Lily pointed out to her sisters.

"Looking at, not lusting," Lorelei automatically corrected in her usual prim voice. The rest of her was prim, too, with her blond hair tumbling perfectly over the shoulders of her perfectly fitted turquoise-colored top. "I'm allowed to look."

Nola made a grunting sound of agreement. No primness for her. Her long blond hair was scooped in a disordered ponytail, with just as many strands falling out as there were gathered up. No makeup and, judging from her stained jeans and old Roper boots with burnt specks, she'd been blowing her glass art right before she'd made this visit.

"Besides, Wyatt will benefit from any lustful urges I get from gawking at a hot guy," Nola added.

Wyatt, Nola's husband and the love of her life. In their case, that particular label was actually true since they'd started their romance way back in high school, and after some bumps and hitches, some of which had been plenty serious, their relationship had continued and led to marriage.

Lily cleared her throat, looking for a change of subject. A change of mindset, too, since she didn't want to be mentally stripping off any more of Jonas's clothes. "Where are Stellie and Charlie?" Stellie was Lorelei's daughter, and Charlie was Nola's son.

"With Dax and Wyatt," Nola answered.

Dax and Wyatt Buchanan were not only Jonas's brothers, but they were also married to Lily's siblings, which made this sort of a *Seven Brides for Seven Brothers* deal. Minus Jonas and her, of course, since they'd never ever hooked up in any kind of way. Probably never would, either, because while Jonas was hands-off for Lily, she was no doubt hands-off for him, too, because she had been his kid brother's girlfriend.

"Dax is having a daughter-daddy playdate with Stellie," Lorelei said, keeping her gaze on Jonas as he made his way toward them.

Nola groaned softly when Jonas pulled on his shirt, covering those amazing abs and six-pack. "Well, since Alma got rid of your visitors, I guess our services aren't needed right now."

"Yes, but call us if things get too wild," Lorelei added. She brushed a kiss on Lily's cheek. Nola gave Lily a light punch on the arm, and her sisters headed back to Lorelei's car.

Alma was parked right next to them, and the woman appeared to be looking through file folders in a box. *Appeared to be*, Lily noted. But Alma also kept glancing back at her in a way that made Lily think she was waiting for everyone else to leave so they could talk alone. Maybe Alma intended to emphasize to Lily just how important this research would be.

"You okay?" Jonas asked Lily when he stepped up beside her.

Lily nodded, and because she was still doing some lusting, she didn't look up at him. Best not to make eye contact until she was certain she'd temporarily squashed those smutty thoughts about him.

"I got Hezzie's name in the Last Ride Society drawing," Lily explained.

"Yeah, I heard. I was checking fences in the east pasture when I got a call from Larry, whose wife was at the meeting. I rode back because I thought you might need help getting rid of the folks coming here. Then I saw you had it all under control."

Larry Davidson, one of the horse trainers, who was married to Lily's distant cousin, Ellie, and yes, Ellie would have definitely been at the drawing and probably would have come with the crowd of well-wishers if she hadn't had to get back to their twin toddlers.

"When I first got the call from Larry," Jonas went on, "I thought he was going to tell me that you'd drawn Maddie's name."

Lily made a quick sound of agreement. "I thought the same thing when I spotted the crowd." She didn't add they'd dodged a bullet by it not being Maddie because she had a bad feeling in the pit of her stomach there might be a bullet of a different kind headed her way.

"I think it would have been hard on Eli to have Maddie's life dissected," Jonas added.

"Yes," she verified. Because such dissecting would have brought up her death.

"What's Alma doing?" he asked, tipping his head to the woman. Since only Alma's overalls-clad butt and legs were showing, Jonas no doubt recognized her from her car.

"Getting some research stuff on Hezzie." Lily didn't add that Alma was also acting weird. Then again, Alma had begun her stand-up comic career at a point in her life when most people would have been winding down, so weird was usually Alma's default behavior.

"Alma, you need help carrying that?" Jonas called out to her.

"Nope. It's not heavy. I'm just making sure it's all here before I give it to Lily." Alma glanced back at them and kept aiming those glances at her while she continued to thumb through the box. It seemed to Lily, though, that Alma was stalling more than verifying the box's contents.

Since Jonas was studying Alma, too, Lily expected him to remark on her odder-than-usual behavior. But he didn't.

"Once Alma's gone, we need to talk," Jonas said, keeping his voice low. "I found something in the mailbox."

Now Lily had to risk that eye contact when she turned toward him. "What?"

Her mind started doing more whirling with speculation. Some kind of prank maybe, like poop? After all, she had a teenage daughter and Jonas had a teenage stepson, so one of their kids' *friends* could have thought that was a fun way to pass the last week of summer break.

Jonas didn't answer because Alma chose that exact moment to drag the box from her back seat and head toward them. Despite Alma's assurance that it wasn't heavy, Jonas hurried to help her with it.

"Thanks bunches," Alma said. "If you want to go ahead and set it on Lily's porch, that'd be great."

Of course, Jonas didn't refuse, but Lily saw the suspicion on his face and was sure it was on hers as well. Alma clearly had something she wanted to tell Lily in private.

As Nola and Lorelei had done, Alma watched Jonas as he took the box from her and walked toward the porch. The woman shook her head.

"Not sure how you can get work done when you've got a view like that," Alma remarked.

The *view* was Jonas's butt, which she knew was just as prime as the rest of him. The fit of his jeans verified that.

Alma fanned herself, and then, as if snapping herself out of a lust-induced trance, she cleared her throat and swiveled back to Lily. Her expression went into the "total serious" mode.

"Full disclosure," Alma said after an extremely windy sigh. "Every quarter before the drawing, I make sure to shove Hezzie's name all the way to the bottom of the bowl."

Because of all the speculation Lily had already done over Alma's oddball mood, that didn't come as a surprise. "Because now that Hezzie's name has been drawn, you think people might lose interest in the Last Ride Society."

Alma blinked as if that thought had never occurred to her. Then her forehead bunched up. "No, I put Hezzie's name at the bottom of the bowl because I never wanted it to be drawn. *Never ever*," she emphasized.

Now Lily had to shake her head. "I don't understand."

"I know, but I'm about to explain it to you." Alma gave another of those windy sighs. "Girl, we got to be very, very careful about this big-assed can of worms you're about to open."